THE REVIEWERS HAVE HAILED ALL THE PREVIOUS VOLUMES IN THIS BEST OF THE YEAR SERIES . . .

"A really fine anthology . . . bravo!"

—*Locus*

"A real cream-of-the-crop selection which could persuade readers there's more excitement left in the field than they thought."

—*Publishers Weekly*

". . . Carr never picks an inferior story and misses virtually none of the real "bests!"

—*The Commentator*

"As anthologies go, Terry Carr's Best SFers are among the few in the upper echelon."

—*Science Fiction Review*

. . . AND THIS YEAR'S COLLECTION IS BETTER THAN EVER!

A SCIENCE FICTION BOOK CLUB SELECTION

THE BEST SCIENCE FICTION OF THE YEAR

#8

Terry Carr, Editor

A Del Rey Book

BALLANTINE BOOKS • NEW YORK

Acknowledgments

"The Barbie Murders" by John Varley: Copyright © 1977 by Davis Publications, Inc. From *Isaac Asimov's Science Fiction Magazine*, January–February 1978, by permission of the author and his agents, Kirby McCauley, Ltd.

"A Hiss of Dragon" by Gregory Benford and Marc Laidlaw: Copyright © 1978 by Omni Publications International, Ltd. From *Omni*, December 1978, by permission of the authors.

"Black Glass" by Fritz Leiber: Copyright © 1978 by Fritz Leiber. From *Andromeda 3*, by permission of the author.

"To Bring in the Steel" by Donald Kingsbury: Copyright © 1978 by The Condé Nast Publications, Inc. From *Analog*, July 1978, by permission of the author.

"The Very Slow Time Machine" by Ian Watson: Copyright © 1978 by Ian Watson. From *Anticipations*, by permission of the author.

"Devil You Don't Know" by Dean Ing: Copyright © 1977 by The Condé Nast Publications, Inc. From *Analog*, January 1978, by permission of the author.

"Count the Clock That Tells the Time" by Harlan Ellison: Copyright © 1978 by Harlan Ellison. From *Omni*, December 1978, by permission of the author and his agent, Robert P. Mills, Ltd., New York. All rights reserved.

"View from a Height" by Joan D. Vinge: Copyright © 1978 by Joan D. Vinge. From *Analog*, June 1978, by permission of the author.

"The Morphology of the Kirkham Wreck" by Hilbert Schenck: Copyright © 1978 by Hilbert Schenck. From *Fantasy and Science Fiction*, September 1978, by permission of the author and his agent, Virginia Kidd.

"Vermeer's Window" by Gordon Eklund: Copyright © 1978 by Terry Carr. From *Universe 8*, by permission of the author.

"The Man Who Had No Idea" by Thomas M. Disch: Copyright © 1978 by Thomas M. Disch. From *Fantasy and Science Fiction*, October 1978, and *Winter's Tales 24*, by permission of the author.

"Death Therapy" by James Patrick Kelly: Copyright © 1978 by Mercury Press, Inc. From *Fantasy and Science Fiction*, July 1978, by permission of the author.

Contents

alien planets, plus attackers and guardians from the future.

—TERRY CARR
January 1979

The Barbie Murders

John Varley

Our future offers both challenges and opportunities. For instance, if you're one of the many people who take a jaundiced view of the "cult of individualism"—so often a mask for selfish competitiveness—you may be delighted at John Varley's pocket society in which everyone looks exactly like everyone else and people *really* devote their lives to the common good.

A maverick in such a society would be a serious threat, however. And if a murder were committed—well, how could a police officer identify the guilty party? No names, no fingerprints . . .

Varley, as usual, has considered the problem in thorough detail. His answers aren't simple.

The body came to the morgue at 2246 hours. No one paid much attention to it. It was a Saturday night, and the bodies were piling up like logs in a millpond. A harried attendant working her way down the row of stainless steel tables picked up the sheaf of papers that came with the body, peeling back the sheet over the face. She took a card from her pocket and scrawled on it, copying from the reports filed by the investigating officer and the hospital staff:

Ingraham, Leah Petrie. Female. Age: 35. Length: 2.1 meters. Mass: 59 kilograms. Dead on arrival, Crisium

1

Emergency Terminal. Cause of death: homicide. Next of kin: unknown.

She wrapped the wire attached to the card around the left big toe, slid the dead weight from the table and onto the wheeled carrier, took it to cubicle 659a, and rolled out the long tray.

The door slammed shut, and the attendant placed the paperwork in the out tray, never noticing that in his report the investigating officer had not specified the sex of the corpse.

Lieutenant Anna-Louise Bach had moved into her new office three days ago, and already the paper on her desk was threatening to avalanche onto the floor.

To call it an office was almost a perversion of the term. It had a file cabinet for pending cases; she could open it only at severe risk to life and limb. The drawers had a tendency to spring out at her, pinning her in her chair in the corner. To reach A she had to stand on her chair; Z required her either to sit on her desk or to straddle the bottom drawer with one foot in the legwell and the other against the wall.

But the office had a door. True, it could only be ópened if no one was occupying the single chair in front of the desk.

Bach was in no mood to gripe. She loved the place. It was ten times better than the squad room, where she had spent ten years elbow to elbow with the other sergeants and corporals.

Jorge Weil stuck his head in the door.

"Hi. We're taking bids on a new case. What am I offered?"

"Put me down for half a Mark," Bach said, without looking up from the report she was writing. "Can't you see I'm busy?"

"Not as busy as you're going to be." Weil came in without an invitation and settled himself in the chair. Bach looked up, opened her mouth, then said nothing. She had the authority to order him to get his big feet out of her "cases completed" tray, but not the experience in exercising it. And she and Jorge had worked together for three years. Why should a stripe of gold paint on her shoulder change their relationship? She supposed the informality was Weil's way of saying he wouldn't let her promotion bother him as long as she didn't get snotty about it.

Weil deposited a folder on top of the teetering pile marked "For Immediate Action," then leaned back again. Bach eyed the stack of paper and the circular file mounted in the wall not half a meter from it, leading to the incinerator—and thought about having an accident. Just a careless nudge with an elbow . . .

"Aren't you even going to open it?" Weil asked, sounding disappointed. "It's not every day I'm going to hand-deliver a case."

"You tell me about it, since you want to so badly."

"All right. We've got a body, which is cut up pretty bad. We've got the murder weapon, which is a knife. We've got thirteen eyewitnesses who can describe the killer, but we don't really need them since the murder was committed in front of a television camera. We've got the tape."

"You're talking about a case which has to have been solved ten minutes after the first report, untouched by human hands. Give it to the computer, idiot." But she looked up. She didn't like the smell of it. "Why give it to me?"

"Because of the other thing we know. The scene of the crime. The murder was committed at the barbie colony."

"Oh, sweet Jesus."

The Temple of the Standardized Church in Luna was in the center of the Standardist Commune, Anytown, North Crisium. The best way to reach it, they found, was a local tube line which paralleled the Cross-Crisium Express Tube.

She and Weil checked out a blue-and-white police capsule with a priority sorting code and surrendered themselves to the New Dresden municipal transport system—the pill sorter, as the New Dresdenites called it. They were whisked through the precinct chute to the main nexus, where thousands of capsules were stacked awaiting a routing order to clear the computer. On the big conveyer which should have taken them to a holding cubby, they were snatched by a grapple—the cops called it the long arm of the law—and moved ahead to the multiple maws of the Cross-Crisium while people in other capsules glared at them. The capsule was inserted, and Bach and Weil were pressed hard into the backs of their seats.

In seconds they emerged from the tube and out onto the plain of Crisium, speeding along through the vacuum, magnetically suspended a few millimeters above the induction rail. Bach glanced up at the Earth, then stared out the window at the featureless landscape rushing by. She brooded.

It had taken a look at the map to convince her that the barbie colony was indeed in the New Dresden jurisdiction—a case of blatant gerrymandering if ever there was one. Anytown was fifty kilometers from what she thought of as the boundaries of New Dresden, but was joined to the city by a dotted line that represented a strip of land one meter wide.

A roar built up as they entered a tunnel and air was injected into the tube ahead of them. The car shook briefly as the shock wave built up; then they popped through pressure doors into the tube station of Anytown. The capsule doors hissed and they climbed out onto the platform.

The tube station at Anytown was primarily a loading dock and warehouse. It was a large space with plastic crates stacked against all the walls, and about fifty people working to load them into freight capsules.

Bach and Weil stood on the platform for a moment, uncertain where to go. The murder had happened at a spot not twenty meters in front of them, right here in the tube station.

"This place gives me the creeps," Weil volunteered.
"Me, too."

Every one of the fifty people Bach could see was identical to every other. All appeared to be female, though only faces, feet, and hands were visible, everything else concealed by loose white pajamas belted at the waist. They were all blond; all had hair cut off at the shoulder and parted in the middle, blue eyes, high foreheads, short noses, and small mouths.

The work slowly stopped as the barbies became aware of them. They eyed Bach and Weil suspiciously. Bach picked one at random and approached her.

"Who's in charge here?" she asked.

"We are," the barbie said. Bach took it to mean the woman herself, recalling something about barbies never using the singular pronoun.

"We're supposed to meet someone at the temple," she said. "How do we get there?"

"Through that doorway," the woman said. "It leads to Main Street. Follow the street to the temple. But you really should cover yourselves."

"Huh? What do you mean?" Bach was not aware of anything wrong with the way she and Weil were dressed. True, neither of them wore as much as the barbies did. Bach wore her usual blue nylon briefs in addition to a regulation uniform cap, arm and thigh bands, and cloth-soled slippers. Her weapon, communicator, and handcuffs were fastened to a leather equipment belt.

"Cover yourself," the barbie said, with a pained look. "You're flaunting your differentness. And you, with all that hair . . ." There were giggles and a few shouts from the other barbies.

"Police business," Weil snapped.

"Uh, yes," Bach said, feeling annoyed that the barbie had put her on the defensive. After all, this was New Dresden, it was a public thoroughfare—even though by tradition and usage a Standardist enclave—and they were entitled to dress as they wished.

Main Street was a narrow, mean little place. Bach had expected a promenade like those in the shopping districts of New Dresden; what she found was indistinguishable from a residential corridor. They drew curious stares and quite a few frowns from the identical people they met.

There was a modest plaza at the end of the street. It had a low roof of bare metal, a few trees, and a blocky stone building in the center of a radiating network of walks.

A barbie who looked just like all the others met them at the entrance. Bach asked if she was the one Weil had spoken to on the phone, and she said she was. Bach wanted to know if they could go inside to talk. The barbie said the temple was off limits to outsiders and suggested they sit on a bench outside the building.

When they were settled, Bach started her questioning. "First, I need to know your name, and your title. I assume that you are . . . what was it?" She consulted her notes, taken hastily from a display she had called up on the computer terminal in her office. "I don't seem to have found a title for you."

"We have none," the barbie said. "If you must think of a title, consider us as the keeper of records."

"All right. And your name?"

"We have no name."

Bach sighed. "Yes, I understand that you forsake names when you come here. But you had one before. You were given one at birth. I'm going to have to have it for my investigation."

The woman looked pained. "No, you don't understand. It is true that this body had a name at one time. But it has been wiped from this one's mind. It would cause this one a great deal of pain to be reminded of it." She stumbled verbally every time she said "this one." Evidently even a polite circumlocution of the personal pronoun was distressing.

"I'll try to get it from another angle, then." This was already getting hard to deal with, Bach saw, and knew it could only get tougher. "You say you are the keeper of records."

"We are. We keep records because the law says we

must. Each citizen must be recorded, or so we have been told."

"For a very good reason," Bach said. "We're going to need access to those records. For the investigation. You understand? I assume an officer has already been through them, or the deceased couldn't have been identified as Leah P. Ingraham."

"That's true. But it won't be necessary for you to go through the records again. We are here to confess. We murdered L. P. Ingraham, serial number 11005. We are surrendering peacefully. You may take us to your prison." She held out her hands, wrists close together, ready to be shackled.

Weil was startled, reached tentatively for his handcuffs, then looked to Bach for guidance.

"Let me get this straight. You're saying you're the one who did it? You, personally."

"That's correct. We did it. We have never defied temporal authority, and we are willing to pay the penalty."

"Once more." Bach reached out and grasped the barbie's wrist, forced the hand open, palm up. "*This* is the person, this is the body that committed the murder? This hand, this one right here, held the knife and killed Ingraham? This hand, as opposed to 'your' thousands of other hands?"

The barbie frowned.

"Put that way, no. *This* hand did not grasp the murder weapon. But *our* hand did. What's the difference?"

"Quite a bit, in the eyes of the law." Bach sighed, and let go of the woman's hand. Woman? She wondered if the term applied. She realized she needed to know more about Standardists. But it was convenient to think of them as such, since their faces were feminine.

"Let's try again. I'll need you—and the eyewitnesses to the crime—to study the tape of the murder. *I* can't tell the difference between the murderer, the victim, or any of the bystanders. But surely you must be able to. I assume that . . . well, like the old saying went, 'all Chinamen look alike.' That was to Caucasian races, of course. Orientals had no trouble telling each other apart. So I thought that you . . . that you people would . . ." She trailed off at the look of blank incomprehension on the barbie's face.

"We don't know what you're talking about."

Bach's shoulders slumped.

"You mean you can't—not even if you saw her again?"

The woman shrugged. "We all look the same to this one."

Anna-Louise Bach sprawled out on her flotation bed later that night, surrounded by scraps of paper. Untidy as it was, her thought processes were helped by actually scribbling facts on paper rather than filing them in her datalink. And she did her best work late at night, at home, in bed, after taking a bath or making love. Tonight she had done both and found she needed every bit of the invigorating clarity it gave her.

Standardists.

They were an offbeat religious sect founded ninety years earlier by someone whose name had not survived. That was not surprising, since Standardists gave up their names when they joined the order, made every effort consistent with the laws of the land to obliterate the name and person as if he or she had never existed. The epithet "barbie" had quickly been attached to them by the press. The origin of the word was a popular children's toy of the twentieth and early twenty-first centuries, a plastic, sexless, mass-produced "girl" doll with an elaborate wardrobe.

The barbies had done surprisingly well for a group that did not reproduce, that relied entirely on new members from the outside world to replenish their numbers. They had grown for twenty years, then reached a population stability where deaths equaled new members—which they called "components." They had suffered moderately from religious intolerance, moving from country to country until the majority had come to Luna sixty years ago.

They drew new components from the walking wounded of society, the people who had not done well in a world that preached conformity, passivity, and tolerance of your billions of neighbors, yet rewarded only those who were individualistic and aggressive enough to stand apart from the herd. The barbies had opted out of a system where one had to be at once a face in the crowd and a proud individual with hopes and dreams and desires. They were the inheritors of a long tradition of ascetic withdrawal, surrendering their names, their bodies, and their temporal aspirations to a life that was ordered and easy to understand.

Bach realized she might be doing some of them a disservice in that evaluation. They were not necessarily all losers. There must be those among them who were attracted simply by the religious ideas of the sect, though Bach felt there was little in the teachings that made sense.

She skimmed through the dogma, taking notes. The Standardists preached the commonality of humanity, denigrated free will, and elevated the group and the consensus to demi-god status. Nothing too unusual in the theory; it was the practice of it that made people queasy.

There was a creation theory and a godhead, who was not worshiped but contemplated. Creation happened when the Goddess—a prototypical earth mother who had no name—gave birth to the universe. She put people in it, all alike, stamped from the same universal mold.

Sin entered the picture. One of the people began to wonder. This person had a name, given to him or her *after* the original sin as part of the punishment, but Bach could not find it written down anywhere. She decided that it was a dirty word which Standardists never told an outsider.

This person asked Goddess what it was all for. What had been wrong with the void, that Goddess had seen fit to fill it with people who didn't seem to have a reason for existing?

That was too much. For reasons unexplained—and

impolite to even ask about—Goddess had punished humans by introducing differentness into the world. Warts, big noses, kinky hair, white skin, tall people and fat people and deformed people, blue eyes, body hair, freckles, testicles, and labia. A billion faces and fingerprints, each soul trapped in a body distinct from all others, with the heavy burden of trying to establish an identity in a perpetual shouting match.

But the faith held that peace was achieved in striving to regain that lost Eden. When all humans were again the same person, Goddess would welcome them back. Life was a testing, a trial.

Bach certainly agreed with that. She gathered her notes and shuffled them together, then picked up the book she had brought back from Anytown. The barbie had given it to her when Bach asked for a picture of the murdered woman.

It was a blueprint for a human being.

The title was *The Book of Specifications. The Specs*, for short. Each barbie carried one, tied to her waist with a tape measure. It gave tolerances in engineering terms, defining what a barbie could look like. It was profusely illustrated with drawings of parts of the body in minute detail, giving measurements in millimeters.

She closed the book and sat up, propping her head on a pillow. She reached for her viewpad and propped it on her knees, punched the retrieval code for the murder tape. For the twentieth time that night, she watched a figure spring forward from a crowd of identical figures in the tube station, slash at Leah Ingraham, and melt back into the crowd as her victim lay bleeding and eviscerated on the floor.

She slowed it down, concentrating on the killer, trying to spot something different about her. Anything at all would do. The knife struck. Blood spurted. Barbies milled about in consternation. A few belatedly ran after the killer, not reacting fast enough. People seldom reacted quickly enough. But the killer had blood on her hand. Make a note to ask about that.

Bach viewed the film once more, saw nothing useful, and decided to call it a night.

The room was long and tall, brightly lit from strips high above. Bach followed the attendant down the rows of square locker doors which lined one wall. The air was cool and humid, the floor wet from a recent hosing.

The man consulted the card in his hand and pulled the metal handle on locker 659a, making a noise that echoed through the bare room. He slid the drawer out and lifted the sheet from the corpse.

It was not the first mutilated corpse Bach had seen, but it was the first nude barbie. She immediately noted the lack of nipples on the two hills of flesh that pretended to be breasts, and the smooth, unmarked skin in the crotch. The attendant was frowning, consulting the card on the corpse's foot.

"Some mistake here," he muttered. "Geez, the headaches. What do you do with a thing like that?" He scratched his head, then scribbled through the large letter F on the card, replacing it with a neat N. He looked at Bach and grinned sheepishly. "What do you do?" he repeated.

Bach didn't much care what he did. She studied L. P. Ingraham's remains, hoping that something on the body would show her why a barbie had decided she must die.

There was little difficulty seeing *how* she had died. The knife had entered the abdomen, going deep, and the wound extended upward from there in a slash that ended beneath the breastbone. Part of the bone was cut through. The knife had been sharp, but it would have taken a powerful arm to slice through that much meat.

The attendant watched curiously as Bach pulled the dead woman's legs apart and studied what she saw there. She found the tiny slit of the urethra set far back around the curve, just anterior to the anus.

Bach opened her copy of *The Specs,* took out a tape measure, and started to work.

"Mr. Atlas, I got your name from the Morphology Guild's files as a practitioner who's had a lot of dealings with the Standardist Church."

The man frowned, then shrugged. "So? You may not approve of them, but they're legal. And my records are in order. I don't do any work on anybody until you people have checked for a criminal record." He sat on the edge of the desk in the spacious consulting room, facing Bach. Mr. Rock Atlas—surely a *nom de métier*—had shoulders carved from granite, teeth like flashing pearls, and the face of a young god. He was a walking, flexing advertisement for his profession. Bach crossed her legs nervously. She had always had a taste for beef.

"I'm not investigating you, Mr. Atlas. This is a murder case, and I'd appreciate your cooperation."

"Call me Rock," he said, with a winning smile.

"Must I? Very well. I came to ask you what you would do, how long the work would take, if I asked to be converted to a barbie."

. His face fell. "Oh, no, what a tragedy! I can't allow it. My dear, it would be a crime." He reached over to her and touched her chin lightly, turning her head. "No, Lieutenant, for you I'd build up the hollows in the cheeks just the slightest bit—maybe tighten up the muscles behind them—then drift the orbital bones out a little bit farther from the nose to set your eyes wider. More attention-getting, you understand. That touch of mystery. Then of course there's your nose."

She pushed his hand away and shook her head. "No, I'm not coming to you for the operation. I just want to know. How much work would it entail, and how close can you come to the specs of the church?" Then she frowned and looked at him suspiciously. "What's wrong with my nose?"

"Well, my dear, I didn't mean to imply there was anything *wrong*; in fact, it has a certain overbearing power that must be useful to you once in a while, in the circles you move in. Even the lean to the left could be justified, aesthetically—"

"Never mind," she said, angry at herself for having

fallen into his sales pitch. "Just answer my question."

He studied her carefully, asked her to stand up and turn around. She was about to object that she had not necessarily meant herself personally as the surgical candidate, just a woman in general, when he seemed to lose interest in her.

"It wouldn't be much of a job," he said. "Your height is just slightly over the parameters; I could take that out of your thighs and lower legs, maybe shave some vertebrae. Take out some fat here and put it back there. Take off those nipples and dig out your uterus and ovaries, sew up your crotch. With a man, chop off the penis. I'd have to break up your skull a little and shift the bones around, then build up the face from there. Say two days' work, one overnight and one outpatient."

"And when you were through, what would be left to identify me?"

"Say that again?"

Bach briefly explained her situation, and Atlas pondered it.

"You've got a problem. I take off the fingerprints and footprints. I don't leave any external scars, not even microscopic ones. No moles, freckles, warts, or birthmarks; they all have to go. A blood test would work, and so would a retinal print. An x-ray of the skull. A voiceprint would be questionable. I even that out as much as possible. I can't think of anything else."

"Nothing that could be seen from a purely visual exam?"

"That's the whole point of the operation, isn't it?"

"I know. I was just hoping you might know something even the barbies were not aware of. Thank you, anyway."

He got up, took her hand, and kissed it. "No trouble. And if you ever decide to get that nose taken care of . . ."

She met Jorge Weil at the temple gate in the middle of Anytown. He had spent his morning there, going through the records, and she could see the work didn't agree with him. He took her back to the small office where the records were kept in battered file cabinets. There was a barbie waiting for them there. She spoke without preamble.

"We decided at equalization last night to help you as much as possible."

"Oh, yeah? Thanks. I wondered if you would, considering what happened fifty years ago."

Weil looked puzzled. "What was that?"

Bach waited for the barbie to speak, but she evidently wasn't going to.

"All right. I found it last night. The Standardists were involved in murder once before, not long after they came to Luna. You notice you never see one of them in New Dresden?"

Weil shrugged. "So what? They keep to themselves."

"They were *ordered* to keep to themselves. At first, they could move freely like any other citizens. Then one of them killed somebody—not a Standardist this time. It was known the murderer was a barbie; there were witnesses. The police started looking for the killer. You guess what happened."

"They ran into the problems we're having." Weil grimaced. "It doesn't look so good, does it?"

"It's hard to be optimistic," Bach conceded. "The killer was never found. The barbies offered to surrender one of their number at random, thinking the law would be satisfied with that. But of course it wouldn't do. There was a public outcry, and a lot of pressure to force them to adopt some kind of distinguishing characteristic, like a number tattooed on their foreheads. I don't think that would have worked, either. It could have been covered.

"The fact is that the barbies were seen as a menace to society. They could kill at will and blend back into their community like grains of sand on a beach. We would be powerless to punish a guilty party. There was no provision in the law for dealing with them."

"So what happened?"

"The case is marked closed, but there's no arrest, no

conviction, and no suspect. A deal was made whereby the Standardists could practice their religion as long as they never mixed with other citizens. They had to stay in Anytown. Am I right?" She looked at the barbie.

"Yes. We've adhered to the agreement."

"I don't doubt it. Most people are barely aware you exist out here. But now we've got this. One barbie kills another barbie, and under a television camera . . ." Bach stopped and looked thoughtful. "Say, it occurs to me . . . wait a minute. *Wait* a *minute*." She didn't like the look of it.

"I wonder. This murder took place in the tube station. It's the only place in Anytown that's scanned by the municipal security system. And fifty years is a long time between murders, even in a town as small as—how many people did you say live here, Jorge?"

"About seven thousand. I feel I know them all intimately." Weil had spent the day sorting barbies. According to measurements made from the tape, the killer was at the top end of permissible height.

"How about it?" Bach said to the barbie. "Is there anything I ought to know?"

The woman bit her lip, looked uncertain.

"Come on, you said you were going to help me."

"Very well. There have been three other killings in the last month. You would not have heard of this one except it took place with outsiders present. Purchasing agents were there on the loading platform. They made the initial report. There was nothing we could do to hush it up."

"But why would you want to?"

"Isn't it obvious? We exist with the possibility of persecution always with us. We don't wish to appear a threat to others. We wish to appear peaceful—which we *are*—and prefer to handle the problems of the group within the group itself. By divine consensus."

Bach knew she would get nowhere pursuing that line of reasoning. She decided to take the conversation back to the previous murders.

"Tell me what you know. Who was killed, and do

you have any idea why? Or should I be talking to someone else?" Something occurred to her then, and she wondered why she hadn't asked it before. "You *are* the person I was speaking to yesterday, aren't you? Let me rephrase that. You're the body—that is, this body before me . . ."

"We know what you're talking about," the barbie said. "Uh, yes, you are correct. We are . . . *I* am the one you spoke to." She had to choke the word out, blushing furiously. "We have been . . . *I* have been selected as the component to deal with you, since it was perceived at equalization that this matter must be dealt with. This one was chosen as . . . *I* was chosen as punishment."

"You don't have to say 'I' if you don't want to."

"Oh, thank you."

"Punishment for what?"

"For . . . for individualistic tendencies. We spoke up too personally at equalization, in favor of cooperation with you. As a political necessity. The conservatives wish to stick to our sacred principles no matter what the cost. We are divided; this makes for bad feelings within the organism, for sickness. This one spoke out and was punished by having her own way, by being appointed . . . *individually* . . . to deal with you." The woman could not meet Bach's eyes. Her face burned with shame.

"This one has been instructed to reveal her serial number to you. In the future, when you come here you are to ask for 23900."

Bach made a note of it.

"All right. What can you tell me about a possible motive? Do you think all the killings were done by the same . . . component?"

"We do not know. We are no more equipped to select an . . . individual from the group than you are. But there is great consternation. We are fearful."

"I would think so. Do you have reason to believe that the victims were—does this make sense?—*known* to the killer? Or were they random killings?" Bach hoped not. Random killers were the hardest to catch; without motive, it was hard to tie killer to victim, or to sift one person out of thousands with the opportunity. With the barbies, the problem would be squared and cubed.

"Again, we don't know."

Bach sighed. "I want to see the witnesses to the crime. I might as well start interviewing them."

In short order, thirteen barbies were brought. Bach intended to question them thoroughly to see if their stories were consistent, and if they had changed.

She sat them down and took them one at a time, and almost immediately ran into a stone wall. It took her several minutes to see the problem, frustrating minutes spent trying to establish which of the barbies had spoken to the officer first, which second, and so forth.

"Hold it. Listen carefully. Was this body physically present at the time of the crime? Did these eyes see it happen?"

The barbie's brow furrowed. "Why, no. But does it matter?"

"It does to me, babe. *Hey, twenty-three thousand!*"

The barbie stuck her head in the door. Bach looked pained.

"I need the actual people who were *there*. Not thirteen picked at random."

"The story is known to all."

Bach spent five minutes explaining that it made a difference to her, then waited an hour as 23900 located the people who were actual witnesses.

And again she hit a stone wall. The stories were absolutely identical, which she knew to be impossible. Observers *always* report events differently. They make themselves the hero, invent things before and after they first began observing, rearrange and edit and interpret. But not the barbies. Bach struggled for an hour trying to shake one of them, and got nowhere. She was facing a consensus, something that had been discussed among the barbies until an account of the event had emerged and then been accepted as truth. It was probably a close approximation, but it did Bach no good. She needed discrepancies to gnaw at, and there were none.

Worst of all, she was convinced no one was lying to her. Had she questioned the thirteen random choices, she would have gotten the same answers. They would have thought of themselves as having been there, since some of them had been and they had been told about it. What happened to one happened to all.

Her options were evaporating fast. She dismissed the witnesses, called 23900 back in, and sat her down. Bach ticked off points on her fingers.

"One. Do you have the personal effects of the deceased?"

"We have no private property."

Bach nodded. "Two. Can you take me to her room?"

"We each sleep in any room we find available at night. There is no—"

"Right. Three. Any friends or co-workers I might . . ." Bach rubbed her forehead with one hand. "Right. Skip it. Four. What was her job? Where did she work?"

"All jobs are interchangeable here. We work at what needs—"

"*Right!*" Bach exploded. She got up and paced the floor. "What the hell do you expect me to *do* with a situation like this? I don't have *anything* to work with, not one snuffin' *thing*. No way of telling *why* she was killed, no way to pick out the *killer*, no way . . . ah, *shit*. What do you expect me to *do*?"

"We don't expect you to do anything," the barbie said quietly. "We didn't ask you to come here. We'd like it very much if you just went away."

In her anger Bach had forgotten that. She was stopped, unable to move in any direction. Finally she caught Weil's eye and jerked her head toward the door.

"Let's get out of here." Weil said nothing. He followed Bach out the door and hurried to catch up.

They reached the tube station, and Bach stopped outside their waiting capsule. She sat down heavily on a bench, put her chin on her palm, and watched the ant-like mass of barbies working at the loading dock.

"Any ideas?"

Weil shook his head, sitting beside her and removing his cap to wipe sweat from his forehead.

"They keep it too hot in here," he said. Bach nodded, not really hearing him. She watched the group of barbies as two separated themselves from the crowd and came a few steps in her direction. Both were laughing, as if at some private joke, looking right at Bach. One of them reached under her blouse and withdrew a long, gleaming steel knife. In one smooth motion she plunged it into the other barbie's stomach and lifted, bringing her up on the balls of her feet. The one who had been stabbed looked surprised for a moment, staring down at herself, her mouth open, as the knife gutted her like a fish. Then her eyes widened, and she stared horror-stricken at her companion and slowly went to her knees, holding the knife to her as blood gushed out and soaked her white uniform.

"*Stop her!*" Bach shouted. She was on her feet and running, after a moment of horrified paralysis. It had looked *so* much like the tape.

She was about forty meters from the killer, who moved with deliberate speed, jogging rather than running. She passed the barbie who had been attacked— and who was now on her side, still holding the knife hilt almost tenderly to herself, wrapping her body around the pain. Bach thumbed the panic button on her communicator, glanced over her shoulder to see Weil kneeling beside the stricken barbie, then looked back—

—to a confusion of running figures. Which one was it? *Which one?*

She grabbed the one that seemed to be in the same place and moving in the same direction as the killer had been before she looked away. She swung the barbie around and hit her hard on the side of the neck with the edge of her palm, watched her fall while trying to look at all the other barbies at the same time. They were running in both directions, some trying to get away, others entering the loading dock to see what was going on.

It was a madhouse scene with shrieks and shouts and baffling movement.

Bach spotted something bloody lying on the floor, then knelt by the inert figure and clapped the handcuffs on her.

She looked up into a sea of faces, all alike.

The commissioner dimmed the lights, and he, Bach, and Weil faced the big screen at the end of the room. Beside the screen was a department photoanalyst with a pointer in her hand. The tape began to run.

"Here they are," the woman said, indicating two barbies with the tip of the long stick. They were just faces on the edge of the crowd, beginning to move. "Victim right here, the suspect to her right." Everyone watched as the stabbing was re-created. Bach winced when she saw how long she had taken to react. In her favor, it had taken Weil a fraction of a second longer.

"Lieutenant Bach begins to move here. The suspect moves back toward the crowd. If you'll notice, she is watching Bach over her shoulder. Now. Here." She froze a frame. "Bach loses eye contact. The suspect peels off the plastic glove which prevented blood from staining her hand. She drops it, moves laterally. By the time Bach looks back, we can see she is after the wrong suspect."

Bach watched in sick fascination as her image assaulted the wrong barbie, the actual killer only a meter to her left. The tape resumed normal speed, and Bach watched the killer until her eyes began to hurt from not blinking. She would not lose her this time.

"She's incredibly brazen. She does not leave the room for another twenty minutes." Bach saw herself kneel and help the medical team load the wounded barbie into the capsule. The killer had been at her elbow, almost touching her. She felt her arm break out in goose pimples.

She remembered the sick fear that had come over her as she knelt by the injured woman. *It could be any of them. The one behind me, for instance . . .*

She had drawn her weapon then, backed against the wall, and not moved until the reinforcements arrived a few minutes later.

At a motion from the commissioner, the lights came back on.

"Let's hear what you have," he said.

Bach glanced at Weil, then read from her notebook. " 'Sergeant Weil was able to communicate with the victim shortly before medical help arrived. He asked her if she knew anything pertinent as to the identity of her assailant. She answered no, saying only that it was "the wrath." She could not elaborate.' I quote now from the account Sergeant Weil wrote down immediately after the interview. ' "It hurts, it hurts." "I'm dying, I'm dying." I told her help was on the way. She responded: "I'm dying." Victim became incoherent, and I attempted to get a shirt from the onlookers to stop the flow of blood. No cooperation was forthcoming.' "

"It was the word 'I,' " Weil supplied. "When she said that, they all started to drift away."

" 'She became rational once more,' " Bach resumed, " 'long enough to whisper a number to me. The number was twelve-fifteen, which I wrote down as one-two-one-five. She roused herself once more, said "I'm dying." ' " Bach closed the notebook and looked up. "Of course she was right." She coughed nervously.

"We invoked section 35b of the New Dresden Unified Code, 'Hot Pursuit,' suspending civil liberties locally for the duration of the search. We located component 1215 by the simple expedient of lining up all the barbies and having them pull their pants down. Each has a serial number in the small of her back. Component 1215, one Sylvester J. Cronhausen, is in custody at this moment.

"While the search was going on, we went to sleeping cubicle number 1215 with a team of criminologists. In a concealed compartment beneath the bunk we found these items." Bach got up, opened the evidence bag, and spread the items on the table.

There was a carved wooden mask. It had a huge nose

with a hooked end, a mustache, and a fringe of black hair around it. Beside the mask were several jars of powders and creams, greasepaint and cologne. One black nylon sweater, one pair black trousers, one pair black sneakers. A stack of pictures clipped from magazines, showing ordinary people, many of them wearing more clothes than was normal on Luna. There was a black wig and a merkin of the same color.

"What was that last?" the commissioner asked.

"A merkin, sir," Bach supplied. "A pubic wig."

"Ah." He contemplated the assortment, leaned back in his chair. "Somebody liked to dress up."

"Evidently, sir." Bach stood at ease with her hands clasped behind her back, her face passive. She felt an acute sense of failure, and a cold determination to get the woman with the gall to stand at her elbow after committing murder before her eyes. She was sure the time and place had been chosen deliberately, that the barbie had been executed for Bach's benefit.

"Do you think these items belonged to the deceased?"

"We have no reason to state that, sir," Bach said. "However, the circumstances are suggestive."

"Of what?"

"I can't be sure. These things *might* have belonged to the victim. A random search of other cubicles turned up nothing like this. We showed the items to component 23900, our liaison. She professed not to know their purpose." She stopped, then added, "I believe she was lying. She looked quite disgusted."

"Did you arrest her?"

"No, sir. I didn't think it wise. She's the only connection we have, such as she is."

The commissioner frowned and laced his fingers together. "I'll leave it up to you, Lieutenant Bach. Frankly, we'd like to be shut of this mess as soon as possible."

"I couldn't agree with you more, sir."

"Perhaps you don't understand me. We have to have a warm body to indict. We have to have one soon."

"Sir, I'm doing the best I can. Candidly, I'm beginning to wonder if there's anything I *can* do."

"You still don't understand me." He looked around the office. The stenographer and photoanalyst had left. He was alone with Bach and Weil. He flipped a switch on his desk, turning a recorder *off*, Bach realized.

"The news is picking up on this story. We're beginning to get some heat. On the one hand, people are afraid of these barbies. They're hearing about the murder fifty years ago, and the informal agreement. They don't like it much. On the other hand, there's the civil libertarians. They'll fight hard to prevent anything happening to the barbies, on principle. The government doesn't want to get into a mess like that. I can hardly blame them."

Bach said nothing, and the commissioner looked pained.

"I see I have to spell it out. We have a suspect in custody," he said.

"Are you referring to component 1215, Sylvester Cronhausen?"

"No. I'm speaking of the one you captured."

"Sir, the tape clearly shows she is not the guilty party. She was an innocent bystander." She felt her face heat up as she said it. Damn it, she had tried her best.

"Take a look at this." He pressed a button and the tape began to play again. But the quality was much impaired. There were bursts of snow, moments when the picture faded out entirely. It was a very good imitation of a camera failing. Bach watched herself running through the crowd, there was a flash of white, and she had hit the woman. The lights came back on in the room.

"I've checked with the analyst. She'll go along. There's a bonus in this for both of you." He looked from Weil to Bach.

"I don't think I can go through with that, sir."

He looked like he'd tasted a lemon. "I didn't say we were doing this today. It's an option. But I ask you to look at it this way, just look at it, and I'll say no more.

This is the way *they themselves* want it. They offered you the same deal the first time you were there. Close the case with a confession, no mess. We've already got this prisoner. She just says she killed her, she killed all of them. I want you to ask yourself, is she wrong? By her own lights and moral values? She believes she shares responsibility for the murders, and society demands a culprit. What's wrong with accepting their compromise and letting this all blow over?"

"Sir, it doesn't feel right to me. This is not in the oath I took. I'm supposed to protect the innocent, and she's innocent. She's the *only* barbie I *know* to be innocent."

The commissioner sighed. "Bach, you've got four days. You give me an alternative by then."

"Yes, sir. If I can't, I'll tell you now that I won't interfere with what you plan. But you'll have to accept my resignation."

Anna-Louise Bach reclined in the bathtub with her head pillowed on a folded towel. Only her neck, nipples, and knees stuck out above the placid surface of the water, tinted purple with a generous helping of bath salts. She clenched a thin cheroot in her teeth. A ribbon of lavender smoke curled from the end of it, rising to join the cloud near the ceiling.

She reached up with one foot and turned on the taps, letting out cooled water and refilling with hot until the sweat broke out on her brow. She had been in the tub for several hours. The tips of her fingers were like washboards.

There seemed to be few alternatives. The barbies were foreign to her, and to anyone she could assign to interview them. They didn't want her help in solving the crimes. All the old rules and procedures were useless. Witnesses meant nothing; one could not tell one from the next, nor separate their stories. Opportunity? Several thousand individuals had it. Motive was a blank. She had a physical description in minute detail, even tapes of the actual murders. Both were useless.

There was one course of action that might show re-

sults. She had been soaking for hours in the hope of
determining just how important her job was to her.

Hell, what else did she want to do?

She got out of the tub quickly, bringing a lot of water
with her to drip onto the floor. She hurried into her
bedroom, pulled the sheets off the bed, and slapped the
nude male figure on the buttocks.

"Come on, Svengali," she said. "Here's your chance
to do something about my nose."

She used every minute while her eyes were function-
ing to read all she could find about Standardists. When
Atlas worked on her eyes, the computer droned into an
earphone. She memorized most of the *Book of Standards*.

Ten hours of surgery, followed by eight hours flat on
her back, paralyzed, her body undergoing forced regeneration, her eyes scanning the words that flew by on
an overhead screen.

Three hours of practice, getting used to shorter legs
and arms. Another hour to assemble her equipment.

When she left the Atlas clinic, she felt she would pass
for a barbie as long as she kept her clothes on. She
hadn't gone *that* far.

People tended to forget about access locks that led to
the surface. Bach had used the fact more than once to
show up in places where no one expected her.

She parked her rented crawler by the lock and left it
there. Moving awkwardly in her pressure suit, she entered and started it cycling, then stepped through the
inner door into an equipment room in Anytown. She
stowed the suit, checked herself quickly in a washroom
mirror, straightened the tape measure that belted her
loose white jumpsuit, and entered the darkened corridors.

What she was doing was not illegal in any sense, but
she was on edge. She didn't expect the barbies to take
kindly to her masquerade if they discovered it, and she

knew how easy it was for a barbie to vanish forever. Three had done so before Bach ever got the case.

The place seemed deserted. It was late evening by the arbitrary day cycle of New Dresden. Time for the nightly equalization. Bach hurried down the silent hallways to the main meeting room in the temple.

It was full of barbies and a vast roar of conversation. Bach had no trouble slipping in, and in a few minutes she knew her facial work was as good as Atlas had promised.

Equalization was the barbie's way of standardizing experience. They had been unable to simplify their lives to the point where each member of the community experienced the same things every day; *The Book of Specifications* said it was a goal to be aimed for, but probably unattainable this side of Holy Reassimilation with Goddess. They tried to keep the available jobs easy enough that each member could do them all. The commune did not seek to make a profit; but air, water, and food had to be purchased, along with replacement parts and services to keep things running. The community had to produce things to trade with the outside.

They sold luxury items: hand-carved religious statues, illuminated holy books, painted crockery, and embroidered tapestries. None of the items were Standardist. The barbies had no religious symbols except their uniformity and the tape measure, but nothing in their dogma prevented them from selling objects of reverence to people of other faiths.

Bach had seen the products for sale in the better shops. They were meticulously produced, but suffered from the fact that each item looked too much like every other. People buying hand-produced luxuries in a technological age tend to want the differences that non-machine production entails, whereas the barbies wanted everything to look exactly alike. It was an ironic situation, but the barbies willingly sacrificed value by adhering to their standards.

Each barbie did things during the day that were as close as possible to what everyone else had done. But someone had to cook meals, tend the air machines, load the freight. Each component had a different job each day. At equalization, they got together and tried to even that out.

It was boring. Everyone talked at once, to anyone that happened to be around. Each woman told what she had done that day. Bach heard the same group of stories a hundred times before the night was over, and repeated them to anyone who would listen.

Anything unusual was related over a loudspeaker so everyone could be aware of it and thus spread out the intolerable burden of anomaly. No barbie wanted to keep a unique experience to herself; it made her soiled, unclean, until it was shared by all.

Bach was getting very tired of it—she was short on sleep—when the lights went out. The buzz of conversation shut off as if a tape had broken.

"All cats are alike in the dark," someone muttered, quite near Bach. Then a single voice was raised. It was solemn, almost a chant.

"We are the wrath. There is blood on our hands, but it is the holy blood of cleansing. We have told you of the cancer eating at the heart of the body, and yet still you cower away from what must be done. *The filth must be removed from us!*"

Bach was trying to tell which direction the words were coming from in the total darkness. Then she became aware of movement, people brushing against her, all going in the same direction. She began to buck the tide when she realized everyone was moving away from the voice.

"You think you can use our holy uniformity to hide among us, but the vengeful hand of Goddess will not be stayed. The mark is upon you, our one-time sisters. Your sins have set you apart, and retribution will strike swiftly.

"There are five of you left. Goddess knows who you are, and will not tolerate your perversion of her holy truth. Death will strike you when you least expect it. Goddess sees the differentness within you, the different-

ness you seek but hope to hide from your upright sisters."

People were moving more swiftly now, and a scuffle had developed ahead of her. She struggled free of people who were breathing panic from every pore until she stood in a clear space. The speaker was shouting to be heard over the sound of whimpering and the shuffling of bare feet. Bach moved forward, swinging her outstretched hands. But another hand brushed her first.

The punch was not centered on her stomach, but it drove the air from her lungs and sent her sprawling. Someone tripped over her, and she realized things would get pretty bad if she didn't get to her feet. She was struggling up when the lights came back on.

There was a mass sigh of relief as each barbie examined her neighbor. Bach half expected another body to be found, but that didn't seem to be the case. The killer had vanished again.

She slipped away from the equalization before it began to break up, and hurried down the deserted corridors to room 1215.

She sat in the room—little more than a cell, with a bunk, a chair, and a light on a table—for more than two hours before the door opened, as she had hoped it would. A barbie stepped inside, breathing hard, closed the door, and leaned against it.

"We wondered if you would come," Bach said tentatively.

The woman ran to Bach and collapsed at her knees, sobbing.

"Forgive us, please forgive us, our darling. We didn't dare come last night. We were afraid that . . . that if . . . that it might have been you who was murdered, and that the wrath would be waiting for us here. Forgive us, forgive us."

"It's all right," Bach said, for lack of anything better. Suddenly the barbie was on top of her, kissing her with a desperate passion. Bach was startled, though she had expected something of the sort. She responded as best she could. The barbie finally began to talk again.

"We must stop this, we just have to stop. We're so frightened of the wrath, but . . . but the *longing!* We can't stop ourselves. We need to see you so badly that we can hardly get through the day, not knowing if you are across town or working at our elbow. It builds all day, and at night we cannot stop ourselves from sinning yet again." She was crying, more softly this time, not from happiness at seeing the woman she took Bach to be, but from a depth of desperation. "What's going to become of us?" she asked helplessly.

"Shhh," Bach soothed. "It's going to be all right."

She comforted the barbie for a while, then saw her lift her head. Her eyes seemed to glow with a strange light.

"I can't wait any longer," she said. She stood up and began taking off her clothes. Bach could see her hands shaking.

Beneath her clothing the barbie had concealed a few things that looked familiar. Bach could see that the merkin was already in place between her legs. There was a wooden mask much like the one that had been found in the secret panel, and a jar. The barbie unscrewed the top of it and used her middle finger to smear dabs of brown onto her breasts, making stylized nipples.

"Look what *I* got," she said, coming down hard on the pronoun, her voice trembling. She pulled a flimsy yellow blouse from the pile of clothing on the floor, and slipped it over her shoulders. She struck a pose, then strutted up and down the tiny room.

"Come on, darling," she said. "Tell me how beautiful I am. Tell me I'm lovely. Tell me I'm the only one for you. The only one. What's the *matter*? Are you still frightened? I'm not. I'll dare anything for you, my one and only love." But now she stopped walking and looked suspiciously at Bach. "Why aren't you getting dressed?"

"We . . . uh, I can't," Bach said, extemporizing.

"They, uh, someone found the things. They're all gone." She didn't dare remove her clothes because her nipples and pubic hair would look too real, even in the dim light.

The barbie was backing away. She picked up her mask and held it protectively to her. "What do you mean? Was she here? The wrath? Are they after us? It's true, isn't it? They can see us." She was on the edge of crying again, near panic.

"No, no, I think it was the police—" But it was doing no good. The barbie was at the door now, and had it half open.

"You're her! What have you done to . . . no, no, you stay away." She reached into the clothing that she now held in her hands, and Bach hesitated for a moment, expecting a knife. It was enough time for the barbie to dart quickly through the door, slamming it behind her.

When Bach reached the door, the woman was gone.

Bach kept reminding herself that she was not here to find the other potential victims—of whom her visitor was certainly one—but to catch the killer. The fact remained that she wished she could have detained her, to question her further.

The woman was a pervert, by the only definition that made any sense among the Standardists. She, and presumably the other dead barbies, had an individuality fetish. When Bach had realized that, her first thought had been to wonder why they didn't simply leave the colony and become whatever they wished. But then why did a Christian seek out prostitutes? For the taste of sin. In the larger world, what these barbies did would have had little meaning. Here, it was sin of the worst and tastiest kind.

And somebody didn't like it at all.

The door opened again, and the woman stood there facing Bach, her hair disheveled, breathing hard.

"We had to come back," she said. "We're so sorry that we panicked like that. Can you forgive us?" She was coming toward Bach now, her arms out. She looked so vulnerable and contrite that Bach was astonished when the fist connected with her cheek.

Bach thudded against the wall, then found herself pinned under the woman's knees, with something sharp and cool against her throat. She swallowed very carefully and said nothing. Her throat itched unbearably.

"She's dead," the barbie said. "And you're next." But there was something in her face that Bach didn't understand. The barbie brushed at her eyes a few times, and squinted down at her.

"Listen, I'm not who you think I am. If you kill me, you'll be bringing more trouble on your sisters than you can imagine."

The barbie hesitated, then roughly thrust her hand down into Bach's pants. Her eyes widened when she felt the genitals, but the knife didn't move. Bach knew she had to talk fast and say all the right things.

"You understand what I'm talking about, don't you?" She looked for a response, but saw none. "You're aware of the political pressures that are coming down. You know this whole colony could be wiped out if you look like a threat to the outside. You don't want that."

"If it must be, it will be," the barbie said. "The purity is the important thing. If we die, we shall die pure. The blasphemers must be killed."

"I don't care about that anymore," Bach said, and finally got a ripple of interest from the barbie. "I have my principles, too. Maybe I'm not as fanatical about them as you are about yours. But they're important to me. One is that the guilty be brought to justice."

"You have the guilty party. Try her. Execute her. She will not protest."

"*You* are the guilty party."

The woman smiled. "So arrest us."

"All right, all right. I can't, obviously. Even if you don't kill me, you'll walk out that door and I'll never be able to find you. I've given up on that. I just don't have the time. This was my last chance, and it looks like it didn't work."

"We don't think you could do it, even with more time. But why should we let you live?"

"Because we can help each other." She felt the pressure ease up a little, and managed to swallow again. "You don't want to kill me, because it could destroy your community. Myself . . . I need to be able to salvage some self-respect out of this mess. I'm willing to accept your definition of morality and let you be the law in your own community. Maybe you're even right. Maybe you *are* one being. But I can't let that woman be convicted when I *know* she didn't kill anyone."

The knife was not touching her neck now, but it was still being held so that the barbie could plunge it into her throat at the slightest movement.

"And if we let you live? What do you get out of it? How do you free your 'innocent' prisoner?"

"Tell me where to find the body of the woman you just killed. I'll take care of the rest."

The pathology team had gone and Anytown was settling down once again. Bach sat on the edge of the bed with Jorge Weil. She was as tired as she ever remembered being. How long had it been since she slept?

"I'll tell you," Weil said, "I honestly didn't think this thing would work. I guess I was wrong."

Bach sighed. "I wanted to take her alive, Jorge. I thought I could. But when she came at me with the knife . . ." She let him finish the thought, not caring to lie to him. She'd already done that to the interviewer. In her story, she had taken the knife from her assailant and tried to disable her, but had been forced in the end to kill her. Luckily, she had the bump on the back of her head from being thrown against the wall. It made a black-out period plausible. Otherwise, someone would have wondered why she waited so long to call for police and an ambulance. The barbie had been dead for an hour when they arrived.

"Well, I'll hand it to you. You sure pulled this out. I'll admit it, I was having a hard time deciding if I'd do as you were going to do and resign, or if I could have stayed on. Now I'll never know."

"Maybe it's best that way. I don't really know, either."

Jorge grinned at her. "I can't get used to thinking of *you* being behind that godawful face."

"Neither can I, and I don't want to see any mirrors. I'm going straight to Atlas and get it changed back." She got wearily to her feet and walked toward the tube station with Weil.

She had not quite told him the truth. She did intend to get her own face back as soon as possible—nose and all—but there was one thing left to do.

From the first, a problem that had bothered her had been the question of how the killer identified her victims.

Presumably the perverts had arranged times and places to meet for their strange rites. That would have been easy enough. Any one barbie could easily shirk her duties. She could say she was sick, and no one would know it was the same barbie who had been sick yesterday, and for a week or month before. She need not work; she could wander the halls acting as if she was on her way from one job to another. No one could challenge her. Likewise, while 23900 had said no barbie spent consecutive nights in the same room, there was no way for her to know that. Evidently room 1215 had been taken over permanently by the perverts.

And the perverts would have no scruples about identifying each other by serial number at their clandestine meetings, though they could not do it in the streets. The killer didn't even have that.

But someone had known how to identify them, to pick them out of a crowd. Bach thought she must have infiltrated meetings, marked the participants in some way. One could lead her to another until she knew them all and was ready to strike.

She kept recalling the strange way the killer had looked at her, the way she had squinted. The mere fact that she had not killed Bach instantly in a case of mistaken identity meant she had been expecting to see something that had not been there.

And she had an idea about that.

She meant to go to the morgue first, and to examine the corpses under different wavelengths of lights, with various filters. She was betting some kind of mark would become visible on the faces, a mark the killer had been looking for with her contact lenses.

It had to be something that was visible only with the right kind of equipment, or under the right circumstances. If she kept at it long enough, she would find it.

If it was an invisible ink, it brought up another interesting question. How had it been applied? With a brush or spray gun? Unlikely. But such an ink on the killer's hands might look and feel like water.

Once she had marked her victims, the killer would have to be confident the mark would stay in place for a reasonable time. The murders had stretched over a month. So she was looking for an indelible, invisible ink, one that soaked into pores.

And if it was indelible . . .

There was no use thinking further about it. She was right, or she was wrong. When she struck the bargain with the killer she had faced up to the possibility that she might have to live with it. Certainly she could not now bring a killer into court, not after what she had just said.

No, if she came back to Anytown and found a barbie whose hands were stained with guilt, she would have to do the job herself.

A Hiss of Dragon

Gregory Benford and Marc Laidlaw

Terraforming of alien planets is a valid notion that's been explored in many sf stories,
but there are limits to what's practical. Imagine
a planet that's totally lacking in heavy metals:
would it be more likely for us to adapt the
world to humanity, or to use the sciences of
bioengineering to make *us* capable of living
comfortably on that planet?

Gregory Benford, whose novels include *In
the Ocean of Night* and *The Stars in Shroud*,
is a major sf writer of the 1970s. Marc Laidlaw
had just graduated from high school when he
met Benford, discussed this idea with him (Benford had been thinking about it for some time),
and collaborated on the story below. The result
was an entertaining adventure on a thoroughly
realized world far from our own.

"Incoming Dragon!" Leopold yelled and ducked to the
left. I went right.

Dragons come in slow and easy. A blimp with wings,
this one settled down like a wrinkled brown sky falling.
I scrambled over boulders, trying to be inconspicuous
and fast at the same time. It didn't seem like a promising beginning for a new job.

Leopold and I had been working on the ledge in
front of the Dragon's Lair, stacking berry pods. This
Dragon must have flown toward its Lair from the other

side of the mountain spire, so our radio tag on him didn't transmit through all the rock. Usually they're not so direct. Most Dragons circle their Lairs a few times, checking for scavengers and egg stealers. If they don't circle, they're usually too tired. And when they're tired, they're irritable. Something told me I didn't want to be within reach of this one's throat flame.

I dropped my berry-bag rig and went down the rocks feet first. The boulders were slippery with green moss for about twenty meters below the ledge, so I slid down on them. I tried to keep the falls to under four meters and banged my butt when I missed. I could hear Leopold knocking loose rocks on the other side, moving down toward where our skimmer was parked.

A shadow fell over me, blotting out Beta's big yellow disk. The brown bag above thrashed its wings and gave a trumpeting shriek. It had caught sight of the berry bags and knew something was up. Most likely, with its weak eyes, the Dragon thought the bags were eggers— off season, but what do Dragons know about seasons?—and would attack them. That was the optimistic theory. The pessimistic one was that the Dragon had seen one of us. I smacked painfully into a splintered boulder and glanced up. Its underbelly was heaving, turning purple: anger. Not a reassuring sign. Eggers don't bother Dragons that much.

Then its wings fanned the air, backwards. It drifted off the ledge, hovering. The long neck snaked around, and two nearsighted eyes sought mine. The nose expanded, catching my scent. The Dragon hissed triumphantly.

Our skimmer was set for a fast takeoff. But it was 200 meters down, on the only wide spot we could find. I made a megaphone of my hands and shouted into the thin mountain mist, "Leopold! Grab air!"

I jumped down to a long boulder that jutted into space. Below and a little to the left I could make out the skimmer's shiny wings through the shifting green fog. I sucked in a breath and ran off the end of the boulder.

Dragons are clumsy at level flight, but they can drop

like a brick. The only way to beat this one down to the skimmer was by falling most of the way.

I banked down, arms out. Our gravity is only a third of Earth normal. Even when falling, you have time to think things over. I can do the calculations fast enough—it came out to nine seconds—but getting the count right with a Dragon on your tail is another matter. I ticked the seconds off and then popped the chute. It fanned and filled. The skimmer came rushing up, wind whipped my face. Then my harness jerked me to a halt. I drifted down. I thumped the release and fell free. Above me, a trumpeting bellow. Something was coming in at four o'clock and I turned, snatching for my blaser. Could it be that fast? But it was Leopold, on chute. I sprinted for the skimmer. It was pointed along the best outbound wind, flaps already down, a standard precaution. I belted in, sliding my feet into the pedals. I caught a dank, foul reek of Dragon. More high shrieking, closer. Leopold came running up, panting. He wriggled into the rear seat. A thumping of wings. A ceiling of wrinkled leather. Something hissing overhead.

Dragons don't fly, they float. They have a big green hydrogen-filled dome on their backs to give them lift. They make the hydrogen in their stomachs and can dive quickly by venting it out the ass. This one was farting and falling as we zoomed away. I banked, turned to get a look at the huffing brown mountain hooting its anger at us, and grinned.

"I take back what I said this morning," Leopold gasped. "You'll draw full wages *and* commissions, from the start."

I didn't say anything. I'd just noticed that somewhere back there I had pissed my boots full.

I covered it pretty well back at the strip. I twisted out of the skimmer and slipped into the maintenance bay. I had extra clothes in my bag, so I slipped on some fresh socks and thongs.

When I was sure I smelled approximately human, I tromped back out to Leopold. I was damned if I would let my morning's success be blotted out by an embarrassing accident. It was a hirer's market these days. My training at crop dusting out in the flat farmlands had given me an edge over the other guys who had applied. I was determined to hang on to this job.

Leopold was the guy who "invented" the Dragons, five years ago. He took a life form native to Lex, the bloats, and tinkered with their DNA. Bloats are balloonlike and nasty. Leopold made them bigger, tougher, and spliced in a lust for thistleberries that makes Dragons hoard them compulsively. It had been a brilliant job of bioengineering. The Dragons gathered thistleberries, and Leopold stole them from the Lairs.

Thistleberries are a luxury good, high in protein and delicious. The market for them might collapse if Lex's economy got worse—the copper seams over in Bahinin had run out last month. This was nearly the only good flying job left. More than anything else, I wanted to keep flying. And *not* as a crop duster. Clod-grubber work is a pain.

Leopold was leaning against his skimmer, a little pale, watching his men husk thistleberries. His thigh muscles were still thick; he was clearly an airman by ancestry, but he looked tired.

"Goddamn," he said. "I can't figure it out, kid. The Dragons are hauling in more berries than normal. We can't get into the Lairs, though. You'd think it was mating season around here, the way they're attacking my men."

"Mating season? When's that?"

"Oh, in about another six months, when the puffbushes bloom in the treetops. The pollen sets off the mating urges in Dragons—steps up their harvest, but it also makes 'em meaner."

"Great," I said. "I'm allergic to puffbush pollen. I'll have to fight off Dragons with running eyes and a stuffy nose."

Leopold shook his head absently; he hadn't heard me. "I can't understand it—there's nothing wrong with my Dragon designs."

"Seems to me you could have toned down the behavior plexes," I said. "Calm them down a bit—I mean, they've outgrown their competition to the point that they don't even *need* to be mean anymore. They don't browse much as it is . . . nobody's going to bother them."

"No way—there's just not the money for it, Drake. Look, I'm operating on the margin here. My five-year rights to the genetic patents just ran out, and now I'm in competition with Kwalan Rhiang, who owns the other half of the forest. Besides, you think gene splicing is easy?"

"Still, if they can bioengineer *humans* . . . I mean, we were beefed up for strength and oxy burning nearly a thousand years ago."

"But we weren't blown up to five times the size of our progenitors, Drake. I made those Dragons out of mean sons of bitches—blimps with teeth is what they were. It gets tricky when you mess with the life cycles of something that's already that unstable. You just don't understand what's involved here."

I nodded. "I'm no bioengineer—granted."

He looked at me and grinned, a spreading warm grin on his deeply lined face. "Yeah, Drake, but you're good at what you do, really good. What happened today— well, I'm getting too old for that sort of thing, and it's happening more and more often. If you hadn't been there I'd probably be stewing in that Dragon's stomach right now—skimmer and all."

I shrugged. That gave me a chance to roll the slabs of muscle in my shoulders, neck, and pectorals—a subtle advertisement that I had enough to keep a skimmer aloft for hours.

"So," he continued, "I'm giving you full pilot rank. The skimmer's yours. You can fly it home tonight, on the condition that you meet me at the Angis Tavern for a drink later on. And bring your girl Evelaine, too, if you want."

"It's a deal, Leopold. See you there."

I whistled like a dungwarbler all the way home, pedaling my new skimmer over the treetops toward the city. I nearly wrapped myself in a floating thicket of windbrambles, but not even this could destroy my good mood.

I didn't notice any Dragons roaming around, though I saw that the treetops had been plucked of their berries and then scorched. Leopold had at least had the foresight, when he was gene tinkering, to provide for the thistleberries' constant replenishment. He gave the Dragons a throat flame to singe the treetops with, which makes the berries regrow quickly. A nice touch.

It would have been simpler, of course, to have men harvest the thistleberries themselves, but that never worked out, economically. Thistleberries grow on top of virtually unclimbable thorntrees, where you can't even maneuver a skimmer without great difficulty. And if a man fell to the ground . . . well, if it's on the ground, it has spines—that's the rule on Lex. There's nothing soft to fall on down there. Sky life is more complex than ground life. You can actually do something useful with sky life—namely, bioengineering. Lex may be a low-metal world—which means low technology—but our bioengineers are the best.

A clapping sound to the left. I stopped whistling. Down through the greenish haze I could see a dark form coming in over the treetops, its wide rubbery wings slapping together at the top of each stroke. A smackwing. Good meat, spicy and moist. But hard to catch. Evelaine and I had good news to celebrate tonight; I decided to bring her home smackwing for dinner. I took the skimmer down in the path of the smackwing, meanwhile slipping my blaser from its holster.

The trick to hunting in the air is to get beneath your prey so that you can grab it while it falls, but this smackwing was flying too low. I headed in fast, hoping to frighten it into rising above me, but it was no use. The smackwing saw me, red eyes rolling. It missed a beat in its flapping and dived toward the treetops. At that instant a snagger shot into view from the topmost branches, rising with a low farting sound. The smack-wing spotted this blimplike thing that had leaped into its path, but apparently didn't think it too threatening. It swerved about a meter under the bobbing creature—

And stopped flat, in midair.

I laughed aloud, sheathing my blaser. The snagger had won his meal like a real hunter.

Beneath the snagger's wide, blimplike body was a dangling sheet of transparent sticky material. The smackwing struggled in the moist folds as the snagger drew the sheet upward. To the unwary smackwing that clear sheet must have been invisible until the instant he flew into it.

Within another minute, as I pedaled past the spot, the snagger had entirely engulfed the smackwing and was unrolling its sticky sheet as it drifted back into the treetops. Pale yellow eyes considered me and rejected the notion of me as food. A ponderous predator, wise with years.

I flew into the spired city: Kalatin.

I parked on the deck of our apartment building, high above the jumbled wooden buildings of the city. Now that my interview had been successful, we'd be able to stay in Kalatin, though I hoped we could find a better apartment. This one was as old as the city—which in turn had been around for a great deal of the 1,200 years humans had been on Lex. As the wood of the lower stories rotted, and as the building crumbled away, new quarters were just built on top of it and settled into place. Someday this city would be an archaeologist's dream. In the meantime, it was an inhabitant's night-mare.

Five minutes later, having negotiated several treach-erous ladders and a splintering shinny pole into the depths of the old building, I crept quietly to the wooden door of my apartment and let myself in, clutching the mudskater steaks that I'd picked up on the way home. It was dark and cramped inside, the smell of rubbed wood strong. I could hear Evelaine moving around in the kitchen, so I sneaked to the doorway and looked in.

She was turned away, chopping thistleberries with a thorn-knife.

I grabbed her, throwing the steaks into the kitchen, and kissed her.

"Got the job, Evey!" I said. "Leopold took me out himself and I ended up saving his—"

"It *is* you!" She covered her nose, squirming away from me. "What is that smell, Drake?"

"Smell?"

"Like something died. It's all over you."

I remembered the afternoon's events. It was either the smell of Dragon, which I'd got from scrambling around in a Lair, or that of urine. I played it safe and said, "I think it's Dragon."

"Well, take it somewhere else. I'm cooking dinner."

"I'll hop in the cycler. You can cook up the steaks I brought. Then we're going out to celebrate."

The Angis Tavern is no skiff joint, good for a stale senso on the way home from work. It's the best. The Angis is a vast old place perched on a pyramid of rock. Orange fog nestles at the base, a misty collar separating it from the jumble of the city below. Other spires poke up in the distance, punctuating the dark with crustings of yellow light.

Evelaine pedaled the skimmer with me, having trouble in her gown. We made a wobbly landing on the rickety side deck. It would've been easier to coast down to the city, where there was more room for a glide approach, but that's pointless. There are thick cactus and thornbushes around the Angis base, hard to negotiate at night. In the old days it kept away predators; now it keeps away the riffraff.

But not completely: two beggars accosted us as we dismounted, offering to shine up the skimmer's aluminum skin. I growled convincingly at them, and they skittered away. The Angis is so big, so full of crannies to hide out in, they can't keep it clear of beggars, I guess.

We went in a balcony entrance. Fat balloons nudged

against the ceiling, ten meters overhead, dangling their cords. I snagged one and stepped off into space. Evelaine hooked it as I fell. We rode it down past alcoves set in the rock walls. Well-dressed patrons nodded as we eased down, the balloon following. The Angis is a spire, broadening gradually as we descended. Phosphors cast creamy glows on the tables set into the walls. I spotted Leopold sprawled in a webbing, two empty tankards lying discarded underneath.

"You're late," he called. We stepped off onto his ledge. Our balloons, released, shot back to the roof.

"You didn't set a time. Evelaine, Leopold." Nods, introductory phrases.

"It seems quite crowded here tonight," Evelaine murmured. A plausible social remark, except she'd never been to an inn of this class before.

Leopold shrugged. "Hard times mean full taverns. Booze or sensos or tinglers—pick your poison."

Evelaine has the directness of a country girl and knows her own limitations; she stuck to a mild tingler. Service was running slow, so I went to log our orders. I slid down a shinny pole to the first bar level. Mice zipped by me, eating up table scraps left by the patrons; it saves on labor. Amid the jam and babble I placed our order with a steward and turned to go back.

"You looking for work?" a thick voice said.

I glanced at its owner. "No." The man was big, swarthy, and sure of himself.

"Thought you wanted Dragon work." His eyes had a look of distant amusement.

"How'd you know that?" I wasn't known in the city.

"Friends told me."

"Leopold hired me today."

"So I hear. I'll top whatever he's paying."

"I didn't think business was that good."

"It's going to get better. Much better, once Leopold's out of the action. A monopoly can always sell goods at a higher price. You can start tomorrow."

So this was Kwalan Rhiang. "No, thanks. I'm signed up." Actually, I hadn't signed anything, but there was something about this man I didn't like. Maybe the way he was so sure I'd work for him.

"Flying for Leopold is dangerous. He doesn't know what he's doing."

"See you around," I said. A senso was starting in a nearby booth. I took advantage of it to step into the expanding blue cloud so Rhiang couldn't follow and see where we were sitting. I got a lifting, bright sensation of pleasure, and then I was out of the misty confusion, moving away among the packed crowd.

I saw them on the stairway. They were picking their way down it delicately. I thought they were deformed, but the funny tight clothes gave them away. Offworlders, here for the flying. That was the only reason anybody came to Lex. We're still the only place men can seriously fly longer than a few minutes. Even so, our lack of machines keeps most offworlders away; they like it easy, everything done for them. I watched them pick their way down the stairs, thinking that if the depression got worse, offworlders would be able to hire servants here, even though it was illegal. It could come to that.

They were short as children but heavyset, with narrow chests and skinny limbs. Spindly people, unaugmented for Lex oxy levels. But men like that had colonized here long ago, paying for it in reduced lifetimes. I felt as though I were watching my own ancestors.

Lex shouldn't have any oxy at all, by the usual rules of planetary evolution. It's a small planet, 0.21 Earth masses, a third g of gravity. Rules of thumb say we shouldn't have any atmosphere to speak of. But our sun, Beta, is a K-type star, redder than Sol. Beta doesn't heat our upper atmosphere very much with ultraviolet, so we retain gasses. Even then, Lex would be airless except for accidents of birth. It started out with a dense cloak of gas, just as Earth did. But dim old Beta didn't blow the atmosphere away, and there wasn't enough compressional heating by Lex itself to boil away the gases. So they stuck around, shrouding the planet, causing faster erosion than on Earth. The winds moved dust horizontally, exposing crustal rock. That upset the isostatic balance in the surface, and split open faults. Volcanoes poked up. They belched water and gas onto the surface, keeping the atmosphere dense. So Lex ended up with low gravity and a thick atmosphere. Fine, except that Beta's wan light also never pushed many heavy elements out this far, so Lex is metal-poor. Without iron and the rest you can't build machines, and without technology you're a backwater. You sell your tourist attraction—flying—and hope for the best.

One of the offworlders came up to me and said, "You got any sparkers in this place?"

I shook my head. Maybe he didn't know that getting a sendup by tying your frontal lobes into an animal's is illegal here. Maybe he didn't care. Ancestor or not, he just looked like a misshapen dwarf to me, and I walked away.

Evelaine was describing life in the flatlands when I got back. Leopold was rapt, the worry lines in his face nearly gone. Evelaine does that to people. She's natural and straightforward, so she was telling him right out that she wasn't much impressed with city life. "Farmlands are quiet and restful. Everybody has a job," she murmured. "You're right that getting around is harder—but we can glide in the updrafts, in summer. It's heaven."

"Speaking of the farmlands," I said, "an old friend of mine came out here five years ago. He wanted in on your operations."

"I was hiring like crazy five years ago. What was his name?"

"Lorn Kramer. Great pilot."

Leopold shook his head. "Can't remember. He's not with me now, anyway. Maybe Rhiang got him."

Our drinks arrived. The steward was bribable, though—Rhiang was right behind him.

"You haven't answered my 'gram," Rhiang said directly to Leopold, ignoring us. "I guess he didn't figure I was worth any more time."

"Didn't need to," Leopold said tersely.

"Sell out. I'll give you a good price." Rhiang casually

sank his massive flank on our table edge. "You're getting too old."

Something flickered in Leopold's eyes; he said nothing.

"Talk is," Rhiang went on mildly, "market's falling."

"Maybe," Leopold said. "What you been getting for a kilo?"

"Not saying."

"Tight lips and narrow minds go together."

Rhiang stood, his barrel chest bulging. "You could use a little instruction in politeness."

"From you?" Leopold chuckled. "You paid off that patent clerk to release my gene configs early. Was that polite?"

Rhiang shrugged. "That's the past. The present reality is that there may be an oversupply of thistleberries. Market isn't big enough for two big operations like ours. There's too much—"

"Too much of you, that's my problem. Lift off, Rhiang."

To my surprise, he did. He nodded to me, ignored Evelaine, and gave Leopold a look of contempt. Then he was gone.

I heard them first. We were taking one of the outside walks that corkscrew around the Angis spire, gawking at the phosphored streets below. A stone slide clattered behind us. I saw men duck behind a jutting ledge. One of them had something in his hand that glittered.

"You're jumpy, Drake," Evelaine said.

"Maybe." It occurred to me that if we went over the edge of this spire, hundreds of meters into the thorn scrabble below, it would be very convenient for Rhiang. "Let's move on."

Leopold glanced at me, then back at the inky shadows. We strolled along the trail of volcanic rock, part of the natural formation that made the spire. Rough black pebbles slipped underfoot. In the distant star-flecked night, skylight called and boomed.

We passed under a phosphor. At the next turn Leopold looked back and said, "I saw one of them. Rhiang's right-hand man."

We hurried away. I wished for a pair of wings to get us off this place. Evelaine understood instantly that this was serious. "There's a split in the trail ahead," Leopold said. "If they follow, we'll know . . ." He didn't finish.

We turned. They followed. "I think I know a way to slow them down," I said. Leopold looked at me. We were trying to avoid slipping in the darkness and yet make good time. "Collect some of these obsidian frags," I said.

We got a bundle of them together. "Go on up ahead," I said. We were on a narrow ledge. I sank back into the shadows and waited. The two men appeared. Before they noticed me I threw the obsidian high into the air. In low gravity it takes a long time for them to come back down. In the darkness the two men couldn't see them coming.

I stepped out into the wan light. "Hey!" I yelled to them. They stopped, precisely where I thought they would. "What's going on?" I said, to stall.

The biggest one produced a knife. "This."

The first rock hit, coming down from over a hundred meters above. It slammed into the boulder next to him. Then three more crashed down, striking the big one in the shoulder, braining the second. They both crumpled.

I turned and hurried along the path. If they'd seen me throw, they'd have had time to dodge. It was an old schoolboy trick, but it worked.

The implications, though, were sobering. If Rhiang felt this way, my new job might not last long.

I was bagging berries in the cavernous Paramount Lair when the warning buzzer in my pocket went off. A Dragon was coming in. I still had time, but not much. I decided to finish this particular bag rather than abandon the bagging-pistol. The last bit of fluid sprayed over the heap of berries and began to congeal instantly, its tremendously high surface tension drawing it around the irregular pile and sealing perfectly. I holstered the gun, leaving the bag for later. I turned—

A slow flapping boom. Outside, a wrinkled brown wall.

Well, I'd fooled around long enough—now I dived for safety. The Dragon's Lair was carpeted with a thick collection of nesting materials. None was very pleasant to burrow through, but I didn't have any choice. Behind me I could hear the Dragon moving around; if I didn't move out of his way in a hurry I might get stepped on. The emergency chute on my back tangled in a branch, just as the stench in the Lair intensified. I hurried out of it and went on. I'd just have to be sure not to fall from any great heights. I didn't worry about it, because my skimmer was parked on the ledge just outside the Lair.

I stuck my head up through the nest to judge my position. The bulk of the Dragon was silhouetted against the glare of the sky, which was clear of fog today. The beast seemed to be preening itself. That was something I never thought they did outside of the mating season— which was six months away.

I scrambled backward into the nest. The buzzer in my pocket went off again, though it was supposed to signal just once, for ten seconds. I figured the thing must have broken. It quieted and I moved on, thinking. For one thing, the Dragon that occupied this Lair was supposed to have been far from home right now— which meant that my guest didn't really belong here. Dragons never used the wrong Lair unless it was the mating season.

I frowned. Why did that keep coming up?

Suddenly there was a rush of wind and a low, thrumming sound. The light from outside was cut off. I poked my head into the open.

Another Dragon was lumbering into the Lair. *This* was really impossible. Two Dragons sharing a Lair— and the wrong one at that! Whatever their reasons for being here, I was sure they were going to start fighting pretty soon, so I burrowed deeper, moving toward the nearest wall.

My elbow caught on something. Cloth. I brushed it away, then looked again. A Dragonrobber uniform like my own. It was directly beneath me, half buried in the nesting material. I caught my breath, then poked at the uniform. Something glittered near one empty sleeve: an identification bracelet. I picked it up, shifted it in the light, and read the name on it: *Lorn Kramer.*

Lorn Kramer! So he had been in Leopold's group after all. But that still didn't explain why he'd left his clothes here.

I tugged at the uniform, dragging it toward me. It was limp, but tangled in the nest. I jerked harder and some long, pale things rattled out of the sleeve.

Bones.

I winced. I was suddenly aware that my present situation must be somewhat like the one that had brought him here.

I looked into the Lair again. One of the Dragons was prodding its snout at the other, making low, whuffling sounds. It didn't look like a hostile gesture to me. In fact, it looked like they were playing. The other Dragon wheeled about and headed for the entrance. The first one followed, and in a minute both of them had left the Lair again—as abruptly and inexplicably as they had entered it.

I saw my chance. I ran across the Lair, grabbed my skimmer, and took off. I moved out, pedaling furiously away from the Dragons, and glanced down.

For a minute I thought I was seeing things. The landscape below me was blurred, though the day had been clear and crisp when I'd flown into the Lair. I blinked. It didn't go away, but got clearer. There was a cloud of yellowish dust spreading high above the forest, billowing up and around the Lairs I could see. Where had it come from?

I sneezed, passing through a high plume of the dust. Then my eyes began to sting and I sneezed again. I brought the skimmer out of the cloud, but by this time my vision was distorted with tears. I began to cough and choke all at once, until the skimmer faltered as I fought to stay in control, my eyes streaming.

I knew what that dust was.

Nothing affected me as fiercely as puffbush pollen: it was the only thing I was really allergic to.

I stopped pedaling.

It affected Dragons, too. It set off their mating urges.

But where was the damned stuff coming from? It was six months out of season. I started pedaling again, legs straining. I turned to get a better view.

A flash of light needled past my head, and I knew. Three skimmers shot into view from around the spire of Paramount Lair. The tip of one of my wings was seared away by a blaser. My skimmer lurched wildly, but I held on and brought it up just as the first skimmer came toward me. Its pilot was wearing a filtermask. Attached to the skimmer were some empty bags that must have held the puffbush pollen. But what I was looking at was the guy's blaser. It was aimed at me.

I reeled into an updraft, pulling over my attacker, grabbing for my own blaser. The skimmer soared beneath me, then careened into a sharp turn. It was too sharp. The guy turned straight into the path of his companion. The two skimmers crashed together with a satisfying sound, then the scattered parts and pilots fell slowly toward the treetops. Seconds later, the forest swallowed them up.

I looked for the third man, just as he came up beside me. The bastard was grinning, and I recognized that grin. It was Kwalan Rhiang's.

He nodded once, affably, and before I could remember to use my blaser, Rhiang took a single, precise shot at the chain guard of my skimmer. The pedals rolled uselessly. I was out of control. Rhiang lifted away and cruised out of sight, leaving me flailing at the air in a ruined skimmer.

I had exactly one chance, and this was to get back to the Lair I'd just abandoned. I was slightly higher than the opening, so I glided in, backpedaled for the drop— and crashed straight into the wall, thanks to my ruined pedals. But I made it in alive, still able to stand up and brush the dirt from my uniform. I stood at the mouth of the Lair, staring out over the forest, considering the long climb that lay below me.

And just then the Dragons returned.

Not one, this time—not even two. *Five* shadows wheeled overhead; five huge beasts headed toward the Lair where I was standing. And finally, five Dragons dropped right on top of me.

I leapt back just in time, scrambling into the blue shadows as the first Dragon thumped to the ledge. It waddled inside, reeking. I moved back farther. Its four friends were right behind. I kept moving back.

Well, at least now I knew *why* they were doing this. Kwalan Rhiang had been setting off their mating urges by dusting the Dragons with puffbush pollen, messing up their whole life cycle, fooling with their already nasty tempers. It made sense. Anything less subtle might have gotten Rhiang into a lot of trouble. As it was, he'd doubtless fly safely home, waiting for Leopold's Dragons to kill off Leopold's men.

Out in the cavernous Lair, the Dragons began to move around, prodding at each other like scramble-mice, hooting their airy courting sounds. The ground shook with their movement. Two seemed to be females, which suggested that I might look forward to some fighting between the other three. Great.

I fumbled at my pockets for something that might be of help. My warning buzzer had shattered in my rough landing; I threw it away. I still had my bagging-gun, but it wouldn't do me a lot of good. My blaser seemed okay. I unholstered it and began to move along the wall. If I went carefully, I might be able to get onto the outer ledge.

Two of the males were fighting now, lunging, the sounds of their efforts thundering around me. I made a short run and gained a bit of ground. One of the Dragons retreated from the battle—apparently the loser. I groaned. He had moved directly in my path.

A huge tail pounded at the ground near me and a

female started backing my way, not looking at me. There was no place to go. And I was getting tired of this. I decided to warn her off. I made a quick shot at her back, nipping her in the hydrogen dome. She squawked and shuffled away, confused. I went on.

I stopped. There was a hissing sound behind me. Turning, I could see nothing but the Dragon I'd just shot. She didn't appear to be making the sound, but it was coming from her direction. I peered closer, through the blue gloom, and then saw where the noise was coming from.

Her hydrogen dome was deflating.

I nearly laughed aloud. Here was the answer to my problem. I could deflate the Dragons, leaving them stranded, unable to fly, while I climbed down this spire without fear of pursuit. I lifted my blaser and aimed at the male nearest the rear of the Lair. A near miss, then a hit. Hydrogen hissed out of his dome as well. Then I got the second female, and another male who was directly across from me.

One Dragon to go. The others were roaring and waddling. The Lair was full of the hissing sound.

I turned to my last opponent. He wasn't looking my way, but he was blocking my exit. I moved in closer and lifted my blaser.

Then he saw me.

I flung myself aside just as he bellowed and pounded forward, filling the entrance to the Lair, blocking out the sunlight. I rolled into the thorny nest. I fired once, hitting him in the snout. He swung his head toward me, pushing me around toward the outer ledge, bellowing. I fired again, and once more missed his hydrogen dome. I made a dash around his rump just as he spun my way, tail lashing against me. His dark little eyes narrowed as he sighted me, and his throat began to ripple.

My time was up. He was about to blast me with his throat flame.

The Dragon opened his mouth, belched hydrogen, and ignited it by striking a spark from his molars—

That was the wrong thing to do.

I saw it coming and ducked.

The cavern shuddered and blew up. The orange explosion rumbled out, catching the Dragons in a huge rolling flame. I buried myself in the nesting strands and grabbed onto the lashing tail of my attacker. Terrified by the blast, he took off. My eyebrows were singed, my wrists burned.

The world spun beneath me. A tendril of smoke drifted into view just below, mingled with flaming bits of nesting material and the leathery hide of Dragons. Then my view spun again and I was looking at the sky. It gradually dawned on me that I was clinging to a Dragon's tail.

It occurred to the Dragon at the same time. I saw his head swing toward me, snapping angrily. His belly was flashing purple. Every now and then he let out a tongue of flame, but he couldn't quite get at me. Meanwhile, I held on for my life.

The Dragon flew on, but my weight seemed to be too much for it. We were dropping slowly toward the trees, as easily as if I'd punctured his bony dome with my blaser. But it would be a rough landing. And I'd have to deal with the Dragon afterward.

I spied something rising from the trees below us. It shot swiftly into the air after a high-flying bulletbird, its transparent sheet rippling beneath its blimplike body. It was a huge snagger—as big as my own skimmer. I kicked on the Dragon's tail, dragging it sideways. The Dragon lurched and spun and then we were directly over the snagger.

I let go of the tail and dropped, my eyes closed.

In a second, something soft rumpled beneath me. I had landed safely atop the snagger. I opened my eyes as the Dragon—having lost my weight—shot suddenly upward. I watched it glide away, then looked down at the snagger, my savior. I patted its wide, rubbery body. My weight was pushing it slowly down, as if I were riding the balloons in the Angis Tavern. I looked forward to a comfortable trip to the ground.

"I like your style, kid."

I jumped, nearly losing my place on the snagger. The voice had come out of midair. Literally.

"You," I said. No more was necessary. He was banking around behind me.

Kwalan Rhiang had returned in his skimmer. He circled easily about me as I fell toward the treetops. He came in close, smiling, his huge legs pedaling him on a gentle course. I had to turn my head to keep an eye on him.

"I said before I'd top what Leopold was paying you," he shouted, his thick voice cutting the high air. "After today, I think I'd pay *double*. I could use someone like you."

I felt my face harden. "You bastard. You're responsible for what just happened. Why would I work for someone who's tried to kill me?"

He shrugged. "Gave you a chance to prove yourself. Come on, you're wasting your time with Leopold."

"And you're wasting your time with me."

He shrugged again, utterly sure of himself. "As you wish. I gave you a chance."

I nodded. "Now just go away."

"And leave you to tell Leopold about all this? You don't think I'm going to let you back alive, do you?"

I froze. Rhiang slid a blaser from its holster at his waist and aimed it at my head. His grin widened. The muzzle dropped a fraction, and I breathed a little easier.

"No," he said distantly, "why kill you straight off? Slow deaths are more interesting, I think. And harder to trace."

He aimed at the snagger. If he punctured it, I'd drop into the trees. It was a long fall. I wouldn't make it.

I growled and grabbed for the gun at my waist, bringing it up before Rhiang could move. He stared at me for a moment, then started laughing. I looked at what I was holding.

"What're you going to do with that?" he said. "Bag me?"

It was my bagging-pistol, all right. I'd dropped the

blaser back in the Lair. But it would still serve a purpose.

"Exactly," I said, and fired.

The gray fluid squirted across the narrow gap between us, sealing instantly over Rhiang's hands. He fired the blaser but succeeded only in melting the bag enough to let the weapon break away. It fell out of sight.

His eyes were wide. He was considering death by suffocation.

"No," he choked.

But I didn't fire at his head. I put the next bag right over his feet, sealing the pedal mechanism tight. His legs jerked convulsively. They slowed. Rhiang began to whimper, and then he was out of control. His skimmer turned and glided away as he hurried to catch any updraft he could. He vanished behind Paramount Lair, and was gone.

I turned back to observe the treetops. Rhiang might be back, but I doubted it. First he'd have a long walk ahead of him, over unpleasant terrain, back to his base . . . *if* he could maneuver his skimmer well enough to land in the treetops, and make the long, painful climb down.

But I didn't worry about it. I watched the thorntrees rise about me, and presently the snagger brought me gently to the ground. I dismounted, leaving the snagger to bob back into the air, and began to walk gingerly across the inhospitable ground, avoiding the spines. A daggerbush snapped at me. I danced away. It was going to be a rough walk out. Somewhere behind me, Rhiang might be facing the same problem. And he wanted me dead.

But I didn't have as far to go.

Black Glass

Fritz Leiber

New Yorkers frequently brag that their city is the world's leader and predicts how we'll live in the future—a notion that sometimes frightens that city's visitors. Fritz Leiber, who vacationed there not long ago, came away with haunting memories of a possible future for us all.

Memories of the future? Yes. But futures must be made—and they might yet be unmade.

On a chilly Saturday in late autumn last year I was walking slowly east on 42nd Street in New York, threading my way through the somewhat raunchy throngs and noting with some wonder and more depression the changes a quarter-century had made in the super-metropolis (I'd visited the city several times recently, staying in Greenwich Village and Chelsea, but this was the first time in more than twenty years that I'd walked any distance across midtown Manhattan), when there was borne in on me the preponderance of black glass as a facing material in the newer skyscrapers, as though they were glisteningly robing themselves for an urban funeral—perhaps their own.

Well, there was justification enough for that, I told myself with a bitter smile, what with the grime, the smog, the general filth and pollution, garbage strikes, teachers' strikes, the municipal universities retrenching desperately, municipal financing tottering near bankruptcy, crime in the growling, snarling streets where the taxi drivers, once famed for their wise-guy loquacity, were silent now, each in his front-seat fort, communicating with his passenger only by voice tube and payment slit. For two blocks now I'd been passing nothing but narrow houses showing X-rated films with an emphasis on torture, interspersed with pornographic book stores, leather shops, hardware stores displaying racks of knives, a few seedy drug and cigar stores, and garish junk-food food bars.

Did my gloomy disapproval of all this reflect nothing but my piled-up years? I asked myself. (Those around me were mostly young, though with knowing eyes and used-looking flesh.) I'd reached the age where the rest of life is mostly downhill and more and more alone, when you know that what you haven't gotten already you most likely will never get—or be able to enjoy if you do, and when your greatest insights are apt to transform next moment into the most banal clichés, and then back again and forth still once more, bewildering. And just lately I'd tried and failed to write a book of memoirs and personal philosophy—I'd set out to make a net to capture the universe and ended by creating a cage for my solitary self. Had New York City really changed at all? For example, hadn't Times Square, across which I was now pressing, been for the last seventy-five years a mass of gigantic trick advertisements flaring aloft—monstrous ruby lips that puffed real smoke, brown bottles big as tank cars pouring unending streams of grainy electric whisky? Yes, but then they had evoked wonder and amusement; the illusions had been fun; now they got only a bored acceptance and a dark resentment at the establishment power they represented; the violence seething just below the surface in the city was as real as the filth upon that surface, and the skyscrapers had reason to foresee doom and robe themselves in black.

Of course the glass wasn't really black—an opaque black—although it looked like that from the outside. But when you went inside (as I now did, through revolving doors, into the spacious lobby of the Telephone

Building at 42nd and Sixth Avenue), you saw at once it was only somewhat dusky, as if a swift-traveling storm cloud had blotted out the sun while you were going in. Or as if (it occurred to me with a twinge of fear) the small gray churning edged shadow in my left eye were expanding out to cover the whole visual field—and invading my right eye also. (I'd discovered that evidence of retinal degeneration a year ago, and the optical surgeon had treated it with skillfully aimed bursts of laser light, whose pinpoint cautery had scarred the diseased tissue, arresting the shadow's spread—but for dreary weeks I'd anticipated going blind and practiced for that by feeling my way around my room for an hour each day with my eyes shut tight.)

Now through the dusky glass I saw a young woman in a dark green cloak and gloves and jaunty visored cap pulled down—it was a chilly day, foreshadowing winter—striding along purposefully in the direction I'd been going, and her example inspired me to shake off my dismal thoughts, push out through the dizzying doors, and follow after. I enjoyed passing iron-fenced Bryant Park with its winter-dark bushes and grass, although the wind bit keenly—at least there were no neon promises of sick thrills, no violet-glowing mercury-vapor commands to buy. And then I came to the great Public Library at Fifth Avenue, which always gives me a lift with its semblance of being an island of disinterested intelligence in a dingy, commercial sea—although today, in tune with the times, a small scattered crowd encircled a swarthy man juggling flaming torches on the library's broad steps (encourage local street artists!—it promotes integration) while the two proud stone lions flanking the wide entry seemed to look away disdainfully. Some skinny children ran around the northern one, two rangy blacks conversing earnestly rested themselves against its side, and then my striding young woman in green, coming suddenly out of a crowd, passed in front of the lion, but as she did so, she briefly paused with face averted and laid her hand upon its mane in a gesture that was at once compassionate and

commanding and even had an odd and faintly sinister
note of ritual. I knew I was being imaginative to read so
much into a stranger's gesture seen at a distance, but it
nevertheless struck me as being somehow *important*.

She had reversed directions on me, going back toward Sixth, and once more I took my cue from her for
my own strolling. I wasn't following her with any real
intentness, or at least that's what I told myself then—
why, I hadn't even glimpsed her face either time—but I
did want to see more of those black glass buildings, and
they had seemed to cluster most thickly north on Sixth.
At any rate, by the time I'd reached Sixth again, I'd lost
sight of her, though I somehow had the impression
she'd turned north there.

I reminded myself it isn't called Sixth any more, but
been rather grandiosely renamed the Avenue of the
Americas. Though really it's the same old knock-about
Sixth that once had an elevated and then was forever
being dug up. And it's still Sixth underground—the
Sixth Avenue IND subway.

I found enough black glass as I wended north, peering upward like a hick, to delight my sense of the grotesque. After New York Telephone there was RCA
Corporation and Bankers Trust and West Side Federal
Savings and W. R. Grace and Company, where the dark
glass sloped, and the Stevens Tower, where the black
facings were separated by gravestone pale verticals.
And at 1166 they had black glass with *stars*, by God
(but why were green faceless people painted on the
wooden facing masking the lobby they were rebuilding
there? Here be mysteries, I thought).

But all the time that I was playing my game with the
buildings, I was aware of a not altogether pleasant
change that had begun to take place in the scene around
me after I'd looked out of the lobby of the Telephone
Building and seen the day suddenly darken. That darkening effect had kept up after I'd got outside, as if the
afternoon were drawing to an end sooner than it should,
or as if—melodramatic fantasy!—an inky infection
were spreading from the pernicious black glass to the

air and space around it. The further north I pressed, block by block, the more I noticed it, as though I were penetrating deeper and deeper into some realm of not altogether unfrightening mystery.

As for the girl in green, although I once or twice thought I'd caught sight of her a block or so ahead, I made no effort to catch up with her and verify my guess (or see her face). So she could hardly be responsible for the darkly romantic element (the feeling of playing with mysterious dangers) that had entered my fantasies. Or so I believed at the time.

And then I found I'd arrived at Rockefeller Plaza, where the black tried to disguise itself with dim silvery verticals, and the game became by degrees a little more somber and frightening. I think the transition occurred at the Pool of the Planets. I noted that oddly but not unpleasantly jarring feature (in the midst of the metropolitan commercial, the cosmic) down in a sunken court. I was instantly attracted and descended by means of broad gray granite steps. Nearby were chaste advertisements for a municipal theater offering something called "The New York Experience," which somehow struck me a bit comically, as though London should announce it was going to impersonate London. And there were other features which I have forgotten.

The pool itself was dark and very shallow, perfectly circular and quite wide, and from it rose on slender metal stems, all at their proper distances from the center and in their proper sizes, amazingly, as far as I could determine, the spheres of the planets done in some darkened silver metal and blackish brass. Simple inset plates of the same metals gave the names, symbols, dimensions, and distances. Truly, a charming conceit, but with sinister touches (the theme of darkening, the idea of the planets emerging from, or menaced by, a great unknown sea in space), so that when I finally turned away from it and especially when I'd mounted the stairs again to the sidewalk, I was not altogether surprised to find the scene around me altered still further. The people seemed to have grown fewer and I was unaccounta-

bly hesitant to look at their faces, and it had grown
much, much darker—a sort of grainy blackness sprin-
kled everywhere—so that for the first time in months I
felt for a moment in sharpest intensity the fear I'd had a
year ago of going blind, while in my mind, succeeding
each other rapidly, there unrolled a series of very brief
darting visions: of New York and its high-rises drowned
in a black sea, of the girl in green whirling on me and
showing under her cap's visor no face at all, of the
northern library lion coming suddenly awake at memory
of the girl's touch (post-hypnotic command?) and shaking his pale mane and suppling his stony flanks and setting out after us, the pads of his paws grating on the
steps and sidewalk, like giant's chalk—those fugitive visions and a dozen like them, such as the mind only gets
when it's absorbing presentations from inner space at
top speed, too many to remember.

At the first break in those visions, I wrenched my
attention away from inner space to the sidewalk just
ahead of me and I moved away from the sunken court.
It worked. My surroundings didn't darken any further
(that change was arrested) and the people grew no
fewer, though I didn't yet risk looking at their faces.
After a space I found myself grasping a thick brass railing and gazing down into a larger and—thank God!—
more familiar sunken area. It was the skating rink, and
there, one more figure among the graceful circlers in
the white-floored gloom (a couple of them in rather
flamboyant costumes, a couple of them suggesting animals), was my girl in green with cap pulled down and
cloak swinging behind her, taking the long strokes you'd
have expected from her striding.

I was entranced. I remember telling myself that she'd
had just enough time, while I'd paused at the Pool of
the Planets, to put on her skates and join the others. It
was a delight to watch her moving swiftly without having to chase after her. I kept wishing she'd look up and
I'd see her face and she'd wave. I concentrated so on
her that I hardly noticed the gloom once more on the
increase, and the other skaters growing fewer as they

broke away to glide from the rink, and the low murmur of comment growing around me. It was as if there were an invisible spotlight on her.

And then there entered the rink with a rush, skidding to a near stop at its center, an amazing figure of clownish comedy, so that the murmur around me changed to laughter. It was that of a man in a wonderfully authentic tawny-pale lion's costume with more of a real lion's mask than a man's face, as with the Cowardly Lion in *The Wizard of Oz*, so that for a moment (but a moment only) I recalled my fantasy of the library lion coming to life. The girl in green came smoothly gliding toward him, as if they were supposed to waltz together, and he moved to meet her but then skidded off at an unlikely angle, fighting to keep his balance, and the laughter rose obediently.

It went on like that for a while, the lion proceeding around the rink in a series of staggering rushes and skids, flailing his front paws (his arms) in every direction, the girl circling him solicitously and invitingly, dipping in toward him and out, to the accompaniment of the laughter.

But then the scene grew darker still, as if the invisible spotlights were failing, and the grating of the lion's skates against the ice louder as he skidded (so that my library-lion fantasy came uneasily back to my mind), and he moved more slowly and drooped his great maned mask as if he were sick, so that his efforts to keep balance became more pathetic than comical, and the laughter, and then all the other sounds too, died away as though someone had turned on a tap marked "Silence."

And then he collapsed in a sprawling heap on the ice and the girl reached him in one long glide and knelt low over him, and the darkness became so great that I could no longer see the green in her visored cap or in her cloak trailed on the ice behind her, or in the gloves on her hands cupping his huge jowls, and the gloom closed in completely.

It was then that my trick of concentrating on the

pavement just ahead of me (there was light enough for that, it was lighter up here) and not looking at faces (there were people crowding around me now, though they made no noise) stood me in good stead, so that I was able to get away, step by step, from the sunken court of the skating rink drowned in inky darkness.

I don't know with certainty what my intentions were then. I think they were to get down to her somehow and help her with her unfortunate partner. At any rate, one way or another, letting myself move with the crowd here, clutching along a stair rail there, I did manage to descend several levels, one of them by escalator, until I finally emerged into that brightly lit, somewhat low-ceilinged world of dingy white tile which underlies so much of New York.

There was one difference, however. Although the place was lined with colorful busy store fronts, and marked with arrow-trails leading to various street exits and subways, and although there were throngs and scatters of people following along them, everything went silently, or at most with a seashell-roaring suggestion of muted noise, as if I had actually gone temporarily deaf from a great but unremembered sound, or else descended rapidly from a very great height and my ears not yet adjusted to it.

Just then I was caught up in a hurrying crowd of people coming from one of the subway entrances, so thick a crowd that I was forced to move with it for a ways while I edged sideways to get free. And then this crowd was in turn further constrained by another crowd pushing in the opposite direction—into the subway—so that my efforts to extricate myself were further hampered. And then, while I was in that situation, just being hemmed in and carried along, I saw my young woman in green in the same predicament as myself, apparently, but in the other crowd, so that she was being carried toward and then past me. I saw her face at last: It was rather narrow and somehow knifelike with glowing hazel eyes, and I got the instant impression of invincible youth strangely matured before its time. She looked angry and somewhat disheveled, her green cap pushed back with visor askew and brown hair foaming out from under it. She didn't have her lion man being crowded along with her (*that* would have been a sight, I told myself—and might have gained her some space, too) but she *was* carrying, clutched to her chest, a pale-tan long-haired cat. And then, just when she'd been carried opposite me and I unable for the moment to move a step closer to her—there must have been a dozen people between us; we could only see each other clearly because we were both quite tall—why, just then she looked straight at me and her hazel eyes widened and her brown eyebrows went up, and lifting one cupped hand alongside her lips while she clutched her cat more closely with the other, she twice called something to me, working her lips and face as though she were trying to enunciate very clearly, before she was rapidly carried away out of my sight—and all the lights around me dimmed a little. I made a real effort to get free and follow her then, but it only resulted in a minor altercation that further delayed me—a woman I was squeezing past snarled at me, and as I begged her pardon while still trying to get past, a man beside her grabbed me and told me to quit shoving and I grabbed his elbows and shook him a bit in turn, while still apologizing. By that time the crowd had started to melt away, but it seemed too late now to go tearing after the girl into the subway. Besides, I was still trying to make sure of and puzzle out the cryptic message I thought she'd called to me—actually I was pretty sure of it, what with my hearing having gotten somewhat better and a bit of reading of her lips as they carefully shaped the few words. Twice.

Spoken in the manner of someone who announces a change of rendezvous or a place to get together in case of separation, the repeated message was simply: "Cortlandt Street. Tower Two. The Deck."

Now that wasn't cryptic at all, I told myself, now that I'd hopefully got it down straight. Cortlandt Street was simply a subway address of the World Trade Center, Tower Two was the southernmost of the lofty twins, and the 107th floor was the observation deck with the open-air promenade on the 110th, the roof, to which you could go by a long three-story escalator—I knew all about that. I'd been up there myself only two days ago to enjoy the magnificent view of Manhattan, Queens, Brooklyn, the East River and the Hudson, Staten Island, the Jersey shore. It lay on the same subway line (only a few stations further along) I'd be taking myself in a bit to get back to where I was visiting with my son in Greenwich Village.

For I wasn't going aboveground in this locality again today—that much I was sure of. I was no longer so sure of exactly what had happened up there, how much had been due to a weird weather change or a confusion about time (though a wall clock told me just then that it was still more than an hour until sunset) and how much had been subjective, a matter of my mood and the strange directions my imagination had taken. There are people who get panicky in crowds and narrow places, such as big city streets, they actually go crazy. I'd never had any trouble that way that I knew of, but there's always a first time. In fact, there are all sorts of strange things that happen to you and you find out about yourself as you grow older. Such as playing a game with yourself of pretending to be attracted to younger and younger women and following them in the street. All sorts of nonsense. (Another part of my mind was reminding me that her message to me had been real and that she had touched the library lion and skated with a sick lion-man and been carrying a long-haired cat of the same color when last seen. What was to be made of that?) But however much nonsense or no, nonsense and vivid daydreams, I wasn't going to go up to Rockefeller Plaza again today and look down into the Pool of Planets or the skating rink. No, I wasn't going to do that.

As my thoughts reached that point, the underground lights flickered again, shadows racing across the white tile, and dimmed down another notch. "What's the matter with the lights?" I involuntarily demanded aloud, fighting to keep the note of panic out of my voice.

The man who happened to be shuffling past me at that moment was quite short. He was wearing a black overcoat worn smooth in spots with a dusty-looking astrakhan collar. His head was bowed under the weight of a black derby also worn shiny in spots, and he had it pulled down to his jutting ears, making them jut out still further.

He halted and lifted his face toward mine (it took quite a swing of his head) and I got a considerable minor shock, for covering his entire face below his eyes was a white gauze mask such as the Japanese favor during cold epidemics. But it wasn't altogether white by any means. Centered on it were two coal-black spots where his nostrils would be underneath. Each was surrounded by a wide gray border fading up to white at a distance of about two inches from the dull jet centers. They overlapped, of course. While below them was a horizontal gray-bordered line only less black marking his mouth. I wondered in what atmosphere he could have been all day to have accumulated so much pollution. Or had he worn the same mask for several days?

Then, keeping his fierce dark eyes fixed on mine, he growled somewhat muffledly (the mask) but in the measured tones of an originally mild man grown truculent, even recklessly so, with the years and repeated disillusion, "So what's the matter with the lights? Nothing's the matter with the lights. They're always like that—only sometimes worse. This is a little above average. Where have you been all your life?"

"I'm just visiting New York," I told him. "My son."

"So who visits New York?" he demanded, continuing to eye me suspiciously. "We should be so lucky as to be somewhere else. Your son hasn't gotten away yet? That's terrible. My condolences."

I didn't quite know how to answer that one, so I just continued to look at him sideways. Somehow while talking we'd begun to walk on slowly together toward the subway.

"So what's with *this*, you're asking maybe?" he said challengingly, indicating his mask. "The old schmuck has got the crazies about germs, they're trying to assassinate him? That's what my wife thought, and my brother-in-law the druggist, when I started to wear it." He shook his head slowly and emphatically. "No, my friend, I'm not afraid of germs. Germs and me, we get on all right, we got an understanding, things in common. Because germs are alive. No, it's the dead Dreck I don't want none of, the Guck (that's the goyish word for it), the black foam."

His muffled, muttering voice was indescribably odd. There was nothing wrong about my hearing now, incidentally. I searched for a relationship between the visual and auditory dimmings I'd been experiencing, but there didn't seem to be any, their cycles didn't jibe.

I was going to ask him what industry or business the black foam figured in, though it didn't sound like a very specific thing, but by then we were at the subway. I half expected him to head uptown for the Bronx, but he stuck with me and changed with me a station or two later to the IRT.

"I'm getting off at 14th Street," I volunteered, adding after a moment, "Or maybe I'll go on to Cortlandt. You were saying something about black—"

"So why shouldn't you?" he demanded, interrupting. "Or change your mind as much as you want? Myself, I change at Chambers and keep on to Brooklyn. You're thinking it's maybe queer I live in Brooklyn? That's where my brother-in-law's got his drugstore. He's very ambitious—wants to be a chemist. Now about the black foam, the Dreck, I'm the expert on that, believe me, I'm your rabbi there, because I foresaw its coming before anyone else." And he turned toward me and laid a hand on my forearm and gripped it, and he fixed on me his dark eyes above the filthy mask.

We were sitting side by side on one of the long seats in a car that was more than three quarters empty, the windows and walls crawling with graffiti that were hard to read because the lights were dimming and flickering so. The other passengers paid us no heed, locked in their thoughts or stupefactions. As the train set off with a lurch and a low screech, he began.

"You remember when detergents first started getting in sewage and mounding up in rivers and lakes, killing the fishes—mountains of white foam that wouldn't go away? The Guck, the Dreck began like that, only black, and it came from the air and crawling along the ground and working up from under the ground. The street-washing trucks couldn't pick it up, not all of it, brooms and hoses couldn't move it, it built up in corners and cracks and angles. And people ignored it, pretended it wasn't there, like they always do at first with muggings and trashings and riots and war and death. But I could see it. Sometimes I was sure I was the only one, but sometimes I thought my niece Chana could see it too and admit it to herself—Chana, a very nice, delicate girl, refined and plays the piano—from the way she looked quick out the window and then away and washed her hands over and over. Chana and her cat, who stopped going out. I watched the Dreck getting thicker and thicker, building up higher and higher, blacker and blacker—the black foam."

"But why a foam?" I asked him. "Why not just dirt or dust?"

"Because it clings and smears and creeps, don't blow like dust. Comes through the air, but once it lands, don't blow no more. You know those foams the firemen got that shut in fire, strangle it to death? The Guck works the same with life, you should believe me.

"When I started wearing this mask and making my wife stop opening windows ever and never open an inside door without shutting the outside one, she decides I'm getting sensitive (her nice word for the crazies, maybe) and wants her brother recommend a doctor should give me shots. 'So now I'm sensitive, am I?' I say to her." (He lifted a finger to his mask's center.) " 'Then what's this?' I ask her. 'Poppy seeds? You maybe want to try filling a blintz with it?' "

We ground to a stop at the 14th Street platform and after a while the doors slid shut with hollow thuds and we humped out of it, and I'd had no thought of getting off. I was spellbound by the way this man's grotesque tale of his paranoia, or whatever, fitted with my own experiences and fantasies this afternoon, as if it were the same story (a black story!) told in a different language or as if it were perhaps a contagious insanity manifesting itself differently, but with one basic theme, in each victim.

My Ancient Mariner of the Subway continued, still fixing me with his glittering dark eye, "When the Dreck got so bad everyone had to admit it, then my brother-in-law was the first comes to me, you should expect it, with all sorts of explanations of what it was and why it wasn't so bad as it looked, we should love it maybe.

" 'The scientists understand it and are learning to control it,' he tells me, like we should celebrate.

" 'Which means they can't do anything about it right now?' I say. 'Is that news?'

" 'It is the ultimate para-terminal waste product—' (he says, holding up a finger like a professor. The words he's got! like he's a Doctor of Dreck! and he repeats himself until I've learned them by heart, *Zeeser Gottenyu*!) 'created by a catalytic action of various industrial wastes on each other under conditions of extreme congestion. As a result it has maximum stasis—'

" 'It stays, all right,' I say, 'if that's what you're getting at.'

" '—and is the ultimate in unbiodegradable paraplastics,' he keeps on with.

" 'It's degrading to us,' I agree. 'And it's making us all into paraplegics, *nu*?'

"He tries again with 'In a very general way, simplifying it for the layman, it is as if the organic, under unprecedented pressures, were trying to return to the inorganic, and succeeding only too well.'

" 'If you mean it's black death spreading itself like sour cream, covering everything, I knew it already. Tell me, was it invented at Dachau or Belsen?' "

Christopher Street went by, Houston, Canal. Sluggish passengers braved the dim stations. The car emptied.

The masked man kept on, quoting his brother-in-law.

" 'In structure,' he says, making with the finger again, 'it is a congeries—' (*Oy, Gottenyu*, his words!) '—of microscopic bubbles that are monomolecular, hence black—'

" 'Ah-ha! Like poppy seeds! I was just telling Rivke,' I say.

" '—and in many ways it behaves like a para-liquid, a gas of fixed volume—'

" 'It's fixed us,' I tell him, 'and it's keeping on fixing.'

" '—but it has been proven by scientists,' he keeps up, so I can't get a word in, 'to be absolutely noncarcinogenic, completely inert, and therefore utterly harmless!'

" 'So why won't Chana's cat go out in it?' I ask him."

The train slowed. My companion stood up. "Chambers Street, I should change," he explained. He placed his hands on my shoulders. "You should stay on. Your stop is next, Cortlandt. But, pardon me, you should get yourself a mask if you don't mind me telling you. They've started to carry them at cigar stores, so you shouldn't get Dreck in your tobacco smoke. Goodbye, it's been a pleasure listening to you."

I heard the sliding doors thud shut. I looked around. The car was empty. I wasn't exactly frightened, but I stood up and continued to look around as we surged along, and when the doors opened at the next stop, after having seemed to hesitate deliberately for a long moment, I felt a gust of relief and I slid out quickly.

As I did so, a somewhat silly mood of nervous, high-spirited excitement boiled up in me without warning. The afternoon's happenings would make a great vaudeville act, I told myself, for the young woman in green to tour in—and I'd tell her so if I ever caught up with her, and maybe be her manager. She'd have herself—a graceful girl's always an attraction—and her clumsy lion man, and the little Jewish comedian from the bad old days of broad racial humor. We'd put him on skates too. Would he be afraid of the lion? Of course. But his dirty mask would have to go. On him it might make people think of concentration camps and suffocation. We'd have to do something about that.

The white tile underworld was loftier and cleaner here and brighter too (no dimming or muting, at least at the moment—my eyes and ears seemed working okay). The only thing I wondered about was the absence of hurrying crowds at rush hour—until I remembered it was Saturday.

I wandered with the other mostly solitary movers across those fantastically large underground pleasances, not hurrying particularly but taking long strides, relishing the exercise. We were like ants in a giant's bathroom, each on our separate linear course.

My companions grew fewer as I progressed, and by the time I had purchased my ticket and reached the massive underpinnings of Tower Two, unobtrusive in a vast gleaming, science-fictional, multi-storied hall hung with great panels of aluminum and plates of glass, I was alone. And I alone was lofted on the endlessly mounting steps of the silvery escalator to the high mezzanine, so that I had a comically grandiose vision of myself as Ludwig the Mad King of Bavaria on my way to a performance at the royal theatre that had only one seat in it. On the mezzanine I quickened my stride, thinking of how frustrating it would be to move more slowly and just miss a trip and have to wait, so that by the time I rounded a corner into the alcove of the express elevator I was almost running.

The elevator was in, but its big silvery doors had just begun to close.

I am a man who almost never acts on impulse, but this time I did. I sprinted forward and managed to get aboard, encountering at the last moment an odd physical resistance I had to force my way through with an extra effort, though I was in the clear and didn't have to squeeze past persons or the closing doors—it was something invisible, more like a science-fictional field.

Then the doors closed and the car began to mount and I realized that it was completely dark inside and that I couldn't remember seeing any people in it, my eyes had been only on the closing doors.

No, not completely dark. High on the back wall a small ghostly white light was moving from left to right behind the numbers of the floors. But it wasn't enough light to show anything else, at least not to my unadjusted vision.

I asked myself what the devil could have happened. Was I the only passenger, going up on automatic? But this express elevator always carried an operator, didn't it? Also I recalled there had been a spiel (live or recorded?) about the more-than-quarter-mile nonstop vertical trip lasting less than a minute, the more-than-twenty-mile-per-hour vertical speed, and so on. There wasn't now.

I listened intently. After a bit I began to hear, from the point to my left where I'd recalled the operator standing, a very faint strange croaking and breathy whining, the sort of sound a deaf-and-dumb person makes when he's trying hard to communicate—perhaps as if such a person were thinking hard to himself.

I moved involuntarily to my right and forward without encountering anyone—or thing. I remembered the door at the top was the back of the elevator, opposite to what it was at the bottom. Was the trip going to last forever? The ghost light was hardly halfway across the wall. Would the door at the top open?

I could no longer hear the "deaf-and-dumb" breathing. Was that because of the distance I'd moved or the blood pounding in my ears? Or had the breather stopped thinking and begun to take action? How did one pass time like this while holding still? Playing a routine chess opening in one's head? Reciting the prime numbers under one hundred? Counting the coins in one's pocket by feel? No, they might chink.

The cage stopped. A vertical crack of dull light appeared ahead of me and I squeezed through as soon as it was wide enough. I took a dozen forward steps measuredly, started to turn around, but didn't. I listened uneasily for footsteps behind me.

There was a sound. I turned. The silver doors had closed and the space between me and them was empty.

Then I noticed that the doors themselves were blotched and corroded, the floor under my shoes was faintly gritty, there was an oily, coaly stench in my nostrils, though the air felt dry as a desert's and was *blowing* (indoors!), the place was unnaturally silent except for the air's windy sighing, and there was something very strange about the light.

I turned again and moved cautiously out of the elevator's alcove.

The layout of the enclosed observation deck is very simple. A broad corridor made up of continuous windows on the outside runs all the way around, making a great square. Along the inner wall are murals, displays, booths for attendants, that sort of thing. I was in the corridor on the building's east side.

I looked both ways and didn't see a soul, neither visitors nor the deck's personnel. But I did see trails of footprints and of at least one wheeled vehicle in the dull dust coating the floor.

I couldn't see much of anything out of the windows, at least from where I stood back from them in the middle of the corridor. They seemed to be very dusty, too, and through the dust there wasn't anything visible outside but a dark expanse lightening toward the top and streaked with a dull sunset red. There were no inside lights on.

I didn't approach the windows any closer but walked quietly north in search of an explanation for the incredible transformation that had occurred—or the weird hallucination from which I was suffering. Can one walk through a hallucination one is having? For some reason that question didn't seem nonsensical to me then. Exactly how are inner and outer space related?

The dry, insect-wailing wind brushed my face with its feathery touch. It seemed icy now on my forehead and cheeks because of its rapid evaporation of my sweat of fear. And now, through it, I could hear other noises from ahead: faint rutchings, creakings, and gratings, as if some heavy object were with difficulty being moved. I myself moved more slowly then, in the end hardly at all as, holding my breath, I peered sidewise down the north corridor.

This one wasn't empty. Halfway along it a dozen black-clad figures, black-hooded and black-trousered, were at work where two of the observation windows had been jaggedly smashed open to the dark, reddening sky. Through that large gap came the dry wind that now blew against me more strongly. About half the black figures were busy manhandling a gun (from the first I knew it was a gun) so that it pointed north out the gap. The weapon, formed of a grayish metal, resembled a field piece of the world wars, but there were perplexing differences. The barrel was pointed sharply upward like a mortar's, but was longer, more like that of a recoilless rifle. The breech bulged unnaturally—too big. It was mounted on a carriage with small wheels that seemed to turn with difficulty, judging from the way the black figures strained at it, while beside it on a squat tripod was a steaming cauldron heated by a small fire built on the floor.

The other six or seven figures were closely grouped around the edges of the gap and peering out of it intently and restlessly, as though on watch and guard for something in the sky. Each held ready, close against him, a small missile weapon of some sort.

All the figures were silent, appearing to communicate by some sort of sign language that involved twitchings of the head and grippings of one another's upper arms and legs—perhaps a language more of touch than visual signs.

Despite their silence, there was such a venom and hatred, such a killer's eagerness, about the way the gun-handlers heaved at their cranky weapon, strained and touch-talked, and in the window guards the same, though in them mixed more with dread, that my genitals contracted and my stomach fluttered and I wanted to retch.

Inch by inch I withdrew, thankful for their single-

minded intentness on the gap and for the crepe soles of
my shoes. I retraced my path past the elevator, its
blotched doors still shut at the back of the shadowy re-
cess, and peered with circumspection into the southern
corridor. It seemed as empty as the one I was in. The
windows at its far end glowed red with sunset light. A
short distance along it, the escalator to the open observation deck on the roof three storys above began its
straight-line ascent. Its treads weren't moving (I hardly
needed visual confirmation of that), but up through it
the dry wind, now on my neck, seemed to be blowing
out, escaping from this floor.

I had no desire to explore the red-lit west corridor,
the only one I hadn't peered along, or to wait by the
stained doors of the elevator. The oily, coaly stench was
sickening me. I began the long ascent of the stalled escalator.

At first I went slowly, to avoid noise, then I speeded
up nervously from the dry wind's pressure on my back
and its faint whistlings, and in my feelings a queer mixture of claustrophobia and fear of exposure—the feeling
of being in a long, narrow open. Then I slowed down to
avoid getting winded. And the last few steps I took very
slowly, for fear of running into a guard (or whatever)
at the top—that and a certain hesitation to see what I
would see.

Spying from the entry, I first closely surveyed the
open observation deck—really just a wide, railed, rectangular catwalk, supported by a minimum of metal
framework, about fifteen feet above and twenty feet
back from the edges of the flat roof of the building proper, those edges having a stout high mesh fence, the top
wires of which were electrified to further discourage
would-be suicide jumpers and such. (I knew these details from my earlier visit.)

I didn't spot anyone or anything in the twilight (anyone standing or crouching, at least), though there was
the opposite exit structure matching mine, around
which it would be possible to hide, and at one point the
railing was gone and a slanting ladder led down to the

roof—a crude stairs. Also a good deal of the outer fence appeared to have been torn away, though I didn't try to check that very closely.

Thus reassured (if you can call it that), I straightened up, walked out, and looked around. First to the west where a flattened sun, deep red and muted enough to look at without hurt, was about to go beneath the Jersey horizon. Its horizontal rays gave the low heavens a furnace glow that made "the roof of Hell" a cliché no longer, though lower down the sky was dark.

The horizon all around looked *higher* than it ought to be. From it in toward me stretched an absolutely flat black plain, unbroken save for several towers, mostly toward the north, their western walls uniformly red-lit by the sunset, their long shadows stretching endlessly to the east, a few of the towers rather tall but some quite squat.

I looked in vain for the streets of New York, for the lights that should be coming on (and becoming more apparent) by now, for the Hudson and East rivers, for the bay with its islands and for the Narrows.

None of those things were there, only the dull ebon plain, across which the dry north wind blew ceaselessly. Oh, the utter flatness of that plain! It was like the waters of an absolutely still great lake, not a quiver in it, thickly filmed with coal dust and across which spiders might run.

And then I began to recognize the towers by their tops. That one to the north, the tallest in that direction except for one at almost twice the distance, its somewhat rounded stepbacks were unmistakable—Kong-unmistakable. It was the Empire State shrunken to less than half its height without a corresponding diminishment in breadth. And that still slender spire was the top quarter of the graceful Chrysler Building, its bottom three quarters chopped off by (were they beneath?) the plain. And there was the RCA Building at Rockefeller Center where I'd just been—the top hundred feet of it.

But what were those two structures rather taller (allowing for differences in distance) than the Empire

State? One mostly truncated pyramid, the most distant northern one; the other to the northeast, about where the United Nations enclave would be. Were they buildings built after my . . . well, I had to face up to the possibility of time travel, didn't I?

And there were lights, I began to see now, as the red western walls started to darken—a very few windows scattered here and there among the towers. One of them was in a most modest structure nearby—hardly four storys with a pyramidal roof. I knew it from boyhood, the Woolworth Building, New York's tallest in 1920 and for some years after, which the black plain had almost inundated.

Yes, the black plain, which lay only some five or six hundred feet beneath me, not the thirteen hundred and fifty it ought to be.

And then I knew with an intuitive, insane certainty the black plain's nature. It was the final development of the Guck, the Dreck, the sinister, static, ineradicable foam, the coming of which the old Jew had described to me.

But how in hell could there be *this* much accumulation of waste of whatever sort, seven or eight hundred feet of it? Unless one imagined the whole process as being catalytic in some way and reaching and overpassing some critical value (analogous to fission and fusion temperatures in atomics), after which the process became self-perpetuating and self-devouring—"Death taking over," as he'd said.

And how far, in God's name, did the black plain extend? To the ends of the Earth? It would take more than the melting of a couple of black icecaps to do that to the planet. Oh, I was beginning to think in a crazy way, I told myself . . .

At the same time a line from the cauldron scene in *Macbeth* joggled its way to the surface of my mind: "Make the gruel thick and slab . . ."

But the gruel wouldn't have to be thick, I reminded myself with insane cunning, because it was composed of microscopic *bubbles*. That would stretch the Guck, make it seem that there was much more Dreck than there really was. And it wouldn't be solid and massy like liquids are, but feathery and soft as finest soot or new-fallen snow, hundreds of feet of it . . .

New-fallen black snow . . .

But if the stuff were foam, why didn't it mound up in hillocks and humps, like the life-choking detergent foams the old Jew had talked about? What force, what unnatural surface tension, constrained it to lie flat as a stagnant pond?

And why did I keep coming back to *his* ideas, monotonously? My intuition was insane, all right, as insane as what was happening to me, or as his own paranoid ideas—or mine. I shook my head to clear it of them all and to stir myself to action, and I began to move around the catwalk, studying my closer surroundings. The first thing to catch my eye and almost stop me was the wire-hung narrow suspension bridge connecting the northwest corner of this roof with the nearest corner of the roof of Tower One. It was a primitive affair, the junkyard equivalent of a jungle structure of bamboo and braided vines. The two main wires or thin cables, guyed through holes driven in the roof edges, also served as its rails, from which was flimsily suspended the narrow footway made of sections of thin aluminum sheeting of varying lengths. It swayed a little and creaked and sang in the dry wind from the north.

I could see no figures or movement on the roof of Tower One, though another of its corners was simply gone for twenty feet or so, as if gigantically chopped or bitten off.

I came to the first right-angle turn (to the east) in the catwalk and (just beyond it) the gap in the rail where the ladder went down.

Scanning north again, I saw the last red highlights on the scanty cluster of towers fade as the crouched-down scarlet sun flattened itself completely behind the western horizon, but the hell glow lingered on the low, cramping sky, under which that dry wind from the pole blew on and blew. Squinting my eyes against it, I thought I saw shapes in movement, soaring and flapping, around the most distant northern tower, the tall, unfamiliar, mysterious one. If they were fliers and were really there, they were gigantic, I told myself uneasily.

My gaze dropped down to the lowly pale Woolworth tower with its single dim light and I noticed that its roof edge was damaged somewhat like that of Tower One, and I had a vision (the soaring shapes had paved the way for it) of a vast dragon's head with jaws agape (and mounted on a long neck like that of a plesiosaur) emerging from the black plain and menacing the structure, while great dull black ripples spread out from it in ever-widening circles. Another scrap of poetry came to my mind, Lanier's "But who will reveal to our waking ken/The forms that swim and the shapes that creep/Under the waters of sleep?"

As I mused on that, I heard a not very loud but nevertheless arresting sound, a gasp of indrawn breath. Glancing sharply ahead along the catwalk, I saw, near the exit structure, something that may or may not have been there before (I could have missed it in my survey): a body sprawled flat with that attitude of finality about it which indicates utter exhaustion, unconsciousness, or death. It was clad in what looked in the dusk dark green—cloak, cap, gloves . . . and trousers.

Before I could begin to sort out my reactions to that sight (although I instantly moved softfootedly toward it), another dark-green-clad figure emerged swiftly from the exit-structure and swiftly knelt to the sprawled form in a way that was complete identification for me. I had seen that identical movement earlier today, though then it had been on skates.

When I was less than a dozen feet away, I said, clearing my throat, "Excuse me, but can I be of any help to you?"

She writhed to her feet with the sinuous swiftness of a cobra rearing and faced me tensely across the dead or insensate form, her eyes blazing with danger and menace in the last light from the west. I almost cringed from her. Then there was added a look of tentative recognition, of counting up.

"You're the man in the subway," she said rapidly. "Neutral, possibly favorable, at least not actively hostile —I took a chance on you and that's how I still read you. The man from Elsewhen."

"The subway, yes," I said. "I don't know about the Elsewhen part. I presume from what I see I've time-traveled, but I've always thought that time travel, if such a thing could possibly be, would be instantaneous, not by a weird, crooked series of transformations and transitions."

"Then you were wrong," she said, rather impatiently. "You don't do *anything* all at once in the universe. To get from here to there you traverse a space-time between. Even light moves a step at a time. There are no instantaneous transitions, though there are shortcuts, no actions at a distance. There are no miracles."

"And as for being possibly favorable," I went on, "I've already asked if I could help you."

"You say that as lightly as if it meant tipping your hat or holding a door open. You don't know what you're getting into," she assured me. "You saw the men on the lower deck?"

"The men in black with the gun, yes."

"You mention the gun. That's good," she commented quickly, and for the first time there was a hint in her voice and look that I might be accepted. She went on, "That's the gun my brother and I were going to knock out, when . . . when . . ." Her gaze flickered down toward the flattened form, dark green, death pale, between us, and her voice stumbled.

"I'm terribly sorry—" I began.

"Please!—no sympathy," she interrupted. "We haven't time and I haven't the strength. Now listen to me. In this age the blackness has almost buried New York. We are the sole survivors, we in these two towers and like lonely groups in those out there, a desolate few." She indicated the scattered tops to the north and around. "We should be brothers in adversity. Yet all that those men on the lower deck can feel is hate, hate for all men in other towers than their own, hate and the fears from which their hatred grew—dread of the blackness and of other things. They dress in black because they fear it so and hope so to gain for themselves all the cruel power and exulting evil they read in it, while their avoidance of spoken language is another tribute to their fear—in point, the Guck's their god, their devil-god."

She paused, then commented, "Man lacks imagination, doesn't he? Or even a mere talent for variety in his reactions. Sometimes it seems appropriate he should drown squealing in the dark."

I said, uneasy at this chilly philosophizing, "I'd think you'd be afraid they'd come up here and find us. I wonder that they haven't posted guards."

She shook her head. "They never come out under the sky unless they have to. They fear the birds—the birds and other things."

Before I could ask her another question she resumed the main thread of her talk. "And so all that those men on the lower deck can think to do is to destroy all other towers save their own. That is the business they're about just now (the business of the gun) and one on which they concentrate ferociously—another reason we needn't fear them surprising us here.

"Someday," she said, and for a moment her voice grew wistful, "someday we may be able to change their hearts and minds. But now all we can do is take away their tools, remove their weapon, the gun that's capable of killing buildings.

"And so now, sir," she said briskly, looking toward me, "will you aid me in this venture, knowing the risks? Will you play the part my brother would have played—receive my fire? For I must tell you that *my* weapon requires both a firer and a receiver. One soul can't work it. Also it works only against their weapon, not against them (I would not wish it otherwise), and so it cannot save us from their afterwrath. Escaping will be your own business, with my help. How say you, sir?"

It sounded crazy, but I was in a crazy situation and

my feelings fitted themselves to it—and I remembered the sickening venomousness I had sensed in the black-clad men below.

"I'll help you," I told her in a low, choked voice, swallowing hard and nodding sharply.

She laughed, and with a curtsy to her brother's corpse, knelt by it again and from a pouch at the belt removed something which she held out to me.

"Your receiver, sir," she said gaily, smiling over it. "Your far-focus, yin to the yang of mine. I believe you have seen something like it earlier today. Here, take it, sir."

It was a pale brown cube with rounded corners, about as big as a golf ball and surprisingly heavy. When I looked at it close up I saw that it was the figure of a lioness crouching, quite stylized, the body all drawn together to fit the cubic form—one face of the cube, for instance, was all proud, glaring head and forepaws. It was a remarkable piece, so far as I could make out in the dusk. The eyes appeared to flash, though it seemed all of one material.

"Here is its mate," she said, "my near-focus, my firer," and she held close to my eyes for a long moment a like figure of a maned lion. "And now the plan. It is only necessary that we be on opposite sides of our target, in this case the gun, so that I may weave the web and you anchor it. When we get to the foot of the long stair, you go to the left, I'll to the right. Walk rapidly but quietly as you can to the end corridor they're in. Stand in the middle of it facing them and holding the receiver in front of you. It doesn't matter if it's hidden in your fist, only don't stir then and whatever happens, don't drop it." She chuckled. "You won't have to wait long for me once you get there. Oh, and one other thing. Although your receiver is no weapon against them afterwards, except to weight your fist—no weapon at all without the aid of mine—it has one virtue: If you lack for air (as, *viz.*, they use the Guck on you) hold it close to your nostrils or your lips. That, I believe, is all." She gently clapped her left arm around the back of my waist from where she was standing close beside me and looked up a bit at me and said, "So, sir, let's go.

"But first," she added somewhat comically, "my thanks for your companioning in this venture. Ill met and worse to follow!" And she leaned around laughingly and rather quickly kissed me.

As our lips were pressed together there came a jarringly loud sound from close below. It sounded like a giant cough from very deep in a dark throat. As we pulled apart, turning each toward the north, we saw an incandescent scarlet line rapidly mounting out from the tower beneath, belched from the midst of a spreading smoke puff. It soared across the last darkening carmine streaks of sunset in the top of the sky, seemed to hang there, then fell more and more rapidly through the last of its parabolic course and was extinguished (it seemed) in the black plain short of the Empire State. But then began a churning and a mounding and a glowing in the Guck, ending in a tumultuous eruption of blackness and flame. I was vividly reminded of depth-charging at night, only this glare was redder. And the flash seemed to last longer too, for by its darkening red glow I saw the façade of the Empire State hugely spotched and pied with inky black—napalm that didn't burn.

I was losing my balance—it was my companion dragging at my arm. "Come on," she yelled. "Same plan, only we run."

We ran. Halfway to the stalled escalator we were given an extra shove by the great muffled thunderclap of the explosion. I pounded down the dark silvery, gritty stairs, recklessly for me, watching her draw farther and farther ahead. And then, by God, I heard her *whistling* loud in a fast, rocking rhythm. It was the *cavalry charge*, so help me!

She waited at the bottom to point me left, make sure I got it. And then as I was loping down the west corridor, nearing my goal, the windows ahead of me were painted with a bright red flash against which the small figure of the Empire State was silhouetted. This time they'd struck beyond her, had her bracketed. The third shell . . .

I shot into the north corridor and came to an arm-waving halt just as the dark glass ahead of me bent inward, but did not shatter, with the second muffled thunderclap. And then I faced myself at where the bent black figures were toiling exultantly in their reloading and I held my receiver out in front of me. I remember I held it gripped between right thumb and bent forefinger with the lioness' head looking at them (that seemed important, though the girl hadn't said so) and with my left hand gripped around my right. My legs were bent and spread wide too, so that I must have looked like some improbably elderly macho with a magnum straight out of TV.

I didn't see her arrive beyond them (she was probably there ahead of me) but suddenly my conjoined hands were tingling and there was a narrow sheaf of bright violet lines fanning out from that double fist to touch the extremities of the ugly gun and around it illumine staring ghost eyes and spectral mouths gaping with surprise within black hoods, before they drew together again (the violet lines) into a glowing point which showed me, just above it, very tiny—her face—for all the world as if she and I were playing cat's cradle together with the fluorescent violet string, the gun the figure we'd created.

The tingling spread to my arms and shoulders, but I didn't drop my receiver or writhe around very much.

Then the lines vanished (and my hands stopped tingling) but a swirled Kirlian aura of the same shade of violet hung around the gun, making it glow all over as though new-forged and highlighting the frozen figures around it. Then one of those figures reached out slowly and fearfully and touched the muzzle, and at that point a very fine iridescent violet snowfall began, the individual flakes winking out before they touched the deck, and the snowfall spreading rapidly, eating its way into the glowing metal, until the entire gun had trickled away into dust.

The frozen figures broke then into such a frenzy of arm- and thigh-gripping, and head-twitching, that it was like a battle (or an orgy) in a soundless hell. Then most of them raced away from me, but two toward me, and I heard a high sweet whistling, three mounting notes. She was sounding taps, the *retreat*.

I was already in flight. The west corridor seemed longer than it had coming. She was waiting for me again at the foot of the escalator, but started up as soon as she saw me. I'd not mounted a dozen steps when the faint tattoo of our pursuers' footsteps was abruptly amplified as they poured into the south corridor. It didn't so much frighten me as make me feel wild—an unfamiliar sort of excitement.

I was panting before I was halfway up. I could hear her breathing hard too, though I think she deliberately slowed down so as not to get too far ahead. When I got to the top I did a foolish, show-off thing—I took the deepest gasping breath I could and then turned and bellowed inarticulately down the stairs—roared, you might say, perhaps in honor of the lioness clenched in my fist. And then I went dancing out onto the catwalk, not straight ahead following her, but around the opposite way, with some crazy idea of drawing the pursuit away from her, and pausing to turn and bellow nastily once or twice more.

My storybook ruse didn't work at all. The main body of our silent pursuers went racing after her without even hesitating, though a couple did come skulking after me. She paused at the railing gap to shake her fist at me, or wave me on, I don't know which, and then she ran down the slanting ladder, and across the roof to its northwest corner, and up and out onto the rickety suspension bridge. Two of her pursuers stopped and made hurling motions, there were sharp reports and then two bright white lights were floating above her head and then slowly past her—star-grenades, to give them a name.

She was halfway across the bridge when a swarm of figures appeared at its other end. The glare showed them to be black-clad, black-hooded. She stopped. Then, pausing only for a sweeping gesture of defiance— or a wave of farewell—she ducked under one of the main wires and dove down head first, her green cloak trailing behind her. Almost at once the roof edge cut her off from my sight and there were only the eagerly bent, black-hooded heads peering down.

And then, without warning, there was clapped over my face from behind a double handful of a fine-grained darkness that was soft as soot, intimate as cobweb, somehow oily and dry at the same time, and instantly cutting off all sight and breath. In my convulsive struggles, during which I was thrown down on my back, I lifted my hands to my face and though I did not manage to tear whatever it was away, I became able to see through it dimly and draw shallow breaths. I made a supreme effort and then—

Have you ever begun to wake up from a nightmare that's happening in the same room you're actually sleeping in, and for a while been able to see both rooms at the same time, the nightmare one and the real one, almost coinciding but not quite? It was that way with me. It was night and I was down on my back on the open observation deck of Tower Two at the World Trade Center and there were people bent over me and handling me. And sometimes the sky would be utterly black and the faces hooded ones and the hands gripping cruelly to hurt. And then the dark sky would have a pale cast with reflected light and the faces open and solicitous, and the hands gentle and trying to help. After a brief but dizzying alteration the second scene won out, you might say, and I was drawn to my feet and supported and patted and told that a doctor had been summoned. Apparently I'd been walking along quite normally, enjoying the view (though one person maintained I'd looked troubled), when I'd suddenly collapsed in a faint or a fit. I offered no explanations, suppressed my agitation and astonishment as well as I could, and waited. I remember looking down from time to time at the diamond pattern of New York's street lights (they looked so *very* far below!) and being greatly reassured by that, so much so that once or twice I almost forgot why I felt so bereaved and forlorn.

I let myself be taken to the hospital, where they couldn't find much of anything wrong with me (except that after a bit I felt very tired) and from which my son retrieved me the next day. After a while I told him the whole story, but he's professed himself no more able than I am to decide between what seem to be the two chief possible explanations: that I suffered an extremely vivid and protracted hallucination, during which I moved through the World Trade Center completely blacked out (and possibly through the subway and Rockefeller Plaza in the same state), or that I actually time-traveled.

And if it were a hallucination, when did it begin? (Or if the other, when did *that* begin?) At the Pool of the Planets? Or even earlier, with my first glimpse of the Girl in Green? Or when I dashed into the express elevator and found it dark (there had been my feeling of breaking through a barrier at that point)? There are endless possibilities.

Did I hallucinate the old Jew, was he completely fabricated from materials in my unconscious? Or was he an intermediate stage in my time travel, belonging to an era somewhere between today and that blackly overwhelmed New York of the future? Or was he completely real, just one more freak at large in today's city?

My tired feeling afterwards convinced me of one thing—that whether an experience is real or hallucinatory (or a dream, for that matter, or even something you write), you always have to put the same amount of work into it, it takes the same energy, it takes as much out of you. Does that say something about outer and inner space? (My son says, "Don't dream so strenuously next time," though of course he says that's entirely my choice.)

If it *was* a hallucination, one thing that has to be explained is when and where I acquired the small and very heavy stylized sculpture of a lioness I had tight clenched in my left fist at the end of my experience. No one has been able to identify the tawny material composing it, or its style or school, though resemblances have been noted to Bufano's work and to the stitcheries of Martha McElroy. I've experimented with it a bit, I admit, but it appears to have no mystical or weird scientific properties, though I do think it helps my breathing. I carry it as pocket piece now. Might come in handy some day—though I suppose that's a rather foolish thought.

As for the Young Woman in Green, I have a theory about her. I don't think she plunged to her death when she went off the suspension bridge between the two towers—she'd never have leaped off so lightheartedly unless she'd known she had a way of escape. No, I don't mean she sprouted wings or broke out a small jet or levitation unit after she'd fallen out of my sight. But from what the old Jew told me of the Dreck and from my own observations of it I think it is like soft, powdery new-fallen snow, able to cushion any fall, from no matter how great a height. And I think there are ways of living in it, of moving and breathing, no matter how deeply one is buried. She implied as much when she told me about the additional virtue of my receiver. And she did have her firer with her at the end. I tell myself she survived.

In any case, my feelings about her are such that I would very much like to find her again, even if it were only to begin another hallucination.

To Bring in the Steel

Donald Kingsbury

Not all of the unfamiliar bylines in this book belong to "new" authors. For instance, Donald Kingsbury's first story appeared in *Astounding* in 1952, but it wasn't till 1978 that his next two stories appeared. ("To Bring in the Steel" was his third; you'll find his second story, "Shipwright," in *The Best Science Fiction Novellas of the Year.*)

What was he doing in the years between? He wrote several more sf stories, none of them successful; his agents liked a novel he wrote but said it shouldn't have been set on Venus, so he rewrote it in an Earth setting, spending ten years at it, but never sold it. Meanwhile he was working on a degree in mathematics and writing controversial newspaper articles in the John W. Campbell manner, which "drove people up the walls. It was fun."

He fell in love with "the world's most beautiful potter," who convinced him to take up science-fiction writing again before she "ran away with a charming computer." By this time he'd earned his degree, and currently he's a professor of mathematics at McGill University in Montreal. He also writes science fiction—very successfully now—such as the following story about mining in the asteroid belt, and the people who come to live there.

So his ex was dead. It was like her, too—she'd used the wrong poison and died horribly. Meddrick Kell remembered the time she had been in a rage about him killing animals and had put all his shotgun shells in the fireplace thinking they'd burn gently. God, that was long ago.

The mountains of Earth erupted in his memory, striking him with giddiness. He relished the green mountains for their loneliness; they gave him the same sense of peace as did the bleak desert of an asteroid. His wife hated being alone. She was never happier than when she was partying in a fifteenth-floor penthouse with a dozen desperately elegant drunks who besotted their wit in style with Chivas Regal and Johnny Walker. Probably it was two days of being alone that had driven her to suicide, he thought sarcastically.

Kell toasted the nude on his cabin wall with an imaginary drink—alcohol and drugs were sparingly used in puritan space villages where the members prized clearheadedness because they prized survival. "Here's to the last alimony check!"

Then he returned to the letter from his daughter. He was always astonished by Celia's typewritten prose. She was only seven years old. Two of the paragraphs described her mother's death convulsions. She might grow up to be the System's best horror-story writer if she could learn to avoid words like "eclampsia." *What the hell does "eclampsia" mean? I suppose it's all the fault of that typewriter.*

He'd never met Celia. Helen had never even sent pictures. She just cashed alimony checks. Celia was five years old before Kell received his first letter, in fat, painful child's scrawl. The fax image that had been lasered in from Earth was still glued to the wall beside his nude's left breast. It had made him laugh for days because it was so like all the women he had ever known.

Dear Daddy I want a typwreter

xxxx ooo.

LOVE Celia

Kell didn't know how to buy a gift for a girl. His only experience with children was with his older brothers, all of whom had been raised by their father in a womanless world high in the Sierra Nevada Mountains. Consequently he grappled with the idea of selecting just the right typewriter for Celia as if it were a major Asteroid Belt crisis. The choice was too vast. Finally he had given up in bafflement and ordered for her the most expensive IBM model just to be on the safe side.

You could still get cheap manual-input line printers where one knob selected the typeface and the memory was restricted to a single line, but he hadn't been sure a child could use one. What finally decided him on the IBM Vosowriter 2200 was the hard-wired program that taught children to read while it taught them to type. On top of that it included:

(1) A full screen with editing capabilities.

(2) A hook-up to a 500-page random access cartridge for manuscript revision.

(3) A dictionary with definitions and completely cross-indexed thesaurus.

(4) An auxiliary voicewriter which allowed words to be input via speech. The words appeared on the screen in BFA—Basic Phonetic Alphabet, a slightly expanded version of the long-popular Pitman Initial Teaching Alphabet, handy because it was hardly distinguishable from the Roman alphabet. A parallel program looked up the word in the magnetic bubble dictionary and replaced the phonetic spelling by the standard spelling—if the word was contained in the dictionary.

That was where Celia found words like "eclampsia," "admissibility," and "ingurgitation." But at the bottom of each of her letters was always a hand-scrawled P.S. in very short words. "I want a hole W. Shaekper drama album MGM-LM-5632."

No matter how he tried, Kell had never been able to compose a letter in reply to his daughter and so had delegated that job to his secretary. His secretary's first cute effort had been condescending, distant.

"It's too cold!"

"You're a very cold man," said his secretary with the frankness that was usual between them.

"I don't give a tinker's damn if I'm as cold as the night side of a space corpse, do it over!" Kell had growled.

"What'll I say?"

"David, if I knew what to say, I'd write it! You're an expert at smoothing out all my reports. Not only that but you've been blessed with two younger sisters. You know how the little monsters think! Ask your girl-friend, ask anybody, *just do it*."

And so the correspondence had gone on for two years as they maneuvered in from the Belt toward the orbit of Mars. This, Celia's latest letter, ended with the hand-printed line, "I want to come to Pittsburgh I want to come to Pittsburgh I want to come to Pittsburgh." Pittsburgh was the name of Kell's ship, but the name was applied loosely to the whole symbiotic spaceship-asteroid complex.

What was he going to do with her? It would be a disaster to send Celia off to his brothers, and he'd have to act quickly to keep her out of her grandmother's hands. There were boarding schools, but he didn't know anything about that way of life and didn't trust it. He should talk to a woman; they knew about such things, but he didn't know any women well enough to discuss anything that close to him.

Kell punched out the code for David's bodyphone. "David. I have an Earthside emergency going. Contact Histon McKinner in San Francisco and have him pick up Celia and take her into his personal home right now. Her mother is dead. See that he takes legal action so that I get custody."

"It's dawn at San Francisco right now. I'll take care of everything in three hours."

"Great."

Dawn in San Francisco. The fog would be red in the bay and the white stucco walls along the hillsides would be pink. *What will I do with her?*

There was no dawn on the asteroid called Pittsburgh.

The spaceship that had brought them out to the Belt was leeched to the rock's surface like a great space bird of prey, its huge sunward facing mirror keeping the planetoid in darkness, its talons grasping its victim, its beak devouring her substance. The mirror soaked up energy which had been lasered 400 million kilometers across the solar system from a power station circling the sun well inside Mercury's orbit, energy which out here in this dark energy desert was used to smelt four tons of rock per second, to refine it, and to deliver three tons of waste per second to the vaporizers, where ionized slag was accelerated to eight kilometers per second and blasted out forward along the line of orbit, day after day, year after year, in thundering flame. Twelve years the beast would spiral inward. When the ship finally reached Earth its claws would be clutching the digested remains of its victim, something like 300 million tons of refined metal. Most of it had already been sold to the Japanese.

Kell thought about his daughter all during his inspection tour of the smelter. He constantly wandered over the asteroid poking into everything. He was known as the man to have around during a crisis, probably because he was so perceptive that a part of him was predicting a crisis and planning for it before it ever happened. Today he was slower than usual.

It was the Pittsburgh's second journey to the Belt. She had carried thirty-five veterans from the first trip back with her. Kell was not a veteran—he had signed on as a foreman—but that had not stopped him from rising to second in command. Small space colonies were made for village democracy. Seniority rights and absolute chains of command were not tolerated in an environment where a leader's mistakes could be lethal.

Kell had always had an answer when quick answers were needed, and so he had risen. He always had an answer because he was that engineering freak who was fascinated by obsolete technology. When he was twelve he bought a bag of iron oxide and built himself a forge in the Sierra Nevada and learned to smelt iron. When he was fourteen he turned out a rifle barrel from his own steel on his own lathe. He blew glass and built radio receivers out of homemade vacuum tubes.

In space he was a natural. Hundreds of millions of kilometers from Earth, problems developed that could not be solved by looking up a widget in a catalog and having it flown in. Earth was a year away by the fastest ship. Kell could do things like make an electromechanical gadget that would substitute for a computer. No matter that it was five thousand times as large as it should be; it worked.

The two women he had tried to live with now shunned him. One wouldn't tell him why. The other was a girl whose relationships never lasted more than two months and who herself was mostly a hermit. No use talking to them about Celia. And the women who had babies? The rule was that no children could be brought from Earth and none born during the journey to the Belt and none born while the ship-asteroid symbiosis was being established, but that after rooms had been burrowed in the asteroid, then babies were quite acceptable.

There were eighteen children on the Pittsburgh, the eldest being four and a half. Kell doubted his popularity with their parents. Once he had made a vigorous attempt to legally limit the number of children after a baby had been found lost and injured in one of the machine shops.

No, he had no one to consult, so he consulted himself.

There were no rules about importing children once the smelter had been set up; it had just never been done. He tried to imagine what it would be like to hold Celia in his arms, but he had never held a child in his arms. He tried to imagine himself talking to her but he had never talked to a child. It would be nice to have someone around who loved him, but he had never been loved.

He tried to reach Celia through his own childhood. He remembered himself frying eggs over a wood stove in the Sierra Nevadas, and the time he had stolen an ax and gone into the woods to chop, slicing the leather off his boot toe neatly and earning a beating, and the times he saved the squeezed lemons from the garbage to give flavor to the crystalline shadow-preserved June snow that he loved to suck. But those were boy's memories that he couldn't transfer to the freefall environment of this termite colony. He had no way at all of understanding the girl his vain wife would have spoiled.

His daughter wouldn't like him. If she stayed on Earth at least she could preserve her fantasy about him. But if she stayed on Earth there might be no one who knew *how* to love her.

When he found himself not writing a report that should have been finished in five minutes, he became annoyed. There were ways of ending thoughts that lured you into an endless maze. He pulled out a black die with silver eyes that he knew was perfectly balanced because he had machined it himself. "Odds she stays," he said aloud, "evens she comes." He spun the die off the end of his thumb and it arced over until it was sucked against the ventilation screen: a six. Evens. *So she loses her illusions*, he thought cynically. It was a relief to have the decision made.

But he was vetoed.

The Pittsburgh community had evolved a simple and effective form of democracy, relevant to a group that numbered only 230. Any man could propose a law. He merely had to post it in the computer. A bulletin board might have served as well. If the lawmaker was wise he worked out the wording with three to a dozen supporting friends first. Those that the law affected were then put on a voting list. Debate followed in the form of attached comments and emendations. These were typically formulated by individuals in their spare time or by spontaneous group sessions.

If the issues were controversial a sizable body of comment would appear over a few days. Eventually a compromise version was posted and voting took place at the convenience of the individual voter. Votes were entered on a scale of one to ten, plus for a yes, minus for a no. To pass, a bill had to accumulate more than 50 percent of the eligible votes; however, any issue that polarized the community was placed on the agenda of the monthly town meeting. The vast majority of laws were passed without "going to meeting."

Kell's request to ship Celia out to the Pittsburgh had been denied by the majority. The minority who voted with Kell did not feel strongly enough about it to see that it was sent up to a meeting for debate. There was a wide consensus, cautiously stated, that Kell would not be able to properly perform the functions of a father.

Men in power are often surprised when people refuse to carry out their orders, and can be enraged when it is a simple personal request that is denied. Kell showed his rage by being more distant and by smiling more fixedly.

He had been alone all his life; he enjoyed being alone, but to be *denied* his daughter converted his state of being alone to that of exile and pain. Emotions have two faces. Love can be the peace of union and the agony of having betrayed someone you love. Hate can be the towering triumph over a crushed enemy or the rotting torture of impotence. Grief can be a sobbing relief or the longing for something that can never be.

The pain of his loneliness burned in him, demanding that he bring his daughter here to this barren place. For keeping Celia from him, the rest of them, all 229 of them, could drop like flaring torches into Sol, one by one.

He laughed.

They had given him one small out, a sop to his ego probably—a fatal error, that. He could have her—if he could find someone to take care of her. They didn't think he could do it. He smiled, not trying to force his face into pleasant lines. He smiled for himself. They didn't know how much power he really had.

On Earth the executives at Ventures Metal knew who was jockeying this orebody through the Belt and across the Mars-Earth gulf. Ventures knew who the other captains consulted when there was trouble. On Earth, where the money was, they valued this hunk of metal that when brought to port would line their vaults with more than the gross national product of many nations. So Kell felt in his bones that he could afford multimillion-dollar whims.

He would put in a requisition for a mother for his child with the same care that he might ask for a specialized machine tool. The workpersons of Pittsburgh would get the mother they had so righteously demanded. Would they get a mother!

Lisa Maria Sorenti.

He did not know her personally, and she was not even that notorious unless you followed the San Francisco Bay Area scandals, but he had once seen her in action at a wild party. Three men had fallen in love with her in the few minutes he had watched her flawless performance of the ingenue. But *he* had seen her with his own jaundiced eyes. Her only skill was an electric charm. She was dishonest. She loved to be loved. She did not like men. She was indifferent to women. She was deathly afraid of being poor when she was old. And she would do anything for money, anything.

2

The two San Francisco executives shook hands like old friends who spoke and dealt with each other often, but who just hadn't met solidly for a long time. They both wore lace shirts and short pigtails.

"Histon!"

"Roy!"

"How's Stacy?"

"She's great."

"And the kids?"

"They're great, Roy. Linda's just joined the Little League. She's a great little batter. We've got a new one. That's why I'm here. It's Meddrick Kell's girl; sweetest tyke you ever met. Linda has her out playing baseball right now. Her mother committed suicide. What's not good about it is that I'm afraid Kell has split his can."

"He never had a can to split. How's Celia taking it?"

"Do you know her?"

"Yeah, I had more dealings with her mother than I wanted. Alcoholic bitch and all that."

"Kell wants Celia shipped out."

"Unusual, but what's the problem? We have a supply ship going out."

"Pittsburgh voted him their number one no-good father. They didn't buy it."

"They know they need him! What the hell!" roared Roy.

"They'll agree to her being shipped out if he can get someone to take over as governess—but no one wants the job."

"So ship one in with Celia. Expensive, but then Kell is a billion-dollar man."

"That's what Kell thought of," said Histon morosely.

"He always had an answer. When they add up the debits and the credits, remember I hired him."

"Yeah. Now he wants you to hire Lisa Maria Sorenti. As Celia's governess."

"You're *kidding* me, Histon!"

"I told you he'd split his can."

"Wow. A nice problem."

"You know her? I know *of* her."

"I just happen to have her manager's phone number. Occasionally I give it out to hungry young men who are going into space and need a beautiful memory of Earth to come back to. We pay the bill so they'll want to come back. She's expensive. But her manager gets it all. Some women are dumb."

"She hasn't been in the news for quite some time."

"You're wrong," said Roy. "Last week she had her manager hauled in for assault and battery and then went down with tears in her eyes and bailed him out."

"I see."

"I'll show you her file in living holo." Roy went to the computer terminal. "Her manager sent me these takes to keep my memory fresh." The computer terminal began to display the pictures.

"God, what firm boobs," said Histon, staggering back.

"Nice, but look at those hips! She's a goddess!"

Histon moved his head so that he could get a better view of her tilted face. "She'll never make it as a governess."

"We could send him a bright college girl who loves children and is thrilled by space. I know one who wants to go. She's a chemist."

"Naw, I told you he's split his can. It's got to be Lisa Maria Sorenti. God, look at this one of her in the sea! He doesn't know what he's asking for. She'd blow Pittsburgh apart. I hear she wiggles, too."

"He *always* knows what he's doing. I conclude that he *wants* to blow Pittsburgh apart. If I have judged Kell correctly, he'd take deep affront at being told he doesn't qualify as a father. He's angry about that."

"What'll we do, Roy?"

"You came here just to give *me* this problem, eh?"

"Yeah."

"You bastard."

"Think you can handle it?"

"He's a youngster of thirty-three. I'm sixty-two. Therefore I am twice as smart as he is. Sure I can handle it. I'll bet you one hundred billion dollars that I can handle it."

"Great. And how's your wife?"

"Great. We're going down to Redwood City to visit the grandchildren tonight."

3

Three A.M. Hunting headlights found the shape of her car in the gloom. "That's it." And blinked out. The stocky man kissed her good night, but she had the final say before she left his Mercedes. She held on to his ears and stared into his eyes for a last minute, knowing that he could see the moonlight glowing from hers. "G'night, Punkinhead." And then she was gone.

She had a mnemonic for all of them so that she might never forget a face or a name. Her Pumpkin Head image for Mr. Pokinhet matched his constant grin and the way the silly man lighted up every time he saw her. Some of her other images were not so complimentary, and she dared not use them as endearments. Lisa Maria Sorenti envied the girls who had settled for "darling."

Like the salty skin of a lover, the flavor of the Pacific was on the air. Exhausted, she merely stood by her sports car until the Mercedes was gone, waiting for energy, listening to the whisper of her engine's flywheel. What a beautiful night.

She could remember the days of her childhood when the smog was so pervasive in the Bay Area that you couldn't even see the stars. Now, so a spaceman had told her, you could pick out the Orbital Solar Power Station that fed the San Francisco grid, always at the same point in the sky to the south, unmoving as the stars moved. But she had never been able to differentiate it from a star. Sometimes she caught a factory flowing overhead, they moved so fast.

She eased out of the parking lot on flywheel power and then kicked in the small alcohol motor when she reached the parkway that had grown up over the trail of Spanish priests. It took her twenty minutes to reach San Francisco. She wondered how different her life would be without the earthquake that had killed her mother. Actually she liked San Francisco much better now that the scars of rubble were gone. It was a more peaceful town, more open. Or maybe it only seemed more peaceful without her mother's bitching.

I hope the hell Nick's not home!

She stopped off at an all-night McDonald's for a quick twenty-five-dollar hamburger and kidded the busboy to amuse herself. She always felt comfortable in a hamburger joint when she was depressed. Some of the excitement of her first job as counter girl rubbed off on her, back from the days when her life was less complicated. She had a wry nostalgia for the post-earthquake period when people helped each other.

Her apartment house wasn't far away. It was on a hidden street with trees and a sloping hill. She smiled at their electronic doorman. "Hi, Packard." He hated to be called Tex.

"Good morning, Ms. Sorenti."

One even had to smile at the damn machines these days. They said it was because that made it easier for the pattern recognition circuits. But she suspected the companies of trying to program humans to feel that machines were cute three-year-old children. Then they'd start introducing real machine intelligence.

"Park the car. Charge the flywheel."

"Yes, ma'am." Her car moved away, driverless. "Have a good day," added the machine brightly.

She requested a key-use printout and got it. "Damn!" Nick had been home since ten-thirty. He hadn't used to spend so much time with her. She was tired, but she skipped two up elevators just to be that much longer away from him. When she arrived at her apartment, she inserted the key-card and noiselessly opened the door. She peeked in the bedroom. Yes, there he was all sprawled out in the moonlight. Suddenly she wanted a glass of milk because the kitchen was as far from the bedroom as you could get.

Lisa Maria sipped her milk in the dark, staring for a long moment at the pale whiteness of it between sips. When she needed Nick he wasn't there, he was out floating in the bars. He said he was making contacts for her. She didn't know. Half the time it was probably other women. She didn't care. Now that she was trying to figure out a way to do without him, he was always here. She felt sorry for herself.

They talk about me as if I was the strongest woman in the world, and I can't even get rid of Nick.

The thing that was sending her into an absolute panic was knowing she didn't know how to get along without him. Hamburger Queen of Market Street, that's what she was when he found her. *He* had rented that first opulent apartment where she had learned to hold court and titillate the jaded amidst her exotic array of indoor plants. *His* clever maneuverings brought her to the fringes of society and the warmth of the money that was coming in from space. It was *he* who gave her the books that had opened up those conversations between her and the great minds of California. He even read her poetry when they made love. He still did that. And wrote it. He was composing his magnum opus now that he had beaten her.

She sparred with his memory, trying to understand her trap. Nick was a cunning master of that singular conceit borne by all San Franciscans who think that their city is the only place on God's Earth where one can sin in a state of grace. He had plotted her outrageous escapades with a sure business hand, and had reaped for her the protection that went along with notoriety. "Pure sin," said San Franciscans as they laughed.

He had taught her never to talk about money, that such talk was sordid and would break the magic upon which she existed. In return she had worshipped him with the pride of a woman who *knows* that her man is not one of the suckers.

So Lisa Maria was twenty-five and didn't know how to ask a man for money. She didn't even know how much Nick charged for her. She didn't know how to pay the rent or take out a loan or buy a car. It had taken her a year to muster courage to ask someone who she should see to find out how much money she had. And six months more to comprehend that she was dimeless. She did not know if she loved Nick; she *did* know that she hated him passionately. It was easier to hate him than to hate herself.

She undressed and slipped into bed as silently as a snake in grass, but he woke up anyway, as he always did.

"Big eyes, you have a date tomorrow for lunch at the Robin's Nest. One o'clock sharp. Roy Stoerm. It's a twenty-four-hour date."

"Oh, Christ, Nick! You *know* I can't tolerate twenty-four-hour stands with strangers. I won't even have any sleep by one. And the Robin's Nest is hell-and-gone across town. Give me a break. I'll have wrinkles and I'll be dull."

"I know what I'm doing. He's from Ventures Metal. They could fill in the bay for a golf course. And he's not a stranger. He's sent you some of your best tricks. You were at one of his parties a month ago. The crew of the Glasgow."

She turned her back. *I'm going crazy*. "But I've never met *him*!"

"You will tomorrow."

I wish I was a chemist. But her mind couldn't linger over such an image long, it was too insubstantial and meaningless to her. She saw other pictures—herself welding steel beams, or punching buttons in a space factory with random flashing lights (an image borrowed from TV), or jockeying a horse, or selling hamburgers. Anything. The tears were cascading down her cheeks. For Christ's sake, anything. Anything but this body that carried man-trap scent with it wherever it went.

4

A sarcastic *San Francisco Chronicle* journalist had once described her as the mongrel goddess who had bounced down the steps of a California pantheon after an orgy to which all the Nordic, Roman, Celtic, and Mexican deities had been invited. It was true that Lisa Maria Sorenti had Swedish and Irish and Italian and Mexican blood, and that she was illegitimate, but the rest of what the journalist said was tongue-in-cheek slander.

Her eyes had never decided whether they were Mexican or Swedish—the irises were black rimmed with ocean-foamed interiors; her hair (fresh from the hairdresser) rippled with black light as she flowed through the lunch-hour crowds like driftwood avoiding the boulders of a busy rapid. Her summer dress was Spanish moss being helplessly carried along.

I wonder if he'll like me?

The Robin's Nest had been carved out of some old brick warehouse, and skylights bathed a jungle of greenery. She spotted him immediately—he was the only man seated alone facing the door like a lion waiting beside a mouse hole. And immediately she shifted her eyes, as if to seek someone, allowing him to see her profile, letting him watch her grace as she turned to the hostess. She smiled ravishingly at the hostess, long enough for him to sip of that smile and desire it for himself. She invented a trivial conversation, punctuating it with lively gestures, exaggerated just enough to carry across the room. Only after he had had ample chance to become intoxicated did she allow herself to notice this Stoerm. She met his eyes, held his eyes for a dizzying second, then dropped hers demurely. She spoke to the hostess again, one sentence, then looked back at *him* questioningly, holding off any real reaction until the exact moment he started to rise. Then she rushed forward, delivering her warmest smile full force before she took his hand, gently, tenderly. He was only half out of his seat.

"You must be the Stoerm in my heart."

"Roy," he said, beaming.

He pulled out her chair and seated her and then sat down and appraised her while he discreetly beckoned the wine steward. Instantly she had her mnemonic for him: the Eye of the Stoerm. She could feel the power circling him lazily and the calmness within that circle. *He knows exactly what he's going to do with me.* She hated that in men, but she dared not back away into the violence of the power; she was propelled into the eye, toward closeness. She had an irrational desire to hug him, to cling to him, and that frightened her because she did not see love in his eyes.

"I'll have a Cuban Apricot," he said, "and you?"

"A Daiquiri."

"You've been in the papers again."

"Did you read *that*? That was a *horrible* story. I'm so *embarrassed*." She dropped her eyes in practiced modesty and was surprised to feel a real rush of humiliation. *Oh, God, everyone knows that my man beats me.* Hate for Nick; black hatred.

"I'm interested in your troubles."

She couldn't have spoken about them. She would

have cried. But no one ever topped her or rattled her. "Tell me about your wife," she teased.

"I'm in that worst of all possible situations; my wife understands me."

She laughed. Thank God for a man who can make a woman laugh. He attempted a few more times to open her up, and she gently countered him. She was an old expert at not talking about herself, and she felt him bow graciously to superior force and begin to talk about himself. She learned a lot about his job of recruiting spacemen.

"Why don't you hire me? I'm looking for another job."

"What can you do?" he asked with a chuckle.

She hit him. Affectionately, of course.

He tried to lead her into drunkenness during the lunch conversation which went everywhere pleasant bantering could go, and nowhere, but she *never* gave up control of her body on the job—neither through drugs nor alcohol nor through reactive emotion. Once he stealthily sent a patrol through her guard to destroy the bounds she placed on her anger, and she just as deliberately ambushed the patrol with boredom. *He plays games. He's testing me.* For what purpose? *He's trying to push me into the storm to see if I'll be blown away.* When they left the table she took his arm and kept her body close to his.

In Roy's car, a small Chevrolet of the kind favored by the really rich who liked to maintain a low profile, she puzzled over this man. She could tell he liked her, but he was unusual in that he was indifferent whether she liked him or not.

She did not know where they were going. An upper-class bacchanalia, perhaps? She wondered if she was to be the hors d'oeuvre or the liqueur.

After one pit stop for fuel—an alcohol-synthigas mix—they arced over into the region of the Peninsula that was being heavily invaded by the riches pouring in from space as San Francisco established itself as the multinational capital of space enterprise. In selected areas the middle-class suburban sprawl that had grown like cancer over the Peninsula during the fifties and sixties was being replaced wholesale by the palaces of the very wealthy, leaving only the stately trees that had been planted so long ago. Even the endless winding asphalt streets were gone and the palaces were approached from under the ground through a network that rejected unidentified vehicles.

Roy Stoerm put his Chevrolet's flywheel on charge in the garage. A car could travel 100 kilometers on rotational energy, which came from space-generated electricity, before it had to cut in its ten-horsepower internal combustion engine.

They rose via elevator into a sun-gorgeous room where Roy introduced Lisa Maria to Stacy Garcia, who was an executive at Ventures Metal and wife of Histon McKinner. Stacy wore her charm with the economy of somebody who has had the languid niceties of beautiful trivia atrophied by constant use of precise authority. She was obviously staying home from work just to meet Lisa Maria. She had just as obviously never met a whore before in all her thirty-five years.

"I leave you in good hands," said Roy. "I have some business to conduct this afternoon, but I'll be back for dinner."

Stacy took her hand and gave her a grand tour. The proudest thing she owned was a jade piece given her as a gift by Han Tao Hsia, Commissar of the Red Star Space Fleet. Ventures Metal bought heavy computer-driven mining equipment from them and occasionally rented their space tugs. The Chinese had been the first to use the hybrid chemical-nuclear single-stage Earth-to-orbit freighter, forcing the Americans and then the Russians to follow their lead. Stacy Garcia was a frequent visitor to Peking and spoke fluent Cantonese.

At a den in the back, Lisa Maria met the housekeepers, two enthusiastic English Ph.D.s who maintained this palace and took care of the children, and who were trying to beat each other scripting the Great American Disc Drama when they weren't cooking and gardening and shopping and changing diapers. Stacy said with a twinkle in her eye that she sometimes babysat for them.

And then at the window overlooking the park she pointed out a small naked child running beneath the redwoods below the swimming pool. "Will you do me a favor and take care of Celia while I'm out shopping for dinner? Her mother used to let her run wild, so she bears watching, but she won't give you any trouble. My little brats are at the ballet."

"She looks adorable. I've always wanted children." That was a lie, but Lisa Maria lied easily. "It takes the right man."

"You might say that. Men make good children to practice on before you try raising some real ones. Go swimming if you want."

There were four immense redwoods, probably left over from the vanished suburbia, and ten smaller redwoods no more than six man-heights tall. Beyond that grove was a polyglot woods. She sat on the grass beside the pool, watching the girl. *Seven-year-old girls are so free. I'd love one if I could deep-freeze her on weekends.* Celia would glance up at her, but as soon as their eyes met, Celia dropped hers and busied herself with some stick or task. *Oh, she's a flirt already.* That's when Lisa Maria fell in love with Celia.

"I know that game! You don't fool me one bit! Come here."

Ten minutes later, in her own time, the child appeared in front of the strange woman. She held out one tiny finger at arm's length and let it descend so slowly that her hand trembled. "My daddy lives in a place where things fall *that* slowly," she announced. "He's going to let me live with him." And then she rushed off.

It was another half-hour before Celia delivered herself for further conversation. "Aren't you ever going swimming? I have to swim now every day to get full of the sunshine because where my daddy is the sun is all shrunk." She looked at the intruder disapprovingly. "You can't swim with your clothes on."

"If I took them off I might get caught." Lisa Maria

didn't mind getting caught, but she *did* mind not knowing what the ground rules were in a game of blind man's bluff. Bafflement made her very conventional.

"Last man in is a glyptodont. C'mon."

"In my best dress?"

"Nobody swims with their clothes on, *dummy*."

"Now, that's not really true."

"Oh, maybe in darker suburbia they aren't civilized," she said with impatient disdain, "but not *here*. Here you can only get caught with your clothes off if you are in the house."

I'll ruin my hairdo. But she went swimming anyway and regretted it. Celia used her shoulders as a diving board, and there were games like "spaceship docking," which consisted of Celia ramming her head as hard as she could against Lisa Maria's. It went with a ritual.

"Capowie! Bang!"

"Who's there?" *Oh, my aching head.*

"Linda."

"Linda who?"

"Linda hand with the cargo."

Eventually Roy Stoerm came to the rescue with an enormous bath towel and Celia cuddled up inside it with her new playmate, both shivering in the sunset.

Dinner was served on a long table with candelabra and gold plates, each place set with seven different kinds of knives and forks and spoons and chopsticks of some golden alloy, while the center of the table was recessed to hold the main dishes in special depressions which either heated them or refrigerated them.

The children trooped in. Stacy and Histon had four from ages seven to thirteen, and there was also Celia in an ankle-length white gown. They were remarkably disciplined, all bowing and saying hello to Lisa Maria. They didn't interrupt each other, but were ready to get a word in edgewise as soon as they found a slot. Celia was the most impatient. Once when she did interrupt Histon, she was required to get up and put a red chip in an ancient Chinese lacquered box.

It was a whole evening's mood alien to Lisa Maria

until Roy made a phone call to his wife telling her that he had been detained by business. That touch put her comfortably at ease.

The eldest boy rushed out into the kitchen to fetch something that had been forgotten. The housekeepers chatted with the children. It was fashionable to hire housekeepers with Ph.D.s to train the children in the intricacies of witty table conversation and to select their Drama Discs. They were not allowed to watch TV.

As if by some signal the congregation became silent. Stacy began to say grace in a Spanish so melodious that Lisa Maria was transported in time to the tiny apartment of her scrappy grandmother, whose parents had picked tomatoes in the Imperial Valley and whose daughter was passionately anti-Catholic. The grandmother had kidnapped Lisa Maria one day when she was five and taken her to be baptized in an awesome and nameless cathedral that Lisa Maria had never been able to find again in spite of all the church collecting she did. The only Spanish she knew was the word for sin, "*pecado*."

Histon and Roy controlled the conversation, focusing on her but with the skill of film directors who were out to flatter their star and hide her wrinkles and edit her bad scenes. Stacy played script girl. Even the children, who seemed to know in their worldly way that she was a wicked lady, ad-libbed for her when she forgot her lines. *Sometimes I don't understand notoriety*, she thought. She was basking in their attention and smiling too much and drinking 10 percent faster than she should, always danger signals. *It's a trap*.

"Histon made the dessert. He won't even give *me* the recipe," complained Stacy.

"If you're stuffed, I'll take your portion," whispered Celia into Lisa Maria's ear.

5

They drank Pimpeltjens from tiny ceramic goblets after dinner, the children dispersed, the housekeepers cleaned up, and the four of them retired to the spacious room that was now starlit. They analyzed the Argentinian revolution and how a group of multinationals had banded together to put down the killing and reestablish order. Killing was bad for business. Histon and Roy chuckled over the subtleties of how the French and Socialist arms dealers had been tricked into taking a loss of over twenty-six billion dollars.

All in all, the after-dinner conversation was becoming heavy. Lisa Maria laid her head on Roy's arm and closed her eyes, hinting. Histon and his wife discreetly excused themselves and Roy took her affectionately by the shoulders for a walk through the palace and into a cozy den, where he kissed her. She understood everything now. The den's couch would swallow them and the room was private. This was Roy's night off from his wife.

"How are you doing?" he asked.

"It was a lovely evening." She held him and returned the kiss, stroking his neck under the short braid. "A nice change for me."

"I had Nick thrown in jail this afternoon. Thirty days," he said calmly as if he had been complimenting her on the smoothness of her skin.

She froze. She backed away. She stared at him.

"I said I welded him."

In the middle of her shock she felt her arm swinging—*is this me?*—to slap him viciously. "I don't want Nick hurt! He's my problem!" And she backed away, beyond arms' reach, afraid of that center of calmness which she had not even disturbed. And as she backed up she felt herself caught in the hurricane of power that circled him, then tossed wildly away on the wind. Nick was all she had. She didn't know how to get along without him. "Don't hurt him," she pleaded.

He just stared at her.

"You multinational bastards are all the same. You think you run the world!"

"We try to provide a little leadership where it is necessary."

"I want him back!" she screamed.

"I have absolutely no sympathy for Nick. He beats you. He's taken all of your money; he's stripped you bare." Stoerm opened up a report and threw it on the desk top. "I have a complete financial report on him—and you. It is not hard to find out things about you. You don't even like him."

"You want him out of the way?"

"Yes."

"Because *you* want me?"

"Yes."

"Because you're going to solve all my problems—just like Nick? *I hate you.*"

"Not like Nick. I'm going to solve all of your problems, but I'm going to give you a choice. You can go back to Nick in thirty days if that's what you want. I just want him out of the way while you make up your mind."

"The answer is *no*, you gonorrhea drip!"

"Your salary would be twenty million dollars a year."

Suddenly there was no floor under her feet. She was not sure that Roy's face was upside down or right side up or that he even had a face.

"In noninflationary terms that you can understand, Miss Hamburger Queen, that's eight hundred thousand hamburgers with french fries and coleslaw, retail."

Panic. Roy had dismissed Nick—her protector, her old man—with one blow and in the next moment he had stripped her of her free will, and she didn't want to go *there*. The mere thought terrified her. Space. Only space paid salaries like that. She was being hogtied and shanghaied into space.

"I don't want to go."

"Think of the money."

"You *bastard!*"

"You're broke now. You'll be thirty-two when you get back, still in the prime of your life, and you'll be worth one hundred and forty million dollars."

"Those women who go into space are chemists or electronic engineers or mechanics or something. I can't even get rid of Nick. Why me?"

"We have a mad spaceman out there. He's quite functional. He's worth billions to us. He has that gift for turning disaster into victory. We don't tamper with a good thing. We pamper it. He put in a requisition for you."

"So you're buying me?"

"We're offering you a contract and making it worth your while."

"A dream girl off the shelf."

"You're good at it."

"For seven years? Most guys I can't *stand* after two hours. Does he think I come with a valve in my belly button so that he can deflate me when I'm not in use?"

"It is a much more complicated situation than that. In fact it is a dangerous situation. He didn't want *you*. He wanted his daughter Celia."

"That cute kid? She's a darling."

"Those little asteroid villages are very tight. Probably the Earth hasn't seen anything like them since the New England colonists of the seventeenth century. They voted no. They told him he wasn't a qualified father. I'm sure they are right. His psych profile shows a complete blank on women and children. He grew up without women, and he has had no success with the few short relationships he has had as an adult. He abandoned his child before she was born."

"Sounds like a great guy."

"I had lunch with him once. He has a barrier personality. I don't mean he doesn't have emotions. He does. He smiles when he is filled with hate, things like that. Have you ever met these people who function perfectly in a group and have no friends? He's one of those. I think he took it hard when they wouldn't let him have even the symbol of a one-to-one relationship. They said he could have his daughter if he could find a governess. So he smiled and chose you."

"You're hiring *me* as a babysitter for that innocent girl?"

"Exactly."

"Your mind has been rotted by RPX."

"I'm not worried about Celia. Those colonies are wonderful with their children. I'm worried about the grownups."

"Because of me?"

"He wants you there to generate the hurt he can't inflict himself. And I think he chose his weapon with his usual brilliance. He's going to prove that *they* are emotionally incompetent to handle women, and that *he* is the good father. While he's tending to Celia, you'll be smashing marriages right and left and raising hell."

"You sound like a shrink right out of a Berkeley sewer."

"I'm an aerospace engineer from La Jolla who could never build ships but turned out to be handy with people."

"Men make me sick," she said. She took his hand and held it against her breast. "That's soft! How can you call that a weapon? How can I respect creatures who fall apart when they are smiled at!"

Roy laughed and pulled her body to him. There were tears in his eyes. "I'm a strong man. I've been happily married for forty years and I wouldn't trade in that woman for Nirvana, but I'm already thinking strange thoughts when I've only been with you for a few hours."

"It's not fair," she sulked, "that men are so weak!"

"Then why have you spent every waking hour for the last ten years developing your charm to the exclusion of everything else so there is nothing left of you but the charm?"

"You *bastard!* Here you are wrecking my whole life"—she was crying and horrified because they weren't fake tears—"and telling me that there is nothing behind the makeup that a man might love."

"Name ten things," he smiled.

"Ho, you think you've got me now, and I'm going to tell you everything about myself. I'm not going to tell you a damn thing! You already know too much."

"God, you have beautiful eyes!"

"The better to wreck your colony with!"

"Nope. Here's your contract. Have a lawyer check it

out and make sure that it is ironclad. Notice the clause in there about wrecking colonies. You all have to deliver the steel, all of you together, to collect your monies. That's insurance we take out to assure cooperation. But *you* have a special clause. You're not allowed to do your stuff on any male in the Pittsburgh complex *except* Meddrick Kell. Or you don't get paid. See, I'm smarter than Kell. I've lived longer. He's importing what *he* sees as a deadly weapon, and so all I have to do is make sure that the weapon is going to be pointed only at him."

"What about *me*! What if I don't like him! He sounds like a creep!"

"Think of the money. Your mantra is money."

6

The equatorial Free Port at Tongaro in the Pacific was the world's busiest spaceport. Lisa Maria couldn't believe it when she saw one of the eight-thousand-ton single-stage Boeing freighters sitting like a thirty-five story mushroom on the pad as it was being fueled.

The freighters were lifted by a hybrid chemical-nuclear motor that burned LOX with nuclear-heated hydrogen. The tungsten/U-233 fuel elements were manufactured and reprocessed in space, where the radioactive by-products were collected and mounted on a sail-powered basket that spiraled them into the sun. In the distance, beyond the bulk of the ship, was an electrolysis plant that manufactured LOX and LH from seawater and solar power beamed in from space.

Because Celia's father was in the mining business, Lisa Maria batted her eyes at a handsome drop-ship jockey and he took them out to see one of the drop-ships being scrapped in a flickering of cutting torches. These were perhaps the heaviest spaceships ever built by man, rivaling in weight battleships of the Yamato class, but had only one flight in them, down. The jockeys who rode them to Earth called them rafts. They were assembled crudely of massive metal in a low orbit and needed to be able to perform only two functions: to hold together while they burned off their heat shield in the atmosphere and to float when they hit the water. Sometimes they were scrapped at Tongaro and sometimes towed all the way to San Francisco or San Diego or Yokahama.

More to Lisa Maria's liking was the smaller two-stage passenger ship. The lower module was a sleek hypersonic craft that went to mach-9 on a scram-jet powered by hydrogen and air, and then circled quickly back to Tongaro to pick up another piggy-back rider for up to five trips in one day. The upper module was a compact ship backed by either a hybrid power plant or a LOX/LH power plant. She was less enthusiastic when she was taken inside. It wasn't like an airliner at all. There was no more headroom than in a car.

She could still see a patch of the Pacific through the tiny porthole when she was strapped in. *Goodbye, Earth.* Celia took her hand. She was so frightened while the countdown began that her heart was thumping in her chest.

Think of the money.

Her heart did not stop pounding all during the thundering of the rockets. That lasted no longer than the wait in a bank line. Free-fall came before she was used to the acceleration. She could see a patch of the Earth through the tiny porthole.

Woman and child were given a spartan room in the low-orbit Rockwell Station. They stayed there seven days receiving an intensive space survival course in a class of twenty new recruits. It was 10 percent theory and 90 percent training in automatic reflexes, like how to slap a patch on torn suit webbing in four seconds. The people in the course were mainly new workers. The station's primary function was to rent lofts to businesses that needed zero gravity and vacuum and unlimited power. Once Lisa Maria took Celia to visit the factory where the brains of her typewriter had been manufactured.

Five days of concentrated effort to put her space legs together finally hit Lisa Maria with the incredible gut realization that she was forever free of Nick, her great love, the man who had made a woman of her. Suddenly there was no way to stop grinning. Normally she could control her rather compulsive smile, but that fifth day any attempt to be sober resulted in a mellifluous laugh which activated so many male fantasies that she had to hide in the woman's room to calm the storm.

There she wrote a joyous love letter to Roy, teasing him about being another Nick who was only too willing to arrange her whole life for her. "After all," she penned, wishing she could use her happiness for ink, "you are keeping all *my* money in *your* bank." She had it faxed down to Earth by an operator who fell in love with her when he took the letter, and she ended the evening "on air" in the cabin of her space-survival instructor, learning how to make out in free-fall.

"Lisa Maria! Oh! Come to the window! Look. That's the *C.L. Moore!* That's *our* ship over there!" The ship was essentially a long cylinder attached to a great dish that sucked power, not from the sun, but from a point close to the sun. Celia was bouncing from floor to ceiling, from ceiling to floor. It was the seventh day.

Far away, well inside Mercury's orbit, circling twenty-million kilometers from the flaming surface of Sol the Star, was a power station built by man. The sun clawed at the intruder with erupting solar flares like an angry tiger striking through his gravity bars. It was a dangerous place to be, but it was the right place to be if you wanted power—an energy flux of seventy-eight kilowatts passed through every square meter.

The power station was a strange-looking beast with a delicate appendage of radiators that spread away from the sun like a comet's tail. Mounted behind the shadow of the giant heat exchanger was a graceful laser cannon that poured gigawatts of power across the inner solar system to the birds of prey that mined the Belt. Lesser cannon fed the ships outbound from Earth's orbit. The stations themselves, deep in the sun's gravity well, were supplied by sailing ships that tacked upon a rich photon wind.

Inside the solar power station named Goliath an operations officer was making contact with the *C.L. Moore*. He was scanning with a communications laser, and every time his beam crossed the *Moore*'s parabola, the *Moore* sent out a time signal which fed into a computer on the Goliath that narrowed the scan. It wasn't a fast process. There was a sixteen-minute time lag between output and feedback, but within half an hour the communications beam was centered on the *Moore*'s receiver.

Eight minutes later the *C.L. Moore* was powered. Her drive was essentially a proton accelerator that ionized hydrogen and pushed it to 100 kilometers per second using laser energy drawn from her parabolic mirror. The cabins and freight holds and hydrogen tanks were built around the long accelerator, while the mirror was free-mounted to the starboard. If such a ship were strapped for fuel it might take two years to reach the Belt, but the normal journey took from ten to fourteen months.

The *C.L. Moore* was carrying spare parts to the Pittsburgh, and heavy machinery and thirty persons for the Osaka. Her captain was a computer. She was to return empty to Mars, refuel there and bring home a load of passengers.

Lisa Maria went stir-crazy after only five days. At first she was hyperactive and quietly hysterical. Sex with the other passengers didn't help. Counting off the days by fives on the cabin wall didn't help. Gradually she slipped into a mild catatonic depression. She wrote THINK OF THE MONEY on the wall and stared at it for hours. She hated space. Once she wrote Nick a long letter asking him to take her back but never faxed it. Celia took care of her.

Celia read her bedtime stories like Pooh Bear and when she could get her attention played Shakespeare drama discs. If she skipped a meal, Celia fed her sternly. The spaceship protein was terrible, but the fresh vegetables were juicy and at the peak of flavor.

"You have to eat if you are going to be strong enough to take care of me!"

When Lisa Maria began to come back to life, Celia put her arm around her and spent three days reading to her the classic *Planet of Magic* about the redhead Trudina and the dark Jindaram, Princesses of Zahelan, daughters of the Crimson Moon, defeated candidates for the post of High Enchantress. Their souls had been created by the Red Witch, fresh, without past lives, and the girls had been raised to introduce a new age of innocence to the Planet of Magic. But the old wizard Taslt defeated them at the Temple of T'halil because of their vanity and cleverly shipped off their souls in a silver cage to the Planet of Forgetfulness, Earth, where no one could remember their past lives and were doomed to repeat the same mistakes life after life. Of course, Trudina and Jindaram learned how to conquer their vanity after many trials and tribulations, without even knowing who they were, and finally returned to the Planet of Magic and defeated Taslt and brought on the Age of Innocence.

Lisa Maria started to smile again and wrote poetry steadily for two weeks, which she had never done before in her life. She was feeling the impact of the little girl and understanding why women and men who had children were more mature than those who didn't. Children took you back through your own childhood and gave you a fresh look at decisions you had made in innocence and forgotten about but were still using, and it showed you your own parents in a new light. She found it upsetting to see herself angry when Celia did the things that had once annoyed mother Sorenti and to be *sure* that she was *right* to be angry.

Then one evening, which wasn't any different from the spaceship day, while they were making a game of eating raw carrots together, Lisa Maria began to talk about things that she had kept secret from everybody all her life, even Nick. She didn't mind talking to Celia about the hidden feelings of a whore. She knew Celia would never grow up to be like her. In fact, Celia wanted to be a starship captain, and though she might never be because starships weren't invented yet, she would become something like that. So it was easy to talk to her. Celia just giggled or gasped or put her hand over her mouth. Then Lisa Maria read Celia a bedtime story the girl had never heard out of the favorite book of grandmother Morantes about a woman called Ruth, and their friendship solidified forever. Six months later the journey was over.

They glided in from behind, so they saw Pittsburgh's dish first. Only when they were right on top of the colony did they see the "sunrise" of the slag-jet pouring out, illuminating the shadowed face of the asteroid.

"My daddy! My daddy! You'll love my daddy. He writes better letters than I do!"

Lisa Maria thought about Daddy Kell's very very bad reputation. *I'll strangle him if he doesn't treat her right.* She wasn't worried about him. All she had to do was put on her professional hat and she could handle any man alive from sadist to fool. It wasn't going to matter whether she liked him or not.

She was worried about the women. For every job out here there were a hundred applicants thinking about the money. The women—she had seen the personnel file on the women of Pittsburgh—were so overqualified it made her sick in the pit of her stomach just to think about it. How did a woman ever get to the point where she could build and design machine tools?

She couldn't do *anything* they could do. Even the thing Lisa Maria pretended to do because it was feminine, to be an artist, was fake. She remembered her humiliation while Roy admired the glazes on her pottery, pieces she had bought in an obscure shop in Arizona while she was "doing ceramics," pieces she had lied about to her own group, to Nick, to the *San Francisco Chronicle,* to the world. Sometimes she rigged it so that she took a friend to the pottery to help her remove still warm pots from her kiln. *I can't do it!*

She thought of the money and got ready for the debarkation.

7

When they were through the Pittsburgh's airlock Lisa Maria was wearing the personality she reserved for policemen. Celia spotted her father immediately—the nose and the half-bald head were unmistakable—but immediately she shifted her eyes, as if to seek someone, allowing him to see her profile, letting him watch her grace as she turned to Lisa Maria for emotional support. She smiled ravishingly at her governess, long enough for her father to sip of that smile and desire it for himself. Only after he had had ample chance to become intoxicated did the child allow herself to notice her father. She met his eyes, held them for a second, questioningly, holding off any real reaction until the exact moment he made a slight hand touch against the wall that told her he was going to come forward. Then she launched herself into a glide full force and stopped herself by grabbing him by the ears. She tilted his head and gazed at him. "You're my sugar daddy," she said, smiling. No one noticed Ms. Sorenti.

David showed Lisa Maria the termite digs. Pittsburgh was already old enough to be quite spacious. Each member had his own cave, and the public rooms could be quite enormous. There was jungle park, a series of large caverns filled with tropical vegetation gone slightly insane in free-fall. There was a large spherical room, laced with padded tubing, for four-sided football. The goals were at vertices of a tetrahedron. He didn't show her the working rooms, but she could feel the smelting and the blasting through the rock. The whole complex had a vibrating tone to it.

He sat down with her and took her through the laws. Smoking and drugs were forbidden. All air-seal doors were to be closed after use. She was only allowed in those areas which her key-card would open for her. The captain had absolute authority in all cases where there was no law. And so on and on.

David introduced her to many people. They seemed friendly and proud and curious and small-townish. She was warily friendly in turn. It was like deciding to eat mushrooms and having a badly edited black-and-white guidebook to go by. She was going to eat them one tiny bite at a time and watch for several days to see if she got sick before risking another bite. Somebody had been very kind and put plants in her room. It was spartan but neat.

Kell avoided her for three days. She let him. She lavished Celia with attention, especially when people were watching, but Celia soon lost herself in the labyrinth, sublimely at home; the children she adopted, the adults she adopted, and she joined one of the four-man football teams. Lisa Maria was left alone. Enough. It was time to strike.

She waited for him to return from his rounds with the patience of a spider. Before he knew she was waiting, before he could finish closing his door, she was inside, and closing the door herself. She looked him straight in the eyes without smiling.

He was damned if he was going to look away, but she could sense his fear. "Hello," he said.

She waited until the last echo of his greeting had died before she chose to ignore him. His room was messy, lived in. Socks took a minute to fall if they were dropped. They had been dropped. There were no plants. There was no beauty. The nude on the wall seemed forlornly unhappy in this place without beauty.

"Mr. Kell, I'm flattered that you think I'm worth a hundred and forty million dollars."

"I don't think anything. I wanted my daughter."

"And you just brought *me* here to educate your daughter."

"You've been good to her," he said evasively.

"And my special talents?"

"It was getting dull around here," he said in an uneasy boy's voice.

"So I'm to entertain you?"

"Entertain yourself." He was smiling and she knew he was hostile.

"So I'm to entertain you by entertaining myself?"

"I don't really care what you do."

"Mr. Kell, have we ever met before?"

"Once. At a California orgy."

"Oh, we *have* met! I knew it! Which one!" She smiled for the first time, mischievously, tauntingly.

He snorted.

"No, tell me." She batted her eyes. "Refresh my memory."

"We were at opposite ends of a large terrace with a glass roof. You were wearing a one-piece red bikini."

"One of my more modest days."

"Three men were with you. I remember one of them kissed your hand. You wore a revolting red toenail polish."

"And you never forgot a detail of it."

"They were falling in love with you. All three of them at the same time."

"And you were the fourth?"

"I was thinking what fools they were to be taken in by such superficial charm. You were there for the money."

"That's when you found out I could be bought, is it?" She was drooling venom. She turned and took the nude off the wall. "You won't need her. You've just bought yourself a hundred-and-forty-million-dollar fantasy and you're going to have to live with it. For seven years."

"Not here!"

"You can't handle me?"

"Of course not. I'll introduce you to some of our more competent Romeos." He was grinning. "We have lots of them." He hated them.

"Listen, you centimeter marvel, you don't get out of it that easily. *You* bought me."

"I don't like you any better than you like me," he snapped.

"What woman ever has?"

"Get out. I never made a deal with you."

"You don't understand something, Mr. Kell. It doesn't matter a damn whether I like you or not. It doesn't matter a damn whether you like me." Her eyes were blazing. "You bought me. I was struggling to take control of my own life. Maybe I would have made it. So I didn't. So I'm buyable. So I'm a whore. Thanks for rubbing it in with a hundred-ton stamping press!"

She watched his pain. It was interesting because it was real pain. She let him feel the knives for precisely fifteen seconds. He spoke waves of pain to her but said nothing.

"That'll teach me to wear red monokinis!" she pouted.

He didn't laugh. He was too busy feeling the pain. "Get out."

Without paying any heed to him she carefully disassembled her bitch personality, like a dressing-room makeup take-down. You had to wash under your chin and even get to the very roots of your eyebrows. A quiet sixteen-year-old country girl sat there in front of her mirror selecting a new role. It had to be worked out right down to the motions of the fingers.

For a while he didn't notice that she was smiling at him with warm adoration because the shift was too swift for him to follow. She let the smile grow, powered by her amusement. It was exactly the smile of a woman who has just been proposed to by the man she most wants to spend the rest of her life with. The embarrassed excitement in her hands was just right.

"What makes you suppose I'm going to leave? Do you think I'd come all this way for a man I didn't love?" And she let her eyes fall away so that he could see her lush eyelashes. "You've saved me from a fate worse than death. You just don't know it yet."

Cut. She switched off the lights. Pain. The visual perfection of a woman madly in love. Fade to the physical sensations of love. A tender kiss. A touch of his biceps. Slowly. Not too fast. Let him get used to it. He had become impotent, of course; they always did after that treatment. It didn't matter. Such men had to be taken apart before they would ever fit together sexually. He looked like such an incompetent creep.

She undressed, floating there in the dark, careful not to touch him physically, but careful to let the fabric of her suit brush his skin.

"I'm tired. So are you. We'll just sleep." No pressure at all to begin with. She was willing to wait days until he became used to her body before starting to turn him on erotically.

Think of the money.

Her seduction was interrupted by his work. It was interrupted by his fear. But she knew when to withdraw and when to come back. On the fifteenth evening, he brought her a flower to wear in her hair. He put it there himself and half undressed her and couldn't stop looking at her. She knew she had him hooked.

Later, when he was half asleep as men are apt to be after lovemaking, and so still that he was visibly settling in the asteroid's minute gravitic field, she snuggled up to him, chewing the flower stem. Funny, when they had offered her 140 million to keep this misanthrope happy, the job had seemed like a formidably impossible one, but now that she knew him she wasn't awed at all. If you asked him questions and listened, he answered. He was already confiding in her. Why hadn't other women succeeded? She slipped the flower behind her ear and kissed him all over the cheek. *Women are such fools! Except me.*

David was sighing over her and brushing against her by then. Secretaries had such gall. The chief rocket engineer kept turning up for carrot juice when she was in the cafeteria. And one of the married men who had a baby found excuses to visit when she was with Celia. *Men are such fools! All of them.* They approached the subject of sex like armies of crabs. She teased them. Whenever they made one of their sidewise hints, Lisa Maria lit the lights in her eyes and allowed herself to dream aloud about Kell's sensual prowess until they stopped. It was all a lie, Kell was a lousy lay, but lies never bothered her when they worked. This one kept her admirers muzzled, and of course the stories got back to Kell in the form of leers and cracks and raunchy digs, and so he became more tender and tried his best to live up to his new-found reputation. It was all boringly predictable.

At night she dreamed about being a real human being and doing the things that other women did. She'd seen them driving the rock chewers and setting a broken bone and relining furnaces and troubleshooting the comm equipment and playing a wild game of football.

One evening when Celia and her daddy and Lisa Maria were eating together in her cave-cabin, it drove her crazy to hear this child chatter on about being a starship captain. She sounded so sure of herself! It was the crack that split the rocket engine.

From some distant place in her skull she began to listen to her possessed vocal chords speak about art, using her voice. She had done thus and so with her paintings. Metal sculpturing was very satisfying, but somehow there was no greater thrill than finding a new ceramic glaze that fixed the sunset or captured the essence of a San Francisco fog. Lies, all lies, but she couldn't stop talking about it.

One week later, with the casualness that another man might offer a diamond pendant, Kell took her to an old machine shop that he had fixed up with a kiln and wheel. The kiln would cook pots in either a vacuum, an oxidizing, or a reducing mode with a computer that controlled the time-temperature profile and the amount and kind of atmosphere present.

The wheel had a magnetic frictionless bearing like in the automobile flywheels, and was made out of solid gold, so that once moving, it was difficult to slow down. Metals were not Pittsburgh's problem.

"Nobody drinks out of mugs," she said inanely.

"Make something else."

"What would I use for clay?" she said desperately.

"Ah, I had to do some research on that. But I made you up six different kinds of clay you'll have to try out, different fusing temperatures, different properties. I have the photomicrographs of the particles if that would be of any help." And he showed her the cans. He had prewetted the clay to control dust.

Thus did Lisa Maria Sorenti meet the real Meddrick Kell. She was furious. *Remind me never again to suggest anything to that man that might even remotely sound like a physical problem.* There were no Arizona craft shops to rescue her. She was caught in her lie, and since she had never had that happen before in her life, she had no handy personality to deal with it.

Her first emergency reaction was to make the lie real by transforming herself into a real potter overnight. It didn't work. The shapes that desperation produced were no better than the shapes dabbling had produced when she had her San Francisco studio. And creating a beautiful shape was only the beginning.

She became secretive. "Don't you come into my studio," she told Kell with quavering voice. "I'm the kind of artist who doesn't work well with someone watching." That bought her another week.

Finally she knew she had to face the music. She slaved over a special meal which she cooked in the cafeteria for Kell alone. She wore her best perfume and put a flower in her hair so he wouldn't know she was wearing perfume. She made up her eyes with subtle care in order to conjure an achingly beautiful image.

"You're such a nice man," she said holding his wrist. "And you're *my* old man." She let her fingers be nymphs walking in what was left of his hair. "Do you love me enough to keep a secret?"

"Yeah."

She nibbled at his ears. "I'll be mad at you if you tell *anyone*. I'll be so mad at you I'll never speak to you again."

"Not even when we have sex?" he kidded her.

"I'll *space* myself if you tell anyone!"

"Once you've told me a secret, it's not a secret anymore," he said philosophically.

She let the tears gush from her eyes. "You have to promise!"

"Aw, you know I never talk to anyone."

"I'm not a potter. I'm a fake." She held his face and made him watch her screw up and bawl so that he'd know she was vulnerably feminine and needed protection.

Lisa Maria expected some kind of emotion from him—an angry condemnation, perhaps, or maybe he'd laugh at her. But he didn't do anything. His face went blank. He shifted into what she called his "computer mode."

Pregnant pause. "When *I* lie," said his computer voice, "it is because I want something to be real that isn't. Is that why *you* lie?"

She nodded, not breathing.

"The solution is simple. Become a potter."

"But I can't," she cried. "I've tried!"

"Give me an estimate of the number of hours you've spent potting."

She thought. "Fifty."

"That doesn't qualify as a try. No one can become a potter in fifty hours. You'll *try*. I'll show you how. You have the time."

"Are you going to tell on me?"

"I'll show people the first beautiful thing you do. It took me a thousand hours to make my first iron when I was a kid, and another two thousand hours to learn how to make rifle-barrel steel."

"I've felt so incompetent since I've been here with all these amazing women."

"List for me the things that you'd like to be able to do that they do."

"Everything!" she said defiantly.

Pregnant pause. "If you mean the things they do every day, yes, that's possible for you to learn in seven years. If you mean everything they *can* do, no, that's not possible."

"Is there anything *you* can't do?"

He laughed. "Pot. And I can't write. Celia is teaching me how to write novels these days. We're working on a novel together. She says she hasn't got enough experience to write a novel, so I'm responsible for filling in her blank spots. It's killing me."

Kell set up a simple schedule for her. First she had to master her tools and materials. The goal he gave her was something she felt confident that she could do—learn to make ugly shapes that didn't blow up or crack when bisqued. She was to test her glazes on the successful pieces. A month's work, she thought. No, more like two years, he said and shrugged. Then she could begin.

He began to take her on his rounds. He gave her a stern lecture. On Earth you could go through school and get a C and be promoted. Here if you got a C you got promoted to Death. "Everything you learn to do, bring it up to full competence—or don't do it."

They were eating up the whole asteroid and refining it to metal that had to be stored in such a way that the center of gravity stayed on a line through the slag-jet. He gave her lessons in driving a rock chewer. He put her with a maintenance crew. He showed her how to operate the computer-controlled electron beam machine tools that built their spare parts. No matter how small the task he gave her, he pushed her ruthlessly until she reached full competence.

Sometimes he was too busy to bother with her for days. He left her with her pottery or with Celia. She might be with him only while he slept. Sometimes he went straight around the clock without sleeping.

She got fascinated by metalworking in gold and took lessons from a Swedish engineer who enjoyed her attention. She couldn't resist having an affair with him even though he was married; the temptation to defy Roy Stoerm and get away with it was too strong. She was risking her twenty million a year, but that gave it value in her eyes. She didn't let herself notice that she had picked the most stable and secretive man in all of Pittsburgh.

They made a golden beer stein together as a lark when Lisa Maria bemoaned the fact that it would be useless for her to throw mugs on her wheel. Inventing a beer mug that worked was hilarious. The final version sat on the air (sinking ever so slowly as things did around the asteroid) and had a pleasant inertial feel to it. A special mechanism spun the liquid so that it "fell" to the walls of the stein which when tipped created a gyroscopic resistance that caused a small scoop to throw a sip of liquid from the stein's mouth.

Gently, without any tangled emotion, her Swede withdrew from Lisa Maria, having gotten whatever it was that he wanted, to leave her alone again with Kell, feeling the hostility she felt when she had no one but him. It was dangerous to trust a man, and if you felt like trusting him he was very, very dangerous. Her Swede wasn't dangerous because she *knew* she couldn't trust him.

Wanting to trust Kell reminded her of Carl Chrisholm. Nick had introduced them and rented her to him after his wife's funeral. She was just becoming aware then that Nick was betraying her and Carl seemed so honest. He was older, rich, respected, considerate, gregarious, never dull, and a one-woman man. He took her everywhere. She liked his home, she liked his children. It was strange to love a man and not be cynical about it, to find yourself giving more than you thought you had. Glorious.

She remembered telling Nick goodbye in her mind. *I don't need you. I have Carl!* And one evening she told Carl that she loved him and wanted to be his woman and he'd been so pleased and so loving. The next day he went out and rented a new mistress.

So to hell with Meddrick Kell. Lisa Maria replaced her Swede with David and continued to live dangerously. She had to fake it with Kell because of Stoerm's contract, but nothing in the contract said she had to trust him. She didn't like men who made you love them and all the while were planning to space you.

8

The emergency came suddenly, as they always do. Every eighteen days the solar power station Gilgamesh that supplied Pittsburgh passed behind the sun. Slag-jet

Motor One was shut down for overhaul and Slag-jet Motor Two was fired as soon as Gilgamesh reappeared. But this time Motor Two failed within the hour after start-up.

Every available person was called on to help diagnose the trouble and get repairs operational. While the motors were not firing, the asteroid was not spiraling in toward Earth. Too many delays meant that they would reach Earth when Earth was gone and so their orbit would have to be adjusted to a much later arrival date. The consequence was extra months, perhaps an extra year in space, and grave financial fines for the crew of the Pittsburgh.

Lisa Maria was helping by tending to Kell's comforts and by running errands for him. He was pushing himself mercilessly, planning the whole operation so that all systems would be up in minimum time. She had just brought food to the command center when navigation phoned in a report.

"The single trouble we've got up here is a rock that's going to take out the mirror. The new orbit gives us a collision course. Even if Number Two started firing right now we wouldn't get out of her way in time. She's a small one, but she's got to be taken care of within the hour. Details are coming through your fax right now."

"Shit!" said Kell when he got the charts and read them.

"What's the matter now?"

"Goddamn collision. Lawson, take over. Lisa Maria, suit up. We're going to do in this rock ourselves."

"Kell, you're tired," said Lawson.

"It's okay. It'll relax me. I need a vacation from this mess. I'll be back with you in a couple of hours."

Lisa Maria followed his instant exit like his shadow, but she didn't want to go. "Are you sure I can help?"

"We have your reflexes up to speed. No problem for you."

The skintight tension suits allowed for hard work in space because they sweated like real skin. Both of them stripped and suited up almost faster than the eye could see. "What am I supposed to do?" she pleaded.

"Obey orders. Can't spare anybody else here. Don't worry. It's a picnic. A damn nuisance, but not a real problem."

Seconds later they were blasting off Pittsburgh in one of the open cockpit ships. Only then did Kell relax. "Do you know why they call these things convertibles?"

"They convert people to corpses?" she said, hanging on. Being in the center of a sphere of stars dominated by a single star was an awesome experience.

"They used to drive on the highways of California in these things. The country air feeling. The thrill of the wind in your face."

"Jesus!" said Lisa Maria, hanging on for dear life though she was strapped in.

"We can laser some of these rocks out of the way. But you still have to visit them and cancel the rotation. The laser pits them on a line though the center of gravity, and the back reaction of the vaporized gases acts like a reaction jet. This rock is too big. We've got a rocket with us to do the job. A homemade sparkler, my design, lousy specific impulse, but good enough. We only need to add a quarter of a meter per second to her velocity."

"Do you ever get in collision orbits with other asteroids?"

"Naw. Our navigator is too good for that."

Once the acceleration cut out it was as if they were suspended. Within this glittering sphere she couldn't even tell whether they were mice in a toy rocket car or whether their bodies were as huge as a planet. The human mind cannot comprehend velocity or size without objects that move in relationship to each other.

"You know what they used to do in convertibles?" said Kell. "The object of the game was to run out of gas under the stars. That was an excuse to nuzzle."

"I saw the same disc. It was made in 1947. But there was a moon in the sky."

He began to caress her body.

"Get your electrically heated paws off of me!"

They both laughed inside their helmets.

Forty minutes later they decelerated and the computer brought them to rest beside their slowly tumbling rock. "How far have we gone?" she asked.

"From San Francisco to New York. And shut up. Do everything I say."

The rock was roughly twelve meters in diameter. He fixed a small rocket to its equator and they had a pinwheel flare until the rotation was stopped dead. Then he did some measurements against the stars and drilled a mount for the rocket. Meanwhile she dragged it out and brought it over. She was gliding back to the convertible when she felt an explosion throw her violently until she snapped taut against the ship line. It was all over before she could turn to see what had happened.

"Kell!" she screamed.

By reflex she pulled herself into the cockpit and sent out a radar scan for debris, asking the machine to select a human identity. It picked him up almost immediately. She ordered the convertible to "home" on him, and seconds later was pulling him out of the sky.

There was blood all over, boiling and icing, black in her headlamp. She had no time to ask whether he was dead. She was pulling out her patching equipment at the same time she was deciding what to do with the piece of rocket sticking out of him. Cut it flush to the skin or pull it out? The quickest. Pull it out. Patch instantly. Thank God he wasn't wearing a pressure suit. You couldn't decompress a tension suit unless the helmet shattered. Switch on the physiological monitor. Sudden tears. The pulse was poor, the breathing poor. He was still alive.

And the rock was still heading for a collision with the Pittsburgh mirror. But . . .

He'll die if I don't get him back.

She forgot that she had radio contact with Pittsburgh in her panic to do the right thing which, whatever it was, had to be done swifter than thought. The longer she waited to deflect the rock, the more energy it would take, and if she let it go altogether it might take more energy than Pittsburgh could bring to bear. The only rocket power available was in the convertible's motors.

Crying because Kell was dying, she nosed her vehicle against the rock. Careful! A false move and she'd only start the rock spinning. Free-fall had taught her much physics. Outside the dominating field of Earth, Newton's laws were so evident that they became built into the nervous system. Aim through the center of gravity. Lightly does it; she was nose-heavy by about two or three thousand tons. Lock on the stars so that the gimbles of the motor will act against any spin. Set the accelerometer to stop the firing when they had changed velocity by a quarter of a meter per second. Set for minimum thrust. Fire! The motor roared to life. *God, dear God, let there be some fuel left.*

There was. She had enough fuel remaining in her tanks to take her back to the Pittsburgh in twelve hours. Kell would be long dead. Only then did she remember the radio. She was crying but she turned off the tears because she had that kind of control.

"Convertible Three to Navigation. Come in."

"Come in, Lisa Maria!"

"We've had a terrible accident. I don't know what happened. Kell's hurt, maybe dying. I can't get back." Her voice was rising into hysteria.

"Lisa, listen. I got that. I want to know something. We have a radar fix on the rock. It has moved out of collision orbit. Did you know that?"

"Yes. When the rocket blew up, I used the convertible's fuel."

"Great thinking!"

"I can't get back in time," she cried.

"Lisa. Put Kell's monitor on broadcast. Dr. Hendrick will be right on the line. Home on the Pittsburgh with whatever fuel you've got left. We're coming after you. Flat out. All the delta-vee we've got. Surgery will be set up when you get here. And you, wench, are *you* all right?"

It all went quicker than she thought it possibly could

considering the fact that she was in "New York" and the ambulance was in "San Francisco." The return was a jumble of frantic memories—Kell being whisked away at a rapid glide, Celia's face in pathetic anguish: "Is my daddy dead?" and the two women who helped her de-suit before she fainted, a man trying to shield her while Lawson insisted on debriefing her, a woman she hardly knew reaching out a congratulating hand. Sleep.

When she woke up, David was with her.

"How is he?"

"He's not easy to kill. Rumor has it that his blood is too cold to boil even if you spaced him. Actually, he's better. Lawson is talking about you. He thinks you've soaked up Kell through your pores. He couldn't give you a higher compliment."

"I felt so awkward."

"You didn't make a mistake and everyone knows it."

"It was just reflex."

"Spaceman's reflex."

"Is that another compliment?"

"You're going to get tired of them. Someone put in a commendation for you and everyone has voted yes already at ten on the scale."

"Well, the company is paying me twenty million dollars a year to bring in the steel and if this barge doesn't reach port we don't get paid, right?"

"Right!"

"I want to see Kell."

She found him talking into a hands-off phone about the lining of Motor Number Two. He signed off when she came in. "You're the one who can answer my questions," he said. "How did I get here?"

"I saved you."

"How come the mirror is still there?"

"I saved it."

"What did you bring me along for if you are that competent?"

"I thought the experience would do you some good, but you turned out to be as useful as a bloody corpse. Next time I won't bring you."

"Do you know what my last thought was?" he said. "I thought I had killed you and I loved you."

"Do you know what my last thought was?" she said. "I was worried sick about the mirror. I thought I might not get my hundred and forty million dollars."

She took his hand and looked at his eyes looking into hers. *I'll never tell you I love you,* she thought at him, *because then you'll hire a new mistress and I'll be unhappy again.*

The Very Slow Time Machine

Ian Watson

Yet another time-machine story? Yes, certainly; but not a typical one about murdering your great-great-grandmother or bringing back uninvented inventions from the future. Time-travel concepts continue to fascinate us because they *always* contradict and upset our world view, and this story does so more than most.

Ian Watson, author of *The Embedding*, *Miracle Visitors*, and a number of other remarkable sf novels, is one of the most delightful British writers to enter the science-fiction field in recent years. You'll see why.

(1990)

The Very Slow Time Machine—for convenience: the VSTM*—made its first appearance at exactly midday 1 December 1985 in an unoccupied space at the National Physical Laboratory. It signaled its arrival with a loud bang and a squall of expelled air. Dr. Kelvin, who happened to be looking in its direction, reported that the VSTM did not exactly *spring* into existence instantly, but rather expanded very rapidly from a point source, presumably explaining the absence of a more devastating explosion as the VSTM jostled with the air already present in the room. Later, Kelvin declared that what he had actually seen was the *implosion* of the VSTM. Doors were sucked shut by the rush of air, instead of

* The term VSTM is introduced retrospectively in view of our subsequent understanding of the problem (2019).

bursting open, after all. However, it was a most confused moment—and the confusion persisted, since the occupant of the VSTM (who alone could shed light on its nature) was not only time-reversed with regard to us, but also quite crazy.

One infuriating thing is that the occupant visibly grows saner and more presentable (in his reversed way) the more that time passes. We feel that all the hard work and thought devoted to the enigma of the VSTM is so much energy poured down the entropy sink—because the answer is going to come from him, from inside, not from us; so that we may as well just have bided our time until his condition improved (or, from his point of view, began to degenerate). And in the meantime his arrival distorted and perverted essential research at our laboratory from its course without providing any tangible return for it.

The VSTM was the size of a small caravan; but it had the shape of a huge lead sulphide, or galena, crystal—which is, in crystallographers' jargon, an octahedron-with-cube formation consisting of eight large hexagonal faces with six smaller square faces filling in the gaps. It perched precariously—but immovably—on the base square, the four lower hexagons bellying up and out towards its waist, where four more squares (oblique, vertically) connected with the mirror-image upper hemisphere, rising to a square north pole. Indeed, it looked like a kind of world globe, lopped and sheared into flat planes: and has remained very much a separate, private world to this day, along with its passenger.

All faces were blank metal except for one equatorial square facing southwards into the main body of the laboratory. This was a window—of glass as thick as that of a deep-ocean diving bell—which could apparently be opened from inside, and only from inside.

The passenger within looked as ragged and tattered as a tramp; as crazy, dirty, woebegone, and tangle-haired as any lunatic in an ancient Bedlam cell. He was apparently very old; or at any rate long solitary confinement in that cell made him seem so. He was pallid, crookbacked, skinny, and rotten-toothed. He raved and mumbled soundlessly at our spotlights. Or maybe he only mouthed his ravings and mumbles, since we could hear nothing whatever through the thick glass. When we obtained the services of a lip reader two days later the mad old man seemed to be mouthing mere garbage, a mishmash of sounds. Or was he? Obviously no one could be expected to lip-read backwards; already Dr. Yang had suggested from his actions and gestures that the man was time-reversed. So we videotaped the passenger's mouthings and played the tape backwards for our lip reader. Well, it was still garbage. Backwards, or forwards, the unfortunate passenger had visibly cracked up. Indeed, one proof of his insanity was that he should be trying to talk to us at all at this late stage of his journey rather than communicate by holding up written messages—as he has now begun to do. (But more of these messages later; they only begin—or, from his point of view, *cease* as he descends further into madness—in the summer of 1989.)

Abandoning hope of enlightenment from him, we set out on the track of scientific explanations. (Fruitlessly. Ruining our other, more important work. Overturning our laboratory projects—and the whole of physics in the process.)

To indicate the way in which we wasted our time, I might record that the first "clue" came from the shape of the VSTM which, as I said, was that of a lead sulphide or galena crystal. Yang emphasized that galena is used as a semiconductor in crystal rectifiers: devices for transforming alternating current into direct current. They set up a much higher resistance to an electric current flowing in one direction than another. Was there an analogy with the current of time? Could the geometry of the VSTM—or the geometry of energies circulating in its metal walls, presumably interlaid with printed circuits—effectively impede the forward flow of time, and reverse it? We had no way to break into the VSTM. Attempts to cut into it proved quite ineffective and were soon discontinued; while x-raying it was foiled, conceivably by lead alloyed in the walls. Sonic scanning provided rough pictures of internal shapes, but nothing as intricate as circuitry; so we had to rely on what we could see of the outward shape, or through the window—and on pure theory.

Yang also stressed that galena rectifiers operate in the same manner as diode valves. Besides transforming the flow of an electric current, they can also *demodulate*. They separate information out from a modulated carrier wave—as in a radio or TV set. Were we witnessing, in the VSTM, a machine for separating out "information"—in the form of the physical vehicle itself, with its passenger—from a carrier wave stretching back through time? Was the VSTM a solid, tangible analogy of a three-dimensional TV picture, played backwards?

We made many models of VSTMs based on these ideas and tried to send them off into the past, or the future—or anywhere, for that matter! They all stayed monotonously present in the laboratory, stubbornly locked to our space and time.

Kelvin, recalling his impression that the VSTM had seemed to expand outward from a point, remarked that this was how three-dimensional beings such as ourselves might well perceive a four-dimensional object first impinging on us. Thus a 4-D sphere would appear as a point and swell into a full sphere, then contract again to a point. But a 4-D octahedron-and-cube? According to our maths this shape couldn't have a regular analogue in 4-space; only a simple octahedron could. Besides, what would be the use of a 4-D time machine which shrank to a point at precisely the moment when the passenger needed to mount it? No, the VSTM wasn't a genuine four-dimensional body; though we wasted many weeks running computer programs to describe it as one, and arguing that its passenger was a normal 3-space man imprisoned within a 4-space structure—the discrepancy of one dimension between him and his vehicle effectively isolating him from the rest of the universe so that he could travel hindwards.

That he was indeed traveling hindwards was by now absolutely clear from his feeding habits (i.e., he regurgitated), though his extreme furtiveness about bodily functions, coupled with his filthy condition, meant that it took several months before we were positive, on these grounds.

All this, in turn, raised another unanswerable question: if the VSTM was indeed traveling backwards through time, precisely where did it *disappear* to, in that instant of its arrival on 1 December 1985? The passenger was hardly on an archaeological jaunt, or he would have tried to climb out.

At long last, on midsummer day 1989, our passenger held up a notice printed on a big plastic eraser slate.

CRAWLING DOWNHILL, SLIDING UPHILL!

He held this up for ten minutes, against the window. The printing was spidery and ragged; so was he.

This could well have been his last lucid moment before the final descent into madness, in despair at the pointlessness of trying to communicate with us. Thereafter it would be *downhill all the way,* we interpreted. Seeing us with all our still eager, still baffled faces, he could only gibber incoherently thenceforth like an enraged monkey at our sheer stupidity.

He didn't communicate for another three months.

When he held up his next (i.e., penultimate) sign, he looked slightly sprucer, a little less crazy (though only comparatively so, having regard to his final mumbling squalor).

THE LONELINESS! BUT LEAVE ME ALONE!
IGNORE ME TILL 1995!

We held up signs (to which, we soon realized, his sign was a response):

ARE YOU TRAVELING BACK THROUGH TIME? HOW? WHY?

We would have also dearly loved to ask: WHERE DO YOU DISAPPEAR TO ON DEC. 1 1985? But we judged it unwise to ask this most pertinent of all questions in case his disappearance was some sort of disaster; so that we would in effect be foredooming him, accelerating his mental breakdown. Dr. Franklin insisted that this was nonsense; he broke down *anyway*. Still, if we *had* held up that sign, what remorse we would have felt: because we *might* have caused his breakdown and ruined some magnificent scientific undertaking. . . . We were certain that it had to be a magnificent undertaking to involve such personal sacrifice, such abnegation, such a cutting off of oneself from the rest of the human race. This is about all we were certain of.

(1995)

No progress with our enigma. All our research is dedicated to solving it; but we keep this out of sight of him. While rotas of postgraduate students observe him round the clock, our best brains get on with the real thinking elsewhere in the building. He sits inside his vehicle, less dirty and disheveled now, but monumentally taciturn: a Trappist monk under a vow of silence. He spends most of his time rereading the same dogeared books, which have fallen to pieces back in our past: Defoe's *Journal of the Plague Year* and *Robinson Crusoe* and Jules Verne's *Journey to the Center of the Earth;* and listening to what is presumably taped music—which he shreds from the cassettes back in 1989, flinging streamers around his tiny living quarters in a brief mad fiesta (which of course we see as a sudden frenzy of disentangling and repackaging, with maniacal speed and neatness, of tapes which have lain around, trodden underfoot, for years).

Superficially we have ignored him (and he, us) until 1995: assuming that his last sign had some significance. Having got nowhere ourselves, we expect something from him now.

Since he is cleaner, tidier, and saner now, in this year 1995 (not to mention ten years younger), we have a better idea of how old he actually is; thus some clue as to when he might have started his journey.

He must be in his late forties or early fifties—though he aged dreadfully in the last ten years, looking more like seventy or eighty when he reached 1985. Assuming that the future does not hold in store any longevity drugs (in which case he might be a century old, or more!) he should have entered the VSTM sometime between 2010 and 2025. The later date, putting him in his very early twenties if not teens, does rather suggest a "suicide volunteer" who is merely a passenger in the vehicle. The earlier date suggests a more mature researcher who played a major role in the development of the VSTM and was only prepared to test it on his own person. Certainly, now that his madness has abated into a tight, meditative fixity of posture, accompanied by normal activities such as reading, we incline to think him a man of moral stature rather than a time-kamikaze; so we put the date of commencement of the journey around 2010 to 2015 (only fifteen to twenty years ahead) when he will be in his thirties.

Besides theoretical physics, basic space science has by now been hugely sidetracked by his presence.

The lead hope of getting man to the stars was the development of some deep-sleep or refrigeration system. Plainly this does not exist by 2015 or so—or our passenger would be using it. Only a lunatic would voluntarily sit in a tiny compartment for decades on end, ageing and rotting, if he could sleep the time away just as well, and awake as young as the day he set off. On the other hand, his life-support systems seem so impeccable that he can exist for decades within the narrow confines of that vehicle using recycled air, water, and solid matter to 100 percent efficiency. This represents no inconsiderable outlay in research and development—which must have been borrowed from another field; obviously the space sciences. Therefore the astronauts of 2015 or thereabouts require very long-term life support systems capable of sustaining them for years and decades, up and awake. What kind of space travel must they be engaged in, to need these? Well, they can only be going to the stars—the slow way; though not a *very* slow way.

Not hundreds of years; but decades. Highly dedicated men must be spending many years cooped up alone in tiny spacecraft to reach Alpha Centaurus, Tau Ceti, Epsilon Eridani, or wherever. If their surroundings are so tiny, then any extra payload costs prohibitively. Now who would contemplate such a journey merely out of curiosity? No one. The notion is ridiculous—*unless* these heroes are carrying something to their destination which will then link it inexorably and instantaneously with Earth. A tachyon descrambler is the only obvious explanation. They are carrying with them the other end of a tachyon-transmission system for beaming material objects, and even living human beings, out to the stars!

So, while one half of physics nowadays grapples with the problems of reverse-time, the other half, funded by most of the money from the space vote, preempting the whole previously extant space program, is trying to work out ways to harness and modulate tachyons.

These faster-than-light particles certainly *seem* to exist; we're fairly certain of that now. The main problem is that the technology for harnessing them is needed *beforehand*, to prove that they do exist and so to work out exactly *how* to harness them.

All these reorientations of science—because of *him* sitting in his enigmatic vehicle in deliberate alienation from us, reading *Robinson Crusoe*, a strained expression on his face as he slowly approaches his own personal crack-up.

(1996)

If you were locked up in a VSTM for x years, would you want a calendar on permanent display—or not? Would it be consoling or taunting? Obviously his instruments are calibrated—unless it was completely fortuitous that his journey ended on 1 December 1985 at precisely midday! But can he see the calibrations? Or would he prefer to be overtaken suddenly by the end of his journey, rather than have the slow grind of years unwind itself? You see, we are trying to explain why he did not communicate with us in 1995.

Convicts in solitary confinement keep their sanity by scratching five-barred gates of days on the walls with their fingernails; the sense of time passing keeps their spirits up. But on the other hand, tests of time perception carried out on potholers who volunteered to stay below ground for several months on end show that the internal clock lags grossly—by as much as two weeks in a three-month period. Our VSTM passenger might gain a reprieve of a year—or five years!—on his total subjective journey time, by ignoring the passing of time. The potholers had no clue to night and day; but then, neither does he! Ever since his arrival, lights have been burning constantly in the laboratory; he has been under constant observation. . . .

He isn't a convict, or he would surely protest, beg to be let out, throw himself on our mercy, give us some clue to the nature of his predicament. Is he the carrier of some fatal disease—a disease so incredibly infectious that it must affect the whole human race, unless he were isolated? Which can only be isolated by a time capsule? Which even isolation on the Moon or Mars would not keep from spreading to the human race? He hardly appears to be . . .

Suppose that he had to be isolated for some very good reason, and suppose that he concurs in his own isolation (which he visibly does, sitting there reading Defoe for the nth time), what demands this unique dissection of one man from the whole continuum of human life and from his own time and space? Medicine, psychiatry, sociology, all the human sciences are being drawn in to the problem in the wake of physics and space science. Sitting there doing nothing, he has become a kind of funnel for all the physical and social sciences: a human black hole into which vast energy pours, for a very slight increase in our radius of understanding. That single individual has accumulated as much disruptive potential as a single atom accelerated to the speed of light—which requires all the available energy in the universe to sustain it in its impermissible state.

Meanwhile the orbiting tachyon laboratories report that they are just on the point of uniting quantum mechanics, gravitational theory, and relativity; whereupon they will at last "jump" the first high-speed particle packages over the C-barrier into a faster-than-light mode, and back again into our space. But they reported *that* last year—only to have their particle packages "jump back" as antimatter, annihilating five billion dollars' worth of equipment and taking thirty lives. They hadn't jumped into a tachyon mode at all, but had "möbiused" themselves through wormholes in the space-time fabric.

Nevertheless, prisoner of conscience (his own conscience, surely!) or whatever he is, our VSTM passenger seems nobler year by year. As we move away from his terminal madness, increasingly what strikes us is his dedication, his self-sacrifice (for a cause still beyond our comprehension), his Wittgensteinian spirituality. "Take him for all in all, he is a Man. We shall not look upon his like . . ." Again? We shall look upon his like. Upon the man himself, gaining stature every year! That's the wonderful thing. It's as though Christ, fully exonerated as Son of God, is uncrucified and his whole life reenacted before our eyes in full and certain knowledge of his true role. (Except . . . that this man's role is silence.)

(1997)
Undoubtedly he is a holy man who will suffer mental crucifixion for the sake of some great human project. Now he rereads Defoe's *Plague Year*, that classic of collective incarceration and the resistance of the human spirit and human organizing ability. Surely the "plague" hint in the title is irrelevant. It's the sheer force of spirit which beat the Great Plague of London, that is the real keynote of the book.

Our passenger is the object of popular cults by now—a focus for finer feelings. In this way his mere presence has drawn the world's peoples closer together, cultivating respect and dignity, pulling us back from the brink of war, liberating tens of thousands from their concentration camps. These cults extend from purely fashionable manifestations—shirts printed with his face, now neatly shaven in a Vandyke style; rings and worry-beads made from galena crystals—through the architectural (octahedron-and-cube meditation modules) to life-styles themselves: a Zen-like "sitting quietly, doing nothing."

He's Rodin's "Thinker," the "Belvedere Apollo," and Michelangelo's "David" rolled into one for our world as the millennium draws to its close. Never have so many copies of Defoe's two books and the Jules Verne been in print before. People memorize them as meditation exercises and recite them as the supremely lucid, rational Western mantras.

The National Physical Laboratory has become a place of pilgrimage, our lawns and grounds a vast camping site—Woodstock and Avalon, Rome and Arlington all in one. About the sheer tattered degradation of his final days less is said; though that has its cultists too, its late-twentieth-century anchorites, its Saint Anthonies pole-squatting or cave-immuring themselves in the midst of the urban desert, bringing austere spirituality back to a world which appeared to have lost its soul—though this latter is a fringe phenomenon; the general keynote is nobility, restraint, quiet consideration for others.

And now he holds up a notice.

I IMPLY NOTHING. PAY NO ATTENTION TO MY PRESENCE. KINDLY GET ON DOING YOUR OWN THINGS. I CANNOT EXPLAIN TILL 2000.

He holds it up for a whole day, looking not exactly angry, but slightly pained. The whole world, hearing of it, sighs with joy at his modesty, his self-containment, his reticence, his humility. This must be the promised 1995 message, two years late (or two years early; obviously he still has a long way to come). Now he is Oracle; he is the Millennium. This place is Delphi.

The orbiting laboratories run into more difficulties

with their tachyon research; but still funds pour into them, private donations too on an unprecedented scale. The world strips itself of excess wealth to strip matter and propel it over the interface between sub-light and trans-light.

The development of closed-cycle living-pods for the carriers of those tachyon receivers to the stars is coming along well, a fact which naturally raises the paradoxical question of whether his presence has in fact stimulated the development of the technology by which he himself survives. We at the National Physical Laboratory and at all other such laboratories around the world are convinced that we shall soon make a breakthrough in our understanding of time reversal—which, intuitively, should connect with that other universal interface in the realm of matter, between our world and the tachyon world—and we feel too, paradoxically, that our current research must surely lead to the development of the VSTM, which will then become so opportunely necessary to us, for reasons yet unknown. No one feels they are wasting their time. He is the Future. His presence here vindicates our every effort—even the blindest of blind alleys.

What kind of Messiah must he be, by the time he enters the VSTM? How much charisma, respect, adoration and wonder must he have accrued by his starting point? Why, the whole world will send him off! He will be the focus of so much collective hope and worship that we even start to investigate *Psi* phenomena seriously: the concept of group mental thrust as a hypothesis for his mode of travel—as though he is vectored not through time or 4-space at all but down the waveguide of human willpower and desire.

(2001)
The millennium comes and goes without any revelation. Of course that is predictable; he is lagging by a year or eighteen months. (Obviously he can't see the calibrations on his instruments; it was his choice—that was his way to keep sane on the long haul.)

But finally, now in the autumn of 2001, he holds up a sign, with a certain quiet jubilation:

WILL I LEAVE 1985 SOUND IN WIND AND LIMB?

Quiet jubilation, because we have already (from his point of view) held up the sign in answer:

YES! YES!

We're all rooting for him passionately. It isn't really a lie that we tell him. He did leave relatively sound in wind and limb. It was just his mind that was in tatters. . . . Maybe that is inessential, irrelevant, or he wouldn't have phrased his question to refer merely to his physical body.

He must be approaching his take-off point. He's having a mild fit of tenth-year blues, first-decade anxiety, self-doubt; which we clear up for him. . . .

Why doesn't he know what shape he arrived in? Surely that must be a matter of record before he sets off. . . . *No!* Time can not be invariable, determined. Not even the Past. Time is probabilistic. He has refrained from comment for all these years so as not to unpluck the strands of time past and reweave them in another, undesirable way. A tower of strength he has been. *Ein' feste Burg ist unser Zeitgänger!* Well, back to the drawing board, and to probabilistic equations for (a) tachyon-scatter out of normal space (b) time reversal.

A few weeks later he holds up another sign, which must be his promised Delphic revelation:

I AM THE MATRIX OF MAN.

Of course! Of course! He has made himself that over the years. What else?

A matrix is a mold for shaping a cast. And indeed, out of him have men been molded increasingly since the late 1990s, such has been his influence.

Was he sent hindwards to save the world from self-slaughter by presenting such a perfect paradigm—which only frayed and tattered in the eighties when it did not matter any more; when he had already succeeded?

But a matrix is also an array of components for translating from one code into another. So Yang's demodulation of information hypothesis is revived, coupled now with the idea that the VSTM is perhaps a matrix for transmitting the "information" contained in a man across space and time (and the man-transmitter experiments in orbit redouble their efforts); with the corollary (though this could hardly be voiced to the enraptured world at large) that perhaps the passenger was *not there* at all in any real sense; and he had never been; that we merely were witnessing an experiment in the possibility of transmitting a man across the galaxy, performed on a future Earth by future science to test out the degradation factor: the decay of information—mapped from space on to time so that it could be observed by us, their predecessors! Thus the onset of madness (i.e., information decay) in our passenger, timed in years from his starting point, might set a physical limit in *light-years* to the distance to which man could be beamed (tachyonically?). And this was at once a terrible kick in the teeth to space science—and a great boost. A kick in the teeth, as this suggested that physical travel through interstellar space must be impossible, perhaps because of Man's frailty in face of cosmic ray bombardment; and thus the whole development of intensive closed-cycle life-pods for single astronaut couriers must be deemed irrelevant. Yet a great boost too, since the possibility of a receiverless transmitter loomed. The now elderly Yang suggested that 1 December 1985 was actually a moment of lift-off to the stars. Where our passenger went then, in all his madness, was to a point in space thirty or forty light-years distant. The VSTM was thus the testing to destruction of a future man-beaming system and practical future models would only deal in distances (in times) of the order of seven or eight years. (Hence no other VSTMs had imploded into existence, hitherto.)

(2010)

I am tired with a lifetime's fruitless work; however, the human race at large is at once calmly loving—and frenetic with hope. For we must be nearing our goal. Our passenger is in his thirties now (whether a live individual, or only an epiphenomenon of a system for transmitting the information present in a human being: literally a "ghost in the machine"). This sets a limit. It sets a limit. He couldn't have set off with such strength of mind much earlier than his twenties or (I sincerely hope not) his late teens. Although the teens *are* a prime time for taking vows of chastity, for entering monasteries, for pledging one's life to a cause. . . .

(2015)

Boosted out of my weariness by the general euphoria, I have successfully put off my retirement for another four years. Our passenger is now in his middle twenties and a curious inversion in his "worship" is taking place, representing (I think) a subconscious groundswell of anxiety as well as joy. Joy, obviously, that the moment is coming when he makes his choice and steps into the VSTM, as Christ gave up carpentry and stepped out from Nazareth. Anxiety, though, at the possibility that he may pass beyond this critical point, towards infancy; ridiculous as this seems! He knows how to read books; he couldn't have taught himself to read. Nor could he have taught himself how to speak *in vitro*—and he has certainly delivered lucid, if mysterious, messages to us from time to time. The hit song of the whole world, nevertheless, this year is William Blake's "The Mental Traveller" set to sitar and gongs and glockenspiel . . .

> *For as he eats and drinks he grows*
> *Younger and younger every day;*
> *And on the desert wild they both*
> *Wander in terror and dismay . . .*

The unvoiced fear represented by this song's sweeping of the world being that he may yet evade us; that he may slide down towards infancy, and at the moment of his birth (whatever life-support mechanisms extrude to keep him alive till then!) the VSTM will implode back whence it came: sick joke of some alien superconsciousness, intervening in human affairs with a scientific "miracle" to make all human striving meaningless and pointless. Not many people feel this way openly. It isn't a popular view. A man could be torn limb from limb for espousing it in public. The human mind will never accept it; and purges this fear in a long song of joy which at once mocks and copies and adores the mystery of the VSTM.

Men put this supreme *man* into the machine. Even so, Madonna and Child does haunt the world's mind . . . and a soft femininity prevails—men's skirts are the new, soft, gracious mode of dress in the West. Yet he is now so noble, so handsome in his youth, so glowing and strong; such a Zarathustra, locked up in there.

(2018)
He can only be twenty-one or twenty-two. The world adores him, mothers him, across the unbridgeable gulf of reversed time. No progress in the Solar System, let alone on the interstellar front. Why should we travel out and away, even as far as Mars, let alone Pluto, when a revelation is at hand; when all the secrets will be unlocked here on Earth? No progress on the tachyon or negative-time fronts, either. Nor any further messages from him. But he *is* his own message. His presence alone is sufficient to express Mankind: hopes, courage, holiness, determination.

(2019)
I am called back from retirement, for he is holding up signs again: the athlete holding up the Olympic Flame.

He holds them up for half an hour at a stretch—as though we are not all eyes agog, filming every moment in case we miss something, anything.

When I arrive, the signs that he has already held up have announced:

(*Sign One*) THIS IS A VERY SLOW TIME MACHINE. (And I amend accordingly, crossing out all the other titles we had bestowed on it successively over the years. For a few seconds I wonder whether he was really naming the machine—defining it—or complaining about it! As though he'd been fooled into being its passenger on the assumption that a time machine should proceed to its destination *instanter* instead of at a snail's pace. But no. He was naming it.) TO TRAVEL INTO THE FUTURE, YOU MUST FIRST TRAVEL INTO THE PAST, ACCUMULATING HINDWARD POTENTIAL. (THIS IS CRAWLING DOWNHILL.)

(*Sign Two*) AS SOON AS YOU ACCUMULATE ONE LARGE QUANTUM OF TIME, YOU LEAP FORWARD BY THE SAME TIMESPAN *ahead* OF YOUR STARTING POINT. (THIS IS SLIDING UPHILL.)

(*Sign Three*) YOUR JOURNEY INTO THE FUTURE TAKES THE SAME TIME AS IT WOULD TAKE TO LIVE THROUGH THE YEARS IN REAL-TIME; YET YOU ALSO OMIT THE IN-TERVENING YEARS, ARRIVING AHEAD INSTANTLY. (PRIN-CIPLE OF CONSERVATION OF TIME.)

(*Sign Four*) SO, TO LEAP THE GAP, YOU MUST CRAWL THE OTHER WAY.

(*Sign Five*) TIME DIVIDES INTO ELEMENTARY QUANTA. NO MEASURING ROD CAN BE SMALLER THAN THE INDIVIS-IBLE ELEMENTARY ELECTRON; THIS IS ONE "ELEMEN-TARY LENGTH" (EL). THE TIME TAKEN FOR LIGHT TO TRAVEL ONE EL IS "ELEMENTARY TIME" (ET): I.E., 10^{-23} SECONDS; THIS IS ONE ELEMENTARY QUANTUM OF TIME. TIME CONSTANTLY LEAPS AHEAD BY THESE TINY QUANTA FOR EVERY PARTICLE; BUT, NOT BEING SYNCHRONIZED, THESE FORM A CONTINUOUS TIME-OCEAN RATHER THAN SUCCESSIVE DISCRETE "MOMENTS," OR WE WOULD HAVE NO CONNECTED UNIVERSE.

(*Sign Six*) TIME REVERSAL OCCURS NORMALLY IN STRONG NUCLEAR INTERACTIONS—I.E., IN EVENTS OF ORDER 10^{-23} SECS. THIS REPRESENTS THE "FROZEN

GHOST" OF THE FIRST MOMENT OF UNIVERSE WHEN AN "ARROW OF TIME" WAS FIRST STOCHASTICALLY DETERMINED.

(*Sign Seven*) (And this is when I arrived, to be shown Polaroid photographs of the first seven signs. Remarkably, he is holding up each sign in a linear sequence from *our* point of view; a considerable feat of forethought and memory, though no less than we expect of him.) NOW, ET IS INVARIABLE & FROZEN IN; YET UNIVERSE AGES. STRETCHING OF SPACE-TIME BY EXPANSION PROPAGATES "WAVES" IN THE SEA OF TIME, CARRYING TIME-ENERGY WITH PERIOD (X) PROPORTIONAL TO THE RATE OF EXPANSION, AND TO RATIO OF TIME ELAPSED TO TOTAL TIME AVAILABLE FOR THIS COSMOS FROM INITIAL CONSTANTS. EQUATIONS FOR X YIELD A PERIOD OF 35 YEARS CURRENTLY AS ONE MOMENT OF MACROTIME WITHIN WHICH MACROSCOPIC TIME REVERSAL BECOMES POSSIBLE.

(*Sign Eight*) CONSTRUCT AN "ELECTRON SHELL" BY SYNCHRONIZING ELECTRON REVERSAL. THE LOCAL SYSTEM WILL THEN FORM A TIME-REVERSED MINI-COSMOS AND PROCEED HINDWARDS TILL X ELAPSES, WHEN TIME CONSERVATION OF THE TOTAL UNIVERSE WILL PULL THE MINI-COSMOS (OF THE VSTM) FORWARD INTO MESH WITH UNIVERSE AGAIN—I.E., BY 35 PLUS 35 YEARS.

"But how?" we all cried. "How do you sychronize such an infinity of electrons? We haven't the slightest idea!"

Now at least we knew when he had set off: from thirty-five years after 1985. From *next year*. We are supposed to know all this by next year! Why has he waited so long to give us the proper clues?

And he is heading for the year 2055. What is there in the year 2055 that matters so much?

(*Sign Nine*) I DO NOT GIVE THIS INFORMATION TO YOU BECAUSE IT WILL LEAD TO YOUR INVENTING THE VSTM. THE SITUATION IS QUITE OTHERWISE. TIME IS

PROBABILISTIC, AS SOME OF YOU MAY SUSPECT. I REAL-
IZE THAT I WILL PROBABLY PERVERT THE COURSE OF
HISTORY AND SCIENCE BY MY ARRIVAL IN YOUR PAST
(MY MOMENT OF DEPARTURE FOR THE FUTURE); IT IS
IMPORTANT THAT YOU DO NOT KNOW YOUR PREDICA-
MENT TOO EARLY, OR YOUR FRANTIC EFFORTS TO
AVERT IT WOULD GENERATE A TIME LINE WHICH
WOULD UNPREPARE YOU FOR MY SETTING OFF. AND IT
IS IMPORTANT THAT IT DOES ENDURE, FOR I AM THE
MATRIX OF MAN. I AM THE HUMAN RACE. I AM LEGION.
I SHALL CONTAIN MULTITUDES.

MY RETICENCE IS SOLELY TO KEEP THE WORLD ON
TOLERABLY STABLE TRACKS SO THAT I CAN TRAVEL
BACK ALONG THEM. I TELL YOU THIS OUT OF COMPASSION,
AND TO PREPARE YOUR MINDS FOR THE ARRIVAL OF GOD
ON EARTH.

"He's insane. He's been insane from the start."

"He's been isolated in there for some very good reason. Contagious insanity, yes."

"Suppose that a madman could project his madness—"

"He already has done that, for decades!"

"—no, I mean really project it, into the consciousness of the whole world; a madman with a mind so
strong that he acted as a template, yes, a matrix for
everyone else, and made them all his dummies, his copies; and only a few people stayed immune who could
build this VSTM to isolate him—"

"But there isn't time to research it now!"

"What good would it do shucking off the problem for
another thirty-five years? He would only reappear—"

"Without his strength. Shorn. Senile. Broken. Starved
of his connections with the human race. Dried up. A
mental leech. Oh, he tried to conserve his strength. Sitting quietly. Reading, waiting. But he broke! Thank
God for that. It was vital to the future that he went
insane."

"Ridiculous! To enter the machine next year he
must already be alive! He must already be out there in

the world projecting this supposed madness of his. But he isn't. We're all separate sane individuals, all free to think what we want—"

"*Are we?* The whole world has been increasingly obsessed with him these last twenty years. Fashions, religions, life-styles: the whole world has been skewed by him ever since he was born! He must have been born about twenty years ago. Around 1995. Until then there was a lot of research into him. The tachyon hunt. All that. But he only began to *obsess* the world as a spiritual figure after that. From around 1995 or 6. When he was born as a baby. Only we didn't focus our minds on his own infantile urges—because we had him here as an adult to obsess ourselves with—"

"Why should he have been born with infantile urges? If he's so unusual, why shouldn't he have been born already leeching on the world's mind—already knowing, already experiencing everything around him?"

"Yes, but the real charisma started then! All the emotional intoxication with him!"

"All the mothering. All the fear and adoration of his infancy. All the Bethlehem hysteria. Picking up as he grew and gained projective strength. We've been just as obsessed with Bethlehem as with Nazareth, haven't we? The two have gone hand in hand."

(*Sign Ten*) I AM GOD. AND I MUST SET YOU FREE. I MUST CUT MYSELF OFF FROM MY PEOPLE; CAST MYSELF INTO THIS HELL OF ISOLATION.

I CAME TOO SOON; YOU WERE NOT READY FOR ME.

We begin to feel very cold; yet we cannot feel cold. Something prevents us—a kind of malign contagious tranquility.

It is all so *right*. It slots into our heads so exactly, like the missing jigsaw piece for which the hole lies cut and waiting, that we know what he said is true; that he is growing up out there in our obseesed, blessed world, only waiting to come to us.

(*Sign Eleven*) (Even though the order of the signs was time-reversed from his point of view, there was the sense of a real dialogue now between him and us, as though we were both synchronized. Yet this wasn't because the past was inflexible, and he was simply acting out a role he knew "from history." He was really as distant from us as ever. It was the looming presence of *himself* in the real world which cast its shadow on us, molded our thoughts, and fitted our questions to his responses; and we all realized this now, as though scales fell from our eyes. We weren't guessing or fishing in the dark any longer; we were being dictated to by an overwhelming presence of which we were all conscious—and which wasn't locked up in the VSTM. The VSTM was Nazareth, the setting-off point; yet the whole world was also Bethlehem, womb of the embryonic God, his babyhood, childhood and youth combined into one synchronous sequence by his all-knowingness, with the accent on his wonderful birth that filtered through into human consciousness ever more saturatingly.)

MY OTHER SELF HAS ACCESS TO ALL THE SCIENTIFIC SPECULATIONS WHICH I HAVE GENERATED; AND ALREADY I HAVE THE SOLUTION OF THE TIME EQUATIONS. I SHALL ARRIVE SOON AND YOU SHALL BUILD MY VSTM AND I SHALL ENTER IT; YOU SHALL BUILD IT INSIDE AN EXACT REPLICA OF THIS LABORATORY, ADJACENT TO THIS LABORATORY, SOUTHWEST SIDE. THERE IS SPACE THERE. (Indeed, it had been planned to extend the National Physical Laboratory that way, but the plans had never been taken up, because of the skewing of all our research which the VSTM had brought about.) WHEN I REACH MY TIME OF SETTING OUT, WHEN TIME REVERSES, THE PROBABILITY OF THIS LABORATORY WILL VANISH, AND THE OTHER WILL ALWAYS HAVE BEEN THE TRUE LABORATORY THAT I AM IN, INSIDE THIS VSTM. THE WASTE LAND WHERE YOU BUILD, WILL NOW BE HERE. YOU CAN WITNESS THE INVERSION; IT WILL BE MY FIRST PROBABILISTIC MIRACLE. THERE ARE HYPERDIMENSIONAL REASONS FOR THE PROBABILISTIC INVERSION, AT THE INSTANT OF TIME REVERSAL. BE WARNED

NOT TO BE INSIDE THIS LABORATORY WHEN I SET OUT, WHEN I CHANGE TRACKS, FOR THIS SEGMENT OF REALITY HERE WILL ALSO CHANGE TRACKS, BECOMING IMPROBABLE, SQUEEZED OUT.

(*Sign Twelve*) I WAS BORN TO INCORPORATE YOU IN MY BOSOM; TO UNITE YOU IN A WORLD MIND, IN THE PHASE SPACE OF GOD. THOUGH YOUR INDIVIDUAL SOULS PERSIST, WITHIN THE FUSION. BUT YOU ARE NOT READY. YOU MUST BECOME READY IN 35 YEARS' TIME BY FOLLOWING THE MENTAL EXERCISES WHICH I SHALL DELIVER TO YOU, MY MEDITATIONS. IF I REMAINED WITH YOU NOW, AS I GAIN STRENGTH, YOU WOULD LOSE YOUR SOULS. THEY WOULD BE SUCKED INTO ME, INCOHERENTLY. BUT IF YOU GAIN STRENGTH, I CAN INCORPORATE YOU COHERENTLY WITHOUT LOSING YOU. I LOVE YOU ALL, YOU ARE PRECIOUS TO ME, SO I EXILE MYSELF.

THEN I WILL COME AGAIN IN 2055. I SHALL RISE FROM TIME, FROM THE USELESS HARROWING OF A LIMBO WHICH HOLDS NO SOULS PRISONER, FOR YOU ARE ALL HERE, ON EARTH.

That was the last sign. He sits reading again and listening to taped music. He is radiant; glorious. We yearn to fall upon him and be within him.

We hate and fear him too; but the Love washes over the Hate, losing it a mile deep.

He is gathering strength outside somewhere: in Wichita or Washington or Woodstock. He will come in a few weeks to reveal himself to us. We all know it now.

And then? Could we kill him? Our minds would halt our hands. As it is, we know that the sense of loss, the sheer bereavement of his departure hindwards into time will all but tear our souls apart.

And yet . . . I WILL COME AGAIN IN 2055, he has promised. And incorporate us, unite us, as separate thinking souls—if we follow all his meditations; or else he will suck us into him as dummies, as robots if we do not prepare ourselves. What then, when God rises from the grave of time, *insane?*

Surely he knows that he will end his journey in madness! That he will incorporate us all, as conscious living beings, into the matrix of his own insanity?

It is a fact of history that he arrived in 1985 ragged, jibbering, and lunatic—tortured beyond endurance by being deprived of us.

Yet he demanded, jubilantly, in 1997, confirmation of his safe arrival; jubilantly, and we lied to him and said YES! YES! And he must have believed us. (Was he already going mad from deprivation?)

If a laboratory building can rotate into the probability of that same building adjacent to itself: if time is probabilistic (which we can never prove or disprove concretely with any measuring rod, for we can never see *what has not been,* all the alternative possibilities, though they might have been), we have to wish what we know to be the truth, not to have been the truth. We can only have faith that there will be another probabilistic miracle, beyond the promised inversion of laboratories that he speaks of, and that he will indeed arrive back in 1985 calm, well-kept, radiantly sane, his mind composed. And what is this but an entrée into madness for rational beings such as us? We must perpetrate an act of madness; we must believe the world to be other than what it was—so that we can receive among us a Sane, Blessed, Loving God in 2055. A fine preparation for the coming of a mad God! For if we drive ourselves mad, believing passionately what was not true, will we not infect him with our madness, so that he is/has to be/will be/and always was mad too?

Credo quia impossible: we have to believe because it is impossible. The alternative is hideous.

Soon He will be coming. Soon. A few days, a few dozen hours. We all feel it. We are overwhelmed with bliss.

Then we must put Him in a chamber, and lose Him, and drive Him mad with loss, in the sure and certain hope of a sane and loving resurrection thirty years hence—so that He does not harrow Hell, and carry it back to Earth with Him.

Devil You Don't Know

Dean Ing

Dean Ing is another writer who began in the 1950s, paused for twenty years, and returned to the field only recently; his first two stories were published in 1955 and 1957.

He says that when he began to write, in his early twenties, he was "too preachy." So he turned to designing, building, and racing small-bore sporty cars, gave that up when the aerospace industry appropriated his designs, and went back to school for a doctorate in communication theory. He taught at a Midwestern university for years, but quit when he was told to conform to rigid policy or get out.

He's been a full-time writer for two years now, having returned to science fiction as much an idealist as ever but now realizing that "if you're gonna stand on a soapbox, make it a rhinestone soapbox." The present story was triggered by one of his students, who wrote a paper on maltreated institutionalized children; it's a fast-paced and deeply felt story full of convincing details about The System and those who somehow contrive to live under it. And sometimes to do more . . .

Maffei, brushing at his cheap suit, produced his papers with confidence. They were excellent forgeries. "I

159

dunno the patient from whozis," he said. "Will she need sedation? A jacket?"

The receptionist was your standard sanitarium model: stunning, crisp, jargony, her uniform a statement of medical competence as spurious as Maffei's authorization. "Dina Valerie Clarke," she read. "I did an ops transfer profile on her. If I may see your ID, sir?" It was not really a question.

Both driver's license and psychiatric aide registration were genuine enough. Neither card hinted that this stocky aide, Christopher Maffei, was also M.D., Ph.D., and in his present capacity, SPY. To stay in character he rephrased his question while surrendering the cards. "Will the kid need restraint?"

"It doesn't say," she murmured, returning his ID. "We can sign her over to you after your exit interview."

"*My* interview? Lady, I'm just the taxi to some clinic in Nebraska."

"It's only a formality," she purred, fashioning him a brief bunny-nose full of sexual conspiracy.

Maffei avoided laughing. In three years of residency and five of research, he had observed enough morons to be a passable simulacrum on his own. "I never done that before," he lied. He had listened to these sales pitches only too often. "Can I use your phone? Dr. Carmichael can talk to you from Springfield . . ."

"Sign here, please, and here, and there," in ten-below tones.

Maffei smiled and signed. *You're beaten by invincible ignorance,* he thought. *Maybe we should start a club.* He straightened and looked around, realizing that the receptionist had buzzed for Val Clarke.

She came toward him slowly at first down the long hallway, made smaller by her outsized luggage. It was very expensive luggage, the guilt-assuaging hardware a wealthy parent would provide for an unwanted child. Chris still chafed at what it had cost him.

As Val neared him, he saw that her hair had been shorn almost to the scalp. Lice, probably. Her height was scarcely that of a ten-year-old. The frail angular body, still too large for her head, was yet too small for its oddly misaligned and bovine eyes. She wore the same white ankle socks, slippers, and trousers she'd had when entering Nodaway Retreat two weeks before. Her smiling gaze swept up to his, then past, and she broke into a stumbling skip toward the entrance.

"You must be Valerie Clarke," Maffei said with forced gaiety, catching gently at her pipestem wrist.

The vacant smile foundered. A silent nod. No more skipping; the girl stood awaiting whatever this vast authoritarian world might dictate.

"Let's get you to an ice-cream cone," Maffei said, letting her bring the suitcases. He maintained the running patter while strapping her into his electric four-seater and stowing the luggage behind. "I bet you'd like a Frostylite, hm?"

Tucking his slight paunch under the steering wheel, Maffei whirred them toward the automatic gate. It slid aside, then back, as they emerged onto the highway. Val Clarke slumped in her seat with a lip-blubbering parody of released tension. "Oh, come on, Val, it can't be that bad," Maffei smirked.

"Not for you it can't. It isn't your screwed-up implants, pal, you try running an inside surveillance with an intermittent transceiver short sometime and I'll patronize *you*."

He glanced from the road to her, reached out to her tiny skull and gently stroked behind her ear. "No swelling. If it were a mastoid infection you'd know it for sure."

The girl shrugged upward in her seat, barely able to see over the battery cowl ahead. "I'll survive. Well, what do you make of Nodaway Retreat?"

"Typical ultraconservative ripoff," he mused, barely audible over the hum and tire noise. "From your reports I make it one staff member per twenty patients, minimal life-support for everyone concerned except for the up-front crew; one honest-to-God R.N. and a pair of general practitioners who look in once a month from Des Moines to trade sedatives for fees."

"I've seen worse. Remember Ohio?"

Maffei nodded sagely. Val Clarke had scarcely been admitted when her transmissions began to read like a bedlam litany. Rickettsia and plain starvation, a "bad ward" where three children of normal intelligence were chained, and a nightly victimization of youthful male patients by the staff. "That's what my survey is about; to change all that. It was the worst I ever saw," he admitted.

Val flicked him a quick glance, but Maffei intended no sarcasm. He had seen two staff members wearing masks of outraged innocence, and strap marks on Val's thin calves after the general warrant had been served— really more raid than service, brought on by Val's moment-to-moment account via her minuscule implanted transceiver. In the space of thirty-six hours Val had seen two compound femur fractures on a girl who had jumped from her high window, and a gang assault of one profoundly retarded child by besmocked thugs. The worst Maffei had seen in Ohio was not precisely the worst Val Clarke had seen; but then, Maffei bore no stigmata of retardation.

It was Valerie Clarke's tragedy to have been born with an autosomal dominant inheritance which was instantly diagnosed as mental retardation. The astonishing width between her eyes had a name of its own: hypertelorism. It explained nothing except that Val's great brown orbs were set a trifle too far apart to please a society which, paradoxically, distrusted eyes set too close together. Her lustrous roan hair normally covered a skull which, from its small size, also had a special stigma with label attached: microcephaly. Her ears flared a bit, particularly noticeable now that her hair was shorn, and at twenty-two, Val Clarke passed for twelve even without her training bra.

Any competent specialist could adjust to the fact that Val's intelligence was normal, her motivation superb—a recipe for "genius." The unadjusted expectation was something else again. Val, an early victim of maldiagnosis and parental rejection, knew the signs of a good sanitarium from the inside because she had experienced enough bad ones in childhood.

When Val was thirteen, a supicious young intern named Chris Maffei taught her basic algebra and the scatology of three foreign languages to prove his point. After that, her schooling was more formal if not exactly conventional. Any girl who patterned herself after Chris Maffei could junk the word "convention" at the outset, with the obvious exception of medical conventions, where Chris read scholarly papers and pumped for any grant money he could locate.

Now Chris was a year into a fat HEW grant to study the adequacy of private mental homes; and if he had not actually suggested that Val volunteer for commitment in these places, he had not omitted oblique hints at the notion. Nor turned down her offer. It was a symbiosis: Maffei had his spy, Val her spymaster.

"Hey," she said. He looked around and briefly laid his hand over the one she offered palm up. "Thanks for reeling me in so fast."

One corner of his mouth went up. "Had to. That short was interfering with my favorite live soap opera."

"Schmuck," she said tenderly—Maffei had never entirely managed to socialize her language. "Speaking of soap, you could introduce Nodaway to the idea."

"I'll note it when I debrief you after supper. I was in the army with a G.P. near here. If I know Farr, he'll do an Onward Christian Soldiers when I send him my notes on the place."

"Fine. And by the way, good guru, you just passed a Frostylite. You p'omised," she added, expertly faking a vocal retardation slur.

"First things first. We need a battery recharge to make Joplin tonight."

Startled: "Why Joplin, of all places? That's south."

"Because I have you scheduled for a scrub-up and transceiver check there tonight. And because after that we're going into the Deep South."

She was silent but he lip-read her response: *Oh, my God.*

After the Joplin stop, Maffei's little sedan hummed on barrel tires toward Mississippi. Val failed to concentrate on Durrell's *Clea*. The source of her unease was not the September heat, but the fact that she had slept at the clinic in Joplin. Chris lavished care on her as he would on a rare and exorbitant device, but she did not delude herself on the point. Val needed a secure relationship and physical human warmth. Very well then: he shared motel rooms with her. She also needed passionate attention, as anyone might when in constant proximity to a beloved. Chris dutifully pleased her when, on rare occasions, she was insistent enough. The one thing Valerie Clarke could not elicit from Chris was his desire.

Durrell's velvet prose wasn't helping Val's mood. She studied her reflection in the car window. *Ms. Universe I'm not. If I expect this sex object of mine—okay, twenty pounds overweight and why shouldn't he be?— to come fawning over my Dumbo ears I'm worse than microcephalic, I'm scatocephalic.* She traced a tentative forefinger along the pink smoothness of one ear. At least she had perfect skin. "Chris, why do you put me out before making the transceiver check if you don't make an incision?"

He yawned before answering, flexing strong hands on the wheel. "We do, Val. Those antennae are so fine I can run 'em just inside the dermis, on the fossa of your helix—uh, inside your ear rim. A microscalpel does it; almost no bleeding and it heals quick as boo. But I have to keep you abso-bloody-lutely still. Same for the X-ray check on your implant circuitry. It's a whole lot bigger in area than it might be, since I wanted it spread out for easy maintenance."

"You didn't cut down to the mastoid?"

"No need to fix the resonator; I just incised a tiny slit to your circuit chip. It was a hairline circuit fracture, just right for laser repair. Total heat doesn't amount to a paramecium's hotfoot, using the miniaturized Stanford rig. See, you don't *have* to hurt the one you love." He grinned.

"I'll remind you of that after supper."

He clucked his tongue in mock dismay, still grinning. Message clear, will comply, out. She returned to Durrell as the kilometers hummed away.

The supper hush puppies in Vicksburg were a pleasant surprise, not by being in the least digestible but in their lingering aftertaste. When she and Chris vented simultaneous belches later, her fit of giggles might have caused a lesser man to make war, not love. All credit to the Maffei mystique, she decided still later, as she lazed on the motel bed and watched Chris attack his toenails. "You never told me how you got those mangled toes," she murmured. "We beautiful people are repelled by physical deformity, y'know."

He looked up, preoccupied, then grinned. "Same way I got this," he rubbed his finger over the broken nose that gave him a faintly raffish look. "Soccer. Did I ever tell you I once played against Pelé?"

She fetched him a wondering smile. "Wow; no."

Deadpan: "Well, I never did—but Lord knows what I may've told you." Dodging the flung pillow, he went on. "You'd best save your energy for tomorrow, Val. We'll be delivering you up to the graces of Gulfview Home around noon."

Retrieving the pillow, she placed it in her lap and hugged it, eyes half closed, dreaming awake. "A view of the gulf will be nice. I hope this is a clean place—and please, God, air conditioned."

"Don't count on it. It's forty kilometers from the gulf; how's that for an auspicious start?"

She shrugged. "It figures. But why this place? We're kind of off our itinerary." She wriggled beneath the covers, hiding her thin limbs.

He put away his clippers and reached for the lightplate, waving it to a diffuse nightlight. "A tip from HealthEdWelfare," he said, swinging under the coverlet. After a long pause he added, "You'll have a contact inside: a Ms. May Endicott. She won't know about you, but she knows something, I guess. And an insider's tip is a good place to start. Better the devil you know, and all that. I'll find out what sent her running to HEW after we commit you. Most likely a snoopy old dowager with fallen arches and clammy handshake." He grew silent, realizing that Val's response was the softest of snores. Chris Maffei fell asleep wondering if Gulfview and old Ms. Endicott would fit his preconceptions.

Gulfview Home squatted precisely in the center of its perimeter fencing; held its white clapboard siding aloof like skirts from the marauding grass. Viewing the grounds, it was hard to imagine much organized recreation for patients. Chris identified himself to the automatic gate, then rolled his window back up to escape the muggy air. In silence, they pulled up before the one-story structure.

Their expectations followed earlier studies which, since the 1950s, had always shown higher per capita need for institutional treatment in the Southeast—and lower per capita effectiveness. The region was catching up; but, in 1989, still lagged. To Chris, it was a problem in analysis. To Val, stumbling up Gulfview's steps with her luggage, the first problem was a dread akin to stage fright. It always was; and as always, she hid her fear from Chris. The air conditioning was a relief, but a new fear sidled up to Val when they found the receptionist. She was, and wasn't, old Ms. Endicott.

Chris saw that Ol' Miz Endicott had very high arches for such small feet. He stood watching as May Endicott ushered a vacant-eyed Val Clarke from the reception room. A waist he could span with two hands, but la Endicott hourglassed to very nice extremes. Rather like a pneumatic gazelle by Disney, he judged.

Endicott boasted thick brown curls. "Dye job" was Val's whispered aside as she stumbled, entirely in character, with her luggage. But Chris was not listening.

The Endicott woman returned in moments, to help Chris complete papers placing Val Clarke squarely in the hands of a private jail—or asylum, rehab home, whatever it might prove to be. "We were expectin' you, but the senior staff are busy at the moment. The child's history seems well documented," she remarked in a soft patrician drawl. "Do you think she might be a trainable?"

Chris hesitated. A trainable might have free run of the place, or might be closely watched if it were more of a prison. Suddenly he remembered that May Endicott was, after all, a potential ally. "Depends on how good you are, I guess," he said. "I'm told you're concerned for the patients."

"We try—I think," she said as if genuinely pondering.

"I mean you, personally."

A flicker of subtlety in the dark sloe eyes. "I can't imagine who . . . "

"Just a friend in the discipline," he said easily. "Henry E. Wilks. How's that for a set of initials?"

"I don't . . . " she began, and then she did. "Well," she said in a throaty whisper. It set Maffei atingle. "And what are all the Wilkses doin' these days?"

"Waiting to hear from me," he replied, enjoying the respect in her oval face. "And I'm waiting to hear from you. I don't need to meet the staff just yet."

"I'm in the book, M. A. Endicott, in town. Perhaps this evenin'?"

He nodded and continued with the forms, pointedly sliding a blank set into his disreputable attaché case. As he rose, he noted that May Endicott's hands trembled. Anticipation? Fear?

Chris made a leisurely trip into town, bought a sandwich, then found the Endicott address. It was after five P.M. when he parked. He began to study the commitment forms—the fine print could sometimes raise hackles—and remembered the barbecue sandwich. During his third bite he remembered Val Clarke and fumbled for his comm unit. Although the major amplification and tight-band scrambling modes were built into the car, they also enhanced the signal to and from his pocket unit. Without the car, his range was perhaps two

kilometers. With it, over thirty. Val, behind high fencing and well beyond the town limits, should be within
range. But you never knew . . .

He thumbed the voice actuator. The cassette, as usual,
was recording all transmission into the system. "Val?
How'sa girl? I haven't heard a peep." *Nor thought
about one,* he told himself. He waited for a moment and
was about to try again.

"i gave up on you around suppertime," the speaker
replied. Implant devices did not yet rival conventional
transmission. Val could receive a voice with fair fidelity
but could only transmit by subvocalizing. With lips
parted slightly she could transmit almost silently and as
well as, say, a tyro ventriloquist; but bone conduction
and minute power sources had their limitations. Val
Clarke's nuances of intonation and verbal style were
sacrificed for the shorthand speech of covert work. In
short, she sounded very like a machine. Maffei would
have denied that he preferred it that way.

"I was doing errands. And it's only getting to be suppertime now," he objected.

"not when you're running a money mill," Val replied.
"it's on cassette, these people use patients to serve
meals—and to cook 'em, from the taste of it. yuchhh."

"If you're bitching about the food, you can't have
much worse on your mind."

"yeah? try thinking of me in here on an army cot,
and you outside with miz handy cot."

"Endicott," he chuckled at the mike. "I'll review the
tape later. What else is new?"

"i'm in isolation 'til they figure how to use me, i
think. two males, a female, all young and retarded,
doing chores."

He thought for a moment. "Good therapy for 'em,
unless the chores include lobotomies and group gropes.
Who's in charge?"

"you got me, chris. and i wish you did, this doesn't
smell right. quiet as a tomb in my room with very soft
wallpaper and no view at all. when i say isolated, i
mean locked away. but the kids gave me a toy."

"Something educational?"

"a rubber duckie, swear to god. well, they're nice kids."

"Look; I have some reading to do, and a session with the Endicott lady so we can plan. I'll check with you later. Don't eat your duckie."

"same to you, fella," in monotonic reply. He smirked at the speaker, but no answer seemed very useful. He pocketed the comm unit and returned to his sandwich and forms.

Although commitment forms varied, they generally claimed almost total control over their wards. Chris Maffei had doctored Val's records to assure that she would not be subjected to insulin shock treatment, surgery, or unusual medication. The forms implied that Gulfview could damned well amputate her head if they chose, but there were safeguards against such treatment. For one thing, Val could transmit her plight and get help from Maffei. Or, if it came to that, she could simply admit her charade. In sixteen previous investigations, she had never blown her cover.

Maffei was munching a pickle slice when he saw the steam plume of the bus, two blocks away. It slid past him a moment later, slowing to disgorge the unmistakable form of May Endicott. She had a very forthright stride, he decided, and admired it until she disappeared into her apartment. The pickle disposed of, Maffei crammed the forms into his attaché case and grunted, sweating, from the car. Val was right: he'd have to watch his weight.

At his knock, the door whisked open. May Endicott tugged him in by a sleeve, darting quick looks over his shoulder at her innocent shrubbery. She shut the door just as quickly and jumped at his reaction. "Gentlemen don't usually laugh at me."

"They should, if you treat 'em like jewel thieves," Maffei grinned. Beneath the makeup, he saw, she was quite young. "A poor beginning, ma'am. We really don't have anything to be furtive about, do we?"

The faintest relaxation of erect shoulders, and: "I'm not sure, Mr. Moffo."

"Maffei; Dr. Christopher Maffei, Johns Hopkins, to be insufferable about it," he said, getting the expected response. "Can we sit?"

She had a merry musical laugh of her own, waving him to a couch between stacks of periodicals. He saw several journals on abnormal psychology and special education. Idly he checked the issue numbers as they talked. His first goal was to put this latent centerfold at ease, simply done by asking her to talk about herself.

May was agreeable to the low-key interrogation. Modestly raised in Montgomery; a two-year nursing certificate with notions of an R.N. to come; parents retired; summer work in a state hospital. "I don't know if I have a callin'," she finished, "but I like to feel I'm bein' used well."

"You will be," Maffei said cryptically, and flipped back the journal he held. "Thought I might find myself here. Just a small reference," he added with exaggerated modesty.

She saw him referenced by another author and looked away. "You embarrass me, Dr. Maffei; I should've recognized your name."

"Hey, none of that," he laughed. "I'm Chris and you're May, if you don't mind it. You seemed jumpy and I wanted to reassure you, that's all. Want my full ID?"

She sat back, relaxed, strong calves crossed fetchingly as she glanced through his cards. Maffei had a rising sense that this would be one of his more pleasant investigations. "Understand, May, I hope you're wrong about your job. As you know, private homes run a long gamut from excellent to atrocious." She nodded, beginning to pour an aperitif.

"I can't survey every asylum in the country, but the HEW agreed to pick up the tab for a little"—he searched for an Endicott trigger-word—"chivalrous snooping. I have no official standing beyond what the AMA lends me, which is vague enough, God knows.

But soon I'll have a fair sampling of the virtues and vices of private sanitariums. Who's mistreating patients? What staff training is most needed? Where should the gummint step in? Not exactly cloak-and-dagger stuff, May, but not the questions your average institutional exec likes to hear." He did not add that the book from his research might be a muckraking best seller.

"So you don't ask out loud," she prompted.

"Right; I try to find someone like you, and whisper in her ear."

Rising smoothly, she purred, "Well, now I know you're really a doctor. Developin' your bedside manner." Maffei realized his gaffe too late and refused to admit it was accidental. "Let's say my Freudian half-slip is showing and let it go," he said. "I mean, no, dammit, that's not what I meant." A pause. "Do you have this effect on *every*body?"

She stood quietly, reaching some internal decision. Then, "It's a problem," she admitted, with a sunburst grin that took Maffei by frontal assault. "Physician, heal thyself."

"It may take some patchwork," he chuckled, "but bear with me."

A nod; slow and ageless.

"Professionally, I need you to check on a list of things. You reported that the last receptionist had no specialized training, was lucky to have the job, but seemed anxious to leave. And when she left, she did it in style. Expensive car and so on."

"A Lotus Cellular, no less," May put in. "And I know Lana Jo Fowler's family and they couldn't support that kind of spo'ty habit."

"Maybe she had sugar-daddy support?"

"That's how she let on," May said, "but she wouldn't say that if it were true. I think she was bein' paid off. I don't know what for. Lana Jo was no dumplin', and no brain either.

"Then there's Dr. Tedder," she continued, "I mean both Drs. Tedder, Lurene and Rhea." It did not escape Maffei that she named the woman first. "They live on the grounds and I don't see him much, but he isn't my idea of a doctor, more like a wino, and she—is—a—sight, a proper *sight,*" she finished, rolling her eyes melodramatically.

"You haven't mentioned the honcho."

"Dr. Merkle? Rob Merkle is unmentionable, maybe that's why. Those soft sausage hands; but when he keeps 'em to himself he's competent. I'll say this, he knows where every penny goes."

"No doubt. Well, I need data like where Merkle and the Tedders did their residencies, what's the cost of boarding a patient, the sources of referrals, types of therapy, type and dosage of drugs prescribed and by whom, dietician's schedule . . ."

"Whew," with lips pursed in kissable fashion, Maffei thought. "That's a tall number."

"I haven't begun," he said sadly.

"We both have," she smiled. "I smell cheap barbecue sauce on you, but could you use a shrimp salad anyway?"

"A small one. Need help?"

"It's woman's work," she said, surprising him again by her atavism. By the end of the evening, May had a long list of Maffei's professional needs and a sketchy idea of his personal ones. Never once did he mention Valerie Clarke. He could not have said exactly why.

Val awoke to depressingly familiar voices, muffled by the padding on her walls. It was not the timbre of a remembered person but the quasi-linguistic chanting of mentally retarded children that she recognized. Aware that the staff might be watching by monitor, Val lay on her musty bedding and played with her fingers. She reconstructed the ward's morning by inference from the subdued noises. A parrotlike male recited a holovision commercial with astonishing fidelity: *one* trainable, sure as hell. Footsteps, peals of animal glee, angry hoots in their wake: horseplay, probably unsupervised and therefore dangerous. A bucket dropped (kicked?) hard and a howl of dismay; some poor MR klutzing his cleaning chores. Every few minutes, shuffling thumps at her door. Val gave up on that one and lay back to give her fingers a rest.

Her door swung open so quickly that Val jumped. It was no trick to register a fearful MR grimace. The heavy door seemed a trifle to the dray-horse muscles of Dr. Lurene Tedder. The pale deepset eyes flanked an aquiline Tudor nose, and Val sensed great stamina in Lurene Tedder's hundred and seventy pounds. Yet the most striking feature was hair, seemingly tons of it, a cascade of blue-black tresses spilling over her shoulders, an emblem utterly female crowning the stocky woman.

A voice fortified with testosterone: "Hello, Valerie. Time for us to get up." A practiced smile fled across the face, to be replaced by a gaze that promised to miss very little. "Do we understand?"

Val waited a moment to nod assent, then stood, hands at her sides.

"Can we talk? Dr. Lurene, can we say that? Dr. Lurene," the big woman crooned.

My, but she loves the sound of that, Val thought. She nodded.

"Then *say* it, you . . . try and say it, Valerie."

Val said it in unfeigned fright. Lurene Tedder's ignorance of MR training was so blatant that Val wondered momentarily if she were being baited by a patient. "Docta Luween," she said again, dully, and again.

Lurene Tedder nodded, again treated Val to a smile; but this time it lingered. "I think we're gonna work out fine."

And the operative word is "work," Val thought. She risked a hint of a smile with eyes that begged for acceptance. Only half of it was pretense.

Lurene Tedder motioned Val from the cell, and Val, scurrying to comply, nearly collided with May Endicott. Thrusting a folder brusquely at May, the Tedder woman produced an expensive hairbrush and, sweeping it through her one glory, hurried off. "Find something therapeutic for this one," she flung over a broad shoulder.

May, placing a gentle hand on Val's arm, called,

"Were you going to do an assessment?" Her tone implied that Tedder had merely forgotten.

"Oh, sure, yeah," as the big woman sailed on from the ward, her voice booming louder. "Send her to, uh, our office about three."

Thick steel-faced fiber doors swung to and fro in Lurene Tedder's wake. Val looked straight ahead, half fearing that eye contact with May Endicott would reveal too much. May aspirated a bitter sigh, then brightened as she turned to Val. "I'm goin' to introduce you to some people, Valerie," she promised. These were the first friendly words Val had heard, and almost she began to forgive May Endicott her splendor in gender.

May did not hurry, nor ask questions of Val, but maundered, talking easily, from one patient to another down the row of beds. Val noted the linolamat floor approvingly; you could fall on it without harm, yet May's virginally white, whorishly spiked heels left no indentation. *Why must the woman flaunt it so?* The floor's barely perceptible slope led to a small drainage grate in the ward center; Val thought herself petty to hope a high-style heel might catch in it. She let details register without quick eye movement, indexing data with mnemonic tricks Chris had taught her. This was Val's métier, and doing it well, she outpaced her fears for the moment.

But: *Why doesn't she slip me the high sign,* Val thought. She and Chris always chose a fresh code word for ID and a general all-is-well signal, but May Endicott had not used it.

May broke into the reverie: "Is there anything you'd like to see especially, Valerie?"

After a long pause for pseudoserious pondering: "Chitlins?"

Val privately admitted that the Endicott bimbo had a nice laugh. "Well, not today anyway. We're havin' a fortified soup—" as if to herself adding, "what else?"

Val pointed to a patient May had ignored. "Big Boy," she slurred.

May smiled again at this wholly understated description, then walked to the end bed. Val stepped near and gazed upon a mountain of flesh. It was alive, in a way.

"This is Gerald Rankine," May began. Doubtless, she did not expect Val to understand much, but persisted. Rankine was eighteen, an enormous smooth-faced cherub in cutaway pajamas. Severely retarded, he would vegetate in a clinic for as long as his body might function. May guessed his weight at four hundred pounds, and Val saw, with an old shock of recognition, that the great body was asymmetrical. The limbs and even the head were distinctly larger on the right side. "He can eat when we help," May ended, "and we give him medicine so he won't hurt himself."

Hurt himself? If this great thing was subject to seizures, Val opined silently, he needed better accommodations than these. She wondered if Rankine had bedsores; and if he felt them; and if it were more ethical to maintain him or not to, under the circumstances. It was hopeless to feel assured at any answer. She was saved from further speculation by May's greeting to someone approaching from the ward kitchen. Val knew better than to turn on her own volition.

"Laura, honey," May said happily. "We have a new girl; I think she might be a help." And then May pulled Val around, and Val swept her eyes up a slender girlish form to meet—no eyes at all.

Laura Dunning was in many respects a lissome sixteen. She moved well, spoke with a charming drawl, dressed neatly, with pert nose and an enviable rosebud mouth. But the high forehead continued down to her cheeks with only faint, shallow depressions where her eyes would be in a more rational world. Val cudgeled her memory for a similar case, could find none. And somehow, inexplicably, Laura Dunning was very beautiful to look upon. Perhaps her animated speech helped; an old theorist's prescription for superb speech performance was an intelligent female with good hearing, blind from birth.

Val expected a fleeting fingertip inspection of her face, shoulders, arms and hands by the blind Laura. Instead, she offered her hand to be shaken. Another discard from an embarrassed family, Laura was obviously no more MR than was Val herself.

As Val took the proffered hand, May seemed to shift roles and excused herself. "I'll go double-check that darlin' soup," she said in pleasant sarcasm, and Val was left with the blind girl.

Laura began talking, talking, eliciting brief answers now and then from Val, evidently deciding what chores Val might be willing and able to perform. Disturbingly, the blind girl studied every answer with satisfaction—or was it secret amusement? When Laura turned to lead Val to the ward kitchen, she did so with balletic grace. Val was no stranger to the blind—but in some way, she felt, Laura Dunning was extraordinarily sighted.

Under close supervision, Val had no chance to give a detailed response when Maffei transmitted before noon. She cut in only long enough to respond with their code word. Anxious to begin his paper chase of senior staff documentation, Chris elected to leave Val on her own. "We can count on Endicott," he assured her. "I'll leave the comm unit recorder here at the motel; you can report when you get the chance, even if I'm out of range."

Again Val muttered their code word, loudly enough that May, hovering supportively near, chuckled. Satisfied, Chris keyed out.

Lunch was passable, kitchen chores simple, her three o'clock assessment a misnomer. Val left the Tedder office at suppertime, squired by Laura Dunning and too angry at the Tedder couple to trust herself in an immediate report. Laura, her every gesture as assured as a sighted dancer's, wangled fresh bedding for Val in a ward bed next to Laura's own. Val waited a half-hour, pulled her pillow over most of her head, and began to transmit.

". . . and then i realized they never intended legit tests," she recorded, nearing the crux of her message. "assessment? i scrubbed their deleted floor! rhea tedder's stoned on something; middle-age, middle-size, middlin' scared of docta luween. he'd make a great spy, you can overlook him so easy. i expected him to float up to the ceiling when he wasn't grabbing for my goodies. no sweat, lurene handled him. but they had no motor skills hardware, no nothing for m.r. tests that i saw.

"the rankine boy could be hell on square wheels if he *is* epileptic. can't tell from laura if it's grand mal, akinetic, myoclonic, whatever. i can hear me asking!

"caught sight of morkin nee merkle's goatee and you get the connection. fifty, hefty, soft mouth, dead eyes, voice like the bottom note of a pipe organ. bad-liver skin, i'd say. treats lurene as peer, maybe something going there between 'em.

"drug dispensing: weird but may be okay. there's a lot of it. the blind girl—her you have to meet—does the work and i swear she's efficient. gets dosages from the staff. boy, does she empathize; a girl had a petit mal seizure tonight, laura's ears must be like tuning forks. stopped dead, turned toward the kid shuddering. lucky me, i got to help clean the beddypoo. laura says she doesn't mind, helping the helpers. some help: profound m.r. and epilepsy.

"and what's with miz bandicoot, haven't you told her i'm me? and what the hell keeps you out so long, can't you xmit? sure leaves me out on a long string, and if you infer i'm strung out, you're improving.

"i suspect merkle uses drugs as babysitters; no organized play beyond what laura fixes, they all love her. 'course, some get enough exercise working. i think they do it for laura, and i also think lurene knows it.

"nutrition: okay, i think. hell of a good modern kitchen with equipment they don't need to make soup. m.r.'s keep the stainless shiny. tons of soy flour; so what else is new? tedders and merkle set up meals after lights out, i can hear 'em in there now. merkle doesn't seem the type for menial work, but that's his voice.

"and i ache all over from charlady chores. drop me a postcard someday, i could use good news." Sleep came easily to Val after that; the lax operation at Gulfview had given Val a breadth of insight that ordinarily might take weeks. Surely, she felt, Chris would wrap this job up easily. It was a lullaby thought, a beguiling diversion that left her utterly unprepared for the morrow.

Val tried to doze through the ward's early morning chaos, failed, and feigned sleep to query Chris Maffei. Instantly his reply began in her head. She felt the elation of contact trickle away as he continued.

"Hey, Mata Hari, we're making progress," he began. "I'm transcribing now at, uh, two A.M. Got back from—uh—an interview to the comm unit late and just finished your tape. Great stuff, hon." Val needed one guess to identify his late evening interviewee.

"Nothing on the Tedders yet," he went on. "But data retrieval isn't all that good here in town, I can get to a records center in Biloxi if I'm up bright and early."

So he's already hull-down on the horizon from me this morning, Val thought.

"Keep your eyes open for indiscriminate use of phenobarb, Valium, Zarontin, all the old standby zonkers. You recall the drill: Valium's the same size pill regardless of dose, it's the color—well, you know.

"I haven't blown your cover to May . . . "—the barest of hesitations, then the surname added— "Endicott because what she doesn't know, she can't reveal. What she already knows is incriminating enough. Merkle might be tricky—or worse.

"The rundown on Robin Terence Merkle looked okay at first; bona fides from med school and AMA. But no special work with MR; he went into pharmaceutical research with a chemical company from '71 to '83. Took an enviable vacation, then until starting Gulfview in '85. On a hunch, I dropped in at the local cop shop and asked about the last receptionist before Endicott; Lana Jo Fowler, a local girl. And there's a missing-persons sheet on her. They found her nifty Lotus abandoned in a Hattiesburg parking lot and she'd been dropping school-girl hints about hitting it rich. It occurred to me that maybe something rich hit *her*.

"The desk sergeant said they'd done their number on

the Fowler girl, a plain sort who got her popularity the only way she knew how. One of their many blind leads was a gentleman who'd recently paid for her visa and hovercraft fare to Cancún, down the Yucatán. A very proper professional man. Rob Merkle.

"The police aren't disposed to worry about it, but the girl's family is. Which leaves me with hunches. If any of 'em are right, Merkle knows where Lana Jo Fowler is, and she knows where something expensive is. Mexico? Ironic thing is, I'm in a better position than a small-time police department to spend time on it.

"In case you wonder: I'm not sidestepping to pursue this little mystery. I suspect the Gulfview operation should be shut down, but I don't want to pillory a guy who may be doing his half-assed best." His yawn whispered through Val's head. "If you're as tired as I am, you'll thank me for not waking you. I'll get a few hours' sleep and then head for Biloxi. 'Night."

Val struggled to avoid a sense of being discarded. Told herself that Chris had given so little new instruction because she had done so much so quickly. Took it for granted that Chris was seeing May Endicott at night, and rationalized that he had no better way to confer with the woman. Val's intuition said that Chris was lagging at his forte, the massing of inferences from paperwork. *He's floundering for once, poor love,* she told herself, then felt the gentle touch of Laura Dunning on her arm. She could arise easily enough, but must remember not to shine.

The blind girl seemed pleased that her new retarded helper wanted to accompany her everywhere—even to the bathroom, where Val affected concern that she was made to stand away from Laura's stall. Val sensed no suspicion when Laura allowed her to help dispense the morning's dosages in the ward. Again there was that rarely felt response in deeply retarded patients to a special person. Laura dispensed as much tender loving care as anything, but one oddity began to form a pattern. The more obvious the retardation in a patient, generally the less assured was Laura's deft handling of capsule or liquid suspension. The great vegetative Rankine took a Shetland pony's dose of Dilantin, the cream-yellow suspension given by syringe directly into his slack mouth. Yet Laura fumbled the simple task.

Val was congratulating herself on a complete survey of all-too-heavy ward drug dosage when: "Did we miss anyone?" Laura asked.

Val thought, *How would I know, with an IQ of 40,* and only smiled in answer, a gesture totally lost on Laura.

Laura persisted, "Did we have any medicine left?"

Perspiration began to form at Val's hairline. The questions could be innocent, but they were perfect tripwires for an unwary actress. Val chose the most equivocal response she knew, a murmuring whine that begged relief from stress without imparting any linguistic content. "Mmmmuuhummmaaaahh," she sniveled.

Laura's laugh was merry, guileless. "Well, I guess not." She straightened up from the silent mass of young Rankine, and her hand unerringly found Val's head to pat it, once. "You're a great help. Thank you," she said, and permitted Val to follow her to a holovision set at the end of the ward. Laura, Val found, could enjoy the audio even if she could not receive the images; and she enjoyed company.

Val squirmed as she watched the holo. Suspicions caromed through her head, leaving hot sparks that would not die. It was barely possible that Laura was equipped with some incredibly effective stage makeup and could see—but that seemed wildly unlikely. It was more possible that she had been briefed by the staff to test newcomers for hidden intelligence. Or perhaps Val had somehow conveyed something to this child-woman, something that Laura's sensitivity would respond to, without knowing what that something was. It was also quite likely that Val was overly suspicious; but Valerie Clarke had learned the folly of easily accepting the comfortable answer. She began to hum a repetitious tune from a holo commercial in what she hoped was suitably MR until a male patient shushed her.

Val helped at the noon meal, serving two patients who were unable to eat by themselves. Laura kept one hand on the patient's chin, the other she laid lightly on Val's wrist, until satisfied that Val could complete the chore. The meal and its inevitable cleanup served to lessen Val's ennui while Chris Maffei chased his papers—but Val was not to be idle for long.

The afternoon quiet was punctuated by the skritch of scrub brushes on linolamat as Dr. Robin Merkle made his rounds. Val, part of the work force, entertained a faint hope that Merkle gave adequate attention to his charges. Merkle propped a clipboard on his substantial belly to make occasional notations. The inconspicuous Rhea Tedder cradled more clipboards as he followed behind. Several times the smaller man spoke—Val thought, a little diffidently. Merkle smiled, or did not smile, behind the goatee, but only shrugged in reply. Lurene Tedder stood before the great locked double doors of the ward, preening her dark tresses with her brush, watching her minions scrub. With stolid calm, scrubbing more quietly, Val crept within earshot of the men.

Tedder eased up to exchange clipboards with Merkle. "Lissen, Rob, I could really use a hit," he wheedled. Val paused, addressed a speck of detritus with a trembling fingernail. "Just a little one," Tedder insisted.

Val kept her face down, trying to be invisible, and was rewarded. "One more request," Merkle said in his quietest pleasant basso, "and you get none tonight. We want to be on top of our cycle for tonight's delivery, don't we?" Val thought, *Now I know where Docta Luween gets that "we" crap. Really grooves on Merkle.*

New hope surged in Rhea Tedder's voice. "Then after tonight, again tomorrow with supper?"

A long silence. Val could almost taste the astringent look from Merkle.

"Just checkin' on my cycle," Tedder said. "You're the expert."

An avuncular laugh from the portly Merkle. "Yes,

indeed," he bubbled, "and we'll be friends then, will we not?"

Tedder joined in the laugh, a neurotic *henh, henh* that Val knew from a thousand holo stereotypes of dirty old men. Rhea Tedder was nominally harmless, she thought. *Unless you weigh eighty pounds like I do.*

A crackling slap from across the ward drew the men's attention. Val began to scrub away from them. She could hear, but not yet see, Lurene Tedder at *her* specialty: corporal punishment.

The victim was a young man perhaps twenty-five years old, a quiet one with teeth ruined from habitual gritting together. Val risked a view from her vantage point behind Laura Dunning's bed. Laura sat, knuckles pale as she gripped the coverlet, facing away from the scene.

"You act like a dog, you get treated like a dog," the Tedder woman said in derision. One hand still holding the hairbrush, Lurene Tedder clutched her other hand into the young man's tangled hair. She was plainly pleased that he struggled as she forced his face into something on the floor.

Merkle raised his voice slightly in reproof: "Lurene . . ."

She released her hold with a shrug-and-grin display, satisfied with her punishment of any patient who fouled her ward floor with his excrement. Val mused that it might actually be possible to train a patient away from such pathetic lapses, in the manner of a Lurene Tedder—but at what cost to the patient? Then she saw what the others missed: the youth rising, arms windmilling crazily as the woman looked away. He fell on her without warning. His hands were fouled, too, and while he dealt no serious blows, Val thought his repayment apt.

It was no contest; neither of the male staff tried to help, and in a moment, repeated slaps reduced the youth to a cringing serf at Lurene Tedder's feet.

She then applied further discipline.

In all, the hairbrush hammered only a dozen times;

but Val shuddered each time it fell. She realized that
Lurene Tedder was not using the flat of the brush but
the far more damaging bristles, a thousand dull needles
seeking passage through the coarse fabric of the youth's
ward smock. Seeking, and finding.

The woman paused for breath. Merkle stepped up,
took her hairbrush gently, his face a study in mild
pique. He ignored the sobbing wretch at their feet.
Rhea Tedder, shuffling near them, was the only member of the staff to notice the real victim. He managed to
get the young man to his feet and hauled him toward
the distant bathroom, and Laura moved in swift silence
to help.

Val followed. She paused at the bathroom entrance
to survey the ward. Some patients were unaffected by
the beating, but others contributed to a pulsing obbli-
gato of fear and misery. Over it, Rob Merkle soothed
his dear friend Lurene, who had now taken her brush.
It was faintly stained with blood, but unheeding, she
brushed away her waning fury and punctuated each
stroke with curses. Merkle knew his patients; he drew
Lurene out of the ward with practiced aplomb and a
promise of gin.

In the bathroom, Rhea Tedder had relinquished the
youth to Laura, who peeled the filthy smock from the
patient with infinite care. Val remembered to make a
low repetitive moan without words, though the words
were dangerously close at hand. The youth's back,
neck, and arms oozed bright red pinprick droplets. The
physical damage was only moderate, Val saw as they
bathed their charge in water hot enough to be soporific
as well as cleansing. The damage to a muddled psyche
would be impossible to assess.

When Laura Dunning asked for synthoderm, Tedder
grumbled, but he got it and applied the healing spray
himself, mumbling all the while. His complaints were all
variants on the "Why me, God?" theme, but he was at
least willing to give minimal aid, and for this, Val was
grateful.

As he left them, Tedder paused an instant and Val

felt a grasp on her buttock. It was untimely, covert, somehow more prank than overture. *He's easily pleased,* she thought. Laura would have to wonder why Val chuckled.

But: "Yes, it's too much, Charles Clegg," Laura said. This was the first time Val had heard the youth's name. "She just doesn't know. But," Laura added opaquely, "she will."

Valerie Clarke puzzled over this prediction. Laura, withdrawn into herself and for once less than agile, enlisted Val's aid in getting young Clegg dried, reclothed, and back to his bed. Drugs were again dispensed to some of the patients after supper but this time Laura rejected Val's help. "Go and see the nice holo," she said in no-nonsense tones, and Val played the obedient child.

Alone for all practical purposes, Val signaled Chris Maffei while she watched the distant Laura move among the beds. As she expected, Chris was still out of range. She spoke to the remote cassette. ". . . haven't seen any of the staff since then," she said, completing her account of the ward violence. "didn't see your sweetie-pie at all. she too sleepy today?

"dental care: have i mentioned it? some m.r.'s need caps and there's caries everywhere. and something about laura has me on edge, something i can't specify. yes, i can, too; she isn't on merkle's side but maybe not on ours either. i guess she's just on her own side, and i can't blame her.

"i gave you rhea tedder's conversation with merkle verbatim, and if he's not on a drug maintenance schedule i'm an m.r. for real. and his sweet wife needs a leash; her ordinary interactions are patho, can't guess why merkle keeps either of 'em. maybe you can tell me what delivery merkle expects at night; my guess is, it ain't pepperoni pizza. i get the feeling i'm holding a basketful of cobras and no flute. how soon can you reel me in? i really can't justify a mayday, but i mean, how much do we need to learn beyond this? well, it's your show. just get back to me, okay? all i have to do is play with my fingers and hope the evening stays nice and dull."

Presently, Laura slipped into a tattered seat near Val. Fidgety at first, the blind girl soon began to relax, and Val guessed, incorrectly, that Laura's quietude was a pure effort of will. They watched the holo for hours, becalmed with the surrogate window on a trivial make-believe world. It was quite late when Val heard the staff in the nearby kitchen, and later still when the screaming began.

Val, semientranced before the holovision set, started up violently. The ward lights had automatically cycled off at nine P.M., and only she and Laura lounged before the holo. Vainly she peered down the ward to identify the noise that had aroused her. Was there a spasmodic movement on one of the beds? Val darted a glance at Laura, whose shadowed face and inert form suggested sleep. With the barest whisper of her clothing, Val snaked out of her seat and into the ward's center aisle.

The next moment found her unable to cope. The noise ripped through the ward again: a hoarse, unsexed and dreadful mooing from the nearby ward kitchen. A bombard of metal gongs told her that something flailed among the huge kitchen metalware. She could hear Merkle shouting, and now his voice held tenor over-tones. As the terrible lowing segued to a gasping scream, Val recognized the voice of Lurene Tedder, muffled by blows.

Val glanced quickly toward Laura and had the night-mare sense of duality, two places at once, cause and effect in one. At the same instant, the kitchen door emitted stark light that flooded the ward, followed by the struggling forms of Merkle and the Tedders. Rhea hung from one of Lurene's arms while Merkle pinioned the other. Lurene Tedder's prized hairbrush fell at their feet as the men steered her toward the cell where Val had spent her first night. Valerie Clarke crouched mo-tionless in the aisle, alone and desperately vulnerable—but unseen in the tumult.

Lurene's feet seemed willing enough to follow Merkle's staggering lead, yet her arms strained convulsively for freedom. Val ducked between beds, saw Rhea Tedder lose his grip for a twinkling. Lurene's arm thrashed once, catching herself squarely on the chin. She sagged at the blow and her husband regained his purchase. The big woman subsided into breathless sobs as the men led her into the cell. The cell door remained ajar.

Val saw the vandalized kitchen through its open door. Dark ovals of blood shared spots on the floor with a scattering of white powder that Val supposed was sugar until she heard the voices in the cell.

"I can hold her," came the deep voice between labored breaths. "Get the hypospray and a cartridge of cytovar from my office. Wait: first grab her damnable security brush and toss it in here, it might help. Can you do that much?"

The brush lay two meters from Val. She sank to the floor. A pair of feet shambled near and she heard Rhea Tedder in an old monologue as he retrieved the brush. He stood erect, paused, gave a *huh?* of surprise, and Val gave herself up—too soon. Rhea Tedder strolled back toward the cell, oblivious of the struggle Val could plainly hear in the cell.

Rhea Tedder paused at the cell and tossed the brush in. He spoke calmly, detached. "What about the shipment, it's all over the floor in there. Hell of a waste . . ."

"LATER," Merkle boomed. "Or do *you* want to hold her?"

The smaller man hurried away from this threat, pausing only to unlock the doors at the end of the ward. The big room was awash with light, the cell door still open, a patient moving uneasily in her bed nearby, and Rob Merkle only meters away with a madwoman barely under control, when Valerie Clarke crept to the kitchen door. She held a discarded paper cup pilfered from a wastebasket, and in one scurrying pass she scooped a bit of powder from the floor. Then she was in darkness again, frenziedly duckwalking in deep shadow toward the holo area.

Val thrust the wadded cup far down into the seam of her seat as she settled down beside Laura Dunning. She opened her mouth wide to avoid puffing as she drew lungfuls of sweet air and waited for her adrenalin to be absorbed. She had no pockets, no prepared drop, no confederates—and no delusions of well-being if her petty theft were discovered. She bit her tongue as Laura spoke.

"I've been bad, Valerie, but so were you." The sweet voice scarcely carried between the seats. "We shouldn't be here, we'll have to sneak to bed." With that, the blind girl swirled up from her seat and in an erect glide, quickly found her bed near the kitchen-lit center of the ward. Val trailed her in double-time.

Then: "Pretend sleep," Val heard—or did she imagine it?—from Laura, who took her own advice. Valerie did not, for several minutes, recover enough presence of mind to call Chris Maffei. Instead she lay facing away from the cell where Lurene Tedder lay moaning, tended by Merkle and, at his shuffling return, Rhea. Val was certain that Rhea Tedder had neither the inclination nor the guts to attack his sturdy wife. She wondered how and why Merkle, the only other person with Lurene, had chosen to punish her. Valerie had not yet grasped a shred of the truth.

"chris, oh, god, chris, be there," Val transmitted her prayer of hope from halfway under her pillow.

The response was an intercept code promising live dialogue after a short wait. Then abruptly, with great good cheer: "Hi, Val! I'm working late, believe it or not, but I have a little time . . ."

"you have a mayday, too." Val rushed through her synopsis of the past few minutes, adding, "you wanta come get me? i don't know what's in this cup, but it's part of the shipment—and it bothers this little addict more'n his wife does. if you hurry you might be able to figure what they're up to in the kitchen and storeroom."

After a long pause, Maffei replied, "I don't think Merkle will have time to worry about you tonight. You can slip your sample to May, I'll have her stop by and see you tomorrow."

"tomorrow?" The word was bereft of hope.

"Look, Val, these people are fumbling something; I've only just realized what it might be. You're my eyes and ears while they do it, and you could pick up something a whole lot bigger than either of us ever bargained for."

"e.g., rigor mortis . . ."

"Don't be melodramatic. I have a make on the Tedders; he's a pussycat. Dr. Tedder, all right. Doctor of divinity from a diploma factory in South Texas. The old mail-order business, he may pray you to death but he's a harmless fraud. His wife's a reject physical ed teacher from a girl's military school, with some experience in a chemical plant—curiously, the same company Merkle worked for. My guess is, they're a matched pair of technicians Merkle can count on."

"for what?"

"You ready for this? Sleet! A refrigerated cocaine derivative the feds turned up in New Orleans last year. It avoids most of the side effects of snow—ulcerated sinuses, convulsions, stuff your higher class of cocaine addict will pay to avoid. Potent and highly addictive. Sleet was concocted by somebody pretty bright; pure snow processed with a powdered enzyme and protein. You take it with food, the enzyme comes up to your body temperature, and your stomach lining lays a swell little hit on you when the three components interact."

"you think they're cutting it here?"

"I think Rob Merkle could be the capital-S source. You say soy flour's abundant there? I damn well bet it is, to keep fresh batches of enzyme going. It'd have to be slurried and centrifuged, dried—but, hell, once you had the process and the enzyme, your only problem would be keeping the secret and maybe fighting off your buyers. Merkle may have caught Miz Tedder sneaking some."

Val coded a "hold" signal and emerged slowly from beneath her pillow. She could hear Lurene Tedder speaking with the men, her enunciation mushmouthed but steady. Val employed cloze procedure to mentally fill in the words she missed and listened for several minutes, mystified. When she burrowed under the edge of the pillow again, she brought a new loose end with her. "something's not meshing, chris. merkle's asking lurene what happened and she can't tell him; doesn't blame him for anything. as if the invisible man lambasted her." It was a much closer guess than Val knew.

Maffei used her simile to press his earlier point. "It's *all* been invisible until now. You have a chance to see things I couldn't even get close to, and . . ."

". . . and you can't see past those big boobies." The wrong moment, she knew; but there it was.

Chris answered *sotto voce*, as if to a male friend, and Val knew that May Endicott was within hailing distance of him. "If it'll make you feel better, she, ah, puts up a good front."

"i swoon with delight, you bastard. you could have the good sense to lie about it."

"My work is too important for lies between us, Val."

"but not too important for lays with miz randycu . . ."

"Val!" In dulcet reasonable tones: "A certain—relationship—can enhance motivation on the job." Too late he saw the sweep of that truth.

"don't i know it. but the job isn't a clean scholarly paper, the job is people—a boy who doesn't know the hurt is because nobody cares that his teeth are rotting—a lovely girl with smooth flesh where eyes should be, piecing her world together alone—kids that might be curable if anybody cared."

She could hear anger rising in Maffei's answers. For years she had used that as her motive for retreat. "And the first step is just what I'm doing, Val."

"my, my, do tell me all about it."

"*We're* doing! You know I include you."

"when you think about it." Her tones, she knew, were flat; her words harsh. She should be pleading, begging him to complement her love and need, but Valerie Clarke could not cling this time. "look, you have things to do and i don't need this. send—send may around."

"Right, I . . . you're transmitting oddly. Rhythm's off or something. Trouble?" He rapped out the last word.

She was glad Chris could not see the runny nose, cheeks glistening with her tears. "i'm—jumpy, i guess. forget it."

"Well—if you're sure you don't need bailout." His intonation asked, instead of offering, reassurance.

Despite her growing fear, choking back a reminder that she had clearly sent a mayday, she replied, "i'm sure. go 'way, lemme sleep—please, chris."

For a full half-minute Val lay still, commanding her small frame to stop heaving with sobs that might wake Laura. It was easier than ever, now, to empathize with children who could not expect help from Outside.

Then: "Val?"

"yeah."

"Are you really sure? I'm worried; you don't sound right."

"you want a framed affidavit? i said i was."

"I just sensed . . . as if someone had tied you up and forced you to say it. Give me the word."

"somebody did, a long time ago; and chitlins, god-damnit, chitlins!"

Then the channel was silent. For a long while, sleep evaded Valerie. Self-doubt shored her insomnia. She was both losing Chris Maffei and throwing him away; the hard facts militated against her when opponents were violent and massive; and somehow, she knew, she had been witness to more than she could absorb. Sleep came while she searched for a neglected detail. She should have analyzed them in pairs.

If Valerie Clarke awoke sluggishly, she could take comfort in the notion that the staff had managed even less sleep than she. The kitchen was spotless and Rhea Tedder, not Lurene, superintended the breakfast. When May Endicott appeared in the ward to help him, Val noted the shadows under those seductive eyes and enjoyed a nice mixture of emotions.

Twice May found Val's gaze and twice Val treated her to the briefest of enigmatic smiles. Under Laura's tutelage, Val fed two patients and there was no secret way to retrieve her problematic sample, much less pass it on. Immediately after the cleanup—always necessary with patients who fed like caged creatures—Val made her way to the holo area. May could not know Val's intent and soon followed in a manner much too bright, forthright, and amateurish.

May's greeting was tentative and too loud. Val replied in a mumble. "Beg your pardon," May said, leaning near.

"Quit calling attention to us," Val murmured calmly, "and sit down, and especially, *pipe* down."

May sat as if felled. She was blushing as she studied the holo. "Dr. Maffei said tell you his communication set is damaged," she said finally. Two other patients, sitting near, ignored their entire exchange. "But he's getting it fixed now. And he trusted me as a courier. You do have something for me to bring him?" The naive brown eyes radiated concern.

A nod indistinguishable at any distance. "When I leave, it'll be in my seat. For God's sake, get it out of here. And get me out, too, as soon as you can. Don't delay."

A winsome glance from May. Val wished the woman weren't so likable. "We say 'dawdle' in these parts." Then after a long pause, in kaffeeklatsch camaraderie: "I had no idea he was usin' you like this."

"You're even stealing my lines," Val muttered the multiple entendre with relish. To soften its impact she continued, "That goddam comm set! What's wrong with it?"

"I don't know, Chr—Dr. Maffei said he must've hit it with his heel."

Val examined this datum for a moment. Only the scrambler module, a recent addition, was mounted in Maffei's car where it could be struck by a foot. And then only by someone in the passenger's side by kicking upward with one's toe. But with the heel . . . ?

The heel. Right. Val turned her head with great deliberation and, despite herself, a twitch on her lips. She said nothing, only looked volumes. And saw a furious blush mount the Endicott features as May realized her gaffe to someone intimately familiar with Maffei's car. Suddenly shamed by her meanness, Val arose clumsily without a word and wandered off. She had found the bit of paper cup by blind fumbling and let it drop into the seat in plain sight.

Val adopted a shuffling gait as Lurene Tedder entered the ward doorway with a tray of medication. The big woman did not notice Val's spindly person, so intent was she on something at the far end of the ward. With prickly hot icicles at the back of her head, Val knew that Lurene was studying the holo region.

Quickly the woman stepped out to the hallway and keyed a wall intercom. "Dr. Merkle, Dr. Merkle," she called in smug parody of a hospital page, "you are wanted in the ward. Right *now*," she added with the assurance of a drill sergeant.

The intercom replied, but Val could not hear it clearly.

"No I can't, buddy-boy, I just caught me a stasher and I ain't gonna take my eyes off her." Another faint answer. "You come and see. I'll give you a hint, lover: this makes two in a row. I could be wrong, but can you chance it?"

Lurene Tedder marched into the ward again and, without conversation, relinquished the tray to Laura Dunning. The woman never took her stare from the end of the ward, and Val, playing finger games for camouflage, studied the square Tedder face. Under the telltale gleam of synthoderm the entire face was puffy, facial planes indistinct under localized swellings. Like collodion of old, synthoderm tended to peel around the mouth; the naked skin that showed was freckled with tiny scabs.

A chill scuttled down Val's backbone; Lurene's punishment had been a terrific hiding across her face with her own hairbrush! The eyes glittered even more deeply beneath swollen brows and Val knew that Lurene Tedder was fortunate to retain her eyesight. Yet she could be civil to Merkle—who strode into the ward at the moment Laura chose to begin dispensing dosages.

Val shuddered with relief as the pair moved past her. She hurried to Laura's side to take her "instruction" in dispensing the drugs. A backward glance revealed that Merkle and Tedder, talking quickly, were converging on May Endicott. Val wondered whether May had the good sense to think of a cover activity, and guessed against it. As she saw her guess confirmed, Val began to hope that May would brazen or physically force her way out.

From the first moment, May's fear was emblazoned on her face. The dialogue rose in volume until Laura paused, her head cocked attentively. "She's the only good thing that's happened here," Laura said quietly, "and now she'll be gone."

May exchanged glares with Lurene while Merkle, much the tallest, looked down at May. For a second he craned his head to one side at May's cleavage, then thrust one hand into it in a lightning maneuver. May jerked her hands up—too late. Merkle stepped back to examine his prize and Lurene Tedder moved to intercept May's desperate grab.

While May darted anguished looks around her, Merkle studied the scrap of heavy paper and its contents. Brusquely he gave an order and fell behind as May led a procession toward Val's end of the ward. It seemed that they might pass outside until Merkle, with a silent thumb-jerk, indicated the isolation cell to Lurene Tedder. Val considered, for one instant, the possibility of a diversion. Flinging the tray; anything.

No one was prepared for Laura Dunning's reaction. Screaming, "She doesn't hurt anybody," Laura dived past Val and upset the tray as she flung herself at the sounds of combat.

Merkle spun to catch the lithe girl while Lurene

grappled with May. He took no punishment and, with a backhand cuff, sent Laura squalling to the floor. The blind girl, hopelessly unequal to the fray, moaned as she rolled aside. She nursed her right shoulder as, still sobbing, she found her bed and lay back.

Val knelt in the spill of drugs, terrified and inert. She had never felt so vulnerable to physical violence, and almost transmitted an open "mayday" before remembering that Maffei could not receive it.

May's body was not fashioned for the rough-and-tumble of a Lurene Tedder, and after a brief struggle, May was flung into the cell. The door slammed shut, locked under Tedder's key.

Merkle ignored Val, the drugs, and faint pounding from inside the cell, patting Lurene in the manner of a coach with a favored athlete. "You were right," he grunted. They were three meters from Valerie Clarke. "Where did she get it?"

Val hefted a bottle, wondering which skull to aim for, somehow remembering to keep her jaw slack and her eyes slightly averted. An eternal moment later Lurene hazarded, "Must've hidden it down by the holo someplace. You'll have to ask her when."

"You anticipate me," Merkle said jovially, urging Lurene to the ward entrance. As he paused to lock the ward doors, Val heard him continue. "She has to sleep sometime; it'll be simple to find out then." They receded down the hall, and Val heard a last fragment. "No shortage of time, or of scop. I told you this setup would be ideal for it . . ."

A youth began to take interest in the strewn capsules and Val scooped up the mess quickly before taking it to Laura. A corner of her brain marveled that Merkle could simply stride away from an addict's array of downers, knowing that any of the patients might ingest any or all of the drugs—or simply lie down and wallow in them. She sat down heavily on the side of Laura's bed and leaped up again at Laura's quick gasp.

"Don't, oh, don't! My shoulder," Laura moaned,

and Val realized that her small mass had jarred the bed. "Valerie?"

Val answered guardedly. She could call no one, trust no one; Laura might suspect, but had no proof that Val was equipped with that formidable tool, knowledge. On the other hand, May certainly knew. And if Merkle employed scopolamine on May Endicott, he would soon strip the imposture bare. Val sat on her bed, trembling.

It was clear that Laura could not dispense medication. Val judged it was half-past ten, and thinking of the chaos of a dozen interrupted medication schedules in an unsupervised MR ward, she administered the dosages she recalled. Nor was she really out of character: idiot-savant retardates had been known to demonstrate a memory far beyond that of normal people.

The docile Rankine was one of her failures. Laura had evidently stepped on the big needleless syringe which she would have used to administer his whopping dose of Dilantin suspension. Val wasted half a bottle of the stuff trying to pour it past his lips, then gave it up. Rankine was not disposed to help take the dosage by this unfamiliar method; very well, then. He would simply have to bear it with several others whose dosages Val could not recall.

Val lay back on her bed, vainly transmitting to Chris Maffei every few minutes. Interrupted by a low sobbing from Laura, she suddenly considered the remaining drugs. Surely a yellow Valium, only five milligrams, couldn't hurt. She found one in her leftover cache and laid it to Laura's lips.

Laura took it greedily with an attempted smile. "Not enough," she confided. Val stiffened, then relaxed. Even recognizing the drug by taste or shape, how could the blind Laura know a white two-milligram pill from a potent blue ten? But perhaps even ten would not be too much. If the scapula were broken, Laura's pain was surely intense. Val administered another yellow pill and lay back to narrowcast another blazing "mayday" to Chris Maffei.

Two patients scuffled briefly. Another yodeled for joy. Val studied the narrow clerestory windows, knowing that even her very small head would not fit, presuming that she could smash the glass tiles. And if she tried to signal May, only meters away in the isolation cell, the staff could easily pick it up via monitors.

Laura breathed more regularly now, the Valium taking its effect. Lying full length on her bed, Val found satisfaction in her act of loving kindness. Then, without preamble, a delicious lassitude washed through her body as through gauze. Val saw that her right hand was stroking her thigh. Eerily, it did not respond to her next command. "Stop that," she said aloud. She felt a presence not her own; it was purest intuition to reply.

Val composed another message. Deliberately unformed, not vocalized but simply broadcast thought, a cloudy montage of unease and avoidance. No effect, but her left forearm nuzzled her bud of a breast before she could stop it. On an instant surmise Val thought hard of a putrid slime, mentally smelled it, pictured it. Holding the thought, she felt something slip away. It was like a fever breaking, a fever unannounced but somehow benign, that now began reluctantly to loose its hold. Quickly Val visualized a smile; the smile she valued most, the dimpled puckish leer of Chris Maffei.

Then, despite her effort to halt it, her right hand patted her left wrist, twice. She watched her hands intently, a sham catatonic, for many seconds. Whatever it was, it had withdrawn. To where?

Across from Valerie Clarke lay the girl who was prone to mild epileptic seizures. Charles Clegg, the youth who had taken the hairbrush beating, stood near the girl, pointing, laughing. Below a certain level of socialization there is little empathy, and Clegg's amusement stemmed from the girl's loss of control. It was over now, at any rate, with no harm done.

Val told herself she had her own goose flesh to ponder, then in a fresh surge of adrenalin mentally connected the events. Lurene Tedder did not know the source of her flogging. And Val had a lucid flash of

memory during *that* event: the epileptic girl had jerked
on her bed while Laura Dunning, otherwise inert before
the holo, sat and pounded her hand on her chair arm.
Suddenly Laura's subliminal hand movement was
meaningful.

Just now, the MR girl had suffered another spasm,
while some unseen presence bade Val to caress herself.
Who had reason to thank Val? She rolled over, lying
now on her side, and faced Laura.

"What do you need?" Laura spoke soothingly, in
deep repose. Val had said nothing.

All thought of keeping her cover vanished, Val answered, "You said you'd been bad, Laura. Did *you*
make that woman punish herself?"

"I'm not sorry."

Good Jesus, I'm hallucinating. This isn't real. "And
you thanked me just then—a minute ago?"

"I *am* sorry for that" was the contrite reply. "You're
normal, you didn't need it like that."

Another thought whirled in Val's head. "I don't even
have to talk out loud, do I?"

"Better to talk. Thoughts are so fast they're confusing
sometimes. And it hurts sometimes."

"You don't know your strength," Val confided. "I
believe you trigger those seizures the others have."

Laura could not weep tears, but she could cry.
"Sorry. Sorry. Sorry. So much pain and confusion, I try
to help. I'm sorry."

"You do help," Val said. "You can help now if you
can listen in on those miserable sons of bitches to see
what they're up to."

A long pause, then: "Too far away. I have to take
medicine to make people do things. I steal it. Can't be
sure when the power will come, sometimes it doesn't.
Sorry, sorry," the blind girl wept, her high forehead furrowed in grief.

Val soothed Laura, kneeling next to her, thin fingers
on the girl's wrist. A rattle of keys at the ward doorway,
and Val eased back onto her bed. Merkle came in first,
Lurene next. They held the doors open for Rhea, who

wheeled a gurney into the ward. Val realized then that they did not intend May Endicott to walk out of the cell, and subvocalized a prayerful plea to Maffei. Nothing. *Kicked it with your heel, you turd,* she raged.

There was no desperate speed in the preparations. Val guessed they had simply tired of waiting for answers, and had elected to overpower May Endicott before drugging her. "Laura," she whispered, "can you help May when they open that cell door?"

"It's not coming," Laura breathed as the cell door swung open. The trio stormed the pathetic May and slammed the door.

Val flew to the cell and cursed herself for not having checked the lock mechanism earlier. No use in any case: without a key, she could not lock them in, and she went jelly-kneed at the thought of entering that cell with anything less than a riot gun. From the muffled noises Val knew that May was going under sedation. Merkle's bass resonated in the cell but wall padding strained it of content.

She ran to the ward doors. Metal-faced, securely locked, as was the kitchen. But with enough mass piled on the waiting gurney, it might just possibly be accelerated down the ward to smash the doors. And smashing the wheeled metal cot itself might slow them in getting May from the ward. Val did not need a legal opinion to conclude that, with every additional step a fresh felony, the staff of Gulfview might welcome premeditated murder. Whatever might have happened to the Fowler girl, Val did not relish seeing it repeated. She tugged at the gurney, wheeled it up the center aisle toward the holo area. Perhaps the chairs would serve, if she could pile them on, or enlist patients in her enterprise.

She could get no one to aid in her little game. Patients strolled over to watch, slack-jointed and empty-eyed, as Val managed to tip two seats up into the gurney. Whimpering with the effort, she pulled the vehicle near the ponderous holovision set, all of a meter wide and massing perhaps a hundred pounds. She reached to disconnect the wiring, but at least one patient knew what that meant. He wanted his program, and the skinny girl with frightened eyes wanted to pull its plug. He screamed, face twisted in sudden ferocity, and thrust Val away.

Val raced to the side of Laura Dunning, who seemed asleep but for the mobility of her features. "Laura, is Valium the medicine for your power? Could you make some patients help me smash those doors?"

"Dilantin's the only thing that works," came the soft reply. "I only discovered it recently. Do you have any?"

Val whirled to her cache of unused drugs beneath her pillow. They were gone. Disoriented for the moment, she looked up to see young Charles Clegg. He held capsules in one hand while trying to bite off the safety cap of the Dilantin bottle. He had seen people drink it; maybe it would taste good.

Valerie Clarke did not know she could leap so fast, with such hand-eye coordination. She flashed past Clegg in a two-handed grab and the bottle was hers. Clegg was between her and Laura, but Val thought to circle around behind beds across the ward. It was at this juncture that Dr. Robin Merkle emerged from the cell.

He scanned the ward, saw Val, and then spotted the gurney filled with furniture. He looked almost pleased. Val saw it in his face: her cover was blown.

Val held the crucial Dilantin and Merkle, the advantage. He also wielded the hypospray, which could accept pressure cartridges of anything from saline solution to curare. While he could not know Val's intention, Merkle obviously proposed to take her into custody here and now. Their eyes locked. Neither spoke. Lurene Tedder hurried to cut Val off from her narrow corridor between beds and wall.

"Easy, Rob," Lurene cautioned, and Merkle stopped to listen. Val took a step back, poised. "This li'l thing didn't get here on her own, somebody Outside will be askin'."

"If we wait, it's a sure bust," Merkle rumbled as if reasserting an old position. "On the new schedule, we can process another, oh, say eighty pounds of protein." He beamed at Valerie. "Thirty hours or so at twenty-three Celsius."

At this, even Lurene Tedder blinked. "We're gonna *process* these two?" Val first saw the flicker of revulsion in the woman's face, then realized what it meant to her, Valerie Clarke, and had to steady herself against fainting.

"For more enzyme. Matuase doesn't care what it feeds on," Merkle said, pleased at his logic. "These ladies will complete a perfect irony. Part of the operation, as it were."

Sickened with loathing, Val fanned a faint spark of hope that Lurene would rebel. The lump in Val's throat forbade her any speech; the pounding of her heart was physical pain. Then, with a great sigh, Lurene said, "Well, it's better tactics than planting 'em, like you-know-who," and closed in on Valerie Clarke.

The thought of herself as finely ground fodder in some unknown enzyme production phase nearly robbed Val of consciousness, but the approach of Lurene and Merkle was galvanic. Val spun and ran for the gurney, hoping to get it underway before they could stop her. A quasi-female laugh followed her like a promise of extinction. Val collided against an inert patient, reached the gurney, began to thrust it ahead of her down the center of the ward. Even as it began to roll, she saw that she was simply too small for the task.

Lurene danced almost playfully out into the aisle, hands spread before her to intercept the loaded gurney. Val grabbed the thing she held in her teeth and hurled it at the woman, then was aware of her mistake. Val's missile connected against Lurene Tedder's forehead, but the soft plastic bottle had little effect and Lurene diverted the gurney between two beds. Val saw Merkle stoop to retrieve the Dilantin bottle as it skittered near him. The bottle went into his pocket. She had literally hurled her last hope away, and in a stumbling panic Val fell over the huge form of Gerald Rankine, looming in his bed near the holo.

Rankine stirred slightly and opened unfocused eyes. Val scrambled over the great form and into the holo area, now devoid of its two heaviest seats. Lurene Tedder bawled for Rhea, who trotted up the ward for his instructions.

As Val cowered behind the holovision, mindless with terror, Lurene waved Rhea around while she herself took a frontal approach. Merkle moved to cut off any escape behind the beds; and the very proximity of the three triggered Val as it might any small and cornered animal.

Val flung herself into Rhea Tedder as Lurene crashed against the holo set in pursuit. Rhea found himself grappling with a small demon, all thin sticks and sharp edges, that spat and clawed as he held on. Recovering, the sturdy Lurene thrust herself away from the holo, already tottering on its stand from her impact, and then Lurene tackled Val in a smothering embrace. Merkle had time to laugh once as he saw Lurene's clumsy success, but he did not see the holo as it toppled onto the silently staring young Rankine.

Lifted aloft by the big woman, Val caught a glimpse of the holo set. It leaned drunkenly on Rankine's midriff, its great window facing his eyes, its picture transmuted into bursts of flickering light by the rough handling.

Val took two fistfuls of hair and wrenched, trying to tear it from Lurene Tedder's abundant mop. Val's throat was too constricted to scream and Lurene only snarled. From down the ward, then, floated a dreamlike, ecstatic moan. "Ohhhh, it's a *lovely* one," cried Laura Dunning, borne into an orgasmic flood of silently thundering energy.

Because Merkle was most distant from the melee, he was first to catapult himself down the aisle. Val felt muscular arms relax and, kicking furiously, vacated Lurene Tedder's shoulder. Lurene staggered, nearly fell, then began to accelerate down the center of the ward after Merkle. Rhea Tedder tried to follow but tripped over Val before he began to run.

A welter of impressions clamored in Val's head. The holo, crashing to the floor as young Rankine jerked in the throes of a truly leviathan epileptic seizure. Howls of helpless terror from Merkle and the woman, bleats from Rhea, as the three found themselves sprinting harder down the ward. Laura Dunning's cooing luxuriance in a stream of almost sexual power was lower-pitched, but Val heard it. Valerie Clarke splayed hands over her ears and blanched an instant before Merkle impacted against the great double doors.

Merkle, with a hysterical falsetto shriek, never even raised his hands. He slammed the metal door-facing with a concussive report that jolted every patient, every fixture. Head-first, arms and legs pumping, driven by two hundred and sixty pounds of his beloved protein, Dr. Robin Merkle comprised part one of Laura Dunning's battering ram.

Lurene Tedder's last scream was entirely feminine; she managed to turn her head to one side as she obliterated herself against the sheet steel.

The doors, bent under Merkle's hapless assault, flew ajar; a lock mechanism clattered into the corridor beyond as Lurene fell into the opening. Rhea Tedder, ever the rear guard, called his wife's name as he hurtled into the space. One shoulder caught a door frame with pitiless precision, hurled the door wide as the addict ricocheted into a corridor wall. Val, leaping to her feet, saw Rhea disappear down the corridor, lying on his side, still pantomiming a sprinter's gait on the floor. He did not stop for moments afterward; Val could hear the tortured wheeze of his breath, the ugly measured tattoo of his feet and arms beating against the corridor floor and baseboard.

The patients were shocked into retreat from the violence at the ward doorway, and none seemed tempted to approach it. For one thing—*two*—the remains of Rob Merkle and Lurene Tedder sprawled grotesquely in their way.

With all the caution of a nocturnal animal, Val rifled Merkle's lab smock. She found the hypospray intact and felt armed; then she hefted the Dilantin bottle—and in a moment's reflection, realized that she was doubly armed. As she faced her puzzle, odd pieces began to warp into place, and for the first time in many days, Valerie Clarke knew what it meant to smile in relief.

Quickly, gently Val checked for vital signs. She saw the ruined, misshapen head of Robin Merkle and knew why he had no pulse. Lurene Tedder lay dying, insensible, extremities twitching. In the hallway lay Rhea Tedder, unconscious from shock and fractures, his breathing fetid but steady. She judged that he would live. Her small joy in this judgment was proof that Val could still surprise herself. It was true that Rhea Tedder could answer crucial questions—but it was also true that he could ogle a homely girl. She made a note to tell Chris Maffei: *Blessed are the easily pleased, for theirs is the kingdom of Earth.*

The corridor intercom needed no special key. She punched Outside, idly musing at the closeness of help for anyone who could reach the corridor. In moments, a policewoman was taping her call.

Two minutes later Val reentered the ward. She opened the isolation cell with Merkle's keys, once again tense almost to the point of retching with thoughts of what she might find inside. May Endicott lay sprawled in fetching disarray on the cot, drugged to her marrow but apparently unhurt. That enviable body would decay one day, Val thought; but not today, at twenty-three degrees Celsius. She could see from a distance that Gerald Rankine had passed the tonic stage of his seizure, and was well into the clonic, his body jerking slightly as the effects of the monstrous seizure passed. She moved to Laura Dunning's side. It felt good to smile again.

Val wondered how to begin. "I have news for you, Laura," she said gently.

Laura was awake but, with the Valium, quite mellow.

"I know. I did it without the medicine," the blind girl said proudly.

"Well—yes and no. It's seizures by other people that bring on the power, Laura. No wonder you couldn't tell when the power would come: *it isn't your power!*"

Confusion wrinkled Laura's nose. "But I make people do things."

"Can you ever," Val agreed, "but not alone. You're a—a modulator, I suppose. Rankine did not get his Dilantin today; and that could've brought on a seizure by itself. You see—oh, excuse me—you understand, whenever you stole a dose of Dilantin from Rankine or that young girl, the patient who needed it was in danger of an epileptic seizure. But the surest way to bring on a seizure is a strong blinking light—and that holo set zapped poor Rankine into the grandpaw of all grand mals, thank God."

"My," Laura murmured with a secret smile, "but it was good. But you mean, I never needed the medicine myself?"

"It probably impedes you. You need a carrier wave from some strong source, and you manage to modulate it into commands. You know what electroencephalography is? Anyway, a real thunderation seizure comes with the damnedest electrical brain discharge you can imagine, far more intense than any normal discharge. Of course, that same intensity raises hell with the higher centers of that same brain. Like trying to send Morse code through a flashlight, using lightning bolts." She raised her hands, then let them drop in frustration. "All I know is, you've gotta be sensitized in some way to modulate other people's brain discharges into commands. Normal brain activity just doesn't feature such power; those huge discharge spikes are characteristic of epilepsy. All this is simplistic, but I haven't time to detail it now." *Nor understand it yet*, she thought.

Laura sought Val's hand with her own. "You know something about these things? You'll stay with me?"

The idea settled over Valerie Clarke like a security blanket. "I've learned some from a man. I need to learn more." This astonishingly gifted girl needed her, Val realized. Her smile broadened as she stroked Laura Dunning's brow. "I'm going to claim Rhea Tedder went berserk and stampeded the others into that door. It's a weak story, Christ knows, but it'll accommodate the facts you can see." The ethics of her decision disturbed Val until she remembered Rhea Tedder holding her for the processing team.

A sigh from Laura: "I wish I really could see."

"Don't you? Through other people?"

As if showing a hole card, Laura said, "Kind of." Her hand gripped Val's desperately. "If I could do it better, I could help some of my friends here a lot more. Some of them are trying to climb walls in their heads, to get out to us."

It was possible, Val admitted to herself. And who would be a better tool than an honest-to-God telepath? With a machine-generated carrier wave, could Laura reinforce improved behavior patterns in a trainable MR? The possibilities were untouched, and staggering. Chris Maffei had spoken of Gulfview's problems as the devil he knew, but Val smiled at a new thought: *the devil you don't know may be an angel in disguise.*

"Who've you been talking to at night?" Val realized that Laura had, at the very least, known of the transmissions at her end.

"Dr. Christopher Maffei," Val answered. Curiously, it sounded flat. The name no longer held its familiar emotional lift. She considered this further.

"Can he help us—me?"

"Us." Val's correction was an implicit promise. "Yes, but he's a proud man, Laura. He'll want to make you famous." *Because it'll make him famous,* an inner voice added.

Slowly, Laura replied, "I don't think I want that."

"We may be more useful without it," Val agreed. "But I know Chris, and he has strong opinions." She grinned at a sudden unbidden thought. " 'Course, you could always run his opinions off a cliff—and I'm kidding, by the way."

After a long pause Laura asked, "Do you love him?"

Since Laura could probably sense a lie anyway, Val resolved to use utter candor. "Yes." With a starshell burst of insight Val added, "But now I don't think I need him much. Does that sound harsh?"

"Your thinking isn't harsh. And Dr. Maffei: does he need you?"

Put in such blunt terms, the questions brought answers Val had never formalized. They hurt. "Yes; but you see, he's never loved me much."

"*I* love you." Laura's admission was shy, tentative. "But I don't think it's the same, is it?"

Val chuckled. " 'Fraid not. But it's enough. Was it Vonnegut who said the worst thing that can happen to you is not to get used?" A new resolve sped Val's answer. "In a few minutes a whole raft of people will be here to turn everything upside down and set it right again. You're sedated, baby, so you be goddamn good and sedate! Keep your ability to yourself, don't force any automatic behavior on anybody, don't even hint about it—until I come for you. And I will."

The hand tightened again over Val's thinner one. "You have to leave?"

"For a while. Weeks, maybe. But you and I will figure out how you tick, and we don't want Chris Maffei diddling with your metronome so he can compose a best-selling ditty with it. Later, maybe. And maybe not. The trick is being used properly, isn't it, Laura?"

"You're the boss," Laura said meekly. And listening to police beepers in the distance, Valerie Clarke knew that she was, indeed, ready to assume the leaden mantle of decision-making. She wondered if Maffei's scrambler unit was repaired yet. It was the simplest of matters to find out, but Val could wait. There was plenty of time for her to put Maffei to use.

Count the Clock That Tells the Time

Harlan Ellison

> Harlan Ellison was the Guest of Honor at the 1978 World Science Fiction Convention in Phoenix, Arizona, where in line with his conviction that honored guests should be as visible as possible to the attendees, he sat at a typewriter in the lobby of the convention hotel and wrote the following story, each page being taped on the wall as he finished it.
>
> This was *not* an ideal situation in which to produce an outstanding story, but Ellison is inspired by challenges, self-inflicted or otherwise, and the story that resulted is rich and evocative.
>
> Ellison certainly doesn't waste *his* time on Earth.

When I do count the clock that tells the time,
And see the brave day sunk in hideous night;
When I behold the violet past prime,
And sable curls all silver'd o'er with white;
When lofty trees I see barren of leaves
Which erst from heat did canopy the herd,
And summer's green all girded up in sheaves
Borne on the bier with white and bristly beard;
Then of thy beauty do I question make,
That thou among the wastes of time must go . . .

>   —William Shakespeare,
>   the XIIth Sonnet

Waking in the cool and cloudy absolute dead middle of a Saturday afternoon, one day, Ian Ross felt lost and vaguely frightened. Lying there in his bed, he was disoriented; and it took him a moment to remember when it was and where he was. Where he was: in the bed where he had awakened every day of his thirty-five year old life. When it was: the Saturday he had resolved to spend *doing* something. But as he lay there he realized he had come to life in the early hours just after dawn, it had looked as though it would rain, the sky seen through the high French windows, and he had turned over and gone back to sleep. Now the clock-radio on the bedside table told him it was the absolute dead middle of the afternoon; and the world outside his windows was cool and cloudy.

"Where does the time go?" he said.

He was alone, as always: there was no one to hear him or to answer. So he continued lying there, wasting time, feeling vaguely frightened. As though something important were passing him by.

A fly buzzed him, circled, buzzed him again. It had been annoying him for some time. He tried to ignore the intruder and stared off across Loch Tummel to the amazing flesh tones of the October trees, preparing themselves for Winter's disingenuous attentions and the utter absence of tourism. The silver birches were already a blazing gold, the larches and ash trees still blending off from green to rust; in a few weeks the Norway spruces and the other conifers would darken until they seemed mere shadows against the slate sky.

Perthshire was most beautiful at this time of year. The Scottish travel bureaus had assured him of that. So he had come here. Had taken the time to learn to pronounce the names—Schiehallion, Killiecrankie, Pitlochry, Aberfeldy—and had come here to sit. The dream. The one he had always held: silent, close to him, unspoken, in his idle thoughts. The dream of going to Scotland. For what reason he could not say. He had never been here, had read little of this place, had no heritage of Scotsmen, ancestors calling from the past. But this was the place that had always called, and he had come.

For the first time in his life, Ian Ross had *done* something. Thirty-seven years old, rooted to a tiny apartment in Chicago, virtually friendless, working five days a week at a drafting table in a firm of industrial designers, watching television till sign-off, tidying the two and a half rooms till every picture hung from the walls in perfect true with the junctures of walls and ceiling, entering each checkbook notation in the little ledger with a fine point ink pen, unable to remember what had happened last Thursday that made it different from last Wednesday, seeing himself reflected in the window of the cafeteria slowly eating the $2.95 Christmas Dinner Special, a solitary man, somehow never marking the change of the seasons save to understand only by his skin that it was warmer or colder, never tasting joy because he could never remember having been told what it was, reading books about *things* and *subject matter*, topics not people, because he knew so few people and *knew* none of them, drawing straight lines, feeling deserted but never knowing where to put his hands to relieve that feeling, a transient man, passing down the same streets every day and perceiving only dimly that there were streets *beyond* those streets, drinking water, and apple juice, and water, replying when he was addressed directly, looking around sometimes when he was addressed to see if it was, in fact, himself to whom the speaker was speaking, buying gray socks and white undershorts, staring out the windows of his apartment at the Chicago snow, staring for hours at the invisible sky, feeling the demon wind off Lake Michigan rattling the window glass in its frame and thinking this year he would re-putty and this year failing to re-putty, combing his hair as he always had, cooking his own meals, alone with the memories of his mother and father who had died within a year of each other and both from cancer, never having been able to speak more than a few awkward sentences to any woman but his mother . . . Ian Ross had lived his life like the dust that lay in a film across the unseen top of the tall wardrobe cabinet in his bedroom: colorless, unnoticed, inarticulate, neither giving nor taking.

Until one day he had said, "Where does the time go?" And in the months following those words he had come to realize he had not, in any remotely valuable manner, *lived* his life. He had wasted it. Months after the first words came, unbidden and tremulous, he admitted to himself that he had wasted his life.

He resolved to actualize at least the one dream. To go to Scotland. Perhaps to live. To rent or even buy a crofter's cottage on the edge of a moor, or overlooking one of the lochs he had dreamed about. He had all the insurance money still put by, he hadn't touched a cent of it. Enough interest had been earned; he could buy such a cottage if he chose to do so. And there, in that far, chill place in the north he would live . . . walking the hills with a dog by his side, smoking a pipe that trailed a fragrant pennant of blue-white smoke, hands thrust deep into the pockets of a fleece-lined jacket. He would *live* there. That was the dream.

So he had taken the vacations he had never taken, all of them at one time, saved up from eleven years at the drafting table, and he flew to London. Not directly to Edinburgh, because he wanted to come upon the dream very slowly, creep up on it so it wouldn't vanish like a woodland elf hiding its kettle of gold.

And from King's Cross Station he had taken the 21.30 sleeper to Edinburgh, and he had walked the Royal Mile and gazed in wonder at Edinburgh Castle high on the bluff overlooking that bountiful city, and finally he had rented a car and had driven north out the Queensferry Road, across the bridge that spanned the Firth of Forth, on up the A-90 till he reached Pitlochry. Then a left, a random left, but not so random that he did not know it would come out overlooking the Queen's View, said to be the most beautiful view in the world, certainly in Scotland, and he had driven the twisting, narrow road till he was deep in the hills of Perth.

And there he had pulled off the road, gotten out of the car, leaving the door open, and walked away down the October hills to finally sit staring at the Loch, green and blue and silent as the mirror of his memory.

Where only the buzzing fly reminded him of the past.

He had been thirty-five when he said, "Where does the time go?" And he was thirty-seven as he sat on the hill.

And it was there that the dream died.

He stared at the hills, at the valley that ran off to left and right, at the sparkling water of the Loch, and knew he had wasted his time again. He had resolved to *do* something; but he had done nothing. Again.

There was no place for him here.

He was out of phase with all around him. He was an alien object. A beer can thrown into the grass. A broken wall untended and falling back into the earth from which it had been wrenched stone by stone. A clothed and shod artifact of another culture, trying to regain roots that had never been his to begin with.

He felt lonely, starved, incapable of clenching his hands or clearing his throat. A ruin from another world, set down in foreign soil, drinking air that was not his to drink. There were no tears, no pains in his body, no deep and trembling sighs. In a moment, with a fly buzzing, the dream died for him, and was gone as if it had never been so much a part of him, so much a thing to which he had clung. He had not been saved; had, in fact, come in an instant to understand that he had been a child to think it could ever change. What do you want to be when you grow up? Nothing. As I have always been nothing.

The sky began to bleach out.

The achingly beautiful golds and oranges and yellows began to drift toward sepia. The blue of the loch slid softly toward chalkiness, like an ineptly prepared painting left too long in direct sunlight. The sounds of birds and forest creatures and insects faded, the gain turned down slowly. The sun gradually cooled for Ian Ross.

The sky began to bleach out toward a gray-white news-print colorlessness. The fly was gone. It was cold now; very cold now.

Shadows began to superimpose themselves over the dusty mezzotint of the bloodless day:

A city of towers and minarets, as seen through shallow, disturbed water; a mountain range of glaciers with snow untracked and endless as an ocean; an ocean, with massive, serpent-necked creatures gliding through the jade deeps; a parade of ragged children bearing crosses hewn from tree branches; a great walled fortress in the middle of a parched wasteland, the yellow earth split like strokes of lightning all around the structure; a motorway with hundreds of cars speeding past so quickly they seemed to be stroboscopic lines of colored light; a battlefield with men in flowing robes and riding great-chested stallions, the sunlight dancing off curved swords and helmets; a tornado careening through a small town of slatback stores and houses, lifting entire buildings from their foundations and flinging them into the sky; a river of lava burst through a fissure in the ground and boiled toward a shadowy indication of an amusement park, with throngs of holiday tourists moving in clots from one attraction to another.

Ian Ross sat, frozen, on the hillside. The world was dying around him. No . . . it was vanishing, fading out, dematerializing. As if all the sand had run out of the hourglass around him: as if he were the only permanent, fixed, and immutable object in a metamorphosing universe suddenly cut loose from its time-anchor.

The world faded out around Ian Ross, the shadows boiled and seethed and slithered past him, caught in a cyclonic wind-tunnel and swept away past him, leaving him in darkness.

He sat now, still, quiet, too isolated to be frightened.

He thought perhaps clouds had covered the sun.

There was no sun.

He thought perhaps it had been an eclipse, that his deep concentration of his hopeless state had kept him from noticing.

There was no sun.

No sky. The ground beneath him was gone. He sat, merely sat, but on nothing, surrounded by nothing, seeing and feeling nothing save a vague chill. It was cold now, very cold now.

After a long time he decided to stand and *did* stand: there was nothing beneath or above him. He stood in darkness.

He could remember everything that had ever happened to him in his life. Every moment of it, with absolute clarity. It was something he had never experienced before. His memory had been no better or worse than anyone else's, but he had forgotten all the details, many years in which nothing had happened, during which he had wasted time—almost as a mute witness at the dull rendition of his life.

But now, as he walked through the limbo that was all he had been left of the world, he recalled everything perfectly. The look of terror on his mother's face when he had sliced through the tendons of his left hand with the lid from the tin can of pink lemonade: he had been four years old. The feel of his new Thom McAn shoes that had always been too tight, from the moment they had been bought, but which he had been forced to wear to school every day, even though they rubbed him raw at the back of his heels: he had been seven years old. The Four Freshman standing and singing for the graduation dance. He had been alone. He had bought one ticket to support the school event. He had been sixteen. The taste of egg roll at Choy's, the first time. He had been twenty-four. The woman he had met at the library, in the section where they kept the books on animals. She had used a white lace handkerchief to dry her temples. It had smelled of perfume. He had been thirty. He remembered all the sharp edges of every moment from his past. It was remarkable. In this nowhere.

And he walked through gray spaces, with the shadows of other times and other places swirling past. The sound of rushing wind, as though the emptiness through which he moved was being constantly filled and emptied, endlessly, without measure or substance.

Had he known what emotions to call on for release, he would have done so. But he was numb in his skin. Not merely chilled, as this empty place was chilled, but somehow inured to feeling from the edge of his perceptions to the center of his soul. Sharp, clear, drawn back from the absolute past, he remembered a day when he had been eleven, when his mother had suggested that for his birthday they make a small party, to which he would invite a few friends. And so (he remembered with diamond-bright perfection) he had invited six boys and girls. They had never come. He sat alone in the house that Saturday, all his comic books laid out in case the cake and party favors and pin-the-tail-on-the-donkey did not hold their attention sufficiently. Never came. It grew dark. He sat alone, with his mother occasionally walking through the living room to make some consoling remark. But he was alone, and he knew there was only one reason for it: they had all forgotten. It was simply that he was a waste of time for those actually living their lives. Invisible, by token of being unimportant. A thing unnoticed: on a street, who notices the mail box, the fire hydrant, the crosswalk lines? He was an invisible, useless thing.

He had never permitted another party to be thrown for him.

He remembered that Saturday now. And found the emotion, twenty-six years late, to react to this terrible vanishment of the world. He began to tremble uncontrollably, and he sat down where there was nothing to sit down on, and he rubbed his hands together, feeling the tremors in his knuckles and the ends of his fingers. Then he felt the constriction in his throat, he turned his head this way and that, looking for a nameless exit from self-pity and loneliness; and then he cried. Lightly, softly, because he had no experience at it.

A crippled old woman came out of the gray mist of nowhere and stood watching him. His eyes were closed, or he would have seen her coming.

After a while, he snuffled, opened his eyes, and saw her standing in front of him. He stared at her. She was standing. At a level somewhat below him, as though the invisible ground of this non-existent place was on a lower plane than that on which he sat.

"That won't help much," she said. She wasn't surly, but neither was there much succor in her tone.

He looked at her, and immediately stopped crying.

"Probably just got sucked in here," she said. It was not quite a question, though it had something of query in it. She knew, and was going carefully.

He continued to look at her, hoping she could tell him what had happened to him. And to her? She was here, too.

"Could be worse," she said, crossing her arms and shifting her weight off her twisted left leg. "I could've been a Saracen or a ribbon clerk or even one of those hairy pre-humans." He didn't respond. He didn't know what she was talking about. She smiled wryly, remembering. "First person I met was some kind of a retard, little boy about fifteen or so. Must have spent what there'd been of his life in some padded cell or a hospital bed, something like that. He just sat there and stared at me, drooled a little, couldn't tell me a thing. I was scared out of my mind, ran around like a chicken with its head cut off. Wasn't till a long time after that before I met someone spoke English."

He tried to speak and found his throat was dry. His voice came out in a croak. He swallowed and wet his lips. "Are there many other, uh, other people . . . we're not all alone . . . ?"

"Lots of others. Hundreds, thousands, God only knows; maybe whole countries full of people here. No animals, though. They don't waste it the way we do."

"Waste it? What?"

"Time, son. Precious, lovely time. That's all there is, just time. Sweet, flowing time. Animals don't know about time."

As she spoke, a slipping shadow of some wild scene whirled past and through them. It was a great city in flames. It seemed more substantial than the vagrant wisps of countryside or sea-scenes that had been rib-boning past them as they spoke. The wooden buildings and city towers seemed almost solid enough to crush anything in their path. Flames leaped toward the gray, dead skin sky; enormous tongues of crackling flame that ate the city's gut and chewed the phantom image, leaving ash. (But even the dead ashes had more life than the grayness through which the vision swirled.)

Ian Ross ducked, frightened. Then it was gone.

"Don't worry about it, son," the old woman said. "Looked a lot like London during the big fire. First the plague, then the fire. I've seen its like before. Can't hurt you. None of it can hurt you."

He tried to stand, found himself still weak. "But what *is* it?"

She shrugged. "No one's ever been able to tell me for sure. Bet there's some around in here who can, though. One day I'll run into one of them. If I find out and we ever meet again I'll be sure to let you know. Bound to happen." But her face grew infinitely sad and there was desolation in her expression. "Maybe. Maybe we'll meet again. Never happens, but it might. Never saw that re-tarded boy again. But it might happen."

She started to walk away, hobbling awkwardly. Ian got to his feet with difficulty, but as quickly as he could. "Hey, wait! Where are you going? Please, lady, don't leave me here all alone. I'm scared to be here by myself."

She stopped and turned, tilting oddly on her bad leg. "Got to keep moving. Keep going, you know? If you stay in one place you don't get anywhere; there's a way out . . . you've just got to keep moving till you find it." She started again, saying, over her shoulder, "I guess I won't be seeing you again; I don't think it's likely."

He ran after her and grabbed her arm. She seemed very startled. As if no one had ever touched her in this place during all the time she had been here.

"Listen, you've got to tell me some things, whatever

you know. I'm awfully scared, don't you understand? You have to have some understanding."

She looked at him carefully. "All right, as much as I can, then you'll let me go?"

He nodded.

"I don't know what happened to me . . . or to you. Did it all fade away and just disappear, and everything that was left was this, just this gray nothing?"

He nodded.

She sighed. "How old are you, son?"

"I'm thirty-seven. My name is Ian—"

She waved his name away with an impatient gesture. "That doesn't matter. I can see you don't know any better than I do. So I don't have the time to waste on you. You'll learn that, too. Just keep walking, just keep looking for a way out."

He made fists. "That doesn't tell me *anything*! What was that burning city, what are these shadows that go past all the time?" As if to mark his question a vagrant filmy phantom caravan of cassowary-like animals drifted through them.

She shrugged and sighed. "I think it's history. I'm not sure . . . I'm guessing, you understand. But I *think* it's all the bits and pieces of the past, going through on its way somewhere."

He waited. She shrugged again, and her silence indicated—with a kind of helpless appeal to be let go—that she could tell him nothing further.

He nodded resignedly. "All right. Thank you."

She turned with her bad leg trembling: she had stood with her weight on it for too long. And she started to walk off into the gray limbo. When she was almost out of sight, he found himself able to speak again, and he said . . . too softly to reach her . . . "Goodbye, lady. Thank you."

He wondered how old she was. How long she had been here. If he would one time far from now be like her. If it was all over and if he would wander in shadows forever.

He wondered if people died here.

Before he met Catherine, a long time before he met her, he met the lunatic who told him where he was, what had happened to him, and why it had happened.

They saw each other standing on opposite sides of a particularly vivid phantom of the battle of Waterloo. The battle raged past them, and through the clash and slaughter of Napoleon and Wellington's forces they waved to each other.

When the sliding vision had rushed by, leaving emptiness between them, the lunatic rushed forward, clapping his hands as if preparing himself for a long, arduous, but pleasurable chore. He was of indeterminate age, but clearly past his middle years. His hair was long and wild, he wore a pair of rimless antique spectacles, and his suit was turn-of-the-eighteenth-century. "Well, well, well," he called, across the narrowing space between them, "so good to see you, sir!"

Ian Ross was startled. In the timeless time he had wandered through this limbo, he had encountered coolies and Berbers and Thracian traders and silent Goths . . . an endless stream of hurrying humanity that would neither speak nor stop. This man was something different. Immediately, Ian knew he was insane. But he wanted to *talk*!

The older man reached Ian and extended his hand. "Cowper, sir. Justinian Cowper. Alchemist, metaphysician, consultant to the forces of time and space, ah yes, *time*! Do I perceive in you, sir, one only recently come to our little Valhalla, one in need of illumination? Certainly! Definitely, I can see that is the case."

Ian began to say something, almost anything, in response, but the wildly gesticulating old man pressed on without drawing a breath. "This most recent manifestation, the one we were both privileged to witness was, I'm certain you're aware, the pivotal moment at Waterloo in which the Little Corporal had his fat chewed good and proper. Fascinating piece of recent history, wouldn't you say?"

Recent history? Ian started to ask him how long he

had been in this gray place, but the old man barely paused before a fresh torrent of words spilled out.

"Stunningly reminiscent of that marvelous scene in Stendahl's 'Charterhouse of Parma' in which Fabrizio, young, innocent, fresh to that environ, found himself walking across a large meadow on which men were running in all directions, noise, shouts, confusion . . . and he knew not what was happening, and not till several chapters later do we learn ah, marvelous!—that it was, in fact, the Battle of Waterloo through which he moved, totally unaware of history in the shaping all around him. He was there, while *not* there. Precisely *our* situation, wouldn't you say?"

He had run out of breath. He stopped, and Ian plunged into the gap. "That's what I'd like to know, Mr. Cowper: what's happened to me? I've lost *everything*, but I can *remember* everything, too. I know I should be going crazy or frightened, and I *am* scared, but not out of my mind with it . . . I seem to *accept* this, whatever it is. I—I don't know how to take it, but I know I'm not feeling it yet. And I've been here a long time!"

The old man slipped his arm around Ian's back and began walking with him, two gentlemen strolling in confidence on a summer afternoon by the edge of a cool park. "Quite correct, sir, quite correct. Dissociative behavior; mark of the man unable to accept his destiny. Accept it, sir, I urge you; and fascination follows. Perhaps even obsession, but we must run that risk, mustn't we?"

Ian wrenched away from him, turned to face him. "Look, mister, I don't want to hear all that craziness! I want to know where I am and how I get out of here. And if you can't tell me, then leave me alone!"

"Nothing easier, my good man. Explanation is the least of it. Observation of phenomena, ah, *that's* the key. You can follow? Well, then: we are victims of the law of conservation of time. Precisely and exactly linked to the law of the conservation of matter; matter, which can neither be created nor destroyed. Time exists without end.

But there is an ineluctable entropic balance, absolutely necessary to maintain order in the universe. Keeps events discrete, you see. As matter approaches universal distribution, there is a counterbalancing, how shall I put it, a counterbalancing 'leaching out' of time. Unused time is not wasted in places where nothing happens. *It goes somewhere*. It goes here, to be precise. In measurable units (which I've decided after considerable thought, to call 'chronons')."

He paused, perhaps hoping Ian would compliment him on his choice of nomenclature. Ian put a hand to his forehead; his brain was swimming. "That's insane. It doesn't make sense."

"Makes perfectly *good* sense, I assure you. I was a top savant in my time; what I've told you is the only theory that fits the facts. Time unused is not wasted; it is leached out, drained through the normal space-time continuum, and recycled. All this history you see shooting past us is that part of the time-flow that was wasted. Entropic balance, I assure you."

"But what am *I* doing here?"

"You force me to hurt your feelings, sir."

"What am I doing here?!"

"You wasted your life. Wasted time. All around you, throughout your life, unused chronons were being leached out, drawn away from the contiguous universe, until their pull on you was irresistible. Then you went on through, pulled loose like a piece of wood in a rushing torrent, a bit of chaff whirled away on the wind. Like Fabrizio, you were never really *there*. You wandered through, never seeing, never participating, and so there was nothing to moor you solidly in your own time."

"But how long will I stay here?"

The old man looked sad and spoke kindly for the first time: "Forever. You never used your time, so you have nothing to rely on as anchorage in normal space."

"But everyone here thinks there's a way out. I know it! They keep walking, trying to find an exit."

"Fools. There is no way back."

"But you don't seem to be the sort of person who wasted his life. Some of the others I've seen, yes, I can see that; but *you*?"

The old man's eyes grew misty. He spoke with difficulty. "Yes, I belong here . . ."

Then he turned and, like one in a dream, lost, wandered away. Lunatic, observing phenomena. And then gone in the grayness of time-gorged limbo. Part of a glacial period slid past Ian Ross and he resumed his walk without destination.

And after a long, long time that was timeless but filled with an abundance of time, he met Catherine.

He saw her as a spot of darkness against the gray limbo. She was quite a distance away, and he walked on for a while, watching the dark blotch against gray, and then decided to change direction. It didn't matter. Nothing mattered: he was alone with his memories, replaying again and again.

The sinking of the Titanic wafted through him.

She did not move, even though he was approaching on a direct line.

When he was quite close he could see that she was sitting cross-legged on nothingness; she was asleep. Her head was propped in one hand, the bracing arm supported by her knee. Asleep.

He came right up to her and stood there simply watching. He smiled. She was like a bird, he thought, with her head tucked under her wing. Not really, but that was how he saw her. Though her cupped hand covered half her face he could make out a sweet face, very pale skin, a mole on her throat; her hair was brown, cut quite short. Her eyes were closed: he decided they would be blue.

The Greek senate, the age of Pericles, men in a crowd—property owners—screaming at Lycurgus's exhortations in behalf of socialism. The shadow of it sailed past not very far away.

Ian stood staring, and after a while he sat down opposite her. He leaned back on his arms and watched.

He hummed an old tune the name of which he did not know.

Finally, she opened her brown eyes and stared at him.

At first momentary terror, startlement, chagrin, curiosity. Then she took umbrage. "How long have *you* been there?"

"My name is Ian Ross," he said.

"I don't care what your name is!" she said angrily. "I asked you how long you've been sitting there watching me?"

"I don't know. A while."

"I don't like being watched; you're being very rude."

He got to his feet without answering, and began walking away. Oh well.

She ran after him. "Hey, wait!"

He kept walking. He didn't have to be bothered like that. She caught up with him and ran around to stand in front of him. "I suppose you just think you can walk off like that!"

"Yes, I can. I'm sorry I bothered you. Please get out of my way if you don't want me around."

"I didn't say that."

"You said I was being rude. I am *never* rude; I'm a very well-mannered person and you were just being insulting."

He walked around her. She ran after him.

"All right, okay, maybe I was a little out of sorts. I *was* asleep, after all."

He stopped. She stood in front of him. Now it was her move. "My name is Catherine Molnar. How do you do?"

"Not too well, that's how."

"Have you been here long?"

"Longer than I wanted to be here, *that's* for sure."

"Can you explain what's happened to me?"

He thought about it. Walking *with* someone would be a nice change. "Let me ask you something," Ian Ross said, beginning to stroll off toward the phantom image of the hanging gardens of Babylon wafting past them, "did you waste a lot of time, sitting around, not doing much, maybe watching television a lot?"

They were lying down side-by-side because they were tired. Nothing more than that. The Battle of the Ardennes, First World War, was all around them. Not a sound. Just movement. Mist, fog, turretless tanks, shattered trees all around them. Some corpses left lying in the middle of no man's land. They had been together for a space of time . . . it was three hours, it was six weeks, it was a month of Sundays, it was a year to remember, it was the best of times, it was the worst of times: who could measure it, there were no signposts, no town criers, no grandfather clocks, no change of seasons, who could measure it?

They had begun to talk freely. He told her again that his name was Ian Ross and she said Catherine, Catherine Molnar again. She confirmed his guess that her life had been empty. "Plain," she said. "I was plain. I *am* plain. No, don't bother to say you think I have nice cheekbones or a trim figure; it won't change a thing. If you want plain, I've got it."

He didn't say she had nice cheekbones or a trim figure. But he didn't think she was plain.

The Battle of the Ardennes was swirling away now. She suggested they make love.

Ian Ross got to his feet quickly and walked away.

She watched him for a while, keeping him in sight. Then she got up, dusted off her hands though there was nothing on them, an act of memory, and followed him. Quite a long time later, after trailing him but not trying to catch up to him, she ran to match his pace and finally, gasping for breath, reached him. "I'm sorry," she said.

"Nothing to be sorry about."

"I offended you."

"No, you didn't. I just felt like walking."

"Stop it, Ian. I did, I offended you."

He stopped and spun on her. "Do you think I'm a virgin? I'm not a virgin."

His vehemence pulled her back from the edge of boldness. "No, of course you're not. I never thought such a thing." Then she said, "Well . . . I am."

"Sorry," he said, because he didn't know the right thing to say, if there *was* a right thing.

"Not your fault," she said. Which *was* the right thing to say.

From nothing *to* nothing. Thirty-four years old, the properly desperate age for unmarried, unmotherhooded, unloved. Catherine Molnar, Janesville, Wisconsin. Straightening the trinkets in her jewelry box, ironing her clothes, removing and refolding the sweaters in her drawers, hanging the slacks with the slacks, skirts with the skirts, blouses with the blouses, coats with the coats, all in order in the closet, reading every word in *Time* and *Reader's Digest*, learning seven new words every day, never using seven new words every day, mopping the floors in the three-room apartment, putting aside one full evening to pay the bills and spelling out Wisconsin completely, never the WI abbreviation on the return envelopes, listening to talk-radio, calling for the correct time to set the clocks, spooning out the droppings from the kitty box, repasting photos in the album of scenes with round-faced people, pinching back the buds on the coleus, calling Aunt Beatrice every Tuesday at seven o'clock, talking brightly to the waitress in the orange and blue uniform at the chicken pie shoppe, repainting fingernails carefully so the moon on each nail is showing, heating morning water for herself alone for the cup of herbal tea, setting the table with a cloth napkin and a placemat, doing dishes, going to the office and straightening the bills of lading precisely. Thirty-four. *From* nothing *to* nothing.

They lay side-by-side but they were not tired. There was more to it than that.

"I hate men who can't think past the pillow," she said, touching his hair.

"What's that?"

"Oh, it's just something I practiced, to say after the first time I slept with a man. I always felt there should be something original to say, instead of all the things I read in novels."

"I think it's a very clever phrase." Even now, he found it hard to touch her. He lay with hands at his sides.

She changed the subject. "I was never able to get very far playing the piano. I have absolutely *no* give between the thumb and first finger. And that's essential, you know. You have to have a long reach, a good spread I think they call it, to play Chopin. A tenth: that's two notes over an octave. A *full* octave, a *perfect* octave, those are just technical terms. Octave is good enough. I don't have that."

"I like piano playing," he said, realizing how silly and dull he must sound, and frightened (very suddenly) that she would find him so, that she would leave him. Then he remembered where they were and he smiled. Where could she go? Where could *he* go?

"I always hated the fellows at parties who could play the piano . . . all the girls clustered around those people. Except these days it's not so much piano, not too many people have pianos in their homes any more. The kids grow up and go away and nobody takes lessons and the kids don't buy pianos. They get those electric guitars."

"Acoustical guitars."

"Yes, those. I don't think it would be much better for fellows like me who don't play, even if it's acoustical guitars."

They got up and walked again.

Once they discussed how they had wasted their lives, how they had sat there with hands folded as time filled space around them, swept through, was drained off, and their own "chronons" (he had told her about the lunatic; she said it sounded like Benjamin Franklin; he said the man hadn't looked like Benjamin Franklin, but maybe, it might have been) had been leached of all potency.

Once they discussed the guillotine executions in the Paris of the Revolution, because it was keeping pace with them. Once they chased the Devonian and almost caught it. Once they were privileged to enjoy themselves in the center of an Arctic snowstorm that held around them for a measure of measureless time. Once they saw nothing for an eternity but were truly chilled—unlike the Arctic snowstorm that had had no effect on them— by the winds that blew past them. And once he turned to her and said, "I love you, Catherine."

But when she looked at him with a gentle smile, he noticed for the first time that her eyes seemed to be getting gray and pale.

Then, not too soon after, she said she loved him, too.

But she could see mist through the flesh of his hands when he reached out to touch her face.

They walked with their arms around each other, having found each other. They said many times, and agreed it was so, that they were in love, and being together was the most important thing in that endless world of gray spaces, even if they never found their way back.

And they began to *use* their time together, setting small goals for each "day" upon awakening. We will walk *that* far; we will play word-games in which *you* have to begin the name of a female movie star from the last letter of a male movie star's name that *I* have to begin off the last letter of a female movie star; we will exchange shirt and blouse and see how it feels for a while; we will sing every summer camp song we can remember. They began to *enjoy* their time together. They began to live.

And sometimes his voice faded out and she could see him moving his lips but there was no sound.

And sometimes when the mist cleared she was invisible from the ankles down and her body moved as through thick soup.

And as they used their time, they became alien in that place where wasted time had gone to rest.

And they began to fade. As the world had leached out for Ian Ross in Scotland, and for Catherine Molnar in Wisconsin, *they* began to vanish from limbo. Matter could neither be created nor destroyed, but it could be disassembled and sent where it was needed for entropic balance.

He saw her pale skin become transparent.

She saw his hands as clear as glass.

And they thought: *too late. It comes too late.*

Invisible motes of their selves were drawn off and were sent away from that gray place. Were sent where needed to maintain balance. One and one and one, separated on the wind and blown to the farthest corners of the tapestry that was time and space. And could never be recalled. And could never be rejoined.

So they touched, there in that vast limbo of wasted time, for the last time, and shadows existed for an instant, and then were gone; he first, leaving her behind for the merest instant of terrible loneliness and loss, and then she, without shadow, pulled apart and scattered, followed. Separation without hope of return.

There was the faintest keening whine of matter fleeing.

There was the soundless echo of a diminishing moan.

The universe was poised to accept restored order.

And then balance was regained; as if they had never been.

Great events, hushed in mist, swirled past. Ptolemy crowned king of Egypt, the battle of the Teutoburger Forest, Jesus crucified, the founding of Constantinople, the Vandals plundering Rome, the massacre of the Omayyad family, the court of the Fujiwaras in Japan, Jerusalem falling to Saladin . . . and on and on . . . great events . . . empty time . . . and the timeless population trudged past endlessly . . . endlessly . . . unaware that finally, at last, hopelessly and too late . . . two of their nameless order had found the way out.

View from a Height

Joan D. Vinge

As you and I know but NASA evidently doesn't, astronauts don't have to be men; in fact, they don't even have to be people who are physically capable of living comfortably on Earth. Often it may prove useful to choose spacefarers who have urgent reasons for wanting to get away from our planet—as in the case of Emmylou Stewart, a woman born without immunity to Earth's diseases. Having chosen to travel starward, though, such a person might be subjected to some very rude shocks.

Joan Vinge has a degree in anthropology and has worked as a salvage archeologist. She's been writing science fiction for half a dozen years, won a Hugo Award in 1978 for her novelette "Eyes of Amber," and recently published her first novel, *The Outcasts of Heaven Belt.*

Saturday, the 7th

I want to know why those pages were missing! How am I supposed to keep up with my research if they leave out pages—?

(Long sighing noise.)

Listen to yourself, Emmylou: You're listening to the sound of fear. It was an oversight, you know that. Nobody did it to you on purpose. Relax, you're getting Fortnight Fever. Tomorrow you'll get the pages, and an apology too, if Harvey Weems knows what's good for him.

But still, five whole pages; and the table of contents. How could you miss *five* pages? And the table of contents.

How do I know there hasn't been a coup? The Northwest's finally taken over completely, and they're censoring the media—And like the Man without a Country, everything they send me from now on is going to have holes cut in it.

In *Science*?

Or maybe Weems has decided to drive me insane—?

Oh, my God . . . it would be a short trip. Look at me. I don't have any fingernails left.

(*"Arrwk. Hello, beautiful. Hello? Hello?"*)

(*"Ozymandias! Get out out of my hair, you devil." Laughter. "Polly want a cracker? Here . . . gently! That's a boy."*)

It's beautiful when he flies. I never get tired of watching him, or looking at him, even after twenty years. Twenty years. . . . What did the *psittacidae* do, to win the right to wear a rainbow as their plumage? Although the way we've hunted them for it, you could say it was a mixed blessing. Like some other things.

Twenty years. How strange it sounds to hear those words, and know they're true. There are gray hairs when I look in the mirror. Wrinkles starting. And Weems is bald! Bald as an egg, and all squinty behind his spectacles. How did we get that way, without noticing it? Time is both longer and shorter than you think, and usually all at once.

Twelve days is a long time to wait for somebody to return your call. Twenty years is a long time gone. But I feel somehow as though it was only last week that I left home. I keep the circuits clean, going over them and over them, showing those mental home movies until I could almost step across, sometimes, into that other reality. But then I always look down, and there's that tremendous abyss full of space and time, and I realize I can't, again. You can't go home again.

Especially when you're almost one thousand astronomical units out in space. Almost there, the first rung of the ladder. Next Thursday is the day. Oh, that bottle of champagne that's been waiting for so long. Oh, the parallax view! I have the equal of the best astronomical equipment in all of near-Earth space at my command, and a view of the universe that no one has ever had before; and using them has made me the only astrophysicist ever to win a Ph.D. in deep space. Talk about your field work.

Strange to think that if the Forward Observatory had massed less than its thousand-plus tons, I would have been replaced by a machine. But because the installation is so large, I in my infinite human flexibility, even with my infinite human appetite, become the most efficient legal tender. And the farther out I get the more important my own ability to judge what happens, and respond to it, becomes. The first—and maybe the last—manned interstellar probe, on a one-way journey into infinity . . . into a universe unobscured by our own system's gases and dust . . . equipped with eyes that see everything from gamma to ultra-long wavelengths, and ears that listen to the music of the spheres.

And Emmylou Stewart, the captive audience. Adrift on a star . . . if you hold with the idea that all the bits of inert junk drifting through space, no matter how small, have star potential. Dark stars, with brilliance in their secret hearts, only kept back from letting it shine by Fate, which denied them the critical mass to reach their kindling point.

Speak of kindling: the laser beam just arrived to give me my daily boost, moving me a little faster, so I'll reach a little deeper into the universe. Blue sky at bedtime; I always was a night person. I'm sure they didn't design the solar sail to filter light like the sky . . . but I'm glad it happened to work out that way. Sky-blue was always my passion—the color, texture, fluid purity of it. This color isn't exactly right; but it doesn't matter, because I can't remember how anymore. This sky is a sun-catcher. A big blue parasol. But so was the original,

from where I used to stand. The sky is a blue parasol
. . . did anyone ever say that before, I wonder? If anyone knows, speak up—

Is anyone even listening. Will anyone ever be?

("Who cares, anyway? Come on, Ozzie—climb
aboard. Let's drop down to the observation porch while
I do my meditation, and try to remember what days
were like.")

Wccms, damn it, I want satisfaction!

Sunday, the 8th

That idiot. That intolerable moron—how could he do
that to me? After all this time, wouldn't you think he'd
know me better than that? To keep me waiting for
twelve days, wondering and afraid: twelve days of all
the possible stupid paranoias I could weave with my
idle hands and mind, making myself miserable, asking
for trouble—

And then giving it to me. God, he must be some kind
of sadist! If I could only reach him and hurt him the
way I've hurt these past hours—

Except that I know the news wasn't his fault, and
that he didn't mean to hurt me . . . and so I can't
even ease my pain by projecting it onto him.

I don't know what I would have done if his image
hadn't been six days stale when it got here. What would
I have done, if he'd been in earshot when I was listening; what would I have said? Maybe no more than I did
say.

What can you say when you realize you've thrown
your whole life away?

He sat there behind his faded blotter, twiddling his
pen, picking up his souvenir moon rocks and laying
them down—looking for all the world like a man with a
time bomb in his desk drawer—and said, "Now, don't
worry, Emmylou. There's no problem . . ." Went on
saying it, one way or another, for five minutes; until I
was shouting, "What's *wrong*, damn it?"

"I thought you'd never even notice the few pages . . ."
with that sidling smile of his. And while I'm mutter-

ing, "I may have been in solitary confinement for twenty years, Harvey, but it hasn't turned my brain to mush," he said,

"So maybe I'd better explain, first—" and the look on his face; oh, the look on his face. "There's been a biomed breakthrough. If you were here on Earth, you . . . well, your body's immune responses could be . . . made normal . . ." And then he looked down, as though he could really see the look on my own face.

Made normal. Made normal. It's all I can hear. I was born with no natural immunities. No defense against disease. No help for it. No. *No, no, no;* that's all I ever heard, all my life on Earth. Through the plastic walls of my sealed room; through the helmet of my sealed suit. . . . And now it's all changed. They could cure me. But I can't go home. I knew this could happen; I knew it had to happen someday. But I chose to ignore that fact, and now it's too late to do anything about it.

Then why can't I forget that I could have been f—free. . . .

. . . I didn't answer Weems today. Screw Weems. There's nothing to say. Nothing at all.

I'm so tired.

Monday, the 9th

Couldn't sleep. It kept playing over and over in my mind. . . . Finally took some pills. Slept all day, feel like hell. Stupid. And it didn't go away. It was waiting for me, still waiting, when I woke up.

It isn't fair—!

I don't feel like talking about it.

Tuesday, the 10th

Tuesday, already. I haven't done a thing for two days. I haven't even started to check out the relay beacon, and that damn thing has to be dropped off this week. I don't have any strength; I can't seem to move, I just sit. But I have to get back to work. Have to . . .

Instead I read the printout of the article today. Hoping I'd find a flaw! If that isn't the greatest irony of my entire life. For two decades I prayed that somebody would find a cure for me. And for two more decades I didn't care. Am I going to spend the next two decades hating it, now that it's been found?

No . . . hating myself. I could have been free, they could have cured me; if only I'd stayed on Earth. If only I'd been patient. But now it's too late . . . by twenty years.

I want to go home. I want to go home. . . . But you can't go home again. Did I really say that, so blithely, so recently? *You* can't: you, Emmylou Stewart. You are in prison, just like you have always been in prison.

It's all come back to me so strongly. Why me? Why must I be the ultimate victim— In all my life I've never smelled the sea wind, or plucked berries from a bush and eaten them right there! Or felt my parents' kisses against my skin, or a man's body. . . . Because to me they were all deadly things.

I remember when I was a little girl, and we still lived in Victoria—I was just three or four, just at the brink of understanding that I was the only prisoner in my world. I remember watching my father sit polishing his shoes in the morning, before he left for the museum. And me smiling, so deviously, "Daddy . . . I'll help you do that if you let me come out—"

And he came to the wall of my bubble and put his arms into the hugging gloves, and said, so gently, "No." And then he began to cry. And I began to cry too, because I didn't know why I'd made him unhappy. . . .

And all the children at school, with their "spaceman" jokes, pointing at the freak; all the years of insensitive people asking the same stupid questions every time I tried to go out anywhere . . . worst of all, the ones who weren't stupid, or insensitive. Like Jeffrey . . . no, I will not think about Jeffrey! I couldn't let myself think about him then. I could never afford to get close to a man, because I'd never be able to touch him. . . .

And now it's too late. Was I controlling my fate when I volunteered for this one-way trip? Or was I just running away from a life where I was always helpless: helpless to escape the things I hated, helpless to embrace the things I loved.

I pretended this was different, and important . . . but was that really what I believed? No! I just wanted to crawl into a hole I couldn't get out of, because I was so afraid.

So afraid that one day I would unseal my plastic walls, or take off my helmet and my suit; walk out freely to breathe the air or wade in a stream or touch flesh against flesh . . . and die of it.

So now I've walled myself into this hermetically sealed tomb for a living death. A perfectly sterile environment, in which my body will not even decay when I die. Never having really lived, I shall never really die, dust to dust. A perfectly sterile environment—in every sense of the word.

I often stand looking at my body in the mirror after I take a shower. Hazel eyes, brown hair in thick waves with hardly any gray . . . and a good figure; not exactly stacked, but not unattractive. And no one has ever seen it that way but me. Last night I had the Dream again . . . I haven't had it for such a long time . . . this time I was sitting on a carved wooden beast in the park beside the Provincial Museum in Victoria; but not as a child in my suit. As a college girl, in white shorts and a bright cotton shirt, feeling the sun on my shoulders, and—Jeffrey's arms around my waist. . . . We stroll along the bayside hand in hand, under the Victorian lamp posts with their bright hanging flowerbaskets, and everything I do is fresh and spontaneous and full of the moment. But always, always, just when he holds me in his arms at last, just as I'm about to . . . I wake up.

When we die, do we wake out of reality at last, and all our dreams come true? When I die . . . I will be carried on and on into the timeless depths of uncharted space in this computerized tomb, unmourned and unremembered. In time all the atmosphere will seep away; and my fair corpse, lying like Snow White's in inviolate sleep, will be sucked dry of moisture, until it is nothing but a mummified parchment of shriveled leather and bulging bones. . . .

("Hello? Hello, baby? Good night. Yes, no, maybe. . . . Awk. Food time!")

("Oh, Ozymandias! Yes, yes, I know . . . I haven't fed you, I'm sorry. I know, I know . . .")

(Clinks and rattles.)

Why am I so selfish? Just because I can't eat, I expect him to fast, too. . . . No. I just forgot.

He doesn't understand, but he knows something's wrong; he climbs the lamp pole like some tripodal bem, using both feet and his beak, and stares at me with that glass-beady bird's eye, stares and stares and mumbles things. Like a lunatic! Until I can hardly stand not to shut him in a cupboard, or something. But then he sidles along my shoulder and kisses me—such a tender caress against my cheek, with that hooked prehensile beak that could crush a walnut like a grape—to let me know that he's worried, and he cares. And I stroke his feathers to thank him, and tell him that it's all right . . . but it's not. And he knows it.

Does he ever resent his life? Would he, if he could? Stolen away from his own kind, raised in a sterile bubble to be a caged bird for a caged human. . . .

I'm only a bird in a gilded cage. I want to go home.

Wednesday, the 11th

Why am I keeping this journal? Do I really believe that sometime some alien being will find this, or some starship from Earth's glorious future will catch up to me . . . glorious future, hell. Stupid, selfish, shortsighted fools. They ripped the guts out of the space program after they sent me away; no one will ever follow me now. I'll be lucky if they don't declare me dead and forget about me.

As if anyone would care what a woman all alone on a lumbering space probe thought about day after day for decades, anyway. What monstrous conceit.

I did lubricate the bearings on the big scope today. I

did that much. I did it so that I could turn it back toward Earth . . . toward the sun . . . toward the whole damn system. Because I can't even see it; Everything out to Saturn is crammed into the space of two moon diameters, and too dim and small and faraway below me for my naked eyes, anyway. Even the sun is no more than a gaudy star that doesn't even make me squint. So I looked for them with the scope. . . .

Isn't it funny how when you're a child you see all those drawings and models of the solar system with big, lumpy planets and golden wakes streaming around the sun. Somehow you never get over expecting it to look that way in person. And here I am, one thousand astronomical units north of the solar pole, gazing down from a great height . . . and it doesn't look that way at all. It doesn't look like anything, even through the scope. One great blot of light, and all the pale tiny diamond chips of planets and moons around it, barely distinguishable from half a hundred undistinguished stars trapped in the same arc of blackness. So meaningless, so insignificant . . . so disappointing.

Five hours I spent, today, listening to my journal, looking back and trying to find—something, I don't know, something I suddenly don't have anymore.

I had it at the start. I was disgusting; Pollyanna Grad-student skipping and singing through the rooms of my very own observatory. It seemed like heaven, and a lifetime spent in it couldn't possibly be long enough for all that I was going to accomplish, and discover. I'd never be bored, no, not me. . . .

And there was so much to learn about the potential of this place, before I got out to where it supposedly would matter, and there would be new things to turn my wonderful extended senses toward . . . while I could still communicate easily with my dear mentor Dr. Weems, and the world. (Who'd ever have thought, when the lecherous old goat was my thesis advisor at Harvard, and making jokes to his other grad students about "the lengths some women will go to to protect their virginity," that we would have to spend a lifetime together.)

There was Ozymandias's first word . . . and my first birthday in space, and my first anniversary . . . and my doctoral degree at last, printed out by the computer with scrolls made of little x's and taped up on the wall. . . .

Then day and night and day and night, beating me black and blue with blue and black . . . my fifth anniversary, my eighth, my decade. I crossed the magnetopause, to become truly the first voyager in interstellar space . . . but by then there was no one left to *talk* to anymore, to really share the experience with. Even the radio and television broadcasts drifting out from Earth were diffuse and rare; there were fewer and fewer contacts with the reality outside. The plodding routines, the stupifying boredom—until sometimes I stood screaming down the halls just for something new; listening to the echoes that no one else would ever hear, and pretending they'd come to call; trying so hard to believe there was something to hear that wasn't *my* voice, *my* echo, or Ozymandias making a mockery of it.

("Hello, beautiful. That's a crock. Hello, hello?")

("Ozymandias, get *away* from me—")

But always I had that underlying belief in my mission: that I was here for a purpose, for more than my own selfish reasons, or NASA's (or whatever the hell they call it now), but for Humanity, and Science. Through meditation I learned the real value of inner silence, and thought that by creating an inner peace I had reached equilibrium with the outer silences. I thought that meditation had disciplined me, I was in touch with myself and with the soul of the cosmos. . . . But I haven't been able to meditate since—it happened. The inner silence fills up with my own anger screaming at me until I can't remember what peace sounds like.

And what have I really discovered, so far? Almost nothing. Nothing worth wasting my analysis or all my fine theories—or my freedom—on. Space is even emptier than anyone dreamed, you could count on both hands the bits of cold dust or worldlet I've passed in all this time, lost souls falling helplessly through near-perfect vacuum . . . all of us together. With my absurdly long astronomical tape measure I have fixed precisely the distance to NGC 2419 and a few other features, and from that made new estimates about a few more distant ones. But I have not detected a miniature black hole insatiably vacuuming up the vacuum; I have not pierced the invisible clouds that shroud the ultra-long wavelengths like fog; I have not discovered that life exists beyond the Earth in even the most tentative way. Looking back at the solar system I see nothing to show definitively that we even exist, anymore. All I hear anymore when I scan is electromagnetic noise, no coherent thought. Only Weems every twelfth night, like the last man alive. . . . Christ, I still haven't answered him.

Why bother? Let him sweat. Why bother with any of it. Why waste my precious time.

Oh, my precious time. . . . Half a lifetime left that could have been mine, on Earth.

Twenty years—I came through them all all right. I thought I was safe. And after twenty years, my façade of discipline and self-control falls apart at a touch. What a self-deluded hypocrite I've been. Do you know that I said the sky was like a blue parasol eighteen years ago? And probably said it again fifteen years ago, and ten, and five—

Tomorrow I pass 1,000 AUs.

Thursday, the 12th

I burned out the scope. I burned out the scope. I left it pointing toward the Earth, and when the laser came on for the night it shone right down the scope's throat and burned it out. I'm so ashamed. . . . Did I do it on purpose, subconsciously?

("Good night, starlight. Arrk. Good night. Good . . .")

("Damn it, I want to hear another human voice—!")

(Echoing, "voice, voice, voice voice . . .")

When I found out what I'd done, I ran away. I ran and ran through the halls. . . . But I only ran in a circle: This observatory, my prison, myself . . . I can't escape. I'll always come back in the end, to this green-walled room with its desk and its terminals, its cupboards crammed with a hundred thousand dozens of everything, toilet paper and magnetic tape and oxygen tanks. . . . And I can tell you exactly how many steps it is to my bedroom or how long it took me to crochet the afghan on the bed . . . how long I've sat in the dark and silence, setting up an exposure program or listening for the feeble pulse of a radio galaxy two billion light-years away. There will never be anything different, or anything more.

When I finally came back here, there was a message waiting. Weems, grinning out at me half bombed from the screen—"Congratulations," he cried, "on this historic occasion! Emmylou, we're having a little celebration here at the lab; mind if we join you in yours, one thousand astronomical units from home—?" I've never seen him drunk. They really must have meant to do something nice for me, planning it all six days ahead. . . .

To celebrate I shouted obscenities I didn't even know I knew at him, until my voice was broken and my throat was raw.

Then I sat at my desk for a long time with my jack-knife lying open in my hand. Not wanting to die—I've always been too afraid of death for that—but wanting to hurt myself. I wanted to make a fresh hurt, to take my attention off the terrible thing that is sucking me into myself like an imploding star. Or maybe just to punish myself, I don't know. But I considered the possibility of actually cutting myself quite calmly, while some separate part of me looked on in horror. I even pressed the knife against my flesh . . . and then I stopped and put it away. It hurts too much.

I can't go on like this. I have duties, obligations, and I can't face them. What would I do without the emergency automechs? . . . But it's the rest of my life, and they can't go on doing my job for me forever—

Later.

I just had a visitor. Strange as that sounds. Stranger yet—it was Donald Duck. I picked up half of a children's cartoon show today, the first coherent piece of nondirectional, unbeamed television broadcast I've recorded in months. And I don't think I've ever been happier to see anyone in my life. What a nice surprise, so glad you could drop by. . . . Ozymandias loves him; he hangs upside down from his swing under the cabinet with a cracker in one foot, cackling away and saying, "Give us a kiss, *smack-smack-smack*." . . . We watched it three times. I even smiled, for a while; until I remembered myself. It helps. Maybe I'll watch it again until bedtime.

Friday, the 13th

Friday the Thirteenth. Amusing. Poor Friday the Thirteenth, what did it ever do to deserve its reputation? Even if it had any power to make my life miserable, it couldn't hold a candle to the rest of this week. It seems like an eternity since last weekend.

I repaired the scope today; replaced the burnt-out parts. Had to suit up and go outside for part of the work . . . I haven't done any outside maintenance for quite a while. Odd how both exhilarating and terrifying it always is when I first step out of the airlock, utterly alone, into space. You're entirely on your own, so far away from any possibility of help, so far away from anything at all. And at that moment you doubt yourself, suddenly, terribly . . . just for a moment.

But then you drag your umbilical out behind you and clank along the hull in your magnetized boots that feel so reassuringly like lead ballast. You turn on the lights and look for the trouble, find it and get to work; it doesn't bother you anymore. . . . When your life seems to have torn loose and be drifting free, it creates a kind of sea anchor to work with your hands; whether it's doing some mindless routine chore or the most intricate of repairs.

There was a moment of panic when I actually saw

charred wires and melted metal, when I imagined the damage was so bad that I couldn't repair it again. It looked so final, so—masterful. I clung there by my feet and whimpered and clenched my hands inside my gloves, like a great shining baby, for a while. But then I pulled myself down and began to pry here and unscrew there and twist a component free . . . and little by little I replaced everything. One step at a time; the way we get through life.

By the time I'd finished I felt quite calm, for the first time in days; the thing that's been trying to choke me to death this past week seemed to falter a little at my demonstration of competence. I've been breathing easier since then; but I still don't have much strength. I used up all I had just overcoming my own inertia.

But I shut off the lights and hiked around the hull for a while, afterwards—I couldn't face going back inside just then: looking at the black convex dish of the solar sail I'm embedded in, up at the radio antenna's smaller dish occluding stars as the observatory's cylinder wheels endlessly at the hub of the spinning parasol. . . .

That made me dizzy, and so I looked out into the starfields that lie on every side. Even with my own poor, unaugmented senses there's so much more to see out here, unimpeded by atmosphere or dust, undominated by any sun's glare. The brilliance of the Milky Way, the depths of star and nebula and farthest galaxy breathlessly suspended . . . as I am. The realization that I'm lost for eternity in an uncharted sea.

Strangely, although that thought aroused a very powerful emotion when it struck me, it wasn't a negative one at all: it was from another scale of values entirely, like the universe itself. It was as if the universe itself stretched out its finger to touch me. And in touching me, singling me out, it only heightened my awareness of my own insignificance.

That was somehow very comforting. When you confront the absolute indifference of magnitudes and vistas so overwhelming, the swollen ego of your self-important suffering is diminished. . . .

And I remembered one of the things that was always so important to me about space—that here *anyone* has to put on a spacesuit before they step outside. We're all aliens, no one better equipped to survive than another. I am as normal as anyone else, out here.

I must hold on to that thought.

Saturday, the 14th

There is a reason for my being here. There is a reason.

I was able to meditate earlier today. Not in the old way, the usual way, by emptying my mind. Rather by letting the questions fill up the space, not fighting them; letting them merge with my memories of all that's gone before. I put on music, that great mnemonic stimulator; letting the images that each tape evoked free-associate and interact.

And in the end I could believe again that my being here was the result of a free choice. No one forced me into this. My motives for volunteering were entirely my own. And I was given this position because NASA believed that I was more likely to be successful in it than anyone else they could have chosen.

It doesn't matter that some of my motives happened to be unresolved fear or wanting to escape from things I couldn't cope with. It really doesn't matter. Sometimes retreat is the only alternative to destruction, and only a madman can't recognize the truth of that. Only a madman. . . . Is there anyone "sane" on Earth who isn't secretly a fugitive from something unbearable somewhere in their life? And yet they function normally.

If they ran, they ran toward something, too, not just away. And so did I. I had already chosen a career as an astrophysicist before I ever dreamed of being a part of this project. I could have become a medical researcher instead, worked on my own to find a cure for my condition. I could have grown up hating the whole idea of space and "spacemen," stumbling through life in my damned ugly sterile suit. . . .

But I remember when I was six years old, the first time I saw a film of suited astronauts at work in space . . . they looked just like me! And no one was laughing. How could I help but love space, then?

(And how could I help but love Jeffrey, with his night-black hair, and his blue flight suit with the starry patch on the shoulder. Poor Jeffrey, poor Jeffrey, who never even realized his own dream of space before they cut the program out from under him. . . . I will not talk about Jeffrey. I will not.)

Yes, I could have stayed on Earth, and waited for a cure! I knew even then there would have to be one, someday. It was both easier and harder to choose space, instead of staying.

And I think the thing that really decided me was that those people had faith enough in me and my abilities to believe that I could run this observatory and my own life smoothly for as long as I lived. Billions of dollars and a thousand tons of equipment resting on me, like Atlas holding up his world.

Even Atlas tried to get rid of his burden; because no matter how vital his function was, the responsibility was still a burden to him. But he took his burden back again too, didn't he; for better or worse. . . .

I worked today. I worked my butt off getting caught up on a week's worth of data processing and maintenance, and I'm still not finished. Discovered while I was at it that Ozymandias had used those missing five pages just like the daily news: crapped all over them. My sentiments exactly! I laughed and laughed.

I think I may live.

Sunday, the 15th

The clouds have parted.

That's not rhetorical—among my fresh processed data is a series of photo reconstructions in the ultra-long wavelengths. And there's a gap in the obscuring gas up ahead of me, a break in the clouds that extends thirty or forty light-years. Maybe fifty! Fantastic. What a view.

What a view I have from here of everything, with my infinitely extended vision: of the way ahead, of the passing scene—or looking back toward Earth.

Looking back. I'll never stop looking back, and wishing it could have been different. That at least there could have been two of me, one to be here, one who could have been normal, back on Earth; so that I wouldn't have to be forever torn in two by regrets—

("*Hello. What's up, doc? Avast!*")

("Hey, watch it! If you drink, don't fly.")

Damn bird. . . . If I'm getting maudlin, it's because I had a party today. Drank a whole bottle of champagne. Yes, I had *the* party . . . we did, Ozymandias and I. Our private 1,000 AU celebration. Better late than never, I guess. At least we did have something concrete to celebrate—the photos. And if the celebration wasn't quite as merry as it could have been, still, I guess it will probably seem like it was when I look back on it from the next one, at 2,000 AUs. They'll be coming faster now, the celebrations. I may even live to celebrate 8,000. What the hell, I'll shoot for 10,000—

After we finished the champagne . . . Ozymandias thinks '98 was a great year, thank God he can't drink as fast as I can . . . I put on my Strauss waltzes, and the *Barcarolle*: Oh, the Berliner Philharmonic; their touch is what a lover's kiss must be. I threw the view outside onto the big screen, a ballroom of stars, and danced with my shadow. And part of the time I wasn't dancing above the abyss in a jumpsuit and headphones, but waltzing in yards of satin and lace across a ballroom floor in nineteenth-century Vienna. What I wouldn't give to be *there* for a moment out of time. Not for a lifetime, or even a year, but just for an evening, just for one waltz.

Another thing I shall never do. There are so many things we can't do, any of us, for whatever the reasons—time, talent, life's callous whims. We're all on a one-way trip into infinity. If we're lucky we're given some life's work we care about, or some person. Or both, if we're very lucky.

And I do have Weems. Sometimes I see us like an old married couple, who have grown to a tolerant understanding over the years. We've never been soul mates, God knows, but we're comfortable with each other's silences. . . .

I guess it's about time I answered him.

The Morphology of the Kirkham Wreck

Hilbert Schenck

This is a story about the use of time, but it's
not a time-travel story; rather, it has to do
with peoples of the future who will learn how
to bend time to their will in many ways. The
story itself, however, takes place in our past;
it centers on a crisis that occurred when a
sailing ship was driven aground during a
fierce storm off the New England coast. The
sailors were in mortal danger—but no less so
than Earth's time line, and the "time-using
people" who patrolled it.

Hilbert Schenck is the director of the ocean
engineering program at the University of
Rhode Island; this is his second science-fiction
story.

The Riches of the Commonwealth
Are free strong minds, and hearts of
       health;
And more to her than gold or grain,
The cunning hand and cultured brain.
—Robert B. Thomas,
    The Old Farmers Almanack,
    1892, William Ware and Company,
    Boston, Mass.

When the three-masted schooner *H.P. Kirkham*
stranded on Rose and Crown Shoal southeast of Nan-

tucket Island on January 19, 1892, the Coskata Life
Saving Crew, led by Keeper Walter Chase, responded.
The ensuing rescue attempt involved alterations in the
local time flow of magnitudes never before observed
within this continuum. Evolutionary physical forces
were changed beyond the control of time-using peoples,
and a fundamental question was introduced into the information matrix of this continuum, having, apparently,
no resolution.

Time-using societies had always recognized the possibility that energy-users might attain significant mastery
of time manipulation. Indeed, even occasional members
of Keeper Chase's world group had, under the impetus
of some violent or emotional event, been able to perform some limited and simple feats of time engineering,
usually associated with mood and incentive control of
others in the immediate situation. What became evident
when the *Kirkham* stranded was that extreme-value
probability theory could not set a limit on such activity
by an energy-user totally motivated and having what
Keeper Chase's peoples would incorrectly call a high
level of "psychic" ability but what in fact is simply the
ability to make information transfers within an altered
time domain.

The northern gale blew shrieking along the back of
Great Point, driving the spume off the wave tops and
over the bitter beach. The patrolman crouched behind a
sand hill, hunched to keep an occasional swirl of snow
out of his collar, staring dully out at the white and gray
sea. The wind had built up through the night, and now
the shreds of dawn were blowing south over Nantucket,
and the wind spoke continuously of urgent death.

The beach patrol, a hulking dark figure, turned to
put the blast behind him and started back toward the
station, where watchers in the cupola could relieve him
in the light of day. It was twelve degrees above zero,
with the wind gusting over forty.

Inside the Coskata Station the dark, shadowed panel-
ing glowed faintly pink, reflecting the luminous bril-

liance of a huge coal stove in the center of the big common room. Nyman was cookie that week, and the wheatcakes were piling up on the cookstove in the small galley under the stairs. Four men sat silent, waiting for their breakfast, not trying to speak against the whines and rattles of the wind gusts. Yet they clearly heard the telephone tinkle in the cupola. A moment later, Surfman Eldridge appeared at the top of the stairs. "Skipper? It's Joe Remsen at Sankaty Light."

Keeper Walter Chase rose in the dark glow of the station, a giant, almost seven feet tall; his huge shadow startlingly flew up to obscure the walls and ceiling as he moved in front of the ruddy stove and up the stairs.

And Surfman Perkins, toying with his coffee mug, listening to the wind snapping and keening around the station, knowing that dawn calls from the lighthouse meant only one thing, suddenly realized for the first time in his life that he might die. He coughed, sharp barks of sound contrasting with the heavy, measured tread of Keeper Chase mounting the two flights to the cupola.

"Walter Chase here. Is that you, Joe?"

"Walter!" An urgent tone. Chase sensed that time was beginning to run away from him. "Masts on Bass Rip. We saw a flare last night late, but couldn't tell where. She's leaning some. Seems steady, but it's awful far to tell."

"What's her true bearing, Joe?"

"Just about due east from us. That would put her on the north end of Bass Rip."

Keeper Chase consulted a chart and compared angles. He looked out over the station pointer with powerful glasses. "Joe, I can't make her out. She *has* to be further out. We've got forty feet here and I could sure see her if she was laying on Bass Rip. She's got to be on Rose and Crown. South end from your bearing."

A pause. "Well . . . I don't know, Walter. I doubt we'd see her so clear that far. She may have lost her topmasts."

There was no point in arguing. Chase knew the wreck was fifteen miles out, on Rose and Crown Shoal.

A sudden gust blew through the stout government sashes and swirled its chill into the cupola. The little tower rattled and shook. Walter Chase looked out at the ragged dawn, across at Eldridge, then down at the phone. "Joe, hang on. I'm getting the surfboat ready. We'll haul to the backside and launch there. I'll be back to you before I leave the station." Chase rose, ducking his head instinctively in the small room, and slowly climbed down the ladder, his mind fragmenting, working the launch, estimating the tide rips, laying beside the stranded vessel. "Eat quick!" shouted Walter Chase down the stairs. "We got a wreck on Rose and Crown!"

The difficulty in predicting improbable, time-controlling events by energy-users stems from these people's unlikely and illogical motivations and perception. One might assume that Keeper Chase's need to "defeat" the seas of the Nantucket South Shoals flowed from some sense of vengeance or hatred on his part resulting from the loss of a loved parent or a woman in some sea disaster. In fact, Keeper Chase suffered no such loss. Distant family members had, through the years, died on various whaling and trading voyages, but they were only names to Keeper Chase with little emotional attachment. Yet where the winter storms easily broke and ruined other capable men, for Keeper Chase the natural variation of wind and sea, so implacable and daunting to most of Chase's world group, only resonated with his self-image. In essence, Chase did not strongly believe in the "God" concepts so typical of energy users, but he strongly believed in a "Devil"—that is, the continual temptation of his world group by easy choices and safe paths. Keeper Chase saw the variability of the ocean as a natural test of behavior, as a kind of "Devil's assistant." That this naive motivation coupled with his great physical strength and the urgent and marginal situation at the stranded *Kirkham* should have produced such an unprecedented control over time flow cannot now be understood. Keeper Chase's meaning and purpose in this continuum thus remains inexplicable, as in fact he himself was to realize.

Surfman Flood ducked around the corner of the station, finally relieved of the wind blast at his back. He saw the stable door was open, and in the dim interior, Perkins and Gould were fastening a long wooden yoke across the neck of the silent ox. Harness bells tinkled, sound pinpoints in the rush and scream of the wind. Flood's heart seemed hollow. "Where's it at?" he asked at the door.

Josiah Gould peered from under his slicker hat. "Rose and Crown."

Flood sighed. "Fifteen miles downwind."

"Ayeh. Better get some breakfast."

Flood pushed open the station door and felt the relative warmth and stillness of the dark interior suck at his resolve. Nyman was steadily lifting forkfuls of flapjack into his mouth, alternating with steaming coffee from a huge cup in his left hand. Across the table was Flood's place set with a heaping meal.

"We got some rowin' to do, George. Better feed your face quick," said John Nyman. As they ate, rapidly and silently, the two wide doors of the apparatus room opened on the other side of the station, and swirls and draughts of chill rushed everywhere. They heard the shouts and tinkles as the stolid ox was backed over the sills and the harness lashings connected to the surfboat cart.

"Gawd, John, hits just awful on the beach!"

Nyman grinned and winked in the dark, chilling room. "The govinmint only pays you to go out, George," he said quoting the old wheeze. "You got to get back any way you can."

"Fifteen miles to windward! Hell's delight, we won't row a hundred yards in this smother!"

They heard Keeper Chase's deep voice in the apparatus room as the creak of the wheels signaled the surfboat's movement out into the wild dawn. He came into the common room and looked at the two men. "You fellers follow across the neck when you're finished and bring back the ox. I'm going to call Joe Remsen at Sankaty and have him order a tug from Woods Hole. We hain't going to row very far in this blow after we get them fellers off the wreck."

"Amen," said Surfman Flood under his breath. The wind was penetrating everywhere in the station, and the commotion was restless and insistent.

Walter Chase climbed back up into the cupola and cranked the phone magneto.

"Sankaty Light, Keeper Remsen."

"Joe, Walter Chase again. We'll be launching pretty quick. Can you still see her out there?"

"Hang on . . . yep. No change in her heel, as far as I can tell."

"Joe, will you call the town and have them telegraph Woods Hole for a tug. I think this storm's got another day to run, and we just hain't going to row back against it."

"Walter, I'll do my best . . . Them salvage fellows . . . they're hardly what you'd call heroes, you know."

Walter Chase grinned in the dark tower, which was suddenly shaking like a wet terrier. "Rats, vultures, buzzards, and skunks is what I usually hear them called, Joe. But we'll get back. Listen, Joe, I'm taking a line and drail. Might be some squeteague in those shallows in this rough weather."

But Joe Remsen made no sudden answer. He had rowed in the surfboat with Walter Chase under old Captain Pease when the Coskata Station had opened eight years before. Together they had worked the wreck of the infamous brig *Merriwa*, manned by a crew of New York City thugs who attempted to shoot up the station soon after they were landed. Walter Chase and an ax handle had secured the pistols, and then he and Joe had gone with them, now drunk as lords, to town in Wallace Adams' catboat. And Joe Remsen, feeling the tough and solid tower of Sankaty Light vibrate as a thin scream of icy air pierced the solid masonry, smiled in spite of himself, remembering the lunch at the Ameri-

can House. One of the drunken hoodlums had shoved
his hand under a waitress's dress, and she had let him
have a full tray of food plumb in the face. Back to back,
he and Walter Chase had fought the six of them, chairs
flying, crockery smashing everywhere. Joe Remsen's
throat had a catch. He had to say something. "Walter
. . . old friend, take care . . . God bless."

The walk across the neck took only a few blustery
minutes, and Walter Chase met Nyman and Flood mid-
way in that walk leading the ox home. Chase strode
through the tidal cut between two high dunes, and the
full wind caught his slicker and blew it suddenly open
so that for a moment he seemed impossibly huge in the
gray, fitful light. The surfboat lay above high water, and
the men around it huddled together, their backs against
the cutting wind.

Surfman Jesse Eldridge was number one in the Coskata crew. He walked, hunched and stolid, to Walter
Chase. "It's going to be a tough launch, Skipper. Them
waves are running almost along the beach," he shouted.

Chase nodded. "We're getting some lee from Point
Rip, Jesse, but we'll have to launch across them, hold
her head to the east. Otherwise, we'll be back ashore
before we know it." They watched the breaking curls
running toward them from the north.

Nyman and Flood came back, and the men, three on
a side, began to shift the surfboat into the backwash.
The wind blustered at them. "We got to go quick . . .
when we go, boys!" shouted Walter Chase.

The blow was slightly west of north, but the waves
were running directly south and meeting the beach at a
sharp angle. "Take her out about nor'east!" shouted
Walter Chase. "Ready. . . . Now, jump to it!"

The six men lifted the boat by its gunwales and ran
into the waves. A large group had passed and now the
nearshore was a confused and choppy mess. The leading surfmen, Cathcart and Perkins, were almost up to
their waists, and over the sides they vaulted, lifting and
dropping their oars in the rowlocks. Now Gould and
Nyman scrambled in, then Eldridge and Flood. Walter

Chase pushed the surfboat out alone, deeper in, and now a curl appeared more from the east than the others and slapped the surfboat's bow to port back towards shore. Walter Chase moved his right hand forward along the starboard gunwale and pulled sharply. The twenty-three-foot boat gave a hop and her bow shifted eastward again. Then Chase was gracefully over the stern and the men were rowing strongly while he put out the long steering oar. They were clear of the shore break and moving into deeper water. Yet even here the waves were huge, rolling by under the boat and now and again breaking unexpectedly under the keel or beside them as they pulled together.

George Flood, cheerful and round-faced, was rowing port oar next to Jesse Eldridge. "Say, Skipper," he shouted up at Walter Chase. "I'm sure glad your ma never stinted you food. We must have been in a fathom of water before you climbed in."

Walter Chase thought a moment. "Actually, George, I hain't all that big, as Chases go," he boomed. "My great-uncle Reuben Chase was harpooner with Cap'n Grant on the *Niger*, and he went over seven feet. They claimed he could play a bull walrus or a whale on a harpoon line like you or I would a blue or striped bass." Chase paused, then . . . "'Course, that would be a *small* whale, you understand."

Josiah Gould, seated directly ahead of Eldridge, lifted his head, his huge mustache blowing every which way. "Hain't that awful!" he yelled. "He's not just taking us out here to catch our death from pee-nu-monia, but now we're going to listen to more of them Chase family lies, too!"

Flood grinned over his shoulder and shouted back. "Them's not exactly lies, Josiah. Them's what's called 'artistic license.' "

Walter Chase looked benignly at Flood, his small eyes bright and his sideburns wild and full in the whipping wind. "I wisht I had your education, George. It's a plain wonder how you fellers with schooling can call one single thing by so many names. Now my daddy always said there was just three kinds: plain lies; mean, dirty, awful lies; and what's in the *Congressional Record*."

Gould and Nyman looked sideways at each other, winking. If they could get Skipper Chase going on them "govinment fellers," it would be a short and cheerful run to Rose and Crown.

But the wind was worse. They were completely clear of any lee from Great Point. Even Chase's huge voice would be torn away and mutilated. "We're . . . far enough . . . out! Get . . . the sail up!" The four stern oarsmen continued to row, now more northerly into the teeth of the blasting wind. Cathcart and Perkins brought their oars inboard and wrestled the sail, tied in a tight bundle, out from under the thwarts and up into the wind. With Gould's and Nyman's help they finally stepped the mast and then unfurled and dropped the small lateen rig. It caught and filled with a snap, and Walter Chase wrenched the steering oar so hard to port that it described a long arc between the water and the steering notch in the transom. The boat darted off. Eldridge manned the sheet, and the other men huddled on the floorboards, their heads hunched inside the thick issue sweaters and stiff slickers.

Chase, at the steering oar, and Eldridge, on the stern thwart, had their heads close together; and now, running with the wind on the stern quarter, they could suddenly speak less stridently.

"I'm going to head for the lightship south of Great Round Shoal, Jesse," said Walter Chase, his arms in constant motion. "If it comes on to blow worse, we'll just have to go on board her. If we decide to keep going, we'll lay off sou'east and run down to Rose and Crown."

Eldridge was silent, then: "When do you figure we decide, Skipper?"

Chase looked at the jagged seas, whitecaps everywhere to the horizon. "Much beyond the Bass Rip line, we could never fetch the lightship. This lugger hain't much to windward."

The two men looked out ahead as the surfboat, heavily driven, wallowed and yawed and fought the pull of Walter Chase and his tough hickory steering oar.

Now they were three miles out, and looking south, Walter Chase saw that Bass Rip was clear and that the wreck was certainly on Rose and Crown. "We got to decide, Jesse," said Walter Chase.

Surfman Eldridge looked down at his high gumrubber boots and nodded. "It hain't got worse, Skipper."

Chase's small eyes glittered. "Let out the sail, Jesse," he said, and the surfboat bounced and slapped and rolled, but now it was better, for the waves were astern. Off they dashed southeast, surfing down the long rollers in the deep water, then struggling up the shifting water hills. Between the Bass Rip line and McBlair's Shoal, Walter Chase first saw the masts of the wreck. She was at the south end of Rose and Crown, probably in that one-fathom spot there, and leaning to the south perhaps twenty degrees. He headed a bit more southerly and they left the choppy white smother of McBlair's Shoal behind.

Now the three masts were clearly visible. The vessel lay roughly east and west with her stern to Nantucket. She had struck and then bilged, and now the waves were breaking cleanly over her. They had driven the hull over to starboard so that a spectacular line of surf would suddenly appear all along her port side that canted up to face the seas. They were too far away to count the men, but Chase could see dark forms in the ratlines. He peered intently at the wreck. Was it shifting now? It was a bad stranding! If she were facing the seas, even quartering, but broadside they were wrenching her. And the tide was coming. The seas would enlarge and she'd be hit even harder. Chase peered and peered at the wreck, and the surfboat drove along the line made by his eyes.

Chase Two was aware of the *H.P. Kirkham* in a total sense. She was not going to stay together any longer.

Chase Two detected unbalanced forces within the ship-sand-wind-water field matrix. He penetrated the force structure around the *Kirkham*, but there was no TIME! The surfboat was running down the seas. The *Kirkham* was twisting as the combers, steepened and shortened by the shoal, boarded her with shuddering blows. Chase Two clinched, and time flowed more slowly. The waves moved like molasses. The shocks were stretched out, and he could trace the force imbalances. SLOWER! He could not speed the finite duration of impulses flowing between his billions of neural cells, but he could slow time and process data that way. Fiercely he clinched. Time, he realized, could be traded for information. He saw the *Kirkham* completely, and yet simultaneously in every relevant detail. The mizzenmast was shaky, split. Not much had shown on the mast's surface, but now the stick was resonating with the wind, and the splitting was worse. It would soon bring down the main and fore-mast, and the men as well.

There was no solution within the energy matrix alone, and neither time nor information domains extended directly into the energy system. The mast would have to be replaced.

Chase Two stooped like a hawk down the *Kirkham*'s time line. He saw her leave Rose and Crown Shoal and flow backwards to Halifax and leave her lading. Then faster, backwards to other voyages in her brief year of life. Now the masts were out and the hull was coming apart on the stocks of a boatyard near the tiny town of Liverpool on the south coast of Nova Scotia. The masts suddenly grew branches, and in a twinkling, Chase Two watched a French timber cruiser looking up at a tall pine deep in the Nova Scotia forests. The cruiser turned to his associate, the shipyard boss's young son on his first wood-buying trip into the woods. "By gar, dat's one fine tree, eh?"

The young man nodded. It was the tallest in the area. But now Chase Two showed the Frenchman something he had not seen before, that other time. The tree had been struck by lightning. The scar was grown over, but you could just make it out curling from the top and disappearing around the trunk.

"Look," said the timber cruiser. "Dat tree been struck. We walk around." And on the other side they saw the faint scar traveling down to the ground. "Risky, dose ones," said the Frenchman in a superior way. "Hmmmmm." And as he looked around, Chase Two showed him a shorter but perfectly branched mast tree on the other side of the clearing, and the French cruiser pointed and smiled. "Not so beeg, dat one, but plenty tough, I teenk."

And back down the time line, Chase Two dropped like a stone. He saw the new mizzen erected on the Liverpool ways, then, faster and faster, the loading and unloading and movement until the *Kirkham* again struck on Rose and Crown Shoal, bilged, and lay through the stormy night with her men in her rigging.

When Keeper Chase learned that informational and temporal entropy flows could be interchanged, his power to influence events grew at an unprecedented pace. In the course of replacing the *Kirkham*'s mast, Keeper Chase solved a variety of hydrodynamic and structural problems of extreme complexity and entirely by inspection and processing of data. Much more significant, he dealt surely with the philosophical and practical problems of time-information interchange and realized that if time flow could be slowed, it could be controlled in other ways. His ability to arrest time flow within his local region was now so pronounced that a detectable chronologic entropy gradient existed within the entire continuum.

The surfboat blew down on the stricken schooner from the north, heading directly for her battered port side, where white spume flew up twenty feet or more when a big wave took her full on.

"You bow men," shouted Walter Chase. "Get the anchor ready." The positioning had to be done correctly the first time. There would be no clawing back up from the schooner's lee to reanchor if they did it badly. Walter Chase watched the choppy, surging space shorten between the surfboat and the schooner. The current was running to the northeast with the wind a bit west of north and the waves about from due north. He decided to anchor upwind of the vessel's stern and then lay back south and easterly to come under the mainmast and her center ratlines, where the crew was now clustered.

Chase's small eyes gleamed in the gray, dull light. He watched the distance shorten and the schooner widen and her masts grow up and, in them, the men now clearly seen.

"Watch your head, Jesse!" shouted Walter Chase. "We're rounding up now!" He put the steering oar hard over, and again it formed a bow of iron-hard hickory, arched against the forces that drove the boat halfway around, heeling and wallowing wildly until it faced the screaming wind and sharp seas. "Anchor over!" shouted Walter Chase, then, "Oars out, all of you!"

They were up on the thwarts holding her head against the wind as she slipped back with Perkins paying out the anchor line over a smooth, maple cleat. The surfboat lay on her tether about southeast, and Walter Chase guided her back and back until they were a few yards from the schooner and just beyond where the big rollers broke and shuddered the vessel all along her length. The surge was ten feet or more. The surfboat lay down in a trough, and they could look up and see several feet of the schooner's side, then up until they were above the rail and a great wave was sliding out from under them and creaming white and lovely over the vessel's port rail in a burst of foam and a sound of roaring and groaning that made Walter Chase flinch his cheek muscles, for he knew how weak the schooner was.

Chase cupped his hands and bellowed directly into the wind. "Perkins, throw them the heaving stick."

Perkins heard and readied the stick and its loops of line. The surge picked the surfboat up, and as they came level with the schooner's rail, Perkins hurled the stick into the rigging, with the thin line paying smoothly out behind in a graceful arc. One of the crew crawled up the ratlines to where the stick was entangled in the shrouds and turned toward the surfboat.

"You . . . bend a line on that! Use your topsail clew line." The roar of Walter Chase's voice flew downwind, and in moments, the clew line was fast to the stick, and back it came, hand by hand, through the smother to Perkins, who bent it on the same cleat as the anchor warp.

The other end of the clew line was in the hands of the sailor and two others who had crawled over to join him. Walter Chase shouted again. "Tie that line to a shroud, you men!"

They stared stupidly at him, and sudden spray flew up in their faces. Walter Chase turned back to Perkins. "Start to haul in on that slowly. You rowers, ease us toward her side."

But the schooner's crew had waited long enough, and they, or three of them, began to pull fiercely on the clew line themselves. Walter Chase felt the boat jerk roughly toward the schooner and begin a deep roll broadside in a trough. He crammed the steering oar violently over and spun around, pointing at the schooner. "Stop hauling! Stop, I say! Make your end fast. If you make one more pull on that line, we'll cut it!" And as he spoke, Chase pulled a big clasp knife from his slicker pocket and opened the blade with a snick that pierced the duller voice of the gale. Then he passed the big silver knife forward to Perkins, who brandished it above the clew line. The men on the schooner saw the great dark figure with the knife and heard the huge voice driven down by the wind, and they tied off the line and huddled, dully watching the Coskata crew, using both rope and oars, begin to move toward the wreck.

Suddenly the schooner shuddered and inexplicably rolled to windward. She came almost upright and then went back over to starboard, stopping her breathtaking swing at the same list as before. The mizzen gaff snapped off and fell, thudding against its mast on the way down. The schooner began another roll to port, and Perkins looked directly at the men in the ratlines, and his eyes and theirs met. He remembered a Sunday six years ago when, after church, he and his mother had driven in the wagon over to Little Mioxes Pond where, everyone said, a large vessel had blown ashore. They had spent the day with hundreds of others watching the men in the rigging, too weak to grasp the lines shot over the vessel by the surfside crew, falling one after another into the raging sea. The vessel had stranded well out so the crew were only small black figures and they did not move very much when they fell, but Perkins never after that time shot another crow or grackle with the .22 Winchester pump that his mother had saved for a year to buy him. Even if they were just birds, they fell the same way, black against the far sky. And now these men were about to fall, blackly still, but he would see their eyes clearly this time.

"Gawd help us, Skipper! She'll shake her sticks out!" shouted Perkins in a choking, coughing voice, strident with terror.

Walter Chase had followed that roll with bright, keen eyes. She could not withstand much more of that! "No!" he said sharply.

Chase Three surveyed the flow field under the wreck and processed the observations. He clamped intensely on the time flow, and the *Kirkham* was motionless in a sea of stationary fluid and a sky of stationary wind. He explored the flow characteristics of the near shores in every particular, considering the special character of the *Kirkham*'s fields of forces. The current, shifting clockwise during the flood as it did in the area, had undermined the sand bed on which the *Kirkham* lay. But worse, the current, now running more and more counter to the wind, was moving the hull as well.

Chase Three considered how the force and energy relationships could be corrected. The wind was beyond manipulation, deriving as it did from such a disparate mass of variables as to make significant time-based alteration impractical. But the flows of gravity and wind-driven water were another matter. As Chase Three studied these fields of flow, he gradually realized that the natural relationships allowed a bifurcation within the viscosity functions. There were at least two flow-field configurations that had equal probability, and most important, either could exist with no change in total energy level within the continuum. The present field system allowed a strong easterly current to move in over the shoal against the *Kirkham*, but with the alternate field the flow would be slightly damped and diverted more northerly, and the wind force on the schooner would be sufficient to hold her against the sand and damp the roll forces.

Since there was no energy gradient involved, Chase Three immediately altered the continuum to the new flow field, this information gradient being offset by the altered time flow in the local area. The *Kirkham* shuddered but did not roll again.

With his introduction of the Chase Field into the information matrix of our continuum, Keeper Chase was reaching the peak of his astonishing powers. That any alternate description of the fluid-dynamic field existed was not even known, and that Keeper Chase should have found a solution at equal energies was quite marvelous. He did not, when utilizing time-information entropy balances to make the shift, consider that these same laws govern the development and evolution of galactic and supra-galactic motion and that the field shift must occur there as well. Thus Keeper Chase, in addition to sustaining an extraordinary temporal gradient within the continuum, had now inadvertently but irrevocably altered the way in which the energy universe would develop. Those time-using peoples who existed outside the gradient now convened and considered the immediate situation. We too could work within altered time, but the randomness of what was occurring put us beyond normal information transfer procedures. The storm on the Nantucket South Shoals had spawned a gradient storm in time itself. If the rescue attempt should become unlikely within any statistically allowed alternate energy structure, we would have to consider Keeper Chase's reaction to that perception and what an impossible but certainly powerful reaction by Keeper Chase to breach the energy-time-information barriers would cause within these boundaries.

Perkins, bent in a fit of coughing, saw that the schooner was stationary again. "Cathcart," shouted Walter Chase. "Bend a bowline in our painter and get ready to heave it over."

Now they edged closer, hanging like a lunging pony against the whipping anchor line. "Throw!" shouted Chase and the line flew across. "One man at a time," shouted Chase down the screaming wind to the schooner. "Put that bight around your waist."

A large, hulking Negro who had caught the painter passed it to a smaller figure, evidently the cabin boy. The youngster put the line over his head and waited, staring frozenly into the wind.

"Now . . ." and Chase's voice boomed under and around the wind's cry. "When I say jump, you come! You hear!"

The boy nodded, staring out at the marching lines of water foaming towards them.

"Cathcart, haul us in a bit . . . Now, steady, boys!" The surfboat was caught by a comber and lifted, up and up, and the wave was pushing the boat toward the schooner. They were on the peak and the curl was slipping past.

"JUMP!"

The boy flung himself off the ratlines, his legs flailing. Cathcart and Perkins handed in the painter as he fell, thudding, into the space between the bow and center thwarts. "Ease that bow line quick!" shouted Walter Chase, and the surfboat lay off to the east before an early break could turn them over at the schooner's rail.

The boy looked up from the floorboards, his ankle hurting, his teeth chattering; and over him loomed a gigantic figure, sideburns wild and blustery, eyes small and intensely bright, beacons against the wild gray sky. "We count six more, son. Have you lost anyone yet?"

Somehow the boy was able to speak. "No, sir. Seven in all. The cap'n—the cap'n ain't so well. We—we been in the rigging since eight last night. Gawd, it's . . ."

"What ship?" asked George Flood, turning suddenly around.

"*H.P. Kirkham*," said the boy. "From Halifax with fish. Bound to New York."

Walter Chase stood up. "Let's get the next one. You starboard rowers, bring us in slow. Cathcart, bring her head in."

Each time, they approached the *Kirkham* and waited for the proper wave to lift them up and slide the boat close. Then a black tumbling figure would come down into the surfboat every which way, limp with fear and exhaustion and dazed by the sudden, unexpected hope.

Now there were three left and the surfboat rolled more heavily and more water slopped over the gunwales. "Sir," shouted the cabin boy. "I think the cap'n's coming next. They're going to have to sort o' throw him."

Walter Chase peered at the three figures in the ratlines. The wind had slackened a bit and it seemed brighter. He could see an old man, conscious but unable to hold his head up, supported and held against the ratlines by a huge Negro and another big man in bulky clothes. "Josiah, Johnny . . . get ready to help when this fellow comes across."

The center rowers shipped oars and waited. Cathcart carefully pulled them in, a bit at a time. Then he cleated the clew line and hurled the painter back across the foamy gap. They put the loop over the old man's head and shoulders. The boat was rising. "Get ready!" shouted Walter Chase to the three men. "Now!"

The two men threw the captain feet first into the boat. He came down crossways, catching John Nyman across the cheek with his fist as he fell. His head thumped a thwart and he slumped, a bundle of rags, into the bottom of the boat.

Walter Chase quickly knelt and lifted the old man's head. "Keeper Walter Chase. Coskata Life Saving Station. Can you understand me, Captain?"

The old man, his whiskers white with frost and brown with frozen tobacco juice and spittle, stared back unseeing. "Aye. Captain McCloud, master, *H. P. Kirkham* out of Nova Scotia. Thank God . . ."

Chase's eyes pierced the old man's own eyes, and he nodded. "Captain McCloud, we cannot save your vessel. She is breaking up and this storm will grow worse by nightfall."

"I know," said McCloud and his head fell forward and his eyes shut and he shivered in cold and pain and despair. Then . . . "This bloody, foul, awful coast!" His eyes briefly lost their dullness. "Worse than Scotland! Worse than the Channel! These rotting shoals stick out so bleeding far . . . God Almighty . . ." The effort exhausted him. He did not speak again.

The next man was the first mate, hard, grizzled; Cockney-tough enough to sit up after his jump and stare at the young, slender Perkins, bent over in a fit of coughing. "Well, you blokes don't look like bloody much, but you bloomin' well know your business out here!"

And on their final surge up over the schooner's rail the huge black crewman flew between the great and little boats with a sudden grace, and he, like the mate, sat up immediately and peered about from huge white eyes. But he said nothing.

"Now, lads," boomed Walter Chase, as the surfboat lay off easterly, bobbing and pitching in the smother like a logy cork. "Oars out. We got to clear this shallows afore the wind comes on. Lively now."

The four stern oarsmen pulled mightily while Perkins and Cathcart heaved on the anchor warp. Slowly they moved to windward, their efforts sending rivers of sweat inside the heavy sweaters and slickers in the twelve-degree, forty-knot blast.

"Anchor up, Skipper!" shouted Cathcart while Perkins suddenly bent double, both hands over his mouth.

Walter Chase looked back, his side whiskers black spikes, his huge slicker masking the *Kirkham*. He hated to give the gale an inch, but to get past her stern to the west would be a near thing, and the wind was rising again. He put the steering oar over and they fell off on a big soft wave to starboard. "Pull, boys, we got to stay ahead of these combers."

They rowed eastward, then more southerly and cleared the *Kirkham*'s smashed and sagging bow by forty feet. Walter Chase put his oar to starboard and they pulled under the schooner's lee. It was easier there. The schooner was acting as a breakwater, taking the big ones before they reached the surfboat, and they pulled strongly to the west, the wind hard and vicious on their starboard quarter and the sea confused and breaking everywhere, an endless mouth filled with shifting teeth.

But once beyond the schooner's length it was impossible. Chase put her more toward the south, taking the wind on the beam with the current still northeast and running those great, curling rips in the very shallow spots.

"Jesse," said Walter Chase, leaning forward. "We got to clear this shoal afore the high tide this afternoon. Them rollers'll start to break and we couldn't lay at anchor. And the wind's making up again. Them clouds are coming back."

Jesse Eldridge only nodded. He was pulling too hard to talk. They were moving southeast, but only barely. The *Kirkham* was close behind them, and the surfboat was slopping about, taking splash on every wave.

Walter Chase looked at the men they had rescued. His little bright eyes fixed on the first mate and the Negro, their heads buried in coats against the chill. "You fellers. Yank that sail and mast out of there and pitch it over the side. Our sailing days are done!"

The men moved slowly, as best they could, helped by a hand from this or that rower, and finally the outfit went over the side in a piecemeal fashion, trailing astern and finally pulling loose.

George Flood looked up and winked at Walter

Chase. "Skipper," he panted, "how you going to explain throwing that valuable govinmint property over the side to the inspector?"

Walter Chase, at that moment fighting a great, half-breaking wave that threatened to broach the surfboat, suddenly winked a gleaming eye back. "George, I'll just tell that feller that we met this here bureaucrat adrift on his very own desk looking for Washington, D.C., and we just plumb did the Christian thing and loaned him our sail."

Charles Cathcart, leaning intently forward as he pulled, burst into a roar of laughter. "Hell's fire, Skipper! They'd just say you didn't get him to fill in the right forms."

Perkins's oar trailed astern, and he leaned over the side, vomiting and coughing great, deep, sharp barks above the gale. Cathcart reached towards him, and the surfboat lost way and began to bounce and shift southerly into the troughs. Walter Chase looked piercingly at his men. They *must* clear the shoal now. It would only get worse.

Chase Four entered Perkins's continuity of self-awareness. The boy was sick, probably pneumonia, for his lungs were very wet. He was beaten. The cockney mate's praise had got him through the anchor recover, but now he was completely involved with his cough and nausea.

Chase Four dropped down Perkins's time line seeking a point that would reverberate with the *Kirkham* rescue. . . .

Each year on the last day of July along the islands, the life-saving crews return from a two-month off-duty period to a ten-month routine of patrols and watches. On that night the previous summer, the Coskata crew had produced their usual party. They had hired a banjo and violin from town, asked their wives, relatives, friends, and suppliers to the festive evening, and cleared out the dark apparatus room of its large gear. Colored streamers hung from the suspended life car, and festoons of buoys made arches beneath which the dancers turned. The girls, slim and pretty in ankle-length dresses, puffed sleeves, and swinging hair ringlets, smiled at the tall men in their government blue. Before the light went, they trooped outside to the breeches buoy training tower, and the girls climbed, one above the other up the ladder, and all looked back smiling while George Flood pressed his Kodak button and gave a happy shout.

But the prettiest there was Abigal Coffin with Roland Perkins. When the others returned in the dusk to the laughter and screech of the fiddler's bow, he caught her arm. "Let's go look at the ocean, Abby," he said. She was the nicest girl in the town, always smiling, her eyes so bright and full; and as they walked away from the station, Perkins could barely breathe, his chest was so full of love and hope. "Abby . . . could I . . . would you . . . ?" and he leaned toward her and brought his other arm up behind her back.

Chase Four did not wait for the sharp and hurtful reaction; he had skimmed by it once. Instead, he showed Abby Coffin that Roland Perkins was actually a fine, handsome boy. As she looked at him, she realized how sensitive and brave he would always be, how good and gentle his thoughts were toward her. She turned her face upward and they kissed. Later, under a bright moon, she said breathlessly, "Yes, you can touch me there, Roland."

Perkins, his coughing fit mastered, nodded at Cathcart and began to row strongly. Walter Chase urged them on. "We got to make some depth, boys." Perkins, grinning to himself, pulled and pulled. He knew they would get these men back. Chase was too good a boatman to fail, whatever the wind. They would all get government medals. And he thought of Abby and the medal and how she would hold him when he told her. Slowly the surfboat left the *Kirkham* behind.

George Flood's eyes popped open. "Look back quick, Skipper!" he shouted. Walter Chase spun around. In that instant, the *Kirkham* was dissolving.

Her foremast was halfway down, with her main following. The taut and snapping shrouds ripped the quarter-boards completely off the starboard side, and the deck buckled in several large pieces. The mizzen fell, and before it struck the water, the entire hull had disappeared. She had gone like smoke in a gale. Flood looked up at Walter Chase. "Dang lucky we didn't wait for another cup of coffee at the station, Skipper!" he shouted.

Walter Chase, fighting the steering oar continually in the heavy and confused seas, still stared back at the unchecked rollers now streaming over the *Kirkham's* last berth. They had taken the last man off less than an hour before. His eyes narrowed and he wondered about the rescue. Everything was so damn near, so chancy.

The Coskata crew rowed and rowed on Rose and Crown Shoal. Sometimes the boat moved west and sometimes it paused and pitched. Noon was past and the sky had darkened again. The wind was rising with the tide, but they were slowly getting into deeper water, into the twelve-fathom channel that cut aimlessly between Rose and Crown and Bass Rip. The waves were longer and not so steep, but the wind was too heavy. They were hardly moving and the men were exhausted. And the current had revolved almost due easterly and was actually setting them back away from Nantucket. This would have to do for now.

"Cathcart! We got to anchor. Handy now!" They lay back with the winds hammering their starboard quarter, all the scope they could muster laid out to their biggest anchor. The men slumped over their shipped oars while Walter Chase shoved the steering oar this way and that, using the current run to steer his boat up and over the combers. The wind was building again, and its scream and slash was icy and terrible. Jesse Eldridge, hunched in a nest of sweaters and slicker, looked up at Walter Chase. "Skipper, we didn't even make a mile in three hours. You think that tug'll get out here?"

"I figure he will as long as he thinks there might be some loot on the schooner, Jesse," said Walter Chase. He sensed, in fact, that the tug would not come into these wild shoals. Bitterly he thought of the wonderful strength of her cross-compound steam engine driving that big powerful screw. Yellow, rotten cowards! What was the point of even building such a vessel if you could not find men to man it? The surfboat jumped and tugged at the snapping anchor line, while the crew bailed as the spume and spray came in on them with every wave. Perkins and Cathcart gently tended the anchor line, wrapping it in rags, shifting it a few inches now and then to relieve the chafing.

The sky grew darker as the afternoon wore on and the wind built up again. There was so much agitation and violent activity, so many unexpected swoops and thumps, so many waves that appeared from odd directions and with surprising steepness.

Chase pulled and fought the oar, staring out at the screaming bowl of energy around him while a coldness and fierceness steadied his heart and mind. He would bring these men home, all of them. Nothing anywhere was more important than that. The tug, the lifesaving service, the men at their desks in Washington and Boston, the sea and its commerce, the life cars and motor-driven surfboats, the rescues of the past and future, men adrift on the seas of the world and foundering forever in the gales and currents along the coasts, meant nothing beside these few in the Coskata surfboat. He focused his great strength on this single purpose and found a balance between the forces of the storm and his own resolve. They pitched and waited in the freezing blast for the tide to turn.

Dusk comes early to Nantucket in January, and it was almost dark by the time the surfboat had swung clockwise on her tether and now lay a bit west of south. Chase knew they had to go whenever the tide could drive them, and he shouted and joshed the men. Tiredly they put out oars, pulled up the anchor, then struggled off to the west. Chase used his rowers to hold a northerly set, counting on the southeast current to give them a general westerly direction. They took plenty of slop with the waves on their starboard bow, and Chase urged the *Kirkham*'s mate and her black crewman to bailing. The boat moved into deeper water, and as the night came on, Chase suddenly saw, on the very rim of his world, the tiny, flashing point of Sankaty Light.

"Hey, boys!" he shouted. "There's old Sankaty and Joe Remsen having fried bluefish for supper with a bit of Medford rum and lime in hot water."

"Dang me, Skipper," said George Flood, "I wouldn't mind the rum, but Joe can keep the bluefish."

"George," said Walter Chase shaking his head sadly, "I can't make out how you fellers can call yourselves Nantucketers when you like that awful, smelly cod bet-ter'n a little fried blue."

This discussion, which ebbed and flowed at the sta-tion depending on who was cook that week, somehow cheered Jesse Eldridge immensely. "Walter," he said, loudly and firmly, "even them rich Boston summer folk won't give a nickel a pound for blues. You know that as well as I do."

Chase leaned on the oar and turned them a bit more northerly, staring off at the lighthouse. He roared with laughter. "Jesse, them Boston folk smack their lips over three-day boiled cabbage and corn beef, flaked cod that would turn a hog's stomach, and fin and haddy so hard it would break a shark's jaw. Hell's delight, they wouldn't even *notice* a nice hot little blue laying in a nest of parsley, new potatoes, and melted butter."

They rowed on and on toward the light, and the men turned now and then to stare at the pinpoint, so bright and yet so tiny against the black swirl of wind. When they turned back to where the *Kirkham* had been, they saw answering bright and tiny spots in Walter Chase's eyes somehow reflecting and focusing Sankaty.

By ten that night the wind was blowing a three-quarter gale, and the current was rotating to the north-east. They could not go against it, and Walter Chase ordered the anchor down again. Now the wind, filled with a fitful snow, was bitter, and the men slumped against each other, their sweat drying coldly under their clothes, their heads nodding. Chase continually worked the steering oar, roused the men as they drifted off into frozen sleep, ordered the bow crewmen to watch the chafing of the line, and continually rotated his head seeking the great seas moving in the dark. They suddenly appeared as dim, faintly phosphorescent mountains that dashed out of and into the dark at terrifying speeds.

In the intense and shouting dark, the seas loomed huge and unsuspected. There was a wildness about them, a wholly random cruelty. The storm had blown for two days and unusual current motions had been set going. Walter Chase's head swiveled back and forth. He sensed the movement, the surge and backflow. The chill ate at his bones, but his own cold resolve was more arctic still.

Chase Five examined the lumpy and stationary sea. He then examined the rate of change of the water profiles. This was a deadly business! The circulation due to wind stress had rotated the current further than usual to the east. This set up a possible amplification with the flow between Bass Rip and McBlair's Shoal. There was a statistical possibility of one or more resonant occurrences that night! Yet they were still relatively unlikely. No! Chase Five clamped the time flow even tighter and increased the gradient. Within minutes a resonance would actually occur! The wave would build at the north end of Rose and Crown, receiving energy from the cross flow and a sudden wind gust stress. It would break in a mile-long line just north of them and reach them cresting at eighteen feet. The chance of their staying upright was one in three. The chance of their not swamping was . . . nil!

Chase Five, within the theoretical bounds set by entropy flow requirements, stopped time utterly. The continuum waited as Chase Five's neural interconnections achieved a higher level of synthesis. He saw a single possibility. If this resonant wave was unlikely enough . . . yes . . . that was it! Extreme value probability theory could be modified within the time domain, providing that no significantly less likely event was occurring at that instant in the energy continuum. He could lower the expectation and make the wave more unlikely without interaction within the energy domain. Furthermore, it was not just the wave itself that was unlikely, but the wave interpreted by Chase Five, himself a most unlikely event.

That was it! He changed the probabilities, and the wave, instead of building towards its terrifying height, received its new energies at slightly different times and . . . No!

The wave was suddenly building again! Chase Five sensed some other manipulation. Staggered, he clamped tightly on the time flow and asked his first question:

"Who?"

When Keeper Chase modified the laws of extreme value probability within the continuum, he forced us time-using observers to become participants in his struggle with the storm. While highly unlikely events occur infrequently, they exercise a hugely disproportionate effect on the evolution of the continuum. Just as a coastline on Keeper Chase's world will lie unchanged for a hundred years, to be altered drastically by a single unlikely storm lasting a few hours, so the improbable but possible events in the evolution of stellar and information systems often determine the long-term character of huge volumes of energy and temporal space. We could not, then, allow such essential probabilities to be manipulated at the whim of energy storms and energy-users. Thus we intervened and canceled the change. Keeper Chase detected us at once and asked his first question. We decided to answer him . . . almost totally.

Chase Five received the full brunt of the information dump. Like the sky falling in from every angle, the answer to his question flowed faster than thought into his mind. It was an implosion of data, a total, sudden awareness of the continuum, of time and energy and information and their interactions. Of worlds and stars, creatures and spaces, hidden truths and intricate in-sights.

Chase Five was staggered. He clamped on the time flow and tried to organize it all. Like a swimmer, thrown deeply into the dark blue of the deep ocean, he fought and rose toward the light of day, moving through a boundless mass of data. Yet what was happening? Why was he so deeply involved with these others? How did the *Kirkham*, one in ten thousand among such schooners, and these men, a few among millions, come to be at the center of all this? Chase Five assimilated the focal points of the continuum, but he did not yet understand himself or the nature of his adversaries. Clamping and clamping on the time stream, he desper-ately asked his second question:

"God?"

Irony, in the sense understood by those in Keeper Chase's world group, is not a normal component of time-using organizations and duties. Yet Keeper Chase's second question to us achieved the exact essence of that special quality. For if there was a single conscious entity within the entire continuum at the moment who quali-fied as "God," in the sense of Keeper Chase's question, it was Keeper Chase himself. We could not determine how large an information excess Keeper Chase could tolerate, but his confusion seemed to offer us an oppor-tunity. We responded with the remaining information that we had withheld the first time: we showed Keeper Chase how the continuum was organized within its var-ious aspects and, finally, the nature of consciousness within this organization and its relationship with the in-formation, time, and energy aspects of the whole.

The second dump of information was not as exten-sive, but far more staggering. For Chase Five finally saw himself within the total continuum. He saw the cir-cularity and hermetic nature of his activity at the *Kirk-ham,* the unlikely, really senseless character of the rescue and how unimportant, really meaningless were the men now barely alive in the wet and pitching boat. Good Lord, what was the point anyway? His control wavered and time began to slip. The wind moved back towards its own natural pace. The seas became more independent. . . .

Now wait! Chase Five, in his puzzlement and despair, still processed data. And suddenly he saw the fallacy, the problem with their attacks against him. He steadied and clamped time. Yes! Yes, of course! He was stronger! The circularity didn't matter! What mattered was *only* the event! Everything led to that. And the more *unlikely* it was, the more *essential* it became. Yes! He, Walter Chase, Keeper of the Coskata Life Saving Station, was exactly and completely his own justification. And now Chase Five struck back at them. Masterful in his total control of information, gigantic astride the interlaced worlds of energy and time, he stated his third and final question. But because he completely dominated the continuum in all its aspects, he no longer asked. For he knew with complete certainty that none of them could deny what he stated.

"I am central to the evolution of the continuum. My control and my improbability are proof of that!"

At once the growing wave received its various inputs in harmless and likely sequences and passed under the Coskata boat as a huge but almost unnoticed roller. And with that, the storm on the Nantucket South Shoals began to die. For it, like all storms, had to obey the laws of probabilities, and after two harsh days, it was moving off and softening as it went.

Walter Chase, the steering oar now inboard as the wind slackened, saw that dawn and the new tide were coming together. "All right, boys! This time we'll get there!" he shouted. In came the anchor and off they went, the great seas cresting no longer, the wind lessening, and the temperature rising as snow squalls came and went, gray against a dull dawn.

On and on they rowed, and Walter Chase now became aware that Perkins looked odd. His eyes were shining, liquid and bright, and his cheeks were much too red and also shining strangely. The boy rowed as strongly as any, but Chase watched him with more and more concern.

"Perkins," shouted Walter Chase, "see if that mate from the *Kirkham* can relieve you for a while."

But Perkins was thinking of Abby on the beach. She would probably be there when they came in, for her brother was in the surfside crew and he would have told her that they were out. "I'm okay, Skipper," he said in a voice that Chase could barely hear. Chase peered through the snow at the rowers. Perkins was very sick. Perkins must . . .

Chase Six realized that Perkins was dying. The boy's level of consciousness integration had slipped drastically. Desperate, Chase Six plummeted down Perkins' time line seeking solutions everywhere. But the lessening of the storm had sapped his abilities. He could no longer clamp on time or integrate his hard-won information to tasks like this. Yet his very agony gave him the control to achieve the data that crushed, and crushed again, his hopes. How tenuous and marvelous self-awareness was in the continuum! How delicate, beyond yet embedded within the energy system, linked with loops of information, operating within and yet outside of time. Perkins had driven himself, and been driven by Chase, beyond reintegration. And yet Perkins was filled with joy! Within himself, Chase Six finally wept. And as he did, his powers fled away in an unending stream like the fog of a harsh night evaporating as the morning sun pierced through and through it.

Keeper Chase's great time-based powers failed as the emergency abated. Unable to maintain the temporal gradient without the urgency of the storm, he could no longer retrieve or even sustain his vast information resource in any practical sense. Yet he had defeated us and dominated the continuum at almost every moment of his adventure. Staggered after his second question and the implications of our answers, he went on to his final and greatest feat. He dared us to prove that he was not an essential evolutionary force within the continuum. Since such a determination would require understanding of other continuums, if such exist, and that necessary understanding would involve an information entropy gradient so vast that it could not even be theoretically sustained, he effectively blocked all further intervention.

But in the end he could not save his youngest crewman. He learned that conscious self-awareness is the most improbable and delicate balance of all within the continuum. Even his great strengths could not bring Surfman Perkins back from the temporal disintegration toward which he had slipped. If the energy-users of Keeper Chase's world group understood how novel and tenuous such consciousness actually is, they would surely behave far differently than they do.

The actual effects of his alterations within the continuum will only become evident in distant times and through much statistical activity on our part. But his greatest effect was the introduction of his third question, to which we may never have a complete or satisfactory answer. Of course, the so-called heroes of Keeper Chase's world group always have this as their primary purpose—that is, the introduction of central and intractable questions.

At a little after nine in the morning of the twenty-first of January, the Coskata boat was sighted through the fading snow from the bluffs of Siasconset, eight miles south of the shore they had left the day before. Soon the entire community was out on the beach, silently watching the surfboat moving toward them, steered by Walter Chase standing at the stern.

The 'Sconset schoolteacher, a young, thin man who had spent two years reading literature at Harvard College, ran up the bluff, a dozen children behind him. As he topped the rise, the thin sun suddenly pierced the damp air and illuminated the tiny boat and its huge captain, looming back even a half mile out.

"Godfreys mighty!" exclaimed the young man to no one in particular. "It's Captain Ahab himself!" for he believed that literature and life were contiguous.

"Naw, tain't," said Widow Tilton. "Hit's Skipper Chase and the Coskata surfboat." She turned to stare at the young man and laughed. "Hit's the only red surfboat around. Skipper painted it red after the Muskeget boat was almost lost in the ice last December, 'cause no one could see it. They wrote from Boston. Said it was nonregulation. Skipper Chase, he wrote back. Don't remember all he wrote, but there was something in his letter about them desk navigators whose experience with ice amounted to sucking it out of their whiskey and sodas at lunch."

The schoolteacher had been only half listening, but now he turned and grinned at Widow Tilton. "He said that to them, did he?" The young man stared again at the approaching boat and then ran down the sand hill. "Come on, boys!" he shouted back at his class. "Let's help get this boat up!"

The Coskata boat grounded silently in a long swell, and a huge crowd waded into the backwash and pulled her up the slick sand. Everyone tried to help the men get out, yet still no one cheered. Instead, soft and kind words flew everywhere, and joy and comfort seemed to warm the very beach.

Walter Chase boomed at the Macy boys to get their oxen and haul the boat up to the dunes. Then he turned and saw Perkins helped and held by Abby Coffin. The boy could no longer speak. Chase smiled at the girl. "Abby, don't take him home. Get him to your sister-in-law's house here in 'Sconset and put him to bed. Get him warm, quick as you can!"

But Abby knew. She could see the emptiness in Roland Perkins's eyes, his fevered cheeks. She wept, so full of grief and pride and love that she could not speak either. But always afterwards she remembered how sharp and yet sad Skipper Chase's eyes had been when he spoke to her and how completely he dominated the beach in those moments at the end of the rescue.

"Isaiah!" shouted Walter Chase. The youngster dashed up, beaming all over his face, so proud that Skipper Chase had picked him out of the great crowd.

"Yessir, Skipper!" He grinned.

"How's that hoss of yours, Isaiah?" said Walter Chase, and now he grinned too.

"Fastest hoss on Nantucket, Skipper," replied the boy promptly. "She'll win at the summer fair for sure!"

"Well, you climb aboard that nag and hustle for town. Find my wife and tell her we got back safe. Then find the rest of them. You know where the crew's folks live?"

The boy nodded and dashed off. Everyone was now moving up the beach toward the village. Each crewman of the *Kirkham* or man of Coskata was surrounded by residents helping them along, throwing coats or blankets over their shoulders, talking at them about the impossible miracle of the rescue.

Captain McCloud of the *Kirkham* staggered along between his huge black crewman and the Widow Tilton, herself well over six feet and two hundred and fifty pounds. Suddenly the old man pitched forward on his knees, pulling the weakened Negro down with him. "Dear God!" he shouted. "Thank Thee for this deliverance! Thank Thee for sparing Thy humble servants. Thank Thee . . ."

Widow Tilton pulled the old man to his feet and, looking back, saw Walter Chase, huge against the dull sun, his tiny eyes like daytime stars. "You better not worry about thanking God, mister," she suddenly said loudly. "It was Skipper Chase got you back here, and don't ever forget that!"

"Walter." It was his uncle beside him. "When they said you was coming in, I put on a gallon of coffee. Come on. Why, man, you're shaking like a leaf!"

Indeed, Walter Chase suddenly was shaking. He could not stop it, and he let his uncle lead him over the dune and down to the little house with its roaring driftwood-filled fire and the huge blackened pot of powerful coffee.

"Uncle," said Walter Chase as he sipped from a huge mug, "I'm shaking so damn much I've got to drink this outside."

He opened the door and stepped back into the narrow, rutted 'Sconset street just as Joe Remsen, sharp in his blue uniform and issue cap, driving the dapper black and gold-trimmed buggy of the Light House Service, pulled by a smart, high-stepping bay, whirled around the corner and pulled up short in a cloud of dust.

"God in Heaven, Walter!" shouted Joe Remsen. "You all did get back!"

Walter Chase, his huge hands still shaking continuously in the thin, cold morning, looked smiling up at his old friend. "Joe, that's just the handsomest one-hoss outfit on the island," he said simply.

"Walter, they say she came apart less than an hour after you got them off! I saw her masts go down at noon yesterday from the tower!"

Walter Chase stretched suddenly and stared, quite piercingly, back at Joe Remsen. "Well," he said, "we didn't need her after the crew got off, did we, Joe?"

At the time his old friend thought Walter Chase was joking, and he laughed out loud. But thinking back on that moment in later years, he realized that Walter Chase had meant what he said. The *Kirkham* had been allowed to collapse because she somehow wasn't *needed* any more. Yet he never asked about it again, but only wondered.

Joe Remsen climbed down from the buggy and shook his head. "We figured you were goners. That damn tug went as far as Great Point and then turned back last night. Too blamed rough, they said, the rotten cowards! By God, Walter, there won't never be another rescue like this one! You better believe that! They're going to build that canal one of these days. Them gasoline engines'll get better and they'll put them in the surfboats. God Almighty, you took seven of them off. Not one lost. Twenty-six hours out in that smother! It's a miracle! Why, man, you moved heaven and earth . . ."

The hot coffee drained its warmth through Walter

Chase, and suddenly he felt drowsy. "Joe, we never did try a drail for squeteague out there. Just too blamed busy the whole time . . ."

And the two old friends grinned and chuckled at each other in the winter sunlight on a 'Sconset street.

Vermeer's Window

Gordon Eklund

Artistic creation is a mysterious process to
nearly everyone, artists included. It's even
harder for an unsuccessful artist to understand
how it's done. But science continues to devise
methods of storing and imparting information
in ways that will be more and more useful.

Question: If it were to become possible to
feed into a man's mind so much knowledge
about an artist of the past that the man could
actually paint the pictures just as the original
artist had done it, would this be "useful"?
Perhaps he might paint masterpieces whose
originals have been lost . . .

Gordon Eklund, an artist with words, has
some fascinating thoughts on the matter. His
story of a man who devotes his life to such
an experiment tells us quite a lot—and suggests even more.

The painting emerges like a risen bird from the burnt
substance of light alone. The artist draws no firm
lines—either upon or beneath the painting. The colors—blue and gold predominate—flow automatically.
As, over the course of many days, the face and shoulder
of a wide-eyed young woman appear upon his easel, the
artist reacts with excitement. This is the painting commonly identified as "Girl in a Turban," and it is, he
believes, the most profound achievement of Vermeer's

brief career—a painting as subtle, ambiguous, mysterious, and still as the play of sunlight through a half-open window. The swirl of a pearl earring is created in the sudden, swift motion of his brush. The artist is stricken with awe as the woman's cape, a green, magical garment, appears beneath his hand. He tries to paint with his eyes shut tightly, unable to bear the magnificent sight so near, but, only human, he soon must peek.

Jan Vermeer (1632–75) is the most enigmatic of great artists. Not only do his works defy precise interpretation, but little or nothing is known of his beliefs, influences, theories, or life. Born in Delph, Holland, Vermeer apparently achieved some degree of local fame, if not wealth, during his own lifetime, but it wasn't until the early years of the twentieth century that his fewer than forty works were rediscovered and hailed as the creations of fluent genius that they most undoubtedly are. With few exceptions, Vermeer's paintings depict a few figures—often only one—against the space of a single room. The faces of women predominate, and some critics have seen in these recurring individuals possibly autobiographical figures. Vermeer's work is further marked by a fascination with the shadings of natural sunlight. Some observers have asserted that the quality of the light in Delph must have been different from that found elsewhere in the world. More likely, the difference is in the painter, not his light.

The artist as a young boy is burdened by no ambition except to become a great painter. Born in New York City in 1988, he embarks upon his first pilgrimage to the Old World at the age of fourteen, only a few months subsequent to the untimely deaths of both parents. While in Europe, the artist does little but visit one museum after another, where he sits for hours and hours beneath the glorious creations of the old masters. It has been remarked that few individuals are capable of viewing a single painting for longer than it takes to peel and eat an orange. The artist, even as a youth, is one of these few individuals. At eighteen, his inherited fortune now secure, he revisits Europe to enroll as a student at the most famous of Paris's great art schools. Within two weeks he has left. According to his instructors, the young artist stands totally devoid of profound talent. His hands shake at the easel; he fails to control his brush stroke. His sense of color and paint are acknowledged to be masterful, but he has failed to indicate any ability to transform the gorgeous visions of his mind into a completed canvas. He is called a great critic, a poor painter.

Alone and despondent in twenty-first century Europe, the young artist falls in with a decadent crowd. Kapp, one of this group, tells the artist of a rare process which makes use of computer fine analyses and brain-tapping facilities in order to transform selected people into individuals other than themselves. By means of this process, it is possible for anyone to become nearly anyone he wishes, as long as sufficient data exist concerning the projected new identity. Kapp wished to take advantage of the process himself but was coldly rejected for possible transformation by the corporation marketing the process because of a personal deficiency in funding. The young artist, who is incredibly rich, obtains the name of the corporation from Kapp and immediately books passage to the relevant Eastern European capital. There, a representative of the corporation explains the transformation process in somewhat more detail. "The philosophical foundation which makes our process work," says the representative, "is the concept of character determinism. In other words, given the facts concerning any man—and I mean *all* the facts, about his life, his friends, his family, his world—then that man must nearly always be what he will be. The matter of implanting preselected data within the brain is a simple one indeed—we've been doing it for years, beginning with computers and working up to flesh-and-blood people. Our corporation, through this transformation process, has taken this old technique and applied it to its fullest extent. All we ask you to do is give us a name. Who do you want to be? It may be any man or woman you wish, real and imaginary, though the former is generally preferred, both by us and our usual clientele. Once we have the name, then we set to work. The key factor here is our membership in the International Data Network, which as you probably know links up nearly all the world's largest and most sophisticated computers, including several whose very existence is a closely guarded state secret. What the Data Network is then able to provide us—at an immense cost, I can assure you—is a socio-historical collage of the individual chosen. This collage is put together—no human being or finite group of human beings could ever hope to duplicate the process—from all the data available from any conceivable source concerning the individual and his world. Once this collage is implanted within the memory circuits of your brain, you will then be, I can assure you, that very individual. What is more, as a bonus, because no memory erasure is required, you will be simultaneously aware of your past identity and thus fully able to appreciate the nuances of being two people at once. The process, I admit this candidly, does fail perhaps once in fifty tries. Should that happen in your case, a full refund will gladly be rendered." When the artist, after carefully considering all he has heard, tentatively suggests the name of Jan Vermeer, the representative is at first anxious. He agrees to consult with the corporate engineers, who are equally doubtful but also willing to try. So little is known of the life of the so-called Enigma of Delph that the challenge facing the Data Network is undoubtedly immense. Still, the engineers insist that the possibilities of success remain distinctly high. Vermeer was very much a product of a particular time and place—seventeenth-century Holland—a fact which may prove more consequential to his development as an artist than mere boyhood memories. The artist's own expectations of success do not run high, and yet, returning to Western Europe after the completion of the operation, he is willing to accept that he is now Vermeer. His brain insists upon telling him this is so, and he does not choose, for the moment, to doubt it.

He settles in Amsterdam, a city that lies spiritually distant from the sleepy, silent Delph of Vermeer's one known cityscape but which is, the artist believes, as close as he might hope to come in twenty-first-century terms to that magical vista from the past. He retains, as guaranteed, all his old memories, but it is his identity as Vermeer which quickly comes to dominate his every conscious act. With his few remaining funds, he rents a small room in an old house and sets up his easel beside the single meshed window. He begins to paint, but the results are at first disastrous, as far from the art of Vermeer as the scribbled splashings of any talentless youth. Full of bitterness, he contemplates a demand for the immediate return of his own identity but then recalls that Vermeer's earliest accepted work, the Venetian-influenced "Diana and the Nymphs," was not produced until after Vermeer had turned twenty-two. The artist realizes that he must therefore wait for his own dawning moment of inspiration, and so each day until the last smog-bitten rays of the yellow sun vanish from view, he sits motionlessly in front of his barren easel. He sleeps long hours but eats only infrequently. At last, two months subsequent to his own twenty-second birthday, his fingers begin to move of their own accord. Soon enough, he is actually painting. At the bottom center of the canvas there appears quite magically a small white napkin which resembles in shape the image of a dove about to drink. The artist recognizes this as a crucial element in Vermeer's "Diana." He continues to paint, his fingers moving at a speed quite exclusive of his own free will. After many weeks, the finished work stands before him. Overcome by excitement, he rides his motorbike to The Hague, where he is able to view the original work by the first Vermeer. As far as his sharp eye can deduce, nothing—not even a single casual brush stroke—diverges in the slightest detail from his own recently completed work. Back in Amsterdam, he changes lodgings. With money borrowed from a family lawyer, he purchases a small store, which he opens as an art gallery. The first work that he hangs for sale is his own "Diana and the Nymphs." Soon, in his adjoining studio, his hands are at work creating "The Procuress."

In time the artist takes in marriage a wife, who will eventually bear him eleven children. The appearance neither of the wife nor the children surprises him, for he is aware that one of the few known biographical facts concerning Vermeer is that he was married and had nearly a dozen children. Like Catherina Vermeer, Bonnie, his new wife, is one year older than her husband. She explains how, at twelve, she left the home of her father, an accountant in America, and first came to Europe at the age of sixteen. She admits to two previous marriages, and he often suspects that, prior to their marriage, Bonnie lived as a common street prostitute. Little in her manner or bearing has the least resemblance to the wealthy and respectable Catherina, but the artist bears in mind that it is he who is Vermeer and not Bonnie who is Catherina. She remains loyal to him and he feels an often fervent love and devotion toward her. His children, even though he remains uncertain of their actual names or identities, are equally dear to him. He can never be sure whether this love is being excited in his heart or in Vermeer's. Frequently, on quiet evenings, he sits beside Bonnie, who is experiencing tri-dee television, and studies the contours of her ripe, plump, cowish face. Before his staring eyes, her visage will then transform itself into an image far deeper and more ethereal than her own slack, pink flesh. He is convinced that what he is witnessing at these moments is nothing less than the true face of Vermeer's Catherina. Some of the features he glimpses seem similar to those he will eventually paint as "Girl with a Flute" and "Girl in a Red Hat," but the vision is never sufficiently specific for him to claim to have solved this particular biographical mystery.

The artist's studio consists of a single cramped cockroach-infested room adjacent to his gallery. In truth, the original purpose of the room was to serve as an automotive garage. There is only one window, which faces north and is heavily meshed against possible late-night burglars, and little room for furnishings of any kind. In spite of this, he has no trouble at all from the time of "Young Woman Asleep" onward in painting the sun-bathed room, with its two-paneled window, that serves as a common setting for so much of Vermeer's mature art. It is neither his mind nor his eye which does the actual painting for him; it is his fingers alone that do the work. The muscles twitch ecstatically as the vision of the artist courses wildly through them. He could no more refuse to paint what they demand than he could willingly cease to make his heart pump blood.

His art dealership does not prosper. Because of his refusal to deal in works dated later than the seventeenth century, only art of modest quality comes into his hands. He stocks his own works, too, of course, but the prices he chooses to ask for them are not severe. (Neither were those asked by the first Vermeer.) His patrons are often amused at discovering a work such as "Soldier and Smiling Girl" decorating a tiny corner of the gallery. A few, those most knowledgeable about painting, are more amazed than amused. They will stand staring for minutes at a time before finally turning away with a startled laugh. "Why, that replica is so good it might be the original." He replies honestly, "It is not the original." (It is, of course, *an* original.) In his spare time, while Bonnie or one of the children mind the gallery, he walks the streets of Amsterdam. The stark contrast between this exterior world of the twenty-first century and that interior seventeenth-century world which, as Vermeer, he paints constantly astonishes him. His favorite days are those in which the actual orb of the sun can be glimpsed past the dank yellow cloud which hovers continually above. Crime is, of course, rampant in Amsterdam as elsewhere, and the artist is frequently robbed, mugged, and assaulted. On one occasion, he is stripped of his clothes by young thugs and forced to return home naked. Because of a severe pollution alert, only a few small children wander outside to observe his passage. These soon turn their heads aside in apparent shame and disgust. His dignity as an adult has been shattered in their eyes. Only the knowledge of his true identity—he is Vermeer, one of the half-dozen greatest painters in the history of the world—sustains him. Despite such agonies, the only parts of the city he takes special care to avoid are those housing the city's few remaining museums, even though four of Vermeer's most masterful paintings are hung there, including one, "Woman Pouring Milk," that he has only recently completed. At home in his studio, he keeps detailed notes on all his work. The exact chronology of Vermeer's career has long been a subject of critical dispute, and he hopes to solve this mystery along with many others.

At times a painting will come to him that is a total surprise. These are, of course, the lost works of Vermeer and will in the end total thirteen. Most are similar in subject matter to other known works. He paints: "Woman Seated in Thought," "Two Soldiers and a Girl," "Woman with Pearls," and an unexpectedly religious work, "Christ and Two Apostles." The titles are necessarily of his own devising and sheer guesswork, for his fingers refuse to divulge their secret intentions, even while creating these previously unknown works. He hesitates to place any of the paintings in the gallery but finally relents from curiosity and hangs "Christ and Two Apostles." The sum he is spontaneously offered for the work far exceeds the most he has ever received for a single painting. This gesture pleases him deeply, yet he refuses and thereafter keeps the unknown paintings safely hidden in a dusty corner of his studio.

He is plagued at times by a certain confusion between his earlier self as a painter and his present identity as Vermeer. When he comes to paint "Street in Delph," he removes his easel from the studio for the first time and positions it and himself on a nearby avenue. His view here consists of ruined houses, broken windows, two seedy cheese shops, and three aging women who are most likely prostitutes. His fingers rush to interpret this vision as two adjoining brick houses and three faceless working women. The sky, presently saturated in a thick yellow-brown mist, becomes a lovely, cloud-flecked blue. Since he is Vermeer, he must paint what Vermeer has painted. Still, once the work at hand is complete and ready for sale, he returns to the spot and bravely, as an experiment, attempts to paint what he actually sees, wondering how Vermeer would interpret contemporary reality. In spite of his stern efforts, his fingers soon go stiff and refuse to move until he finally relents, stands, and returns to the studio. He makes a second attempt on a second day but once more fails. Some days after this incident, Bonnie, in bed beside him, says, "If you're such a great artist, how come you've never tried to do a picture of me?" Something makes him agree at once to her suggestion. (Perhaps Vermeer in his time had agreed to a similar request.) The following day, she sits for him, but the portrait soon turns stilted, ugly, and poorly colored; it lacks both unity and purpose. In despair because his fingers have produced such masterpieces, he takes a butcher knife and destroys the unfinished work. Bonnie, in a rage, refuses to speak to him for nine days. He wonders if a parallel might exist with some similar marital rif in Vermeer's own life. If so, this would tend to indicate that his wife's face did not appear among his works. But it is impossible to say for sure.

Soon after he has completed and hung "Two Gentlemen and a Lady with a Glass of Wine," a famous art critic from New York enters his shop. The critic's practiced eye immediately falls upon the recent work and he hastens to a corner to study it. After several minutes silent observation, he beckons the artist to join him. "This," the critic says breathlessly, "is simply amazing. Except for the faces, I'd swear it was the genuine Vermeer." (The artist neglects to point out that the faces visible in the so-called original painting were retouched at a later date by an artist far inferior to Vermeer. What appears on this canvas are Vermeer's original creations.) "Who painted it?" the critic demands. "It was I," the artist admits. The critic stares. "Thank God you're an honest man. I swear you could be greater than Van Meegeren if you wished."

Van Meegeren. Even the hint of such an accusation is enough to startle and then depress the artist. Hans van Meegeren was the great art forger of the middle twentieth century who fooled the art world for years with a succession of fake "Vermeers." The artist believes his own identity to lie far from that of a petty forger: he is as much Vermeer himself as the seventeenth-century Dutchman who first bore that name. Still, he cannot wholly rid his mind of the critic's foul innuendo. At last he boards a jettrain to Rotterdam, where "Meeting at Emmaeus," Van Meegeren's most successful fake "Vermeer," hangs in a secluded museum corner. For some hours, to the bemusement even of a guard, he studies the work. By the time he turns homeward, his heart and soul are much relieved. Van Meegeren, he now understands, was a forger strictly produced by his own limited time; his work, though curious, is utterly without value today. Van Meegeren's brief success lay in his ability to paint works patterned in the mold of how Vermeer was perceived in the 1930s. But Vermeer has since changed, as all great artists must, and Van Meegeren has not. Studying his own works at home in the studio, the artist remains convinced that he is Vermeer, not Van Meegeren. He does not paint in the manner of Vermeer; he paints as Vermeer.

His primary responsibility in the creation of the paintings lies in acquiring the proper tools: paints, canvas, brushes. Once such mechanical ends have been met, the paintings will then flow automatically from his fingertips. He may err in the applications of a particular brush stroke but, when he does, his fingers immediately rise to correct the mistake. There is no need for thought, consideration, or decision. He recalls the considerable critical speculation over the possible use by Vermeer of a spectroscope. His own work can neither deny nor affirm this possibility. He makes no use of such an instrument and yet the odd perspective that led many critics to this theory remains an integral part of the finished paintings. He is Vermeer, but who was Vermeer? As the years pass, this unanswered question disturbs him more and more. He realizes how little he has learned of the man he has become. If he were to write a book on the subject, what could he say that would be new? He could describe in detail the manner by which Vermeer produced a canvas such as "Woman Weighing Pearls" (a work he has only recently completed), but that would be all. He knows the *how* but not the *why*. Theories, principles, motivations, and beliefs continue to elude him. His fingers know but will not speak.

The artist commences a passionate affair with a young bohemian girl who lives next door. She is tall, with a long rectangular face, full lips, and small brown eyes. She claims to work as a civil servant but the clutter of articles in her rooms suggests a life of crime. He finds in her figure and character the subject for his painting of "Woman with a Flute." Bonnie, when informed of the affair by a neighborhood warden, refuses to take legal remedies. The artist, deeply wounded by this inaction, confronts his wife alone in the room they share. Stricken by guilt as well as fury, he unburdens himself as never before. He confesses the fact of his dual identity and demands to know which it is that Bonnie truly loves. She is amazed and shakes her head. "Why, I love you, of course. Who else?" "But that is what I am asking," says the artist. "Which of me is it that you love? Is it me as I was born, or is it me as I have become—Vermeer?" Bonnie remains puzzled. "Why, both of you, I guess. It's the only way I've ever known you." He refuses to be so easily pacified and perseveres. "But you can't love two people at once. It's got to be one or the other." Bonnie laughs. "Are you sure?" She nods toward the adjoining house. "Did she make a choice?" Contrite, the artist breaks off his affair with the young girl. He puzzles over the possibility of a similar act of passion in the life of the earlier Vermeer. Within a few weeks the young girl is conscripted into the army fighting in Yugoslavia. When the conflict is at last resolved, the girl fails to return. He notices her name among a list of casualties but remains unmoved. She was more Vermeer's lover than his own, and Vermeer refuses to mourn.

A leading American astronomer announces the approach toward the earth of a large comet, and this is immediately interpreted by many as an indication of impending doom. As the comet draws closer, the end of the world is generally proclaimed, and a series of disturbances ensues. When the comet first appears in the sky, the turmoil becomes much worse. The artist decides to postpone his walks through the city for the duration of the trouble. One evening, all of the houses on the nearest two city blocks are burned to the ground. His gallery is spared and, in the privacy of his studio, his fingers work to complete two of Vermeer's most distinctive works, "The Geographer," and ironically, "The Astronomer." The artist, who seldom attempts to interpret his own work, is unable not to see in these questing, probing figures all that was once most promising in human science. It was the questions that these men dared to ask which for a time forestalled the horror of existence, but once the questions were answered and the answers found to be lacking, the dark undercurrent of humanity's ocean again rose to the surface. Through the window, the artist observes a black cloud hanging like a wreath above the ruined city. Even the shining comet fails to penetrate this bleak veil, and its disappearance serves to calm the general turmoil. Within a few weeks, an army has appeared to restore order and begin the process of reconstruction. The artist resumes his walks but continues to paint in a furious manner. Inside of a week, he produces "Lady Standing at the Virginals." The sight of it moves him to tears. He attempts to explain the experience to Bonnie but fails. It is not the sight of the painting, he decides, but the sound. In Vermeer's work, harmony can be heard to speak.

On a late summer's Sunday afternoon, while Bonnie is at church and the children at play, a small, withered, bald-headed man with broad eyes and large ears enters the shop. Going at once to the wall upon which such recent creations as "Lady Playing a Guitar" and "The Astronomer" are hanging, the small man laughs sharply. The gallery is empty, as it most usually is on a Sunday, and the two of them are quite alone. Turning away from the wall, the small man approaches the counter by a circuitous route that allows him to peep into every shadowed corner as a precaution against hidden intruders. "Vermeer," he says, extending a hand toward the artist, "I am Picasso." The artist is startled by this unanticipated revelation, but subsequent conversation (conducted by both in harsh, furtive whispers) reveals that this small man has become the great twentieth-century Spanish artist by means similar to those used by the artist in becoming Vermeer. "Well," says the man who is now Picasso, "so what have you found out about the mysterious Vermeer?" The artist is forced to hang his head at this question and reveal his limited success. "I know that he was a very great painter and I know exactly how he applied his paint during the course of each work." "Yes, yes," Picasso says impatiently, "that is all well and good, but what of the man's motivation? What is the character that led him to produce such great works?" "I . . ." The artist feels shamed. "I do not know. The paintings flow automatically from my fingertips—my brain learns nothing." The small man expresses his shock and surprise. "Why, that is how it always must be. It is necessary for one to deduce the truth from, so to speak, the facts at hand. With Picasso, I must admit the task was not difficult." "Oh?" says the artist. "And what then was Picasso's character?" The small man grins (his teeth are unclean): "A charlatan. An absolute charlatan." Irritated by this facile slander, the artist demands a quick explanation. The small man says, "Pablo was no genius—I found that out right away. Do you know why he painted the way he did? Of course you don't, but I'm him, and I know. He painted exactly what the audience of his time demanded, but—and this is the crucial point—what the audience demanded were works of genius. So Pablo, to fill that need, became a genius, but is he the one who deserves the credit? I say no, never. The inspiration lay with the audience, not with the painter. Picasso was a whore with a few tubes of paint—his audience was a creature of true genius." Later the man who claims to be Picasso purchases two inexpensive seventeenth-century landscapes and departs. The artist is greatly disturbed by this visit and goes over and over what he has learned from the small man in hopes of uncovering a fallacy in his thinking. When Bonnie returns, she carries beneath an arm the two landscapes. She glares at the artist and says, "Damn it, what are you up to now? I found these things outside in the trash. We haven't enough money to go throwing such things away." On an impulse, the artist shakes his head sadly. "They are rank forgeries, I am afraid. While you were gone, a man came to me with absolute proof."

He believes he should be seeing the world with the eyes of Vermeer, and yet he finds almost no beauty at all outside his own cloistered studio. The contrast is too immense. The jettrains roar past his home, shaking the studio like a leaf caught in a wind; yet he can observe the stillness and silence of "Maid Holding Out a Letter to her Mistress." He discovers a child of nine starving in a secluded street, and her eyes speak to him of lifetimes endured in the passing of a day; but he also knows the passive otherworldliness of "Girl in a Turban." The streets he walks are a mad cacophony of destruction and construction, falling concrete and rising steel; he views the mysterious orderliness of "View of Delph." The spirit of the artist is like a maddened pendulum, thrust wildly from one extreme to another. A great despair overwhelms him, and in his studio one afternoon after completing Vermeer's masterwork, "An Artist in His Studio," he contemplates suicide and raises a knife to his chest, but before he can successfully plunge the sharp blade into his heart, too many questions rise to assail him. Did the first Vermeer suffer from despair? Did he once—perhaps at this very time in his life—attempt suicide? No, no, the artist realizes. He can become only what has already been lived. Vermeer did not kill himself and neither can he. Dropping the dagger, the artist rushes outside. He runs madly down the garbage-strewn streets of his neighborhood. The contrast remains: beauty and ugliness; order and chaos; pain and love. To survive, he must make his spirit blind to all that his fingers do not paint.

A wizened priest from a nearby cathedral visits the gallery one day and tells the artist, "My wife has told me of the excellence of your work. I would like to offer you a commission, if I may." Because of the nearby hovering presence of Bonnie, the artist agrees to accept the commission. Their poverty has increased with the passing years. The priest desires an allegorical painting on a New Testament theme. That same night, at Bonnie's urging, the artist sets to work in his studio. By the third day, he is aware that what his fingers are creating is the "Allegory of Faith," a work commonly accepted as Vermeer's very last. Surprised at the suddenness of this event, he takes time to calculate and determines that his present age is thirty-eight. Because Vermeer did not die until he was forty-three, that leaves him five full years in which to live without art. Almost deliberately, it takes him six months to complete the finished "Allegory." The wizened priest, angered at the delay, refuses to pay the artist more than half the agreed commission. The artist closes up his studio and never paints again.

During the final five years of his life, the artist finds that his love for his wife has grown stronger. He takes a new and powerful interest in his surviving children and even memorizes, for the first time, their complete names. Often now the entire family takes long walks through the closely guarded paths of the open city parks. At these times, alone with his wife while the children play, the artist reveals many of the concerns that have lately come to dominate his mind. He has spent many hours in the careful study of Vermeer's work; he has discovered little of value but now believes that this failure may be of significance in itself. He explains to Bonnie: "The greatness of an artist lies not in his mind, which may be a very ordinary one indeed, but rather in his fingertips or, to be less concrete, in his soul. Most people, if asked, will say that a great artist must also be a great man, but such is rarely, if ever, the case. When great artists fail to express great thoughts, we either blame ourselves or the limitations of the language, but a great artist must invariably express great thoughts—as they should, through their work. Take, for example, the seventeenth-century Dutch painter Jan Vermeer. His paintings express the thought that our perception of reality really consists of nothing beyond the observable effects of sunlight. Is this a great thought, a truly profound one? I do not think so—not as I have expressed it—not in words. But the paintings Vermeer created in order to express this thought—now they are great works indeed." Bonnie seems puzzled by this outburst. Shaking her head tentatively, she says, "But I thought you were Vermeer. You told me that once." The artist says, "No, I was mistaken." "But you had an operation." "True, but it was a failure." "Then," says Bonnie, "you are not a great artist yourself." He pauses upon the path

and speaks slowly: "No, I think I am. I am a great artist, yes, but I am not Vermeer. There can be only one
Vermeer and he as been dead more than three
hundred years. I am someone else—me. I speak to my
own age, having seen and endured these times." "But
aren't your paintings all the same?" asked Bonnie. "The
same as this other man's—Vermeer's?" "They are the
same," says the artist, "but I am different." In this, the
artist is convinced that he has at last discovered Ver
meer.

The Man Who Had No Idea

Thomas M. Disch

Thomas M. Disch, one of the finest thinkers and stylists in science fiction, has been too long away from the field—but his fans were delighted to see him return in full strength during 1978. Two new sf novels by him will probably be in print by the time you read the following subtle and funny novelette about a young man trying to gain a license to speak in public.

Disch is currently at work, in collaboration with Charles Naylor, on a long historical novel.

At first he'd assumed that he'd failed. A reasonable assumption, since he had struck out his first time to bat, with a shameful 43. But when two weeks had gone by and there was still no word from the Board of Examiners, he wondered if maybe he'd managed to squeak through. He didn't see how he could have. The examiner, a wizened, white-haired fuddy-duddy whose name Barry instantly forgot, had been hostile and aggressive right from the word go, telling Barry that he thought his handshake was too sincere. He directed the conversation first to the possible dangers of excessive sunbathing, which was surely an oblique criticism of Barry's end-of-August tan and the leisure such a tan implied, then started in on the likelihood that dolphins were as intelligent as people. Barry, having entered the cubicle resolved to stake all his chips on a tactic of complete candor, had said, one, he was too young to worry about skin cancer, and two, he had no interest in animals except as meat. This started the examiner off on the psychic experiences of some woman he'd read about in *Reader's Digest*. Barry couldn't get a toehold anywhere on the smooth façade of the man's compulsive natter. He got the feeling, more and more, that *he* was keeping score and the old fart was being tested, an attitude that did not bode well. Finally, with ten minutes left on the clock, he'd just up and left, which was not, strictly speaking, a violation. It did imply that some kind of closure had been achieved, which definitely was not the case; he'd panicked, pure and simple. A fiasco from which he'd naturally feared the worst in the form of a letter addressed to Dear Applicant. ("We regret to inform you, etc. . . .") But possibly the old fart had been making things deliberately difficult, testing him; possibly his reactions hadn't been that entirely inappropriate. Possibly he'd passed.

When another two weeks went by without the Board of Examiners saying boo, he couldn't stand the suspense any longer and went down to Centre Street to fill out a form that asked basically where did he stand. A clerk coded the form and fed it into the computer. The computer instructed Barry to fill out another form, giving more details. Fortunately he'd brought the data the computer wanted, so he was able to fill out the second form on the spot. After a wait of less than ten minutes, his number lighted up on the board and he was told to go to Window 28.

Window 28 was the window that issued licenses: he had passed!

"I passed," he announced incredulously to the clerk at the window.

The clerk had the license with his name on it, Barry Riordan, right there in her hand. She inserted it into the slot of a gray machine which responded with an authoritative *chunk*. She slid the validated license under the grille.

"Do you know—I still can't believe it. This is *my* license: that's really incredible."

The clerk tapped the shut-up button pinned on the neckband of her T-shirt.

"Oh. Sorry, I didn't notice. Well . . . thanks."

He smiled at her, a commiserating guilty smile, and she smiled back, a mechanical next-please smile.

He didn't look at the license till he was out on the street. Stapled to the back of it was a printed notice:

IMPORTANT

Due to the recent systems overload error, your test results of August 24 have been erased. Therefore, in accordance with Bylaw 9(c), Section XII, of the Revised Federal Communications Act, you are being issued a Temporary License, valid for three months from the date of issue, subject to the restrictions set forth in Appendix II of the *Federal Communications Handbook* (18th edition).

You may reapply for another examination at any time. An examination score in or above the eighth percentile will secure the removal of all restrictions, and you will immediately receive your Permanent License. A score in the sixth or seventh percentile will not affect the validity of your Temporary License, though its expiration date may be extended by this means for a period of up to three months. A score in the fifth percentile or below will result in the withdrawal of your Temporary License.

Holders of a Temporary License are advised to study Chapter Nine ("The Temporary License") in the *Federal Communications Handbook*. Remember that direct, interactive personal communications are one of our most valuable heritages. Use your license wisely. Do not abuse the privilege of free speech.

So in fact he hadn't passed the exam. Or maybe he had. He'd never find out.

His first elation fizzled out and he was left with his usual flattened sense of personal inconsequence. Tucking the license into his ID folder, he felt like a complete charlatan, a nobody pretending to be a somebody. If he'd scored in the first percentile, he'd have been issued this license the same as if he'd scored in the tenth. And he knew with a priori certainty that he hadn't done that well. The most he'd hoped for was another seven points, just enough to top him over the edge, into the sixth percentile. Instead he'd had dumb luck.

Not to worry, he advised himself. The worst is over. You've got your license. How you got it doesn't matter.

Oh, yeah, another and less friendly inward voice replied. Now all you need are three endorsements. Lots of luck.

Well, I'll *get* them, he insisted, hoping to impress the other voice with the authenticity and vitality of his self-confidence. But the other voice wasn't impressed, and so instead of going straight from Centre Street to the nearest speakeasy to celebrate, he took the subway home and spent the evening watching first a fascinating documentary on calcium structures and then Celebrity Circus, with Willy Marx. Willy had four guests: a famous prostitute, a tax accountant who had just published his memoirs, a comedian who did a surrealistic skit about a speakeasy for five-year-olds, and a novelist with a speech impediment who got into an argument with the comedian about whether his skit was essentially truthful or unjustifiably cruel. In the middle of their argument Barry came down with a murderous headache, took two aspirins, and went to bed. Just before he fell asleep, he thought: I could call them and tell them what *I* thought.

But what did he think?

He didn't know.

That, in a nutshell, was Barry's problem. At last he had his license and could talk to anyone he wanted to talk to, but he didn't know what to talk *about*. He had no ideas of his own. He agreed with anything anyone said. The skit had been *both* essentially truthful *and* unjustifiably cruel. Too much sunbathing probably was dangerous. Porpoises probably were as smart as people.

Fortunately for his morale, this state of funk did not continue long. Barry didn't let it. The next night he was off to Partyland, a 23rd Street speakeasy that advertised heavily on late-night TV. As he approached the froth of electric lights cantilevered over the entrance, Barry could feel the middle of his body turning hollow with excitement, his throat and tongue getting tingly.

There was only a short line, and in a moment he was standing in front of the box office window. "Ring?" the window asked. He looked at the price list. "Second," he said, and slid his Master Charge into the appropriate slot. "License, please," said the window, winking an arrow that pointed at another slot. He inserted his license into the other slot, a bell went ding, and *mira!* He was inside Partyland, ascending the big blue escalator up to his first first-hand experience of direct, interactive personal communication. Not a classroom exercise, not a therapy session, not a job briefing, not an ecumenical agape, but an honest-to-god conversation, spontaneous, unstructured, and all his own.

The usher who led him to his seat in the second ring sat down beside him and started to tell him about a Japanese department store that covered an entire sixteen and a half acres, had thirty-two restaurants, two movie theaters, and a children's playground.

"That's fascinating, isn't it?" the usher concluded, after setting forth further facts about this remarkable department store.

"I suppose it is," Barry said noncommittally. He couldn't figure out why the usher wanted to tell him about a department store in Japan.

"I forget where I read about it," the usher said. "In some magazine or other. Well, mix in, enjoy yourself, and if you want to order anything, there's a console that rolls out from this end table." He demonstrated.

The usher continued to hover, smiling, over his chair. Finally Barry realized he was waiting for a tip. Without any idea of what was customary, he gave him a dollar, which seemed to do the trick.

He sat there in his bulgy sponge of a chair, grateful to be alone and able to take in the sheer size and glamor of the place. Partyland was an endless middle-class living room, a panorama of all that was gracious, tasteful, and posh. At least from here in the second ring it *seemed* endless. It had a seating capacity, according to its ads, of 780, but tonight wasn't one of its big nights and a lot of the seats were empty.

At intervals that varied unpredictably the furniture within this living room would rearrange itself, and suddenly you would find yourself face to face with a new conversational partner. You could also, for a few dollars more, hire a sofa or armchair that you could drive at liberty among the other chairs, choosing your partners rather than leaving them to chance. Relatively few patrons of Partyland exercised this option, since the whole point of the place was that you could just sit back and let your chair do the driving.

The background music changed from Vivaldi's *Four Seasons* to a Sondheim medley, and all the chairs in Barry's area suddenly lifted their occupants up in the air and carried them off, legs dangling, to their next conversational destination. Barry found himself sitting next to a girl in a red velvet evening dress with a hat of paper feathers and polyhedrons. The band of the hat said, "I'm a Partyland Smarty-pants."

"Hi," said the girl in a tone intended to convey a worldly-wise satiety but achieved no more than blank anomie. "What's up?"

"Terrific, just terrific," Barry replied with authentic warmth. He'd always scored well at this preliminary stage of basic communication, which was why, at the time, he'd so much resented his examiner's remark about his handshake. There was nothing phony about his handshake, and he knew it.

"I like your shoes," she said.

Barry looked down at his shoes. "Thanks."

"I like shoes pretty much generally," she went on. "I

guess you could say I'm a kind of shoe freak." She snickered wanly.

Barry smiled, at a loss.

"But yours are particularly nice. How much did you pay for them, if you don't mind my asking?"

Though he minded, he hadn't the gumption to say so. "I don't remember. Not a lot. They're really nothing special."

"*I* like them," she insisted. Then, "My name's Cinderella. What's yours?"

"Is it really?"

"Really. You want to see my ID?"

"Mm."

She dug into her ID folder, which was made of the same velvet as her dress, and took out her license. It was blue, like his (a Temporary License), and again like his, there was a staple in the upper left-hand corner.

"See?" she said. "Cinderella B. Johnson. It was my mother's idea. My mother had a really weird sense of humor sometimes. She's dead now, though. Do you like it?"

"Like what?"

"My name."

"Oh, yeah, sure."

"Because some people don't. They think it's affected. But I can't help the name I was born with, can I?"

"I was going to ask you—"

Her face took on the intent, yet mesmerized look of a quiz-show contestant. "Ask, ask."

"The staple on your license—why is it there?"

"What staple?" she countered, becoming in an instant rigid with suspicion, like a hare that scents a predator.

"The one on your license. Was there something attached to it originally?"

"Some notice . . . I don't know. How can I remember something like that? Why do you ask?"

"There's one like it on mine."

"So? If you ask me, this is a damned stupid topic for a conversation. Aren't you going to tell me *your* name?"

"Uh . . . Barry."

"Barry what?"

"Barry Riordan."

"An Irish name: that explains it, then."

He looked at her questioningly.

"That must be where you got your gift of gab. You must have kissed the Blarney stone."

She's crazy, he thought.

But crazy in a dull, not an interesting way. He wondered how long they'd have to go on talking before the chairs switched round again. It seemed such a waste of time talking to another temp, since he could only get the endorsements he needed from people who held Permanent Licenses. Of course, the practice was probably good for him. You can't expect to like everyone you meet, as the *Communications Handbook* never tired of pointing out, but you can always try and make a good impression. Someday you'd meet someone it was crucial to hit it off with and your practice would pay off.

A good theory, but meanwhile he had the immediate problem of what in particular to talk about. "Have you heard about the giant department store in Japan?" he asked her. "It covers sixteen acres."

"Sixteen and a half," she corrected. "You must read *Topic* too."

"Mm."

"It's a fascinating magazine. I look at it almost every week. Sometimes I'm just too busy, but usually I skim it, at least."

"Busy doing . . . ?"

"Exactly." She squinted across the vast tasteful expanse of Partyland, then stood up and waved. "I think I've *recognized* someone," she said excitedly, preening her paper feathers with her free hand. Far away, someone waved back.

Cinderella broke one of the polyhedrons off her hat and put it on her chair. "So I'll remember which it is," she explained. Then, contritely, "I hope you don't mind."

"Not at all."

Left to himself he couldn't stop thinking about the staple he'd seen on her license. It was like the seemingly insignificant clue in a detective story from which the solution to the whole mystery gradually unfolds. For didn't it strongly suggest that she too had been given the benefit of the doubt, that she'd got her license not because her score entitled her to it, but thanks to Bylaw 9(c), Section XII? The chagrin of being classified in the same category with such a nitwit! Partyland was probably *full* of people in their situation, all hoping to connect with some bona fide Permanent License holder, instead of which they went around colliding with each other.

A highly depressing idea, but he did not on that account roll out the console to select a remedy from the menu. He knew from long experience that whatever could make him palpably happier was also liable to send him into a state of fugue in which conversation in the linear sense became next to impossible. So he passed the time till the next switchover by working out, in his head, the square roots of various five-digit numbers. Then, when he had a solution, he'd check it on his calculator. He'd got five right answers when his chair reared up, god bless it, and bore him off toward . . . Would it be the couple chained, wrist to wrist, on the blue settee? No, at the last moment, his chair veered left and settled down in front of an unoccupied bentwood rocker. A sign in the seat of the rocker said: "I feel a little sick. Back in five minutes."

Barry was just getting used to the idea of going on to six-digit figures when a woman in a green sofa wheeled up to him and asked what kind of music he liked.

"Any kind, really."

"Any or none, it amounts to much the same thing."

"No, honestly. Whatever is playing I usually like it. What are they playing here? I like that."

"Muzak," she said dismissively.

It was, in fact, still the Sondheim medley, but he let that pass. It wasn't worth an argument.

"What do you do?" she demanded.

"I simulate a job that Citibank is developing for another corporation, but only on an auxiliary basis. Next year I'm supposed to start full-time."

She grimaced. "You're new at Partyland, aren't you?"

He nodded. "First time tonight. In fact, this is my first time ever in any speakeasy. I just got my license yesterday."

"Well, welcome to the club." With a smile that might as well have been a sneer. "I suppose you're looking for endorsements?"

Not from you, he wanted to tell her. Instead he looked off into the distance at the perambulations of a suite of chairs in another ring. Only when all the chairs had settled into place did he refocus on the woman in the foreground. He realized with a little zing of elation that he had just administered his first snub!

"What did Freddy say when you came in?" she asked in a conspiratorial if not downright friendly tone. (His snub had evidently registered.)

"Who is Freddy?"

"The usher who showed you to your seat. I saw him sit down and talk with you."

"He told me about some Japanese department store."

She nodded knowingly. "Of course—I should have known. Freddy shills for *Topic* magazine, and that's one of their featured stories this week. I wonder what they pay him. Last week their cover story was about Ireina Khokolovna, and all Freddy could talk about was Ireina Khokolovna."

"Who is Ireina Khokolovna?" he asked.

She hooted a single derisory hoot. "I thought you said you liked music!"

"I do," he protested. But, clearly, he had just failed a major test. With a sigh of weariness and a triumphant smile, the woman rotated her sofa around one hundred and eighty degrees and drove off in the direction of the couple chained together on the blue settee.

The couple rose in unison and greeted her with cries of "Maggie!" and "Son of a gun!" It was impossible for Barry, sitting so nearby and having no one to talk to himself, to avoid eavesdropping on their conversation, which concerned (no doubt as a rebuke to his ignorance) Ireina Khokolovna's latest *superb* release from Deutsche Grammophon. She was at her best in Schumann, her Wolf was *comme ci comme ça*. Even so, Khokolovna's Wolf was miles ahead of Adriana Motta's, or even Gwyneth Batterham's, who, for all her real intelligence, was developing a distinct wobble in her upper register. Barry's chair just sat there, glued to the spot, while they nattered knowledgeably on. He wished he were home watching Willy Marx—or anywhere but Partyland.

"Mine's Ed," said the occupant of the bentwood rocker, a young man of Barry's own age, build, and hair style.

"Pardon?" said Barry.

"I said," he said, with woozy precision, "my name is Ed."

"Oh. Mine's Barry. How are you, Ed?"

He held out his hand. Ed shook it gravely.

"You know, Barry," Ed said, "I've been thinking about what you were saying, and I think the whole problem is *cars*. Know what I mean?"

"Elaborate," Barry suggested.

"Right. The thing about cars is . . . Well, I live in Elizabeth across the river, right? So any time I come here I've got to drive, right? Which you might think was a drag, but in fact I always feel terrific. You know?"

Barry nodded. He didn't understand what Ed was saying in any very specific way, but he knew he agreed with him.

"I feel . . . free. If that doesn't seem too ridiculous. Whenever I'm driving my car."

"What have you got?" Barry asked.

"A Toyota."

"Nice. Very nice."

"I don't think I'm unique that way," said Ed.

"No, I wouldn't say so."

"Cars *are* freedom. And so what all this talk about an

energy crisis boils down to is—" He stopped short. "I think I'm having a fugue."

"I think maybe you are. But that's all right. I do too. It'll pass."

"Listen, what's your name?"

"Barry," Barry said. "Barry Riordan."

Ed held out his hand. "Mine's Ed. Say, are you trying to pick up an endorsement?"

Barry nodded. "You too?"

"No. In fact, I think I've still got one left. Would you like it?"

"Jesus," said Barry. "Yeah, sure."

Ed took out his ID folder, took his license from the folder, tickled the edge of the endorsement sticker from the back of the license with his fingernail, and offered it to Barry.

"You're sure you want me to have this?" Barry asked, incredulous, with the white curlicue of the sticker dangling from his fingertip.

Ed nodded. "You remind me of somebody."

"Well, I'm awfully grateful. I mean you scarcely know me."

"Right," said Ed, nodding more vigorously. "But I liked what you were saying about cars. That made a lot of sense."

"You know," Barry burst out in a sudden access of confessional bonhomie, "I feel confused *most* of the time."

"Right."

"But I can never express it. Everything I *say* seems to make more sense than what I can feel inside of me."

"Right, right."

The music changed from the Sondheim medley to the flip side of the *Four Seasons*, and Barry's chair lifted him up and bore him off toward the couple in the blue settee, while Ed, limp in the bentwood rocker, was carried off in the opposite direction.

"Goodbye," Barry shouted after him, but Ed was already either comatose or out of earshot. "And thanks again!"

The MacKinnons introduced themselves. His name was Jason. Hers was Michelle. They lived quite nearby, on West 28th, and were interested primarily in the television shows they'd seen when they were growing up, about which they were very well informed. Despite a bad first impression, due to his associating them with Maggie of the green sofa, Barry found himself liking the MacKinnons enormously, and before the next switchover he put his chair in the LOCK position. They spent the rest of the evening together, exchanging nostalgic tidbits over coffee and slices of Partyland's famous pineapple pie. At closing time he asked if they would either consider giving him an endorsement. They said they would have, having thoroughly enjoyed his company, but unfortunately they'd both used up their quota for that year. They seemed genuinely sorry, but he felt it had been a mistake to ask.

His first endorsement proved to have been beginner's luck. Though he went out almost every night to a different speakeasy and practically lived at Partyland during the weekends, when it was at its liveliest, he never again had such a plum fall in his lap. He didn't get within sniffing distance of his heart's desire. Most people he met were temps, and the few Permanent License holders inclined to be friendly to him invariably turned out, like the MacKinnons, to have already disposed of their allotted endorsements. Or so they said. As the weeks went by and anxiety mounted, he began to be of the cynical but widely held opinion that many people simply removed the stickers from their licenses so it would *seem* they'd been used. According to Jason MacKinnon, a completely selfless endorsement, like his from Ed, was a rare phenomenon. Quid pro quos were the general rule, in the form either of cash on the barrel or services rendered. Barry said (jokingly, of course) that he wouldn't object to bartering his virtue for an endorsement, or preferably two, to which Michelle replied (quite seriously) that unfortunately she did not know anyone who might be in the market for Barry's particu-

lar type. Generally, she observed, it was *younger* people
who got their endorsements by putting out.

Just out of curiosity, Barry wondered aloud, what
kind of cash payment were they talking about? Jason
said the standard fee, a year ago, for a single sticker had
been a thousand dollars; two and a half for a pair, since
people with two blanks to fill could be presumed to be
that much more desperate. Due however to a recent dis-
proportion between supply and demand, the going price
for a single was now seventeen hundred; a double, a
round four thousand. Jason said he could arrange an
introduction at that price, if Barry were interested.

"I will tell you," said Barry, "what you can do with
your stickers."

"Oh, now," said Michelle placatingly. "We're still
your *friends,* Mr. Riordan, but business is business. If it
were our own *personal* stickers we were discussing, we
wouldn't *hesitate* to give you an endorsement absolutely
gratis. Would we, Jason?"

"Of course not, no question."

"But we're middlemen, you see. We have only limited flexibility in the terms we can offer. Say, fifteen
hundred."

"And three and a half for the pair," Jason added.
"And that is a rock-bottom offer. You won't do better
anywhere else."

"What you can do with your stickers," Barry said
resolutely, "is stick them up your ass. Your asses,
rather."

"I wish you wouldn't take that attitude, Mr. Riordan," said Jason in a tone of sincere regret. "We do like
you, and we have enjoyed your company. If we didn't,
we would certainly not be offering this opportunity."

"Bullshit," said Barry. It was the first time he'd used
an obscenity conversationally, and he brought it off
with great conviction. "You knew when my license
would expire, and you've just been stringing me along,
hoping I'd get panicky."

"We have been *trying,*" said Michelle, "to help."

"Thanks. I'll help myself."

"How?"

"Tomorrow I'm going back to Centre Street and take the exam again."

Michelle MacKinnon leaned across the coffee table that separated the blue settee from Barry's armchair and gave him a sound motherly smack on the cheek. "Wonderful! That's the way to meet a challenge—head on! You're bound to pass. After all, you've had three months of practice. You've become much more fluent these past months."

"Thanks." He got up to go.

"Hey—" Jason grabbed Barry's hand and gave it an earnest squeeze. "Don't forget, if you *do* get your Permanent License—"

"When he gets it," Michelle amended.

"Right—*when* you get it, you know where you can find us. We're always here on the same settee."

"You two are unbelievable," Barry said. "Do you honestly think I'd sell you my endorsements? Assuming"— he knocked on the varnished walnut coffee table—"I pass my exam."

"It is safer," Michelle said, "to work through a professional introduction service than to try and peddle them on your own. Even though everyone breaks it, the law is still the law. Individuals operating on their own are liable to get caught, since they don't have an arrangement with the authorities. We do. That's why, for instance, it would do you no good to report us to the Communications Control Office. Others have done so in the past, and it did *them* no good."

"None of them ever got a Permanent License, either," Jason added, with a twinkle of menace.

"That, I'm sure, was just coincidence," said Michelle. "After all, we're speaking of only two cases, and neither of the individuals in question was particularly bright. Bright people wouldn't be so quixotic, would they?" She underlined her question with a Mona Lisa smile, and Barry, for all his indignation and outrage, couldn't keep from smiling back. Anyone who could drop a word like "quixotic" into the normal flow of conversation and make it seem so natural couldn't be all wrong.

"Don't worry," he promised, tugging his hand out of Jason's. "I'm not the quixotic type."

But when he said it, it sounded false. It wasn't fair.

Barry was as good as his word and went to Centre Street the very next morning to take his third exam. The computer assigned him to Marvin Kolodny, Ph.D., in cubicle 183. The initials worried him. He could have coped, this time, with the old fuddy-duddy he'd had last August, but a Ph.D.? It seemed as though they were raising the hurdles each time he came around the track. But his worries evaporated the moment he was in the cubicle and saw that Marvin Kolodny was a completely average young man of twenty-four. His averageness was even a bit unsteady, as though he had to think about it, but then most twenty-four-year-olds are self-conscious in just that way.

It's always a shock the first time you come up against some particular kind of authority figure—a dentist, a psychiatrist, a cop—who is younger than you are, but it needn't lead to disaster as long as you let the authority figure know right from the start that you intend to be deferential, and this was a quality that Barry conveyed without trying.

"Hi," said Barry, with masterful deference. "I'm Barry Riordan."

Marvin Kolodny responded with a boyish grin and offered his hand. An American flag had been tattooed on his right forearm. On a scroll circling the flagpole was the following inscription:

Let's All
Overthrow
the United States
Government
by Force &
Violence

On his other forearm there was a crudely executed rose with his name underneath: Marvin Kolodny, Ph.D.

"Do you mean it?" Barry asked, marveling over Marvin's tattoo as they shook hands. He managed to ask the question without in the least seeming to challenge Marvin Kolodny's authority.

"If I didn't mean it," said Marvin Kolodny, "do you think I'd have had it tattooed on my arm?"

"I suppose not. It's just so . . . unusual."

"I'm an unusual person," said Marvin Kolodny, leaning back in his swivel chair and taking a large pipe from the rack on his desk.

"But doesn't *that* idea"—Barry nodded at the tattoo—"conflict with your having this particular job? Aren't you part of the U.S. government yourself?"

"Only for the time being. I'm not suggesting that we overthrow the government *tomorrow*. A successful revolution isn't possible until the proletariat becomes conscious of their oppressions, and they can't become conscious of anything until they are as articulate as their oppressors. Language and consciousness aren't independent processes, after all. Talking is thinking turned inside out. No more, no less."

"And which am I?"

"How's that?"

"Am I a proletarian or an oppressor?"

"Like most of us these days, I would say you're probably a little of each. Are you married, uh . . ." (He peeked into Barry's file.) ". . . Barry?"

Barry nodded.

"Then that's one form of oppression right there. Children?"

Barry shook his head.

"Do you live with your wife?"

"Not lately. And even when we were together, we never talked to each other, except to say practical things like 'When is your program going to be over?' Some people just aren't that interested in talking. Debra certainly isn't. That's why—" (He couldn't resist the chance to explain his earlier failures.) "—I did so poorly on my earlier exams. Assuming I *did* get a low score last time, which isn't certain since the results were erased. But assuming that I did, that's the reason. I never got any practice. The basic day-to-day conversational experiences most people have with their spouses never happened in my case."

Marvin Kolodny frowned—an ingratiating, boyish frown. "Are you sure you're being entirely honest with yourself, Barry? Few people are completely willing to talk about something. We've all got hobbyhorses. What was your wife interested in? Couldn't you have talked about that?"

"In religion, mostly. But she didn't care to talk about it unless you agreed with her."

"Have you *tried* to agree with her?"

"Well, you see, Dr. Kolodny, what she *believes* is that the end of the world is about to happen. Next February. That's where she's gone now—to Arizona, to wait for it. This is the third time she's taken off."

"Not an easy woman to discourage, by the sound of it."

"I think she really *wants* the world to end. And also, she *does* like Arizona."

"Have you considered a divorce?" Marvin Kolodny asked.

"No, absolutely not. We're still basically in love. After all, most married couples end up not saying much to each other. Isn't that so? Even before Debra got religious, we weren't in the habit of talking to each other. To tell the truth, Dr. Kolodny, I've never been much of a talker. I think I was put off it by the compulsory talk we had to do in high school."

"That's perfectly natural. I hated compulsory talk myself, though I must admit I was good at it. What about your job, Barry? Doesn't that give you opportunities to develop communication skills?"

"I don't communicate with the public directly. Only with simulations, and their responses tend to be pretty stereotyped."

"Well, there's no doubt that you have a definite communications problem. But I think it's a problem you can lick! I'll tell you what, Barry: officially, I shouldn't tell

you this myself, but I'm giving you a score of sixty-five."
He held up his hand to forestall an effusion. "Now, let me
explain how that breaks down. You do very well in most
categories—Affect, Awareness of Others, Relevance,
Voice Production, et cetera, but where you do fall down
is in Notional Content and Originality. There you could
do better."

"Originality has always been my Waterloo," Barry
admitted. "I just don't seem to be able to come up with
my own ideas. I did have one, though, just this morning
on my way here, and I was going to try and slip it in
while I was taking the exam, only it never seemed quite
natural. Have you ever noticed that you never see baby
pigeons? All the pigeons you see out on the street are
the same size—full-grown. But where do they come from?
Where are the little pigeons? Are they hidden somewhere?" He stopped short, feeling ashamed of his idea.
Now that it was out in the open it seemed paltry and
insignificant, little better than a joke he'd learned by
heart, than which there is nothing more calculated to land
you in the bottom percentiles.

Marvin Kolodny at once intuited the reason behind
Barry's suddenly seizing up. He was in the business,
after all, of understanding unspoken meanings and eval-
uating them precisely. He smiled a sympathetic, mature
smile.

"Ideas . . ." he said, in a slow, deliberate manner,
as though each word had to be weighed on a scale before it was put into the sentence. ". . . aren't . . .
things. Ideas—the most authentic ideas—are the natural, effortless result of any vital relationship. Ideas are
what happen when people connect with each other crea-
tively."

Barry nodded.

"Do you mind my giving you some honest advice,
Barry?"

"Not at all, Dr. Kolodny. I'd be grateful."

"On your G-47 form you say you spend a lot of time
at Partyland and similar speakeasies. I realize that's
where you did get your first endorsement, but really,

don't you think you're wasting your time in that sort of place? It's a tourist trap!"

"I'm aware of that," Barry said, smarting under the rebuke.

"You're not going to meet anyone there but temps and various people who are out to fleece temps. With rare exceptions."

"I know, I know. But I don't know where *else* to go."

"Why not try this place?" Marvin Kolodny handed Barry a printed card, which read:

INTENSITY FIVE
A New Experience in
Interpersonal Intimacy
5 Barrow Street
New York 10014
Members Only

"I'll certainly try it," Barry promised. "But how do I get to be a member?"

"Tell them Marvin sent you."

And that was all there was to it—he had passed his exam with a score just five points short of the crucial eighth percentile. Which was a tremendous accomplishment but also rather frustrating in a way, since it meant he'd come *that* close to not having to bother scouting out two more endorsements. Still, with another three months in which to continue his quest and an introduction to Intensity Five, Barry had every reason to be optimistic.

"Thank you, Dr. Kolodny," Barry said, lingering in the doorway of the cubicle. "Thanks terrifically."

"That's all right, Barry. Just doing my job."

"You know . . . I wish . . . Of course, I know it's not permissible, you being an examiner and all . . . but I wish I knew you in a personal way. Truly. You're a very heavy individual."

"Thank you, Barry. I know you mean that, and I'm flattered. Well, then—" He took his pipe from his mouth and lifted it in a kind of salute. "So long. And Merry Christmas."

Barry left the cubicle feeling so transcendent and relaxed that he was five blocks from Centre Street before he remembered that he'd neglected to have his license revalidated at Window 28. As he headed back to the Federal Communications Building, his senses seemed to register all the ordinary details of the city's streets with an unnatural, hyped clarity: the smell of sauerkraut steaming up from a hot dog cart, the glint of the noon sun on the mica mixed into the paving blocks of the sidewalk, the various shapes and colors of the pigeons, the very pigeons, perhaps, that had inspired his so-called idea earlier that day. But it was true, what he'd said. All the pigeons were the same size.

A block south of the Federal Communications Building, he looked up, and there strung out under the cornice of the building was the motto, which he had never noticed before, of the Federal Communications Agency:

PLANNED FREEDOM IS THE
ROAD TO LASTING
PROGRESS.

So simple, so direct, and yet when you thought about it, almost impossible to understand.

Barrow Street being right in the middle of one of the city's worst slums, Barry had been prepared (he'd thought) for a lesser degree of stateliness and *bon ton* than that achieved by Partyland, but even so the dismal actuality of Intensity Five went beyond anything he could have imagined. A cavernous one-room basement apartment with bare walls, crackly linoleum over a concrete floor, and radiators that hissed and gurgled ominously without generating a great deal of heat. The furniture consisted of metal folding chairs, most of them folded and stacked, a refreshment stand that sold orange juice and coffee, and a great many free-standing, brimful metal ashtrays. Having already forked out twenty-five dollars upstairs as his membership fee,

Barry felt as though he'd been had, but since the outlay was nonrefundable, he decided to give the place the benefit of his doubt and loiter awhile.

He had been loitering, alone and melancholy, for the better part of an hour, eavesdropping to his right on a conversation about somebody's drastic need to develop a more effective persona and to his left on a discussion of the morality of our involvement in Mexico, when a black woman in a white nylon jumpsuit and a calf-length very good imitation mink swept into the room, took a quick survey of those present, and sat down, unbelievably, by him!

Quick as a light switch he could feel his throat go dry and his face tighten into a smile of rigid insincerity. He blushed, he trembled, he fainted dead away, but only metaphorically.

"I'm Columbine Brown," she said, as though that offered an explanation.

Did she expect him to recognize her? She was beautiful enough, certainly, to have been someone he ought to recognize, but if he had seen her on TV, he didn't remember. In a way she seemed almost *too* beautiful to be a noted personality, since there is usually something a little idiosyncratic about each of them, so they can be told apart. Columbine Brown was beautiful in the manner not of a celebrity but of a deluxe (but not customized) sports car.

"I'm Barry Riordan," he managed to bring out, tardily.

"Let's put our cards on the table, shall we, Mr. Riordan? I am a Permanent Card holder. What are you?"

"A temp."

"It's fair to assume then that you're here to find an endorsement."

He began to protest. She stopped him with just one omniscient and devastating glance. He nodded.

"Unfortunately, I have used up my quota. However"—she held up a single perfect finger—"it's almost the New Year. If you're not in a desperate hurry . . . ?"

"Oh, I've got till March."

"I'm not promising anything, you understand. Unless we hit it off. If we do, then fine, you have my endorsement. Fair enough?"

"It's a deal."

"You feel you can trust me?" She lowered her eyes and tried to look wicked and temptress-like, but it was not in the nature of her kind of beauty to do so.

"Anywhere," he replied. "Implicitly."

"Good." As though of its own volition her coat slipped off her shoulders onto the back of the folding chair. She turned her head sideways and addressed the old woman behind the refreshment counter. "Evelyn, how about an orange juice." She looked at him. He nodded. "Make it two."

Then, as though they'd been waiting for these preliminaries to be concluded, tears sprang to her eyes. A tremor of heartfelt emotion colored her lovely contralto voice as she said, "Oh Jesus, what am I going to do? I can't take any more! I am just so . . . so goddamned wretched! I'd like to kill myself. No, that isn't true. I'm confused, Larry. But I know one thing—I am an *angry* woman and I'm going to start fighting back!"

It would have been inconsiderate to break in upon such testimony by mentioning that his name was not, in fact, Larry. What difference does one letter make, after all?

"Have you ever been to the Miss America Pageant on 42nd Street?" she asked him, drying her eyes.

"I can't say I have. I always mean to, but you know how it is. It's the same with the Statue of Liberty. It's always there, so you never get around to it."

"I'm Miss Georgia."

"No kidding!"

"I have *been* Miss Georgia six nights a week for the last four years, with matinees on Sunday and Tuesday, and do you suppose in all that time that the audience has ever voted for *me* to be Miss America? Ever?"

"*I* would certainly vote for you."

"Never once," she went on fiercely, ignoring his supportiveness. "It's always Miss Massachusetts, or Miss

Ohio, who can't do anything but play a damn jew's-harp, if you'll excuse my language, or Miss Oregon, who still can't remember the blocking for *Lovely to Look At,* which she has been dancing since before *I* graduated from high school. There's no one in the whole damn line-up who hasn't been crowned once. Except me."

"I'm sorry to hear it."

"I am a *good* singer. I can tap dance like a house on fire. My balcony scene would break your heart. And I can say objectively that I've got better legs than anyone except, possibly, Miss Wyoming."

"But you've never been Miss America," Barry said sympathetically.

"What do you think that *feels* like, here?" She grabbed a handful of white nylon in the general area of her heart.

"I honestly don't know, Miss . . . " (He'd forgotten her last name.) ". . . Georgia."

"At Intensity Five I'm just plain Columbine, honey. The same as you're just Larry. And not knowing isn't much of an answer. Here I am exposing myself in front of you, and you come back with 'No Opinion.' I don't buy that."

"Well, to be completely candid, Columbine, it's hard for me to imagine your feeling anything but terrific. To be Miss Georgia and have such a lot of talent—isn't that *enough?* I would have thought you'd be very happy."

Columbine bit her lip, furrowed her brow, and evidenced, in general, a sudden change of heart. "God, Larry—you're right! I've been kidding myself: the pageant isn't my problem—it's my excuse. My problem"—her voice dropped, her eyes avoided his—"is timeless and well-known. I fell in love with the wrong man for me. And now it's too late. Would you like to hear a long and very unhappy story?"

"Sure. That's what I'm here for, isn't it?"

She smiled a meaningful, unblemished smile and gave

his hand a quick, trusting squeeze. "You know, Larry—you're an all-right guy."

Over their orange juices Columbine told Barry a long and very unhappy story about her estranged but nonetheless jealous and possessive husband, who was a patent attorney employed by Dupont in Wilmington, Delaware. Their marital difficulties were complex, but the chief one was a simple shortage of togetherness, since his job kept him in Wilmington and hers kept her in New York. Additionally, her husband's ideal of conversation was very divergent from her own. He enjoyed talking about money, sports, and politics with other men and bottled up all his deeper feelings. She was introspective, outgoing, and warm-hearted.

"It would be all right for a while," she recalled. "But the pressure would build until I had to go out and find someone to talk to. It is a basic human need, after all. Perhaps *the* basic need. I had no choice."

"And then he'd find out, I suppose," said Barry.

She nodded. "And go berserk. It was awful. No one can live that way."

Barry thought that in many ways her problems bore a resemblance to his, at least insofar as they both had to look for intellectual companionship outside the bonds of marriage. But when he began to elaborate upon this insight and draw some interesting parallels between his experience and hers, Columbine became impatient. She did not come right out and tell him that he was in breach of contract, but that was definitely the message conveyed by her glazed inattention. Responsive to her needs, he resisted the impulse to make any further contributions of his own and sat back and did his level best to be a good listener and nothing more.

When Columbine had finally run the gamut of all her feelings, which included fear, anger, joy, pain, and an abiding and entirely unreasoning sense of dread, she thanked him, gave him her address and phone number, and said to get in touch in January for his endorsement.

Jubilation, he thought. Bingo. Hallelujah.

But not quite. He still had to get one more endorsement. But now it seemed possible, likely, even inevitable. A matter, merely, of making the effort and reaping the reward.

Dame Fortune had become so well disposed to him that he got his third endorsement (though in point of hard fact, his second) the very next night. The fated encounter took place at Morone's One-Stop Shopping, a mom-and-pop mini-grocery on Sixth Avenue right next to the International Supermarket. Although Morone's charged more for most items, Barry preferred shopping there because it offered such a limited and unchallenging range of choices (cold meats, canned goods, beer, Nabisco cookies) that he never felt intimidated and ashamed of his selections at the check-out counter. He hated to cook, but was that any reason he should be made to feel inadequate? Morone's was made to order for people like Barry, of which there are great numbers.

That night, as he was hesitating between a dinner of Spam and Chef Boy-ar-dee ravioli or Spam and Green Giant corn niblets, the woman who had been standing in front of the frozen food locker suddenly started talking to herself. The Morones looked at each other in alarm. Neither of them were licensed talkers, which was a further attraction of their store, since one's exchanges with them were limited to such basic permissible amenities as "How are you," "Take care," and giving out prices.

What the woman was saying was of a character to suggest that she had just that minute gone crazy. "The pain," she explained calmly to the ice cream section of the freezer, "only comes on when I do this." She stooped closer to the ice cream and winced. "But then it's pure hell. I want to cut my leg off, have a lobotomy, anything to make it stop. Yet I know the problem isn't in my leg at all. It's in my back. Here." She touched the small of her back. "A kind of short circuit. Worse than bending over is twisting sideways. Even turning my head can set it off. Sometimes, when I'm alone, I'll start crying just at the thought of it, at knowing I've become so damned superannuated." She sighed. "Well, it happens to everyone, and I suppose it could be worse. There's no use complaining. Life goes on, as they say."

Having come round to a sensible, accepting attitude, she turned from the freezer to witness the effect of her outburst on the Morones, who looked elsewhere, and on Barry, who couldn't resist meeting her eyes head-on. Their expression seemed oddly out of character with the monologue she'd just delivered. They were piercing (as against vulnerable) steely-gray eyes that stared defiance from a face all sags and wrinkles. Without the contradiction of such eyes, her face would have seemed ruined and hopeless; with them, she looked just like an ancient centurion in a movie about the Roman Empire.

She grimaced. "No need to panic. It's not an emergency. I'm licensed."

Barry proffered his most harmless smile. "I wasn't even thinking of that."

She didn't smile back. "Then what were you thinking?"

"I guess I was feeling sorry."

To which her reaction was, alarmingly, to laugh.

Feeling betrayed and pissed off, he grabbed the nearest can of vegetables (beets, he would later discover, and he hated beets) and handed it to Mr. Morone with the can of Spam.

"That it?" Mr. Morone asked.

"A six-pack of Schlitz," he said, quite off the top of his head.

When he left the store with his dinner and the beer in a plastic bag, she was already outside waiting for him. "I wasn't laughing at you, young man," she told him, taking the same coolly aggrieved tone she'd taken toward the ice cream. "I was laughing at myself. Obviously, I *was* asking for pity. So if I should get some, I shouldn't be surprised, should I. My name's Madeline, but my friends call me Mad. You're supposed to laugh."

"Mine's Barry," he said. "Do you drink beer?"

"Oh, I'm not drunk. I discovered long ago that one

needn't actually drink in order to have the satisfaction of behaving outrageously."

"I meant, would you like some now, with me? I've got a six-pack."

"Certainly. Barry, you said? You're so *direct* it's almost devious. Let's go to my place. It's only a couple blocks away. You see—I can be direct myself."

Her place turned out to be four street numbers away from his and nothing like what he'd been expecting, neither a demoralized wreck heaped with moldering memorabilia nor yet the swank, finicky *pied-à-terre* of some has-been somebody. It was a plain, pleasant one-and-a-half-room apartment that anyone could have lived in and almost everyone did, with potted plants to emphasize the available sunlight and pictures representing various vanished luxuries on the wall, the common range of furniture from aspiring to makeshift, and enough ordinary debris to suggest a life being carried on, with normative difficulty, among these carefully cultivated neutralities.

Barry popped the tops off two beer cans, and Madeline swept an accumulation of books and papers off a tabletop and onto a many-cushioned bed. They sat down at the table.

"Do you know what it's called?" he asked. "The disease you've got?"

"Sciatica. Which is more a disorder than a disease. Let's not talk about it, okay?"

"Okay, but *you'll* have to think of what we do talk about. I'm no good at coming up with topics for conversation."

"Why is that?"

"No ideas. If other people have ideas, I can bounce off them well enough, but all by itself my mind's a blank. I envy people like you who are able to start talking out of the blue."

"Mm," said Madeline, not unkindly, "it's odd you should put it like that; it's almost a definition of what I do for a living."

"Really, what's that?"

"I'm a poet."

"No kidding. You can make a living by being a poet?"

"Enough to get by."

Barry refused to believe her. Neither the woman nor her apartment corresponded with his preconceptions of poets and the necessarily indigent life they must lead. "Have you ever published a book?" he asked craftily.

"Twenty-two. More than that, if you count limited editions and pamphlets and such." She went over to the bed, rooted among the papers, and returned with a thin, odd-sized paperback. "This is the latest." The front cover said in tasteful powder-blue letters on a ground of dusky cream: MADELINE IS MAD AGAIN: New Poems by Madeline Swain. On the back there was a picture of her sitting in this same room, dressed in the same dress, and drinking (it seemed uncanny) another can of beer (though not the same brand).

Barry turned the book over in his hands, examining the cover and the photo alternately, but would no more have thought of looking inside than of lifting Madeline's skirts to peek at her underclothes. "What's it about?" he asked.

"Whatever I happened to be thinking at the moment I wrote each poem."

That made sense but didn't answer his question. "When do you write them?"

"Generally, whenever people ask me to."

"Could you write a poem right now? About what you're thinking?"

"Sure, no trouble." She went to the desk in the corner of the room and quickly wrote the following poem, which she handed to Barry to read:

A Reflection

Sometimes the repetition of what we have
just said will suggest a new meaning
or possibilities of meaning
we did not at first suppose to be there.
We think we have understood our words,

then learn that we have not,
since their essential meaning
only dawns on us the second time round.

"This is what you were thinking just now?" he asked skeptically.

"Are you disappointed?"

"I thought you'd write something about me."

"Would you like me to do that?"

"It's too late now."

"Not at all."

She went to her desk and returned a moment later with a second poem:

Aubade
I was sorry to hear
That you've got to be going.
But you're not?
Then I'm sorry to hear that.

"What does the title mean?" he asked, hoping it might modify the unfriendly message of the four short lines that followed.

"An aubade is a traditional verse form that a lover addresses to his (or her) beloved at dawn, when one of them is leaving for work."

He tried to think of a compliment that wouldn't be completely insincere. "Heavy," he allowed at last.

"Oh, I'm afraid it's not much good. I can usually do better. I guess I don't trust you enough. Though you're quite likable; that's another matter."

"Now I'm likable! I thought"—he dangled the poem by one corner—"you were just hinting that I should leave?"

"Nonsense. You haven't even finished your beer. You *mustn't* hold what I write against me. Poets can't be held responsible for what they say in their poems. We're all compulsive traitors, you know."

Barry said nothing, but his expression must have conveyed his disapproval.

"Now don't be like that. Treason is a necessary part of the job, the way that handling trash cans is a part of being a garbage man. Some poets go to a great deal of trouble to disguise their treacheries; my inclination is to be up-front and betray everyone right from the start."

"Do you have many friends?" he asked, needlingly.

"Virtually none. Do you think I'd go around talking to myself in grocery stores if I had friends?"

He shook his head, perplexed. "I'll tell you, Madeline, it doesn't make sense to me. Surely if you were nice to other poets, they'd be nice to you, on the basic principle of scratch-my-back."

"Oh, of course. Minor poets do nothing else. They positively swarm. I'd rather be major and lonely, thank you very much."

"Sounds arrogant to me."

"It is. I am. *C'est la vie.*" She took a long, throat-rippling sip of the Schlitz and set her can down on the table, empty. "What I like about you, Barry, is that you manage to say what you think without seeming the least homicidal. Why?"

"Why do I say what I think? It's easiest."

"No: why are you so accommodating to me when I'm being such a bitch? Are you looking for an endorsement?"

He blushed. "Is it that obvious?"

"Well, as you don't appear to be either a mugger or a rapist, there had to be some reason you followed a dotty old woman home from her latest nervous breakdown. Let's make a deal, shall we?"

"What sort of deal?"

"You stay around and nudge some more poems out of me. I'm feeling the wind in my sails, but I need a muse. If you give me twenty good ideas for poems, I'll give you your endorsement."

Barry shook his head. "Twenty different ideas? Impossible."

"Don't think of them as ideas, then, think of them as questions."

"Ten," he insisted. "Ten is a lot."

"Fifteen," she countered.

"All right, but including the two you've already written."

"Done!"

She sat down and waited for Barry to be inspired. "Well?" she inquired, after a long silence.

"I'm trying to think."

He tried to think of what most poems were about. Love seemed the likeliest subject, but he couldn't imagine Madeline, at her age and with her temperament, being in love with anybody. Still, that was her problem. He didn't have to write the poem, only propose it.

"All right," he said. "Write a poem about how much you're in love with me."

She looked miffed. "Don't flatter yourself, young man. I may have inveigled you into my apartment, but I am *not* in love with you."

"Pretend then. And don't make it anything flip like that last one. Make it sad and delicate and use some rhymes."

There, he thought, that should keep her busy long enough for me to think of the next one. He opened a second beer and took a meditative swallow. Did poets ever write poems about drinking beer? Or was that too general? Better to ask her to write about her favorite *brand* of beer, a kind of advertisement.

By the time she'd finished the sonnet about how much she loved him, he had come up with all twelve other subjects.

1. A poem about her favorite beer, written as though it were an ad.

2. A poem in the form of a Christmas-shopping list.

3. A poem embodying several important long-range economic forecasts.

4. A poem about a rabbit (there was a porcelain rabbit on one of the shelves) suitable to be sung to a baby.

5. A very short poem to be carved on the tombstone of her least favorite president, living or dead.

6. A poem apologizing to the last person she had been especially rude to.

7. A poem for a get-well card to someone who has sciatica.

8. A poem analyzing her feelings about beets.

9. A poem that skirts all around a secret she's never told anyone and then finally decides to keep it a secret.

10. A poem giving an eyewitness account of something awful happening in Arizona, in February.

11. A poem justifying capital punishment in cases where one has been abandoned by one's lover. (This in its final, expanded form was to become the longest poem in her next collection, "The Ballad of Lucius McGonaghal Sloe," which begins:

> I fell head over heels just four evenings ago
> With a girl that I'm sure you all know,
>> But I couldn't hold her,
>> And that's why I sold her,
> To Lucius McGonaghal Sloe.

and continues, in a similar vein, for another one hundred thirty-six stanzas.)

12. A poem presenting an affirmative, detailed description of her own face.

Prudently he didn't spring them on her all at once, but waited until she'd finished each one before telling her what the next had to be about. She didn't raise any further objections until he came to Number 8, whereupon she insisted she didn't have any feelings about beets whatsoever. He refused to believe her, and to prove his point he cooked up a quick dinner on her hot plate of Spam and canned beets (it was rather late by then, and they were famished). Before she'd had three mouthfuls, the poem started coming to her, and by the time she'd got it into final shape, five years later, it was far and away the best of the lot.

For the next many days Barry didn't speak to a soul. He felt no need to communicate anything to anyone. He had his three endorsements—one from a poet who'd published twenty-two books—and he was confident he could have gone out and got three more a day if he'd needed to. He was off the hook.

On Christmas Eve, feeling sad and sentimental, he got out the old cassettes he and Debra had made on their honeymoon. He played them on the TV, one after the other, all through the night, waxing mellower and mellower and wishing she were here. Then, in February, when the world had once again refused to end, she did come home, and for several days it was just as good as anything on the cassettes. They even, for a wonder, talked to each other. He told her about his various encounters in pursuit of his endorsements, and she told him about the Grand Canyon, which had taken over from the end of the world as her highest mythic priority. She loved the Grand Canyon with a surpassing love and wanted Barry to leave his job and go with her to live right beside it. Impossible, he declared. He'd worked eight years at Citibank and accrued important benefits. He accused her of concealing something. Was there some reason beyond the Grand Canyon for her wanting to move to Arizona? She insisted it was strictly the Grand Canyon, that from the first moment she'd seen it she'd forgotten all about Armageddon, the Number of the Beast, and all the other accouterments of the Apocalypse. She couldn't explain: he would have to see it himself. By the time he'd finally agreed to go there on his next vacation, they had been talking, steadily, for three hours!

Meanwhile, Columbine Brown had been putting him off with a variety of excuses and dodges. The phone number she'd given him was her answering service, the address was an apartment building with guard dogs in the lobby and a doorman who didn't talk or listen. Barry was obliged to wait out on the sidewalk, which wasn't possible, due to a cold wave that persisted through most of January. He left a message at the Apollo Theater, where the pageant was held, giving three different times he would be waiting for her at Intensity Five. She never showed. By mid-February, he'd begun to be alarmed. Early one morning, defying the weather, he posted himself outside her building and waited (five miserable hours) till she appeared. She was profusely apologetic, explained that she *did* have his sticker, there was no problem, he shouldn't worry, but she had an appointment she had to get to, in fact she was already late, and so if he'd come back tonight, or better yet (since she had to see somebody after the pageant and didn't know when she'd be home), at this time tomorrow? Thoughtfully, she introduced him to the doorman so he wouldn't have to wait out in the cold.

At this time tomorrow Columbine made another non-appearance, and Barry began to suspect she was deliberately avoiding him. He decided to give her one last chance. He left a message with the doorman saying he would be by to collect his you-know-what at half past twelve the next night. Alternately, she could leave it in an envelope with the doorman.

When he arrived the following evening, the doorman led him down the carpeted corridor, unlocked the elevator (the dogs growled portentously until the doorman said *"Aus!"*), and told him to ring at door 8-C.

It was not Columbine who let him in, but her understudy, Lida Mullens. Lida informed Barry that Columbine had joined her husband in Wilmington, Delaware, and there was no knowing when, if ever, she might return to her post as Miss Georgia. She had not left the promised sticker, and Lida seriously doubted whether she had any left, having heard, through the grapevine, that she'd sold all three of them to an introduction service on the day they came in the mail. With his last gasp of self-confidence Barry asked Lida Mullens whether *she* would consider giving him an endorsement. He promised to pay her back in kind the moment he was issued his own license. Lida informed him airily that she didn't have a license. Their entire conversation had been illegal.

The guilt that immediately marched into his mind and evicted every other feeling was something awful. He knew it was irrational, but he couldn't help it. The

whole idea of having to have a license to talk to someone was as ridiculous as having to have a license to
have sex with them. Right? Right! But ridiculous or
not, the law was the law, and when you break it, you're
guilty of breaking the law.

The nice thing about guilt is that it's so easy to re-
press. Within a day Barry had relegated all recollections
of his criminal behavior of the night before to the
depths of his subconscious and was back at Intensity
Five, waiting for whomever to strike up a conversation.
The only person who so much as glanced his way, however, was Evelyn, the woman behind the refreshment
stand. He went to other speakeasies, but it was always
the same story. People avoided him. Their eyes shied
away. His vibrations became such an effective repellent
that he had only to enter a room in order to empty it of
half its custom. Or so it seemed. When one is experiencing failure, it is hard to resist the comfort of paranoia.

With only a week left till his temporary license ex-
pired, Barry abandoned all hope and all shame and
went back to Partyland with fifteen hundred dollars in
cash, obtained from Beneficial Finance.

The MacKinnons were not in their blue settee, and
neither Freddy the usher nor Madge of the green sofa
could say what had become of them. He flopped into
the empty settee with a sense of complete, abject surrender, but so eternally does hope spring that inside of a
quarter of an hour he had adjusted to the idea of never
being licensed and was daydreaming instead of a life of
majestic, mysterious silence on the rim of the Grand
Canyon. He rolled out the console and ordered a slice
of pineapple pie and some uppers.

The waitress who brought his order was Cinderella
Johnson. She was wearing levis and a T-shirt with the
word "Princess" in big, glitter-dust letters across her
breasts. Her hat said: "Let Tonight Be Your Enchanted
Evening at Partyland!"

"Cinderella!" he exclaimed. "Cinderella Johnson!
Are you *working* here?"

She beamed. "Isn't it wonderful? I started three days ago. It's like a dream come true."

"Congratulations."

"Thanks." Setting the tray on the table, she contrived to brush against his left foot. "I see you're wearing the same shoes."

"Mm."

"Is something the matter?" she asked, handing him the uppers with a glass of water. "You look gloomy, if you'll forgive my saying so."

"Sometimes it does you good to feel gloomy." One of the pills insisted on getting stuck in his throat. Just like, he thought, a lie.

"Hey, do you mind if I sit down on your couch a minute? I am frazzled. It's a tremendous opportunity, working here, but it does take it out of you."

"Great," said Barry. "Fine. Terrific. I could use some company."

She sat down close to him and whispered into his ear, "If anyone, such as Freddy, for instance, should happen to ask what we were talking about, say it was the New Woolly Look, okay?"

"That's *Topic*'s feature story this week?"

She nodded. "I guess you heard about the MacKinnons."

"I asked, but I didn't get any answers."

"They were arrested, for trafficking, right here on this couch, while they were taking money from the agent that had set them up. There's no way they can wiggle out of it this time. People say how sorry they are and everything, but I don't know: they *were* criminals, after all. What they were doing only makes it harder for the rest of us to get our endorsements honestly."

"I suppose you're right."

"Of course I'm right."

Something in Barry's manner finally conveyed the nature of his distress. The light dawned: "You have *got* your license, haven't you?"

Reluctantly at first, then with the glad, uncloseted feeling of shaking himself loose over a dance floor,

Barry told Cinderella of his ups and downs during the past six months.

"Oh, that is so terrible," she commiserated at the end of his tale. "That is so unfair."

"What can you do?" he asked, figuratively.

Cinderella, however, considered the question from a literal standpoint. "Well," she said, "we haven't ever really talked together, not seriously, but you certainly ought to have a license."

"It's good of you to say so," said Barry morosely.

"So—if you'd like an endorsement from me . . . ?" She reached into her back pocket, took out her license, and peeled off an endorsement sticker.

"Oh, no, really, Cinderella." He took the precious sticker between thumb and forefinger. "I don't deserve this. Why should you go out on a limb for someone you scarcely know?"

"That's okay," she said. "I'm sure you'd have done just the same for me."

"If there is anything I can do in return . . . ?"

She frowned, shook her head vehemently, and then said, "Well . . . maybe . . . "

"Name it."

"Could I have one of your shoes?"

He laughed delightedly. "Have both of them!"

"Thanks, but I wouldn't have room."

He bent forward, undid the laces, pulled off his right shoe, and handed it to Cinderella.

"It's a beautiful shoe," she said, holding it up to the light. "Thank you *so* much."

And that is the end of the story.

Death Therapy

James Patrick Kelly

People have been trying to figure out ways to prevent crime since before the first Egyptian moved the markers denoting the boundaries of his neighbor's crop, but so far we've had very little success. Even capital punishment doesn't seem to have deterred barbaric crimes such as rape and murder . . . but what if a convicted murderer could be put through the trauma of execution and then brought back to life?

James Patrick Kelly is twenty-seven and lives in New Hampshire; he says he used to be invisible until he gave up a paying job to write science fiction and prove he exists. "Death Therapy" was one of his first sales; in view of his talent for characterization and plotting, it's obvious that there'll be many more to come.

Carla Walsh stayed in bed as long as she could, trying to put off the start of her day. She considered calling in sick but knew she wouldn't; she had never taken a sick day in her life. At nine-thirty the clock radio buzzed and the man on the government station began to announce the news. She went into the kitchen and filled a cup with steaming water from the tap. While her tea steeped, she made a miso and bean sprout sandwich for lunch; the institute's cafeteria closed on weekends. Carla was getting bored with her new diet, but the thought of eating dead flesh repelled her. She drank the tea slowly, lighting up a trank when the cup was half empty. Then she showered and began to dress.

Carla Walsh was a tall, lean woman who at one time might have been strikingly pretty. Now she stood slump-shouldered and her delicate features had hardened into a thin, bony mask. She chose from her small wardrobe impatiently; she found it difficult to be interested in clothes today.

At the end of her driveway she stopped to check the mail and found a letter from Jack among the bills and advertisements. She put the mail on the seat beside her and pulled onto the narrow highway.

Before she and Jack had separated, Carla had planned to take a staff position at Massachusetts General Hospital in Boston. Now she was no longer sure that that was what she wanted. She hated the idea of giving up her position at the institute almost as much as she hated the idea of losing Jack for good. Carla had always believed that a doctor should keep her personal and professional lives separate. As she sped down the twisting back roads, she thought grimly that it was much easier now that she had only one life to manage.

She liked to think that Challant was partly to blame. He had recruited her away from teaching and had steered her into her studies of the metabolism of dying. She had been flattered by his personal, almost paternal interest in her career. His praise, however, did little to melt that cold, detached feeling she had whenever she and Jack made love after she had spent the day cutting up cadavers.

Her space in the parking lot had her name stenciled on it in yellow paint. She trudged into the main office building, a ferroconcrete dome that nestled into the landscaped grounds like the egg of some great stone bird. In her office she opened Jack's letter and read it with growing disappointment. It was just another matter-of-fact report: a party at Harvard; news of Sherry Fallows, one of Carla's students; gripes about Eggleston, the head of his department at Northeastern.

The closest he came to mentioning their problem was to ask when she planned to submit her paper; he wanted to come up and visit when it was done. Despite herself, she was pleased at the thought of seeing him again so soon. The weeks since he had been gone had been long ones.

She opened the rest of her mail slowly, even taking time to read over the titles of the University of Virginia surplus-book flyer. Meyers interrupted her at eleven-fifteen.

"I just gave her the last isotope injection."

"I'm coming."

Clear plastic tubes snaked from the respirator into Alica Bowen's open mouth. Her bluish lips were coated with dried mucus; her sunken chest rose and fell to the machine's rhythm. The room smelled like dirty laundry.

Carla and Meyers dressed for the autopsy. Meyers finished first and went next door to prepare the post-mortem room. Carla drifted reluctantly over to the respirator.

Although still hooked up to the machine, the woman was legally dead. Carla had never known her, but she had come to know the empty husk that Alica Bowen had left behind quite well. She had been found in a Boston alleyway, raped and near death. Only the respirator had kept her alive the past three months. Carla had hoped to bring Alica Bowen's massively damaged brain back to life, or failing that, to show that her techniques could at least begin to replace dead cells. Only last week Carla had been forced to admit that despite signs of cellular regeneration, not even a shadow of a person still huddled in Alica Bowen's ruined brain. The woman on the bed was now only a body, just like the hundreds of dead bodies she had seen in sixteen years of practicing medicine. It was a thing, not a woman, she reminded herself fiercely. In the next room she could hear the muted rumble of the scanner being moved into place, casters scraping over the floor.

Meyers came back in and nodded.

She felt very calm and in control as she turned the

respirator off. It was much simpler than she had imagined. The body gurgled, twisted. Its eyes opened abruptly, glaring without sight. Its legs kicked out weakly, then fell twitching into stillness. The luminous curve on the electrocardiograph went flat, matching the flat line on the electroencephalograph.

They slid the tubes from its throat, loaded the wasted body onto a gurney, and wheeled it into the next room. Beside the marble operating table was a long, lead-lined plastic box. They lowered the body into it, fitting the neck into a rubber collar at one end so that the head hung limply outside the box. Meyers closed the lid and the head jerked upright. Carla pulled the remote unit of the isotope scanner toward the box and positioned it over the forehead. Then they retreated to the control area, a small space filled with computer-linked instrumentation and protected from the rest of the room by a shield of six-inch permaglass. Carla watched as Meyers worked at the computer console. The scanner swiveled on its flexible arm and began to weave a hemispherical pattern around the head of the dead woman.

Tiny beads of light raced across the main readout, diagramming a delicate tracery of veins and arteries. It looked to her like the clash of frozen lightning.

"Looks like everything is there," Meyers said.

Carla remained silent.

"The first time cranial blood vessels have regenerated."

"Yeah."

"Ready to open her up yet?"

She took a deep breath. "Give me a few minutes. I'm going out into the hall for a smoke."

She tried not to look at the box and its contents as she walked by. Out in the hall she took a crumpled pack of tranks from her surgical gown. The pack felt empty as she fumbled at it, but there was one left. She lit it eagerly. The mildly soothing smoke helped to distance her from what she had just done. She knew that she could not avoid her guilty horror, only postpone it.

Meyers opened the door. She dropped the butt and

crushed it with the toe of her shoe. She could hear the sound of water splashing in the sink.

There was a note on her desk on Monday morning. Challant wanted to see her.

Dr. Edward deQuincey Challant was the most celebrated of the "pragmatic" behaviorists. He had reached the height of his fame in 1982 when his book, *Punished in the Sight of Men*, was a best seller for nine weeks. Challant was asked to serve on a presidential commission to study the federalization of the prison system and three years later was named director of the Institute for the Study of Modern Man.

His office at the apex of the dome was the largest in the institute. It was decorated with a simple elegance that came naturally to Challant, whose breeding was an easy mix of Brahmin and Harvard. In the center of the room was a slab of quarter-inch permaglass mounted on a sculptured chrome pedestal. Challant always kept it scrupulously free of clutter; the only papers he allowed on his desk were the ones he was working on. The curved wall behind the desk was floor-to-ceiling permaglass filled with a magnificent view of Mounts Washington and Jefferson. Challant was surveying his view when Carla entered. He swiveled in his chair and motioned her into one of the chrome and leather Eames chairs in front of his desk. He had a full head of silky white hair and a pink wrinkled face. Tinted rimless glasses made his gray eyes seem vague and slightly out of focus.

"Good morning, Doctor," he said. "How was your weekend?"

"Terrible."

"Insomnia again?"

"Yeah."

He sighed. "I know it's not my place to say this, but you really should consider cutting down the time you spend here. Six days a week is too much—even for you."

"I don't think it's too much," she said stiffly. "I have a job to do and I do it."

Challant paused, then nodded with reluctant approval. "Have the Bowen tissue samples come back from biopsy yet?"

"Not that I've heard."

"Meyers came in this morning raving about the deep circulation."

"Oh, the circulation was great. I bet we find some trace isotopes in the brain cells themselves." Her voice was flat, uninterested.

"Did you have any of the problems we discussed? You still feel that this was the only way to end the experiment?"

"I felt that way on Saturday."

"And today?"

She thought for a moment. "Today, I'm glad that it's over. For her. For me."

"I've notified the family. They're coming for the body this afternoon."

She gazed out at the mountains.

"How's the paper coming?"

She grimaced. "I'm out of practice, I forgot how hard it is to put words down on paper."

"I know what you mean." He chuckled. It was a dry, humorless sound. "But there's no rush to get it out. As a matter of fact, there's something else I'd like you to look at. Something important." He pushed a thin book bound in plastic across the desk to her. She glanced at the cover: "Proposal to Study Certain Behavior Modification Techniques, submitted by ISMM, Inc., September 11, 1988." Stamped across the bottom of the cover in green was the word "Secret."

"When did we get into the spy business?"

"You'll understand when you read the proposal. I heard from the Justice Department this morning; they've given a verbal commitment to the project. I want you to head the medical team." His smile was meant to be disarming; Carla hated it. "Spend some time looking this over, and when you finish it, we'll talk."

Challant's manner irked her. Whenever he gave her an assignment, he acted as if he were doing her a favor.

"I'll try to get back to you sometime today."

Back in her office, she began to read the proposal resentfully, thinking more of the summary chapter of her paper than of the words in front of her. By the end of the first page she had forgotten all about her own work.

" . . . In the case of sex criminals, statistically the group most resistant to rehabilitation, you can attempt to shape their behavior into a normal pattern of sexuality, or you can punish deviant behavior. While the former is impractical in a prison situation, the latter has never enjoyed statistical success. The problem is that negative reinforcement has never been powerful enough to overcome the primal drives which give rise to deviant behavior. The acts of the sex criminal are expressions both of sexuality and the instinct for aggression. Such primal drives cannot be bottled up by relatively weak negative reinforcements such as prison and electroshock.

"The proposed treatment counters the sexual and aggressive drives with an aversion stimulus of greater magnitude. It has been theorized that all anxieties in the human organism are derived from the fear of death. Yet Arkad and Fritz's studies with alpha-capability telepaths demonstrate conclusively that the death penalty is not an effective deterrent to crime because the human organism is incapable of conceptualizing its own death. The proposed treatment permits the sex criminal to undergo a death experience in a therapeutic context. Revivification under controlled circumstances is a straightforward application of existing medical technology."

She read the proposal through twice. When she finished with it she threw it at the wall. It skidded across the floor on crumpled pages. Her hand trembled as she lit a trank.

At first she was tempted to tear the proposal up and

dump the shreds on Challant's desk. That's what Jack would have told her to do. She realized that he was right about one thing at least; some part of her which she rarely let to the surface had always distrusted Challant.

She left her desk and paced. This was not an experiment; it was torture. She remembered something that Betty Kerin, her advisor at med school, had told her. She said that no one becomes a doctor unless she has very strong and very personal feelings about dying, and no one becomes a good doctor until she tries to understand those feelings. At the time Carla had thought it very wise. Recently she hadn't thought much about it at all. The realization chilled her.

She crossed over to where the proposal lay, picked it up, brushed the gray wisps of floor dust from it, and straightened its pages. She placed it next to her typewriter and sat down to type her letter of resignation.

There was still a page in the carriage with half a dozen lines of typing on it: her final report on the Bowen experiment. She stared at the long blank stretch of paper, then reached to pull it out of the machine—too late. She looked right through the blankness on the page into Alica Bowen's mindless, haunting stare. An accusation? Who was she to judge this experiment?

She got up and began to pace again. She carried a tissue in her hand, crumbling it tirelessly. Finally, when she calmed down, she sat at her desk and tried to consider Challant's proposal objectively.

She drew a line down the middle of a sheet of graph paper and put a plus sign at the top of one column, a minus on the other. On the minus side she wrote the name Betty Kerin in bold letters. She studied it for a few minutes, then circled it. In the plus column she wrote:

Death Penalty favored in polls—will pass soon
Let prisoners make own decisions
Possible success of therapy $= ?\%$
Who finishes paper? Meyers? Challant?

As she stared at her list, she realized that there was no good reason she could give Challant for refusing his offer, because her decision would not be based on professional standards, but on personal prejudices.

"Ah, Carla. I'm glad you're back," Challant said, stacking the papers he had been reading and placing them in his briefcase. "Have a seat."

She remained standing. Challant's smile of greeting died painlessly. "Was it a difficult decision?" he said.

"I'm not sure I've made a decision yet."

"Oh?" He stared at his shoes through the desk.

"What I mean is, I'm not convinced by this." She placed the proposal on the desk distastefully. "What makes you think this can work?"

"Oh, I see." He rose and walked around her towards the door. "Have a seat on the couch over there and we'll talk. Coffee?"

"No," she said icily.

He was gone briefly. She heard him tell his secretary not to disturb them as he backed slowly into the room. He pushed the door shut behind him with his foot while balancing a thick green file and a mug of coffee. When he turned to face her, she was still standing at the desk.

"Come now, Doctor," he said shuffling over to her carefully. "No confrontations. Please." He smiled and sat on the long, low-slung couch which faced the window wall. She crossed the room reluctantly and took the opposite end.

"Well?" she said.

"You want me to justify the project, is that it?"

She nodded grimly.

"All right." He took a sip of coffee. "When I was with the prison commission, I was shown intelligence reports on the Soviet prison system. I can't say how the information was obtained, because I didn't want to find out." He shrugged. "But I—we all accepted it as valid.

"They started experimenting with the treatment in the early eighties. Apparently they now have some sort of prototype facility in operation in Aikhal, Siberia.

They claim a success rate of about 70 percent, working almost exclusively with political prisoners. Just what they call a success, I can't really say."

"And that's it?"

"Oh, no. There's much more," he said dryly. "You see, I soon found out that they expected me to evaluate the Soviet therapy for application to our own prisons." He glanced at her, then looked away. "I expect you know how I felt when this happened. After all, we're not Nazis. We don't torture people just to try out some lunatic scheme. But I had second thoughts. Aside from killing my chances of ever working with federal money, what would I accomplish by quitting? Wouldn't it be better to put this ridiculous theory to rest myself?"

He took another sip of coffee. "Two things have happened since. I served out my appointment to the commission. I toured most of our larger prisons, talked to the staff, the prisoners. I saw that we were already involved in torture, more subtle perhaps, but torture all the same. When you lock a man up in a dead-storage bin and tell him that he's damaged goods. . . . And they're crowded. Oh, Lord, they're jammed in there like cattle in a slaughterhouse."

He paused. Carla thought sourly that sometimes his act was just a little too slick to be believable.

"After that," he continued, "I didn't want to judge the Soviets. I still thought their approach was wrong, but I didn't want to judge them. I convinced the people at Justice that I would need time and resources to study the therapy properly. They generously arranged for me to come here. I've been at it three years now, and I've done everything short of running a test subject through the therapy. And I'm convinced that it can work."

"You can document that?"

Challant hefted the fat green file and laid it on the couch. She made no move for it. His face was expressionless; he was waiting.

"Okay," she said. "But even if it does work, so what? It's still not worth it. People get out of prison eventually. You want to burn a trauma in their minds that they can't forget, ever."

"You already know the answer to that," he said softly. "They're going to pass it, Carla. They've held off as long as they dared, but too many people want the death penalty legalized. People with money. People with votes. The economics of our system demand another way of handling criminals, and the only other way is to kill them."

He leaned forward, looking directly at her. His gaze flustered her slightly; Challant never made and held eye contact so aggressively. Her face began to feel uncomfortably warm.

"I've spent three years preparing for this experiment. Helping you along with your studies of dying was part of my preparation. No matter what you think of it, your work has been important. In time you will succeed with it. Science will be richer for your success, and you—you will probably be famous." He looked away. "I'm sorry to have to say this, Carla, because I like and respect you. But if you don't work on this project, someone else will. The institute wouldn't be able to afford both of you."

Carla didn't reply for several minutes. "All right," she said finally. The words seemed to stick in her throat. "But skip the threats from now on. I'm with you only as long as I can see positive results."

"You're sure?"

"I'm sure for now, Doctor. I'm not making any promises."

Challant took off his glasses and rubbed his eyes. "It's been a hard day, Carla. First Washington, now you." He put them back on. "I believe in this project. I believe in Dr. Carla Walsh. I'd like a firmer commitment, but I guess I'll take what I can get. For now." He slid toward her end of the couch, and they shook hands without enthusiasm.

"If you have some time," he said. "I'd like to get your opinions on some technical matters."

"Go ahead."

"I take it you have no problem with electrocution as the means of death."

"No. That seems the best way. What you want is ventricular fibrillation, disruption of the heart's coordination. Cardiac arrest usually takes place within three to five minutes."

"Cardiac arrest isn't what we want, though. The Soviet experiments used brain death as a determinant. I think we should count on at least five minutes of flat EEG. They report a phenomenon they call 'cellular shock' after that, which is what we want."

"That's very tricky. You run the risk of brain damage."

Challant stood and strolled over to the window wall, hands clasped behind his back. In a flat voice he said, "There's another team, in New Mexico, working along similar lines. They've already done several cardiac-arrest experiments, and they're not getting anything near the behavior modification that the Soviets report. They're looking for a brain-death expert now."

"I see. Okay, flat EEG," Carla thought briefly. "Is there any reason why we can't depress the central nervous system? Barbiturate poisoning impedes the decay process."

Challant turned to face her. "I'm not sure that's possible. I'll be using memory drugs for hypnotherapy, so I'll need at least some kind of stimulant for the final phase of the experiment."

"No, no, that's okay. We could use an amphetamine sulfate—say, amobarbital. And we could probably cover ourselves by reducing body temperature to, say, ninety degrees, right after cardiac arrest. Now, what about subjects?"

He crossed the room and opened his files. "I've already solicited volunteers. I've selected"—he checked the name—"Michael Huxol as our first subject. Judging from his interviews with the prison psychologists, he should be receptive to this kind of therapy. Here's his file. Take it home, look it over, and get back to me as soon as possible if you have any objections."

"What are you going to tell him?"

"Well, we can't very well tell him exactly what the experiment is about. He was told when he volunteered that there would be personal risk involved. He was also told that there was a chance that his sentence would be commuted if the experiment was successful. The rest he'll just have to find out as it happens."

Carla nodded and thrust completely out of her mind what little sympathy she had for the volunteers.

She built a fire in the fireplace that night and made herself a rum toddy. As the drink began to burn into her, she remembered the letter from Jack. She would have to write and tell him that she was getting involved with a new project. She imagined him reading her reply; the thought made her uneasy. He would take it the wrong way. He would think that she wasn't serious about wanting to try again. She thought of calling him but knew she wouldn't. She disliked talking to people she couldn't see, and she dreaded long silences on the telephone. There had been too many long silences the last time.

She realized that she wanted to see him, to have him sitting there next to her so that she could explain exactly the way she felt with her hands, her mouth, her body. She went over to the mantel. There was a picture on it. The two of them sat, cross-legged and smiling, at the top of Mount Monadnock. Far below them the lowlands rolled to the horizon in a shag of orange, brown and yellow. The longer she stared at them, the more unreal those two smiling faces became. They belonged to a pair of improbable characters in a fairy tale where everyone lived happily ever after and where saying "I love you" was the easiest thing in the world.

She went back into the kitchen to make herself another toddy. When she came back, she opened Huxol's file and began to read.

Michael Huxol was twenty-eight, weighed 140, stood nearly six feet tall, had black hair and brown eyes. Since high school he had lost a variety of jobs in the federal work program. He had been accused of rape twice before the Lorenzo murders; both cases were thrown out for lack of evidence. On February 20, 1986, in Worcester, Massachusetts, he had followed Lenore Lorenzo, a twenty-two-year-old bank teller, home from work, forced his way into her apartment, raped her, and then strangled her and her mother, Maria, age sixty-one. He had been booked for the murders two years later when he had been picked up in Boston for procuring. He was convicted and sentenced to life imprisonment at the U.S. Correctional Institution at Walpole, Massachusetts.

Carla was surprised at the pictures in Huxol's file. They showed him to be a rather ordinary-looking man. She couldn't see rape and murder in his thin, frightened face.

She put the file away and tried to read herself to sleep. Halfway through a text on cerebral localization, she realized that it was useless; she was only getting bored. She fixed herself a toddy with a double shot of rum and began a long and loving letter to Jack.

Carla stepped into the doorway and saw that they were waiting. Huxol was sitting on the examination table, naked. His gaunt body was partly covered by the thick black hair which curled from his pasty skin. His newly shaven head made his face seem impossibly large. A gray-uniformed security guard stood off to one side of the table, smoking a trank and tapping the ashes on the floor.

Huxol saw her first.

"Who's that?" His surprisingly low-pitched voice shook.

The guard turned, dropped the smoke behind him, and stepped on it as unobtrusively as he could. Carla ignored him.

"I'm Dr. Walsh," she said, approaching Huxol. "And you're . . . "

"Go away. Please. You're not the doctor." He shrank from her, sliding backwards on the table and covering his groin with his hand. He looked to the guard for support.

"It's all right, Huxol. This won't take long. It's just a routine examination." She edged into his line of sight; he jerked his head away.

"You, Huxol. Get up! And pay attention to the doctor." The guard came up behind him and shoved him off the table. Only the balls of Huxol's feet touched the floor as he hunched over, eyes lowered. His face flushed with embarrassment.

Carla was getting impatient. "Come on now, Huxol. I'm not going to hurt you." He did not respond. "Look at me when I talk to you."

He raised his head until he met her gaze directly. She felt her throat tighten; a wave of revulsion washed over her. She was looking at a different man. He was shockingly ugly: just being near him made her feel unclean, nauseated. The muscles of his jaws began to work hypnotically. She had trouble breathing. His eyes raked down her body like claws, and his hunger, perverse in its animal ferocity, became her hunger.

He looked away.

She staggered as if he had let go of a rope on which she was pulling with all her strength. The guard moved quickly, grabbed Huxol's shoulder, and spun him back against the table.

"Hey! Can't I trust you for a second? What did you do to her?"

"Nothing. I didn't do nothing."

Carla leaned against the wall, breathing heavily. "It's okay. I just feel a little . . . faint. I'll be fine in a minute." She managed a grim smile.

The guard backed away uncertainly, and Huxol got up, resuming his normal slouch and rubbing his back. She waited uneasily for another storm of horror to burst inside her. Nothing happened. Huxol seemed now as he had before: scared, helpless, inoffensive. All she felt for him was pity. She told herself reasonably that she had imagined the whole thing and carefully avoided looking him in the eye again.

She ran through the standard tests quickly: lung check by percussion, blood pressure, reflexes, eye, ear, and throat inspections. She took blood and urine samples and scraped some tissue from the inside of his mouth. As usual she saved the most difficult for last. She pushed his head to one side and then felt his groin for lumps.

His penis started to get hard.

"Cough . . . again . . . again. Good."

It stuck straight out. She glanced at his face. His eyes were clamped shut and there were tears on his cheeks.

"Okay, Mr. Huxol. We're finished in here."

He looked like a little boy caught by his mother playing with himself in the closet. She put on her best professional smile for him, dug into her pocket, pulled out her pack of tranks, and offered him one. He goggled at her, astonished. He let her light it for him and then sucked greedily at it.

"Let me find you a dressing gown and then we'll take some x-rays. Okay?"

There was no compelling professional reason why Carla had to see Huxol once she completed her examination. Yet she found that she was with him several times each day, if only for a few minutes. In the mornings he struggled through the battery of tests which the staff had prepared for him; in the afternoons there were long and exhausting hypnotherapy sessions with Challant. Carla insisted that she, and not Challant, administer the memory drugs before hypnotherapy. Often she monitored their sessions on closed circuit; Challant's relentless skill at stripping away Huxol's defenses made a fascinating, if somewhat repellent, show. She made daily stops at Huxol's heavily guarded room when she arrived at the institute and when she left for home. He asked for a trank whenever he saw her. Once he even smiled and said, "Thanks."

The week of preparation went quickly. Challant predicted that Huxol would respond to the death scenario as if it were real. He was still confident that the experiment would succeed. Carla was less sure.

The moment of terror she had experienced the first time she had seen Huxol haunted her. She steadily lost her battles with insomnia, especially after she dreamed that Huxol raped her. She wanted to discuss her reaction with Challant, but not until she understood it better herself. She pored over Huxol's files again, this time paying closer attention to all the clinical data in his psychological profile.

She spent a whole morning on the phone with the court-appointed psychologist who had testified at Huxol's trial. She borrowed some books from the institute's library. When she was sure of herself, she went to see Challant.

She found him watching a tape of the day's hypnotherapy session. Despite the rows of folded seats, the audiovisual theater did not seem quite empty. The room swallowed up sound as if it were jammed with people. Huxol's outsized face filled the screen, soundlessly convulsed with laughter. She crossed the back of the theater and climbed the stairs to the projection room. The muffled hysteria of Huxol's taped voice filtered through the door. She knocked.

The laughter stopped and the face on the screen froze. Its eyes bulged, its cheeks bunched tightly, its mouth gaped. It was a face in transition; Carla could imagine it continuing to laugh or beginning to cry when the tape started again. She heard footsteps. The door opened.

"Carla?" Challant's brow wrinkled with annoyance. "Who were you expecting?"

"No one. I wasn't expecting . . . come in. Come in and have a seat. Did you see anyone at the door?"

She shook her head.

Challant scowled and turned away into the brightness of the projection room. Carla entered, blinking, as he picked up a phone at the control desk, jabbed out four digits, spoke briefly into the receiver, then slammed it into its place.

"Sorry. There's supposed to be a guard out there." They sat facing each other on folding chairs. "Now what can I do for you?"

"I have some questions I hope you have the answers to."

"I'll do what I can."

"Does Huxol show up on any of the psi scales?"

"Why, yes. He's at least two standard deviations above the mean on all of them."

"Could he project?"

"Project? Thoughts? Perhaps, after a few months training at one of the psi labs."

"I don't mean with training. I mean now."

He leaned his chair back, studying her curiously. "I doubt it. No, I take that back. He definitely couldn't do it now. There has never been any documentation of psi capability without biofeedback training."

"I think we have some here." She told him about the incident with Huxol in the examination room and her discussion with the court psychologist. He listened politely but impassively. She wondered anxiously what he thought of her story, then decided it was too late to stop.

"Okay," she said. "So there's not much question that Huxol has psi potential. Suppose he has much more than shows on your tests. Suppose he's fighting an alpha-capability just as hard as he can. Why? It gets out of control; it wrecks his life. Sometimes he does project his mental states, when influenced by specific stimuli. Sexual stimuli. I bet he can't approach a woman in a sexual context without transmitting his—his lust. Pent-up, ugly, frightening lust; I've experienced it. He's probably never been able to have a loving relationship with a woman."

"So?"

"So! Did any of what I just said make sense to you?"

"Some. I'm interested in your conclusions."

"My conclusions. Okay. If I'm right, then this whole therapy is wrong for Huxol. He needs to control his ability before he can resolve his sexual problem." She paused, frowning. "Also your experimental results will be worthless if you don't look at the relationship between the telepathy and the criminal record."

"Anything else?"

"No. Yes, yes, I think that the experiment could be dangerous. How do we know he won't broadcast his death experience? And what would that do to anyone who received it?"

"And so you'd like me to postpone the experiment."

"You don't believe a word of this, do you?"

"I believe that you're serious." Carla tried to hold in her anger; she hated, above all things, to be patronized. Challant seemed to think she was a little crazy. "But to answer your question," he said gently, "no, I think you're mistaken. I can't believe Huxol has psi capabilities until you can tell me where he was trained. I've been with him for six days now, and I know some things about him that even he doesn't know. I've seen no evidence of alpha-capability telepathy. And even if he had it, which he doesn't, he would still need this therapy. I'm convinced of that. As for broadcasting his death experience, it's impossible. He'll be heavily drugged; all studies indicate that drugs effectively inhibit the alpha-capability."

Carla was subdued. "And what about my reaction to Huxol?"

"I have my own theory about that. You won't like it."

"Try me."

He shifted uncomfortably in his chair. "Alica Bowen died the night she was raped. You couldn't accept that, you thought she was still alive. When your experiment failed, you felt like a murderer." He paused. She sat very straight, very still. Her eyes were two pools of blackness. She nodded tightly for him to continue. "Michael Huxol is a rapist and a murderer. He didn't kill the Bowen girl, but some part of you would like to think that he did. That part of you needs to find the real murderer so that you can share your guilt. You meet Huxol for the first time. Something happens between you. I heard that Huxol had an erection when you examined him. In your mind, this becomes the psychic rape you talk about. Your guilt . . . "

"Stop it." She spit the words out.

They sat, not looking at each other, for several minutes. The silence was as painful as a scream. Finally Challant got up and went over to the control desk. He held a button down, and the stopped image of Huxol on the screen accelerated to a blur. When the tape finished rewinding, he pulled the cassette from its slot and pocketed it.

"I'm sorry I had to say that, Carla. Look, things will go off tomorrow without a hitch and we can forget about this."

She said nothing.

"I haven't told you before," he said, sitting next to her again, "but we're in trouble in Washington. They don't understand our work and they're getting impatient. With this team in New Mexico moving so quickly, everything here has to happen on schedule. That means tomorrow we put Huxol through a death experience."

"I'm going now." She rose quickly and turned away from him.

"We can't do it without you, Doctor."

"I'm tired. I'll see you in the morning." She was out the door before he could reply. She trudged blindly through the empty corridors; as usual, she would be one of the last to leave. They should give me some kind of award, she thought bitterly. She stopped at her office to get her briefcase. The phone rang. She tried to ignore it, couldn't.

"Walsh speaking."

"Carla? I guess I should've known you'd be there."

"Hello, Jack." She sank wearily into her desk chair and tried not to sound like she wanted to hang up.

"I got your letter."

Pause.

"Oh."

"Dammit, Carla, don't you have anything else to say?"

"I said it all in the letter."

"No, you didn't say it all. You didn't say anything. You went on and on about how much you missed me, and then you said you weren't coming down here. What's this new project you're on?"

"Oh, come on, Jack. What's the use?"

Pause.

"I'm coming up, let's see . . . uh . . . Thursday's the soonest. Day after tomorrow."

"You can't come then. I've got something important on here."

"Skip it." He sounded angry.

"Can't. It's the new project. I can't talk about it, I can't skip it, and you can't . . . "

"I'm coming up. Thursday afternoon."

She didn't want to make any final decisions over the phone. She still wasn't sure what her final decision was going to be. After she finished tomorrow, there was no reason why she couldn't drop everything, go back to Boston with him that night. It was a nice thought, even though it sounded a little farfetched.

"Okay, Jack. Thursday."

"I want you to take the day off, understand?"

"Okay, Jack."

Pause.

"I still love you, Carla. I want you back."

"I've got to go. Goodbye." She held the receiver away from her ear until she heard his distant "Goodbye," and then she hung up.

Since the mysterious project had been the subject of much gossip, Challant scheduled the final session for Wednesday night. At eight-thirty they brought a pale Huxol down to the infirmary for a final checkup and his injection. He held his slight body defensively throughout the examination, as if he expected someone to hit him. As soon as Carla finished with him, Challant and a security guard whisked him away for a final hypnotherapy session.

She went directly from the infirmary to the makeshift

control center which had been set up in the audiovisual projection room. The room had been completely sealed off from the theater: the only way to see the lecture platform and the screen was through the television monitors in the corner. Challant had ordered that the rear screen projector be used for the experiment. He did not want to take the chance of having any lights distract Huxol from the death scenario.

They had made the lecture platform over to look like a stage. Sue Jacoby, one of the staff assistants, smoked a trank and tried not to look nervous. Behind her, two security guards were using a folding screen to hide a heavy wooden chair. It seemed to Carla that there were more security guards than staff on this project. One of the guards turned to a camera and signaled to Carla. She pushed a button on the control console, and a curtain fell leisurely in front of the rear screen system.

The phone on the console rang and she picked it up. Challant's voice said, "We're bringing him down now," and the receiver clicked into a dial tone. Carla leaned forward to speak into her microphone: "They're coming."

Jacoby dropped her smoke and stepped on it. One of the guards dragged a chair out into the middle of the room and she sat in it. He tied her up and gagged her. Then he unbuttoned her blouse, fumbling in his embarrassment.

Carla watched the two guards leave through a side door. In a few minutes Challant, Huxol, and another guard entered the theater from the rear and passed down the deserted aisles to the stage. Challant supported Huxol, whose step was wobbly and uncertain. At the stairs leading up to the stage Challant gave Huxol some final instruction, and then he and the guard quickly retraced their steps.

Challant burst into the projection room and slid into the chair next to Carla. He paused to catch his breath, then spoke into his microphone.

"All right, Michael. It's time."

Huxol shuddered, then turned around dazedly. Challant had placed a suggestion in Huxol's mind during hypnotherapy that what he could not clearly see did not exist. To his drugged senses there was no darkened theater behind him; his world was reduced to the span of the brightly lit stage.

He saw Jacoby staring at him, horrified. He climbed the stairs and scuffed across the stage as if he were taking a noontime stroll. She started rocking back and forth in her chair. Her fright seemed very convincing to Carla.

Huxol slapped her across the face. Carla touched Challant's arm to protest, but he ignored her. Huxol put his hand to the woman's reddening face.

He whispered something to her. Challant swore and turned up the gain on the amplifier.

Huxol's hand slid around behind her neck and loosened the knot on her gag. "What's happening here?" he said as the gag went limp and fell out of her mouth. She screamed. He slapped her again and she choked the sound back. She began to cry.

"This is perfect," Challant said. There was awe in his voice. "This is just what we want."

"Start it now. He's going to hurt her." Carla tightened her grip on his arm.

"Not yet. He's still suspicious. Let the power of the scenario work on him for a bit longer. Once he gives into it completely, he won't be able to tell projected images from real people."

Huxol stepped to one side of the woman. He put his hand on the other side of her face and twisted her head around toward him.

"Who the hell are you?"

"L–L–Lenore. Lenore Jacoby. Please don't. You're hurting me."

He rubbed his hand on her cheek. "Lenore, Lenore," he said softly. His hand wandered down the line of her jaw. "I once knew a cunt named Lenore." His hand was on the curve of her neck. Her eyes rolled up. "You're nice, Lenore. Like the other. Nice and soft." His hand was on her chest, moving down . . .

Carla clutched at Challant.

. . . slipping inside her bra.

Challant punched a button.

"Lenore."

The three security guards rushed onstage. Huxol spun around just as they reached him. They pulled him from the woman, pushed him against a wall, and handcuffed him. Two of them held him there while the third untied Jacoby. She staggered off the stage, crying hysterically. Then the guard pulled the folding screen aside to reveal the chair. Huxol recognized the danger in its bundles of wires and its plastic cap studded with electrodes; he tried to lash out at his guards. They dodged his clumsy attempt and threw him up hard against the wall. The third guard rejoined them, and the three of them stripped him, unhandcuffed him and locked him into the chair. He got control of himself and yelled, "No, shit, no! I wasn't going to do nothing. I wasn't." They lowered the cap onto his head, then hurried from the stage.

Challant worked at the console. The curtain rose ominously. He spoke into his microphone: "Michael Huxol, you are going to die."

Carla turned the specially installed cooling system up to its maximum.

A picture flashed on the screen. It was a slide of Huxol's mother and father. Challant spoke into his microphone again, his voice distorted so that Huxol wouldn't recognize it.

"Put your clothes on, son. Don't you have any respect for your mother?"

"I can't. Can't you see? I can't do anything?"

Carla spoke into her microphone: "Michael! Have you been playing with yourself *again?* Put your clothes on right now!"

"Can't." He began to cry in his strange way: tears on a totally indifferent face.

"Now," Challant said. Carla turned a knob on the console up to the halfway mark, then flipped a switch.

One, two, three, she counted to herself. She turned the power off.

Huxol writhed in the chair from the jolt. The screen flashed pictures of Huxol in various moods. "Nobody likes you, Michael," Challant said. "Why doesn't anybody like you? Why, Michael?" There was sarcasm in his voice. He motioned to Carla. She turned the knob to three quarters and flipped the switch. One, two, three, four, five, off.

Huxol struggled against the chair, lifting the rear legs off the ground. A white froth gathered at the corners of his mouth and ran down his chin.

Challant swore again. "That chair is too heavy for him to lift. If he disrupts the instrumentation . . . "

The screen flashed to a police photograph of the Lorenzo apartment. It was in a wild state of disarray. There were no bodies visible.

Challant's voice was harsh. "Why does everybody hate you, Michael?"

The picture changed to a close-up of the couch. A bare foot stuck into the top corner of the screen. Huxol screamed.

"Because you . . . "

Flash. The picture showed Lenore Lorenzo's body. Her skirt was bunched around her waist. Huxol's mouth was still open but no sound came out.

" . . . hate . . . "

Flash. A long shot of the mother's body.

" . . . everybody."

Flash. A close-up of the mother's face. There was a ring of purple bruises around her neck. Her bulging eyes were glazed. Carla gasped; the old woman had that same horrible death stare as Alica. Challant reached in front of her, spun the knob all the way to the right, and flipped the switch.

Suddenly she was plunged into a cold, bitter ocean of fear. It seethed with slimy, mindless things like herself. She sensed Huxol and Challant nearby, ripping at each other's faces; and sensing them, she was in the Lorenzo house, killing the two terrified, writhing women with manic glee. As she stood back to admire her gruesome work, Challant, then Huxol took turns killing them again, until the three stood back, admiring death, admiring. A huge claw punched through their admiration, reached down into their guts and pulled them inside out. They were three gory masses of flesh which mewled as one and grew together. They plummeted, faster and faster, toward a huge gaping maw with a tongue of flame. The tongue licked them and they burned. Then Carla tore herself free of the other two and floated just above the maw of blackness, staring into the blackness until they disappeared.

She drowsed back to reality. She peered at the monitors without comprehending the fact that Huxol had finally tipped the chair over. She thought how angry Challant would be when he found out. Slowly, mechanically, she did what she had programmed herself to do. She focused on the timer which said that Huxol's EEG had been flat for six minutes.

Abruptly, she was fully aware of herself. She turned to find Challant slumped over the console. She felt for a pulse; there was none. She picked up the phone and called the hospital, then ran out the door.

The three security guards were still standing outside the door, waiting for the end of the experiment. She yelled at them. "One of you come with me. The others get a stretcher and get Challant out front. Ambulance coming. He's in there. Move!"

Down on the stage, she unlocked Huxol from the chair. The guard helped her drag him to the infirmary. She hooked him up to the respirator and began external massage, pressing into his breastbone as hard as she could. Bones cracked. There was no response. A pale nurse stuck her head in the door.

"Dr. Challant is dead."

"So?"

"Couldn't you try to revive him?"

"Go away. I've got a patient already."

"But . . . "

"He'd be a vegetable. Out!"

There was a tentative thump that died almost immediately. She kept at it; her arm muscles felt as if they were about to snap. Finally his heart began to respond; there was a regular beat. She linked him to the electroencephalograph. The signal was faint, but still detectable.

Some of the staff members said that when Huxol woke up a few hours later, he screamed in a voice that sounded frighteningly like Challant's. They couldn't get Carla to go down and listen. The next morning some men from the Department of Justice took Huxol away.

When Jack arrived on Thursday afternoon, she was waiting in Challant's office. She had been with the police most of the night, and on the phone to Washington all morning. She felt as if she could stay up for a week.

He took a half step through the open door and peered into the office hesitantly, as if he was afraid of what he might see.

"Come in, Jack." She admired her voice. It was so cool, so much in control.

He entered the room awkwardly, carrying a long flat box behind his back. He smiled and strode across the room.

"Carla! Are you all right? They told me downstairs what happened last night."

"I'm fine. Perfect."

He put the box on Challant's desk. "For you," he said.

She pulled at the ribbon. It fell away and she opened the box. There were a dozen white roses and an envelope in it. She could feel his gaze on her as she read his note: "Carla. There's a vase for these in Boston. All my love, Jack." She looked up, her features carefully neutral. The tender look on Jack's face quickly hardened. She found this moment, as well, to be simpler than she had imagined.

"It's no good, Jack. I've made up my mind. I'm sorry."

It did not take long for him to get angry enough to leave. She waited a few minutes for the eavesdroppers in the outer office to calm down. Then she buzzed for Challant's secretary.

"Throw these out," Carla said, glancing up from some of the paperwork on the desk, "or keep them yourself. Just get them out of here." The astonished woman snatched up the box and turned to leave.

"Wait a minute. Give those back for a minute, would you?" Carla opened the box and picked one rose from the bunch. She broke the stem in half.

"Go down to my old office and get my bud vase when you get the chance," she said, absently twirling the stem between thumb and forefinger. "I think I'll keep just one for here."

Recommended Reading—1978

BRIAN W. ALDISS: "A Chinese Perspective," *Anticipations.* "The Small Stones of Tu Fu," *Isaac Asimov's Science Fiction Magazine*, March–April 1978.

GREGORY BENFORD: "In Alien Flesh," *Fantasy and Science Fiction*, September 1978.

MILDRED DOWNEY BROXON: "Singularity," *Isaac Asimov's Science Fiction Magazine*, May–June 1978.

EDWARD BRYANT: "Stone," *Fantasy and Science Fiction*, February 1978.

ORSON SCOTT CARD: "Killing Children," *Analog*, November 1978. "Mikal's Songbird," *Analog*, May 1978.

THOMAS M. DISCH: "Concepts," *Fantasy and Science Fiction*, December, 1978.

RANDALL GARRETT: "Polly Plus," *Isaac Asimov's Science Fiction Magazine*, May–June 1978.

JOHN KESSEL: "The Incredible Living Man," *Galileo*, September 1978.

STERLING E. LANIER: "The Syndicated Time," *Fantasy and Science Fiction*, July 1978.

PAT MURPHY: "Eyes of the Wolf," *Galaxy*, May 1978.

KEVIN O'DONNELL, JR.:   "The Gift of Promothous," *Analog*, January 1978.

PAMELA SARGENT: "The Novella Race," *Orbit 20*.

BOB SHAW: "Amphitheatre," *Anticipations*.

CHARLES SHEFFIELD: "Sight of Proteus," *Amazing Science Fiction*, May 1978.

CORDWAINER SMITH: "The Queen of the Afternoon," *Galaxy*, April 1978.

GEORGE W. S. TROW: "Alani Beach Now," *The New Yorker*, September 25, 1978.

JOAN D. VINGE: "Phoenix in the Ashes," *Millennial Women*.

GENE WOLFE: "The Doctor of Death Island," *Immortal*.

The Science Fiction Year

Charles N. Brown

Every year for the past five years, various experts have predicted a future downtrend or bust in the science-fiction field, and every year the field gets bigger. 1978 was no exception. Over 1,000 science-fiction titles (both new and reprint) were published with better sales and (alas!) higher prices per volume. The most profitable motion picture of all time was a science-fiction movie, the various best-seller lists contained many sf and fantasy titles, and the various movie merchandise tie-ins were primarily science fiction. Commercial success has probably changed the face of the field forever. It may not be any better as literature, but it's no longer shameful to admit you read that Buck Rogers stuff.

Star Wars became the first movie to gross over half a *billion* dollars in ticket sales. *Close Encounters of the Third Kind* unfortunately tied flying saucers back into sf, but the general audiences loved it and considered it pretty deep stuff. *Battlestar Galactica* was hilariously bad, but thanks to various Christmas tie-ins seems to have done very well commercially. *Lord of the Rings* and *Superman* have just opened to mixed reviews but large audiences. Next year, both the *Star Trek* motion picture and the sequel to *Star Wars* will probably be big moneymakers.

Penthouse International started a science/science-fiction magazine, *Omni,* with a reported advertising budget of five million dollars—enough to buy up all the competition. They're paying very high rates for short fiction.

1978 was a very disappointing year for novels. There was a fair number of better-than-average ones, but nothing truly outstanding. My personal favorites were *Journey* by Marta Randall, a successful combination of science fiction and the family-saga novel; *Blind Voices* by Tom Reamy, an exquisite Bradburian fantasy; and *Beloved Son* by George Turner, a modern *Brave New World*.

The White Dragon by Anne McCaffrey, the latest "Dragonrider" novel, was very good but suffered because it was a middle book in a series. *The Courts of Chaos* by Roger Zelazny finally finished the "Amber" series, but was very sketchy as an independent novel. *The Stand* by Stephen King, a sort of post-plague *Lord of the Rings*, was interesting but much too long. The new Ursula K. Le Guin novel, *The Eye of the Heron*, published as part of the original anthology *Millennial Women* edited by Virginia Kidd, was more a coda to *The Dispossessed* than an independent story; it was much too short.

Other recommended novels for 1978 are *The Avatar* by Poul Anderson, *The Stars in Shroud* by Gregory Benford, *Colony* by Ben Bova, *The Far Call* by Gordon Dickson, *Sight of Proteus* by Charles Sheffield, and *Dreamsnake* by Vonda McIntyre.

Though the year's novels were disappointing, the short-story collections were extraordinary. *The Persistence of Vision* by John Varley was probably the best short-story collection of the decade; the title story should have no competition winning the Hugo and Nebula awards for best novella of the year. *Somerset Dreams and Other Fictions* by Kate Wilhelm had a number of non-sf stories, but who cares? Wilhelm was outstanding in all of them. *The Earth Book of Stormgate* by Poul Anderson, a connected collection of some of his "future history" stories, gave an overall impression greater than the sum of its parts—as did *Still I*

Persist in Wondering by Edgar Pangborn, a posthumous collection set in the same world as his classic novel *Davy. Strange Wine* by Harlan Ellison had fifteen stories that took the reader on an emotional roller coaster. *Blood & Burning* by Algis Budrys, *The Redward Edward Papers* by Avram Davidson, and *The Best Short Stories of J.G. Ballard* were also excellent collections.

The anthology market was still depressed. Aside from the various bests of the year, the annual Nebula Awards volume, and the original anthology serieses *Universe, New Dimensions,* and *Orbit,* it was almost a total loss.

There were some very good books *about* science fiction. Frederik Pohl's autobiography, *The Way the Future Was,* was a warm, nostalgic chronicle covering nearly forty years of the field. *The Complete Guide to Middle-earth* by Robert Foster was an exhaustive concordance to characters, places, and things in the world of Tolkien. Volume 2 of *The Encyclopedia of Science Fiction and Fantasy,* compiled by Donald H. Tuck, finally appeared; it's the best general reference work in the field for annotated descriptions of books. *The Hills of Faraway* by Diana Waggoner was a cranky, opinionated, and fascinating guide to modern fantasy literature. *Index to Science Fiction Anthologies and Collections* by William Contento and *The Science Fiction Heroic Fantasy Author Index* by Stuart W. Wells III are basic reference works that should prove useful for many years. The Contento index listed the entire contents of each anthology or collection and its original appearance, as well as the usual author/title cross-index. A new, updated edition of *A History of the Hugo, Nebula, and International Fantasy Awards* is available for $3.00 from Howard Devore, 4705 Weddel, Dearborn MI 48125.

The science-fiction magazine field certainly had its ups and downs in 1978. Despite its reported million-copy sale, *Omni* received only a lukewarm reception by sf readers. It had three sf editors even before its first issue and the fiction turned out to be mostly mediocre; with Ben Bova at the helm, next year should be better.

Isaac Asimov's Science Fiction Magazine posted huge gains in circulation and finally passed *Analog* in total readership. The magazine has gone from bimonthly to monthly publication and has spawned a companion magazine, *Asimov's SF Adventure Magazine,* a sort of updated *Planet Stories. Asimov's* editor George Scithers won a Hugo Award last year.

Analog got a new editor in August: Stanley Schmidt, a Midwestern physics instructor and science-fiction author. Otherwise, the magazine seemed unchanged. *The Magazine of Fantasy & Science Fiction* raised its price to $1.25 and continued its virtual stranglehold on the literate fantasy short story. *Galaxy,* supposedly a monthly magazine, produced eight issues with great difficulty; each one seemed to be a last gasp. Editor John J. Pierce resigned and was replaced by Hank Stine, who announced a new policy (complete with minuscule pay rates!) reminiscent of the 1940 pulps. I doubt the magazine stands any chance of survival. *Amazing* and *Fantastic* have a new publisher, and Ted White, who edited the magazines for ten years, is no longer connected with them. They will apparently go back to reprint stories only in 1979 and will no longer be a market for established science fiction authors.

Galileo, which has no newsstand distribution, claimed a subscription list of 60,000—the highest in the field. *Unearth,* another non-newsstand magazine, also had a successful year. *Destinies,* a magazine in paperback format, published one issue in 1978; if successful, it could start a new trend.

Leigh Brackett, sixty-two, died on March 18 after a long bout with cancer. Her first story, "Martian Quest," appeared in 1940 and was followed by dozens of colorful adventure stories in *Planet Stories* and other magazines. Her Eric John Stark series is considered the epitome of update fantasy adventure in the Burroughs tradition. She collaborated with William Faulkner on the script of *The Big Sleep* and also did scripts for *El Dorado, Rio Lobo,* and *The Long Goodbye.* She married sf writer Edmond Hamilton in 1946. Her mystery and Western novels have won several awards. *The Long Tomorrow,* a sensitive post-holocaust novel published in 1955, is considered a classic in the field. She completed the script for the second *Star Wars* movie shortly before her death.

Eric Frank Russell, seventy-three, died suddenly of a heart attack on February 29. His first published story, "The Saga of Pelican West," appeared in *Astounding* in 1937. In 1938, he wrote a novel, *Forbidden Acres,* which John W. Campbell had him rewrite for a new magazine, *Unknown,* and retitled *Sinister Barrier;* it has proven to be Russell's most enduring book. *Dreadful Sanctuary,* a 1948 novel, was also well received. Russell created two other near masterpieces in the early fifties, "Dear Devil" (1950) and "And Then There Were None" (1951). In the mid-fifties he turned to humorous science fiction and won a Hugo for "Allamagoosa" (1955). His short stories have been collected in *Deep Space* (1954), *Six Worlds Yonder* (1958), *Far Stars* (1961), *Dark Tides* (1964), and *Somewhere a Voice* (1965). Although his novels have not aged well, his short fiction will always be remembered.

Ward Moore, seventy-five, died January 29, 1978, after a long illness. His most famous novel, *Bring the Jubilee,* an alternate time track book about the Civil War, was first published in 1953. Two earlier novels, *Breathe the Air Again* (1942) and *Greener Than You Think* (1947), received much praise but little commercial success. He started writing for the science fiction magazines in 1950 and published about forty short stories; "Lot" and "Lot's Wife" are the most famous of these. An excellent humorous novel, *Joyleg,* a 1962 serial in collaboration with Avram Davidson, was expanded and published as a book in 1971.

Other deaths in 1978 included those of Bob Juanillo, thirty-one, a new fantasy artist; Donald B. Day, sixty-nine, compiler of *The Index to the Science Fiction Magazines 1926–1950*; Winifred Kearns, seventy-two, a short-story writer; Harry Martinson, seventy-three, author of *Aniara* (1956) and winner of the Nobel Prize

(1974); J. Francis McComas, sixty-seven, cofounder of *The Magazine of Fantasy & Science Fiction* and coeditor of *Adventures in Time and Space* (1946), the most famous of the science-fiction anthologies; Mort Weisinger, sixty-three, author and former editor of *Thrilling Wonder Stories, Startling Stories,* and *Superman*; Sylvia Townsend Warner, eighty-four, author of *Kingdoms of Elfin* (1977); Jay Williams, sixty-four, author of the "Danny Dunn" series of sf juveniles; and Robert Moore Williams, seventy, a prolific pulp writer of the forties and fifties.

Much more cheering was the fact that Robert A. Heinlein underwent successful brain surgery in April 1978. He is not only fully recovered but has finished the first draft of a new novel.

The 1978 Nebula Awards were presented at the Nebula Banquet in San Francisco on April 29, 1978. Winners were: Best Novel: *Gateway* by Frederik Pohl; Best Novella: "Stardance" by Spider and Jeanne Robinson; Best Novelette: "The Screwfly Solution" by Raccoona Sheldon; Best Short Story: "Jeffty Is Five" by Harlan Ellison; Special Award: *Star Wars*.

The 1978 Hugo Awards were presented on September 3, 1978, at the 36th World Science Fiction Convention in Phoenix. Winners were: Best Novel: *Gateway* by Frederik Pohl; Best Novella: "Stardance" by Spider and Jeanne Robinson; Best Novelette: "Eyes of Amber" by Joan D. Vinge; Best Short Story: "Jeffty Is Five" by Harlan Ellison; Best Dramatic Presentation: *Star Wars;* Best Professional Artist: Rick Sternbach; Best Professional Editor: George Scithers; Best Fanzine: *Locus;* Best Fan Writer: Richard E. Geis; Best Fan Artist: Phil Foglio. The John W. Campbell Award for Best New Writer was won by Orson Scott Card.

The 1978 *Locus* Awards were announced in August 1978. Winners were: Best Science Fiction Novel: *Gateway* by Frederik Pohl; Best Novella: "Stardance" by Spider and Jeanne Robinson; Best Short Fiction: "Jeffty Is Five" by Harlan Ellison.

The 1978 John W. Campbell Memorial Award was

372 The Best Science Fiction of the Year #8

presented in Dublin on June 25, 1978. The winning novel was *Gateway* by Frederik Pohl.

The 37th World Science Fiction Convention will be held in Brighton, England, August 23–27, 1979. Guests of Honor include Fritz Leiber and Brian Aldiss. For information on membership, write Seacon 79, 14 Henrietta Street, London WC2E 8QJ, United Kingdom.

The 38th World Science Fiction Convention will be held in Boston August 29 to September 1, 1980. Guests of Honor include Damon Knight and Kate Wilhelm. For information on membership, write Noreascon Two, P.O. Box 46, M.I.T. Station, Cambridge MA 02139.

Membership in the World Convention is the only prerequisite for nominating and voting for the Hugo Awards.

Charles N. Brown is the editor of Locus, The Newspaper of the Science Fiction Field. *Copies are $1.00 each; subscriptions in North America are $9.00 per year, payable to Locus Publications, P.O. Box 3938, San Francisco CA 94119.*